ENTANGLED

TRACI HUNTER ABRAMSON

STEPHANIE BLACK

CLAIR M POULSON

GREG LUKE

Covenant Communications, Inc.

ISBN:978-1-52441-088-9

ENTANGLED

OTHER BOOKS AND AUDIO BOOKS
BY TRACI HUNTER ABRAMSON:

BRIDGE OF TRUST

TRACI HUNTER ABRAMSON

CHAPTER 1

ETHAN SCANNED THE QUIET NEIGHBORHOOD as he drove past the rows of identical houses on the south side of Phoenix. The houses weren't much bigger than the guesthouse that had occupied the space near the garage of his childhood home.

A pang stabbed deep into the tender spot where he kept the memories of his parents. His father had worked so hard to build a good life for their family. Unfortunately, his accumulation of wealth hadn't helped him when his heart had given out at the age of fifty-eight, nor had it saved his mother from a distracted driver a year later.

His mom had reached the hospital alive but hadn't lived long enough for Ethan to get there to say goodbye.

He pushed the regret aside, along with the loneliness that often came with it. Sure, he had his sister, but she had a family of her own now. With his move from Chicago to Arizona, he would no longer get to enjoy their weekly visits or the memories they had so often shared.

This was a good move, Ethan reminded himself. He had been ready for a change when the transfer had come, ready for a fresh start. Now he needed to find a way to create a new life for himself here.

He pulled up to the curb when he reached the address of interest, noting the tidy desert landscape surprisingly free of weeds. A path had been worn beside the front walk in the otherwise evenly spread gravel.

A huge saguaro cactus dominated the center of the yard, a vicious-looking prickly pear living in its shadow. He shifted his attention to the currently empty carport and noted the baby stroller parked next to the door. Could he have the wrong address?

He checked his information again and then confirmed the location. If his sources were correct, Lanny Valo had already left town, but the rumor of a big deal pending had brought him to the top of the FBI Phoenix office's priority list.

Perhaps the stroller was a prop Valo had used to hide the fact that this house was being used as a hub for criminal activity. Ethan wasn't sure why he had gone through the trouble of requesting a search warrant for the home of this suspected drug dealer, but something had kept nagging at him until he'd pushed his request through the proper channels.

The street was quiet when he stepped out of the car. The sun beat down, making Ethan appreciate the invention of air conditioning, even though it was only May. Just as that thought passed through his head, he noticed the hum of a window cooling unit. He wondered briefly why it would be on if Valo had left town. Maybe the man had been in too much of a hurry to close down the house.

Ethan knocked on the door, not surprised when it went unanswered. He pulled his tools out of his inside jacket pocket, leaned down to work on the lock, and, thirty seconds later, turned the knob. Always cautious, he pushed the door open and shouted his standard greeting. "FBI!"

The scent of lemon and pine hung in the air as he stepped inside. Furniture gleamed from a recent dusting, and the kitchen sparkled. Ethan barely suppressed the urge to take off his shoes before stepping onto the freshly vacuumed carpet. He took a cursory glance of the living areas before moving into the hallway leading to the bedrooms.

He looked through the open doorway to his left to see bright-blue walls with a rainbow painted from one corner of the room, up across the ceiling, and down the opposite wall. The crib and changing table left Ethan once again questioning the validity of the address he had been given.

Opposite the crib, a toddler bed boasted a Spiderman bedspread, and a soccer ball lay on the floor beside it.

Feeling very much like an intruder, he began formulating an apology in his mind in the event he discovered it was indeed someone else's home. He glanced across the hall to the bathroom, and instantly, his hand went to his gun. A red smear on the otherwise clean floor matched the handprint on the wash basin.

His pistol in hand, he stepped back into the hall, noticing for the first time the faint odor of blood. Quietly, he padded to the last doorway. Sunlight filtered through the closed blinds to give light to the otherwise dark bedroom. He stepped forward, poised for anything he might encounter.

When his gaze dropped to the floor, he realized he hadn't been ready for everything after all. Bruised and battered, a woman in her midtwenties huddled under a blanket in the corner. Across the room, a man was sprawled on the carpet. A pistol lay in the empty space between them.

Ethan flipped on the light, relieved to hear a whimper from the woman. At least she was still alive.

Instinctively, he took a step toward her before his training took over. He finished his search of the bedroom and master bath to confirm his suspicion that no one else was inside. After sheathing his weapon, he checked the man for a pulse, but the skin was cool, the life already drained out of him. The presence of the gun gave him a good clue as to the cause of death, but he would leave that detail to the coroner. For now, all he could do was treat the living.

Crossing to the woman, he knelt beside her. Dried blood matted her blonde hair, and the thin arm that clutched the blanket was darkened with bruises from wrist to shoulder. If he looked close enough, he was sure he would be able to see the outline of the fingers that had done this to her.

He pulled his cell phone from his pocket and called for an ambulance.

"Everything is going to be all right. An ambulance is on the way," Ethan said.

She didn't respond.

He retreated to the bathroom long enough to dampen a washcloth.

"Can you hear me? I'm going to clean this cut so I can see how deep it is."

She winced when he pressed the cold, wet cloth to her temple. Ethan cleaned the blood from her face, finding that the cut had begun to scab over. The woman was lovely, despite her current condition. Delicate features, dark eyelashes against tanned skin.

He drew the blanket down to check for other injuries. There, nestled at the woman's side, was a baby boy, no more than five or six months old.

Free of the blanket, the baby rolled from his side to his back. His big, blue eyes focused on Ethan, and his cherubic face broke into a huge grin. Except for his soaked diaper and clothing, he appeared completely unharmed.

Ethan spoke to the infant, reaching a hand down to touch the soft brown hair. "Hey there, little guy."

The baby gurgled happily, his chubby fingers grabbing onto his mother's arm, which was wrapped securely around his waist.

"He took my baby," the woman whispered desperately. "Please don't let him take my baby."

"Your baby is right here."

She struggled to shake her head. Her voice was barely audible when she spoke again. "There were two."

CHAPTER 2

"What do you mean you didn't get both of them?" Lanny's voice rose a decibel. He looked into the living room, where his three-year-old son, Henry, was curled up on the couch.

"Your wife had a gun. She shot Mario. We weren't going to stick around and let her take target practice on us."

"She did what?"

"Mario roughed her up a bit when we were putting Henry in the car," Nigel said. "She kept screaming and clawing at him. When he tried to get the baby from her, she reached under the bed and came up shooting."

"Unbelievable."

"Ricky stayed behind. He has a friend who is willing to help us out."

"What kind of friend?" Lanny asked, suspicion coloring his voice.

"Just trust me on this one." Nigel glanced at the toddler on the couch. "For now, I suggest you focus on our upcoming deal. You said yourself that this will change everything for us."

"I'll do my part," Lanny said, "but I expect you to finish yours."

"Give me another day. I'll take care of it."

* * *

Something cool on her forehead brought Summer back to the present. Painful memories tumbled over each other, and she prayed it was all a bad dream. The lack of warmth beside her, despite the blanket draped over her shoulders, sent a fresh wave of trepidation and terror through her. The pain in her ribs and ankle throbbed, and she gasped for air as she struggled to sit up.

"Hey, take it easy. The paramedics are on their way."

The voice was meant to soothe, but that didn't stem the new wave of panic that washed over her. "My baby."

"He's right here."

Summer forced her eyes open and looked at the man kneeling beside her. It took her a moment to lower her eyes to the floor where little Wyatt lay on a clean blanket. His soiled clothing had been removed, and he now wore only a fresh diaper.

She reached out and placed her hand on the baby's stomach but didn't have the strength to lift him.

"Don't worry. I'll keep him safe," the man assured her. As if she could stop the worry. Didn't he understand that someone had ripped her heart out, stomped all over it, and left it there to wither and die?

Apparently, this man was completely clueless, because he kept talking.

"My name is Ethan Flanagan. I'm with the FBI." He paused as though waiting for a response. When he got none, he continued. "You said someone took your other baby. Can you tell me who it was?"

A tiny glimmer of hope flickered, and she forced herself to answer. "Ricky was one of them. I didn't know the other three."

"Is that man over there Ricky?"

She shifted her gaze, and the horror came flooding back. The sound of someone at the front door, Ricky charging inside and knocking her to the ground on his way to Henry's bedroom.

She could still hear the echoes of her screams as she fought to put herself between Ricky and her oldest son, another man's hands grabbing her arm and throwing her from the room.

The struggle, the fist to her side when she tried again to get to her oldest, the heartbreaking decision to protect Wyatt to make sure they didn't get both of her children.

"Is that Ricky?" he repeated, pulling her out of the memory.

"No, that's not him."

She heard the deep voice speaking again, but the words slurred into a low hum as she struggled to focus. In the distance, she heard a door open, followed by more voices, but they drifted off as she once again let the darkness take her under.

* * *

Ethan parked outside his office, the scene at the Valo house firmly planted in his mind. He knew he was supposed to keep a professional distance when working a case, but this one tugged at his heartstrings and tied them into a messy knot. The haunted look on Summer Valo's face was something he would remember for a long time.

He passed through the reception area and made a beeline for Ray's desk, the clean surface only interrupted by a desktop computer and a photo of Ray's wife and three kids.

"Did you find anything on Valo?" Ethan asked.

"The alerts are out, but so far, there's no sign of where he's hiding out and nothing yet on the missing child."

"What did you find on Valo's family background?" Ethan asked, anxious to join in the search.

"Married to his wife, Summer Valo, for four years. Two children. Henry just turned three, and Wyatt is five months old."

"Any idea why he would suddenly turn on his wife?"

"Ex-wife. She filed for divorce while she was pregnant with baby number two. The divorce finalized three months ago."

Ethan let this new information sink in. "From everything I saw at the house, it looked like the ex-wife was living there."

"Which means Lanny was living somewhere else." Ray leaned back in his chair. "That would explain why our informant was so quick to give up the address. Either he knew Valo wasn't there, or our informant is still working for the Lobo family."

"Exactly. He wasn't worried about retribution because he didn't expect us to find anything."

"At least not anything useful."

"I'll start checking out known addresses for Valo," Ethan said.

"We have units rolling to two already." Ray grabbed a paper off his desk and offered it to Ethan. "Here's the complete list."

"What's going on with the other two?"

Before Ray could answer, Ethan heard his name called.

"Flanagan."

He turned to see his boss heading toward him. "Hey, Elias. We were just working on known addresses for Valo."

"Ray can handle that. I need you to go to the hospital." Elias motioned him toward the exit. "Mrs. Valo is refusing treatment."

Ethan fell into step beside Elias. "Why?"

"Something about not letting her baby out of her sight."

"I don't know what you expect me to do about it."

"You're the only person who's managed to pull any information out of her," Elias said.

"Wouldn't you rather have me track down her missing child?"

"Ray is already coordinating with the local authorities. For now, I need you to question Mrs. Valo. See if you can get her to cooperate."

Deflated that he wouldn't be able to join in the search, Ethan forced himself to nod. "I'll do my best."

* * *

It never failed. Ruth Bennington should have known better than to fix a nice dinner on a night she was on call. Her husband would undoubtedly enjoy the lasagna she had labored over tonight, but her best-case scenario would be a late-night serving of leftovers.

Four minutes before the timer had gone off, her boss from Child Protective Services had called with an emergency placement order—an injured woman with an infant son who needed to be cared for.

Ruth changed into her work clothes and returned to the kitchen as the timer sounded. She removed the lasagna from the oven, only to have tomato sauce splatter onto her favorite blouse. Furious that she had forgotten to protect herself with an apron, she set her husband's dinner on the stovetop, changed a second time, and hurried out the door.

For the entire ride to the hospital, she played phone tag with three potential emergency foster parents, but when she finally found a couple who would be the perfect fit and confirmed they were available, someone cut her off on the freeway, and Ruth slammed on her brakes. Her phone dropped out of her hand and went flying onto the floor in front of the passenger seat. Great.

She arrived at the hospital five minutes later, circling the parking lot three times in search of a parking spot. The first one to open was literally the farthest away from the entrance.

She parked the car and left the engine running while she reached down and retrieved her phone. She called the foster parents back, apologized for the interrupted phone call, and confirmed they would remain on standby for her. She then collected the paperwork and tucked it into her soft-sided briefcase.

Taking a moment, she reminded herself that she was here to protect the best interest of the child in question. She mentally prepared for the worst but hoped for the best. With any luck, the mother would be unconscious. Ruth really wasn't in the mood for hysterics today.

CHAPTER 3

ETHAN WASN'T SURE WHAT TO expect when he followed the receptionist's directions through the ER to examination room three. He'd been an FBI agent for six years now, yet here he was babysitting the victims instead of searching for the criminals.

Reminding himself that Summer might have knowledge that could lead to the recovery of her son, he knocked on the door, which was hanging slightly ajar. When no one answered, he slowly pushed it open and peeked inside.

Summer Valo lay on the bed with her eyes closed, her arm wrapped around her baby's waist, much like when Ethan had originally found her. A white bandage covered the cut on her forehead, but he couldn't see any other evidence of her receiving treatment.

A middle-aged woman wearing gray dress pants and a fussy white blouse occupied the single chair in the room, a cell phone pressed to her ear.

"I'll let you know as soon as they get here." She looked up at Ethan as though just noticing his presence. "I've got to go." The woman stood. "Who are you?"

"Ethan Flanagan. FBI. Is everything okay here?"

Summer stirred, and the woman waved toward the door. "Perhaps we should discuss this in private."

Ethan followed her out, noticing the way she positioned herself outside the partially open door so she could watch Summer while speaking with him.

"I'm Ruth Bennington, with Child Protective Services. Since Mrs. Valo is refusing treatment for herself and for her son, we are placing the child in protective custody."

"Why?" Ethan asked, unable to fathom how Summer would survive another traumatic incident, especially so soon after having her oldest child stolen from her. "I examined the baby myself. He's perfectly fine."

"But Mrs. Valo isn't. She's in no condition to care for the baby. Once she has undergone treatment, the child can be returned to her."

"This child was nearly kidnapped this morning. She's in this condition because she fought to save him. Not to mention it isn't safe to put the baby in foster care at this time."

"I'm afraid that isn't your call." Ruth straightened and adopted an authoritative air. "If you'll excuse me, I need to get back in there and make sure that baby isn't harmed while I wait for the police to arrive."

Ethan's hand shot into his pocket, and an instant later, he had his boss on the phone. "We have a problem."

"She won't talk?"

"I haven't had a chance to question her yet, but CPS has called the police in to take custody of her baby," Ethan said. "I'm sorry, Elias, but I don't see how we'll be able to gain her cooperation if she sees us as the enemy, and that's exactly what we're about to become."

"I'll make a call. In the meantime, show the police your credentials when they arrive and see if you can buy me some time."

Two uniformed officers turned the corner and headed toward him. "They just got here. Our time is limited."

"I'll call you back."

Ethan flashed his credentials as the men neared. "I'm Ethan Flanagan, FBI."

The senior officer, a man in his early thirties, extended his hand. "Officer Peters. This is Officer Lopez."

"Good to meet you both." Ethan shook hands with both men. "I need a little time before you go in there. Any chance I can buy you guys a cup of coffee or something?"

"I'm a member of The Church of Jesus Christ of Latter-day Saints," Lopez announced. "I don't drink coffee."

"Okay, how about a donut, then?"

"Gluten-free diet," Peters said.

What were the chances? Ethan pocketed his credentials. Deciding to put his cards on the table, he said, "Look, I really need this favor. My boss is making the call now to block CPS, and I need some time for him to work through the red tape."

He saw their hesitation and added, "This woman nearly died trying to save that baby. Don't we owe it to her to protect them both? We need her help to identify the men responsible and recover the child they did kidnap."

Two sympathetic stares met his, and Ethan prayed they would see reason.

* * *

Summer peeked out from beneath her lowered lashes, hoping to find everything had been a nightmare. A ball of lead sank in her stomach, along with an indescribable pain and sense of loss. She'd thought she was finally free of her ex-husband and the evil that always seemed to follow him, but she had been so wrong.

Her naivete and ridiculous sense of happily ever after had gotten her into this mess. She had let herself get swept off her feet by Lanny and had believed all his promises. She should have known he wouldn't keep his promise to let her raise the boys on her own. Hadn't she deliberately hidden her address from him for this exact reason?

She scanned the room, and her despair deepened when she saw the occupied chair. She was still here, that awful woman who kept trying to take her baby from her. Summer wasn't going to let that happen. Not again.

Wyatt wiggled in her arms and tried to roll over. She tightened her grip, her breath catching as a jolt of pain shot through her side.

The woman with the beady eyes and long, narrow nose was out of her seat in a heartbeat. "Why don't you let me hold the baby so you can rest?"

"You're not taking my baby." Summer didn't know how many times she had uttered those words over the past two hours, but she wished someone would record them and press the replay button. Talking hurt.

Voices outside the door caught her attention. She identified the newcomers, and terror clawed through her. The police had arrived.

Immediately, her head began to shake from one side to the other. "No. No, please. Don't take my baby."

Miss Beady Eyes took her plea as permission do the exact opposite. Reinforced by the officers' presence, she moved to Summer's side and reached for Wyatt. "Come on, now. Don't make this any harder on him than it has to be."

"No!" Summer screamed. The sudden volume of her voice startled Wyatt, and his cry joined hers.

"Hey, now." A vaguely familiar male voice drew closer. "Ms. Bennington, there's no need for force."

"She hasn't left us any other choice."

"Let me try." A man approached and stood opposite of Beady. He spoke to her with a reassuring tone, but the fear didn't let the words through. Beady made another attempt to pull Wyatt free of her grip.

Summer tried to shift away from her to use her body to shield Wyatt, but her cry of pain was instant and nearly as loud as Wyatt's continued wails.

"That's enough," the man said sharply. His hand came down to rest on Summer's shoulder, a gesture of comfort. It took Summer a moment to realize the order wasn't aimed at her but rather at the woman trying to take her baby. "Give me a minute alone with her. If I can't get this resolved, we'll consider other options."

"Step aside, and let me do my job," Beady insisted.

One of the police officers stepped forward. "Ms. Bennington, please wait out here with us."

"I'm supposed to stay with the child at all times."

"This is the only door, and the child will be under the protection of a federal officer." The policeman motioned again for her to exit. "Ma'am. Now, please."

With a huff, she turned and left the room. As soon as Beady was gone, the man moved beside Summer so she could see him more clearly.

She remembered him now and grasped to remember his name. Evan, Ian, Ethan? That was it. Ethan. "Have you found Henry? Have you found my son?"

"We're looking." He lowered his voice as though he didn't want to be overheard by the police and Beady. "I need your help, but I also need your cooperation. The doctors need to treat your injuries, and they can't do that while you're holding Wyatt."

"That woman is trying to take him from me."

"If I promise to keep him right here, will you agree to receive treatment?"

She started to shake her head at the same time Wyatt arched his back and dug his shoulder into one of her injured ribs. She gasped and barely managed to keep the baby from rolling off her.

"What if I come with you while you're receiving treatment? He'll be right with you, except when you have your x-rays." Summer was still debating his proposal when he added, "I want to find Henry, but I can't do it without you. Please let me help."

Tears surfaced and dampened her cheeks. Everything in her resisted releasing Wyatt to anyone. How could she be certain he wasn't lying to her? For all she knew, this man would take Wyatt and immediately surrender him to Child Protective Services.

Ethan leaned closer and whispered. "Don't let her win. I'm on your side."

A glance at Beady standing outside the doorway swayed her. Mustering every ounce of strength within her, she leaned down, kissed the top of Wyatt's head, and nodded her assent.

Ethan lifted the baby from her, the sudden lack of warmth sending waves of apprehension through her.

Beady rushed into the room the moment Wyatt was in Ethan's arms. "I'll take him now."

"No!" Summer protested.

Ethan put a hand on her arm to silence her. "Wyatt Valo is now in protective custody. I'm afraid I can't release him to anyone without permission from my boss."

"This is absurd," Beady insisted.

"Officer Lopez, could you please let the nurse know that Ms. Valo has consented to treatment?"

"I'd be happy to."

The other police officer stepped forward. "Ms. Bennington, why don't you come out here, and we'll see if we can get this sorted out."

"This isn't over."

The other policeman nudged Beady outside and pulled the door closed, leaving Summer alone with Ethan.

Settling the baby against his shoulder, Ethan patted Wyatt's back and pinned Summer with his gaze. "We have people looking for Henry, but do you have any idea where your ex-husband might have taken him?"

"I don't know." Tears welled up in her eyes again.

"Where was he living?"

"He didn't tell me. I didn't ask." Summer swallowed hard and let her eyes linger on Wyatt. "He's not going to stop until he gets what he wants. He'll kill anyone who gets in his way."

"I'm here to make sure that doesn't happen."

A nurse opened the door, followed by an orderly. The nurse focused on Ethan and said, "We're going to take her down for an MRI."

Her panic must have been evident when she looked at Ethan and Wyatt because Ethan immediately moved closer. "I'll come with you."

CHAPTER 4

ETHAN DIDN'T MISS THE EVIL eye Ruth Bennington cast in his direction as he followed the orderly out of the room. Ignoring her, he walked beside the gurney where Summer lay. When they passed the nurses' station, Ethan paused long enough to ensure Summer's presence was listed as confidential.

When they reached the imaging lab, the orderly spoke to Ethan. "You'll need to wait here, sir."

Summer's whole body tensed, and she turned toward him, tears moistening her eyes.

"I promise to take good care of him for you. We aren't going anywhere." Ethan felt like he had won another victory when she gave him a subtle nod.

"The waiting room is the next door down," the orderly said.

"Thanks." Ethan started forward. As though Wyatt could sense his mother's fears, he started fussing the moment Summer disappeared from sight.

Ethan bounced the baby in his arms in an attempt to soothe him. He continued into the waiting room, immediately questioning himself. What was he thinking? He was in no position to take care of a baby, and by refusing to let CPS get involved, he had signed up to do exactly that.

It was only for a few hours, he assured himself. As soon as Summer Valo received treatment, she could help determine how to best care for her baby.

Falling back on the trick he'd learned from his sister, he remained on his feet, settled the baby against his shoulder, and patted Wyatt's back as he paced the room. Gradually, the whimpers subsided, and the child relaxed against him, his weight seeming to increase.

Within moments of Wyatt falling asleep, a technician entered to let Ethan know Summer was done with her MRI. Fighting back a sigh, he hoped this nightmare would end for her soon.

* * *

Ruth Bennington stormed through the hospital corridor toward the exit. She was used to the constant battle that came with her job. Rarely did someone voluntarily give up their child, and tears had become something she expected and chose to ignore. After thirty years of watching parents and children at their most vulnerable, she had learned to block out the emotional turmoil of others.

Normally, she could keep her own emotions decidedly neutral, but the FBI agent today had set her blood boiling. How dare he swoop in like that and act like he knew how to do her job better than she. She had found the perfect home for the baby, and now she would have to undo all her efforts.

Not if she could help it.

She passed through the exit, stepping out into the stifling heat. If the hospital would give CPS an office inside, she wouldn't have to leave the building every time she needed to have a confidential phone call. Spending an unsuccessful twenty minutes searching for an empty office she could borrow had soured her mood even further. She dialed her boss twice before she picked up.

"Ruth, I was about to call you," Jennifer said. "I received a call from the FBI a few minutes ago. They are placing Wyatt Valo into protective custody, so we won't need an emergency foster for him after all."

"Can they do that?" Ruth demanded. "The FBI agent who has the baby isn't cleared by us. For all we know, he doesn't have any experience taking care of a child."

"I can't go into details, but the bureau made a compelling argument of why it would not be in the child's best interest to be placed into foster care."

"Seems to me the FBI should stick with catching criminals and leave child care to us."

"The matter has been settled," Jennifer said with authority. "I'll see you tomorrow."

Another burst of anger shot through Ruth, and she nearly threw her phone to the ground. Then she remembered how little she made for this job and decided it wasn't worth it.

"Excuse me. Ms. Bennington?"

"Yes?" Ruth turned around to see a man in his thirties approaching. He sent her a smile, one that she recognized for what it was. A mask.

"I'm Duke Bissett. I received a call that I should meet you here to pick up a foster child."

Ruth looked at him with a fresh perspective. She recognized the name as one of the emergency foster parents she had intended to use, but something in this man's demeanor left her uneasy. "Who told you to come here? We don't have foster parents come to us. We bring the child to you."

"I'm not sure exactly. My wife took the call. Something about a baby who needed to go into emergency foster care."

"There's been a change of plans."

"What kind of change?"

"The child in question is no longer in need of foster care."

"I don't understand."

She knew he was fishing, and she didn't bite. "I'm sorry, but I'm not at liberty to discuss the case."

He stepped closer and lowered his voice. "Perhaps I can convince you to change your mind."

"I find that unlikely."

His hand disappeared beneath the T-shirt he wore. "I don't."

Her eyes followed the movement and widened when she saw his hand return to view holding a pistol. She opened her mouth, but no sound came out.

"Now, why don't we go for a little walk? You can tell me all about this change of plans and who I need to see about adjusting them."

* * *

Ethan stood outside Summer's room while she nursed her baby. They had waited thirty minutes after her scans and x-rays were taken for the doctor to attend to her, but finally, her broken ankle was protected by a cast. Not much could be done for the bruising along her rib cage, but ace bandages now encircled her torso to give extra support to the injury.

Every time he thought about the beating she must have endured, his blood simmered. He knew such violence existed. Working in law enforcement, he faced it every day, but he didn't think he would ever understand how people could stoop to beating a woman.

His phone rang, and the screen indicated Ray was on the other end. "Any news about Valo's whereabouts?" Ethan said after he answered it.

"No, but we have another problem," Ray said.

"What?"

"Elias had me monitoring the security camera feed for the hospital in case Valo showed up looking for his son."

Instantly, Ethan swept the area for any sign of a threat. "Is he here?"

"No, but I think something is going on," Ray said, his words carrying a sense of urgency. "I caught a glimpse of Ricardo Sastre entering the hospital a minute ago."

"Ricardo Sastre? He's one of the guys Valo met with last week."

"Exactly. I've alerted security, and back up is on the way."

"ETA?"

"Five minutes."

Ethan heard Wyatt let out a burp. He peeked into Summer's room, and she was holding the baby against her chest, a grimace on her face. "Are you ready to go? We need to get out of here."

The look of alarm in her expression was instant. "I can't walk."

Ray's voice sounded through his phone. "Ethan, the guy just knocked out the guard by the ER entrance. He's in the building."

Ethan could hear the automatic doors to the ER opening. He looked around frantically; an elderly man standing beside a woman on a gurney, a ten-year-old boy in a wheelchair beside a frazzled-looking mother, and not a single cop or security guard in sight.

His gaze caught the blue fabric of a rolling screen parked beside Summer's door. He reached out and pulled it toward him, positioning it between the main ER entrance and Summer's door.

He crossed to her bed in three strides. "You hold the baby. I'll hold you."

He gave her a brief moment to process his words before he scooped her out of the bed and cradled her against his chest. He heard her gasp of pain, but her hold on Wyatt tightened as he slipped out the door and behind the screen.

Rapid footsteps drew closer. Using the screen to create a visual barrier between him and anyone near the entrance, he skirted along the edge of the wide hallway, past the four remaining treatment rooms. He continued straight into triage room two, using his shoulder to push a privacy curtain out of his way.

A startled nurse looked up at him from beside a bald woman who appeared to be a cancer patient. "Sir, you can't come in here."

"FBI," Ethan puffed out. He continued forward and used his foot to press down the handle of the outer door leading into the ER lobby.

Before the nurse could question him further, Ethan increased his gait and headed for the heart of the hospital.

"What's going on?" Summer managed to ask, her words breathy. "Is Lanny here?"

"We spotted one of his friends on the security feed."

"Oh no." Tears sprang to her eyes.

"I'm going to get you out of here. Just follow my lead." He walked in silence down a long hallway, his mind racing. Every step he took seemed to cause Summer pain, but that was nothing compared to what would happen if she and Wyatt were found.

He noticed three wheelchairs down a short corridor and changed direction. Using his foot to hold the one nearest him steady, he gently settled Summer into it, then pulled his phone out of his pocket and dialed Ray. "Status?"

"He's heading right for you. Ethan, he must be tracking your phone."

Ethan hit the up button for the elevator. The question of how this man had identified him flitted through his mind, but he didn't have time to ponder it now. "How close is he?"

"You've got fifteen seconds. Twenty if you're lucky."

The elevator dinged. Ethan didn't bother to hang up before he tossed his phone on the floor of the elevator and pressed the button for the fourth floor.

Adrenaline slicing through him, he grabbed the handles of the wheelchair and pushed Summer into the corridor, only to find himself facing a set of double doors with a large Restricted sign on them.

He tried the doors anyway, but they were locked.

"What do we do?" Summer managed to ask.

Hurried footsteps approached. Ethan pushed the wheelchair close to the corner, keeping his body between Summer and the approaching danger. He drew his weapon and held his finger to his lips.

Summer nodded, her terror unmistakable. The baby must have felt his mother's tension because he began to stir. Ethan saw the grimace on Summer's face when she shifted Wyatt in her arms and rubbed his stomach to calm him.

The footsteps grew louder and stopped. A muttered oath sounded, followed by the ding of another elevator.

Ethan considered trying to apprehend the man following them, but concern for Summer's and Wyatt's safety dominated. With civilians everywhere, the last thing he wanted was to start a potential shootout, especially without backup.

He pressed himself against the wall by the corner and listened as the elevator doors slid open and then closed again. His hand tightened on the grip of his gun, and he peered around the corner. Finding the area empty, he stepped behind Summer's wheelchair. "Let's get out of here."

* * *

Summer couldn't breathe. The haze of pain clouded her vision, and she tried to think about anything besides the stabbing pain in her ribs. Artwork hanging on the otherwise sterile, white hospital walls blurred by as Ethan pushed her forward at an alarmingly fast pace.

Wyatt lifted his head and arched his back, apparently trying to see everything they passed. Summer swallowed a gasp of agony as she turned him in her arms, settling him on her lap so he could see everything in front of them.

She didn't realize they were heading back to the ER until Ethan pushed his way into the nearly empty waiting room. "What are you doing? They'll find us."

"They?" Ethan asked. "Only one man was spotted coming into the ER."

"These guys never come alone." The words were still hanging in the air when she looked out the ER waiting room windows and saw him. The man responsible for turning her world upside down.

"Stop!" To her surprise, Ethan complied immediately.

"What's wrong?"

"I recognize that guy. He was at my house."

Ethan continued forward and then headed for the treatment area of the emergency room, the same place they had escaped from only minutes before. She repeated her earlier question. "What are you doing?"

"Improvising." He pulled his badge from his pocket and flashed it at the receptionist. "Open the door."

Though confused, the receptionist hit the button that opened the automatic door.

Ethan pushed Summer through, but instead of going toward the triage and treatment rooms, he made an immediate right. Though questions burned on her tongue, Summer remained silent for fear she would draw unwanted attention to herself.

A gasp escaped her when another familiar face appeared to her left. A single word came out in a whisper, but it held force and urgency. "Stop."

CHAPTER 5

ETHAN SAW HIM THE SAME time Summer did. Zacarias Chavez had been on the Interpol watch list for drug trafficking for the past two years. He was blond today and clean shaven, his eyes green instead of their normal brown.

Ethan hesitated for a brief moment before taking the first hiding place he could find: the supply closet.

He pushed Summer inside. After he closed the door, he knelt in front of her. She was nearly hysterical, tears rolling silently down her face.

"He must be working with Lanny," she whispered. "I can't believe this is happening again."

"I know I'm asking the impossible, but I need you to stay calm. I have an idea. We just have to figure out how to get you past that guy."

"How?"

Ethan looked around the room, his gaze falling on a roll of gauze. "I think you're about to become a burn victim."

"Excuse me?"

"If he can't see your face, he won't recognize you."

"But if he sees Wyatt, he'll suspect something."

"My backup should be here by now. Wait here. I'm going to make a call and when I get back, we'll take care of your disguise." He reached for the door. "I'll be right outside the door. Trust me."

Ethan didn't wait for a response before he opened the door and slipped outside. A stunning black woman who was as tall as he was walked into sight, her uniform identifying her as a paramedic.

"Excuse me, ma'am. I think someone was looking for you."

She stopped. "Me?"

Ethan closed the distance between them. He lowered his voice. "I'm with the FBI, and I need your help."

"ID?" She asked, her skepticism evident.

Ethan turned so his back was to the main hall before he drew it from his pocket. He held it close to his chest to make sure no one would see it but her.

"What do you need?"

"First, do you have a cell phone I can borrow?"

"Yeah, sure." She pulled one from a clip on her belt and handed it to him.

"I also hoped you might have access to an ambulance."

"That's what I drive all day."

"I was hoping you would say that."

* * *

The gauze wrapped around Summer's face tickled her nose and left only her mouth and eyes exposed. Her blonde hair was now hidden beneath a dark-brown wig, compliments of the cancer patient in treatment room four, and Ethan held Wyatt to make sure she wouldn't be associated with her son.

The woman who had bandaged her face now stood behind her wheelchair.

"Ready?" Ethan asked.

"I'm ready to be out of here," Summer managed. "And I'm ready to have Henry back."

"First things first," Ethan said. "What are the chances the man out there will recognize Wyatt?"

"He's never seen him, and Lanny hasn't seen the kids in months."

"Good," Ethan said. "I'll go first with Wyatt. I have a friend who is positioned by the main hall. He'll make sure you get through safely."

She drew a deep breath and instantly regretted it as a stab of pain shot through her. Shallowing her breathing, she managed to nod.

Her lips pressed together into a thin line as she watched Ethan carry Wyatt away. She reached up and swiped at her eyes in an effort to stem her tears.

Ninety seconds ticked by. It might as well have been an eternity. Finally, the woman behind her opened the supply closet door and pushed her into the hallway. A moment later, they continued into the main part of the ER, and Summer saw the man who had been sent to get her. Or had he volunteered?

Her chest tightened, as did her grip on the arms of the wheelchair. The gesture was hidden beneath the gauze that had been wrapped around her hands and wrists. Reminding herself to breathe, she kept her eyes trained forward, barely able to see. Ethan had taken position by the door to the ambulance loading area, Wyatt still safely in his arms.

She sensed movement all around her. Nurses, doctors, patients, visitors. A silent plea went through her head and was sent heavenward that they would pass Zacarias without incident. That prayer went unanswered.

Though she forced herself not to look in his direction, she sensed his nearing presence.

"What happened here?" he asked, now standing in their path.

"Kitchen fire," the woman behind her responded.

"Ouch."

"If you'll excuse me, sir, I need to get her upstairs."

"Of course." He moved slightly, but as they started past, Summer could hear footsteps behind her. Another man's voice carried toward them.

"Excuse me, sir. I wonder if I could ask you a few questions," the man said. "Have you been here long? We're looking for a young woman and her infant son. They disappeared from a treatment room about fifteen minutes ago."

"Sorry. Can't help you," Zacarias said.

Summer was pushed past the familiar man, her every breath an effort. After what felt like an eternity, they reached the double doors on the far side of the ER, and she was loaded into the back of an ambulance, where Ethan and Wyatt waited.

The doors slammed shut, and immediately, the ambulance pulled away.

* * *

Summer gripped the arms of the wheelchair, bracing against the moment when one of Lanny's men would figure out where they were. The ambulance slowed and came to a stop without incident.

"Where are we?" she asked.

"This is where we're picking up our ride." Ethan moved to the back door and opened it.

With the help of the EMTs, Summer was lifted, wheelchair and all, out of the ambulance and placed on the pavement of a narrow strip mall.

Ethan shook hands with both EMTs. "Thank you again for your help."

"This was one of our more interesting days," the woman told him.

"In your profession, that's saying something."

"We'd better get going," the driver said. "Good luck."

"Thanks." Ethan stepped behind the wheelchair and pushed Summer toward several cars parked outside a Mexican food restaurant. He stopped next to a sedan that looked like it had seen better days, retrieved a key from beneath the front bumper, and unlocked the driver's side. After he started the car to get the air conditioning going, he opened the back door to reveal an infant car seat strapped inside.

"Did you want to sit in back with Wyatt?"

"Yes, please."

Ethan gently lifted the sleeping infant from her arms and nestled him against his shoulder when he began to fuss. Summer watched with amazement as he efficiently placed Wyatt in his seat and strapped him in.

"You look like you've had practice with this. I assume you have kids?" she asked.

"No, I'm not married."

Summer's gaze dropped to his ring finger to see it was indeed bare. She wondered how he had managed to stay single. Or maybe he wasn't. Not married didn't necessarily mean unattached.

What was she doing? Henry was missing, and here she was entrusting Wyatt's safety to a man she had just met.

Ethan closed the door and pushed her to the other side of the car. After he helped her into her seat and stored the wheelchair in the trunk, he climbed behind the wheel.

"Where are we going now?" Summer asked, her trepidation causing her voice to waver.

"We're going to a friend's house. It's not far."

Exhausted, Summer leaned her head back and put her hand on Wyatt's foot, needing that bit of contact with him. She tried to stay awake, but the emotional and physical exhaustion won out within seconds.

When the car came to a stop, her head jerked up, and she looked around, disoriented. Relief and terror mixed when her gaze landed on Wyatt, and the events of the past twelve hours came rushing back.

An emptiness settled deep within her, and she struggled to perform the simple task of breathing. Wyatt stirred and whimpered beside her.

She patted his leg in an effort to soothe him and looked out the window. Standing before her was a single-story home with arched windows and a peaked roof. She guessed it to be at least twice the size of her house. Palm trees flanked the entrance, and flood lights illuminated the front walk against the setting sun.

One of the three garage doors opened. A man in his seventies emerged and waved for Ethan to pull inside.

Ethan put the car in drive and parked in the open bay. As soon as he climbed from the car, he shook the older man's hand, and they spoke quietly for a moment before Ethan retrieved the wheelchair from the trunk.

The heat in the garage greeted Summer when Ethan opened the door.

"Let's get you two inside." Ethan offered his hand and helped her out of the car and into the wheelchair. As soon as she was seated, he unstrapped Wyatt and settled him in her arms.

"Summer, this is William Blake." Ethan motioned to the older man. "He's agreed to let you stay here while we look for Henry."

Emotions clogged her throat, her imagination racing in a dozen directions as to where her oldest son might be now. Was he as terrified as he had been when Ricky had loaded him into the car? Was he already with Lanny? Did her ex-husband even know how to care for their son? Would he keep him safe?

"It's good to meet you, Summer." William waved toward the door leading into the house.

Common sense broke through her emotional upheaval. "Why am I staying at someone's house? I would have thought you would want to tuck me away in a hotel or safe house."

"Your ex-husband's organization has been known to find witnesses in our safe houses," Ethan said. "We're keeping you out of the system to make sure he doesn't locate you."

"Let me show you your room, and then we can all sit down and have some dinner," William said. "While we eat, we can talk about how we're going to get your son back."

Summer blinked against the tears that swam in her eyes. "Thank you."

* * *

Ethan followed William's directions through the kitchen and down the hallway. They entered a brightly lit bedroom, a queen-sized bed with a brass headboard sat centered beneath a wide window. A pack and play had been set up next to the bed, a bright-yellow blanket hanging over the side. A pair of crutches leaned against the wall.

William's wife emerged from a doorway on the side of the room, where a bathroom was situated.

"Summer, this is my wife, Hannah," William offered.

"So good to meet you," Hannah said before Summer could respond.

"We thought you might want some crutches when you're a bit stronger, so we brought those in for you," William said. "We can help you adjust them to the right height."

"Thank you," Summer said.

Hannah waved at Ethan and William. "Why don't you two go start on dinner? I'll help Summer settle in."

A look of alarm illuminated Summer's face. Ethan's voice was gentle when he added, "It'll be okay. Let Mrs. Blake help you."

She gave a subtle nod.

William put his hand on Ethan's shoulder. "Come on, Ethan. We have hamburgers to grill."

Ethan wheeled Summer farther into the room and stepped in front of her so he could see her more clearly. "I'll see you in a few minutes."

Summer swallowed hard. "Okay."

Ethan turned and followed William out of the room. As soon as they reached the kitchen, Ethan said, "I need to call Elias and let him know where I am. Any chance you have a burn phone I can use?"

"I do, but I already let Elias know you were coming," William said.

"Did he give you an update on the missing boy?"

"They're looking, but nothing yet. None of the neighbors saw anything, or if they did, they aren't talking." William opened the refrigerator and pulled out a plate with a half dozen hamburger patties on it. "Come outside with me, and I'll fill you in."

Ethan followed him through the sliding-glass door and waited impatiently while the older man fired up the grill and proceeded to lay the raw meat on the rack.

"William, you're killing me here. What do you know?"

"No sightings of Valo or any of his associates at any airports or bus stations."

"That's not surprising. Summer said Valo's men arrived in a car. It's been at least eight hours. They could easily be out of the state by now."

"Possibly."

Ethan caught the hint of doubt in William's voice. "But you don't think so."

"No, I don't," William said. "They don't have everything they came for."

Ethan considered the facts and let them fall in a new light.

"Something else you should know," William continued. "I assume you met the social worker who was in charge of Wyatt's case."

"Yeah. Ruth Bennington. What about her?"

"She's missing."

"What?"

"Security footage shows her being forced into an SUV, but the license plate was covered in mud."

"What would anyone want with her?" Ethan asked.

"My guess is that's how those men knew to track your phone." William flipped the burgers before continuing.

"Was the SUV picked up anywhere on traffic cams?"

"Not so far."

"What do you think? Do we bring in the media, or is it too risky?"

"The media is already involved. Photos of Ruth Bennington and Henry Valo are all over the news," William said. "If they are still in the Phoenix area, we need the public's help to find them."

"I doubt the abductors will be parading either of our kidnap victims around in public."

"No, but we have images of the men who abducted the social worker, and we know Valo is involved."

Ethan looked over his shoulder toward the house. "I can't begin to imagine what Summer must be going through right now."

"Elias mentioned you've had more luck working with her than anyone else so far."

"You can understand why she would have trust issues after being married to Valo," Ethan said.

"Elias offered to park a security detail outside . . ."

"That's risky," Ethan said. "We both know Valo has someone feeding him information from the inside, or the last two witnesses against him wouldn't have ended up dead."

"I know. That's why we decided against it."

"Maybe I should take Summer to a hotel or even my apartment," Ethan said. "I don't want to endanger you and Hannah."

"No one besides Elias knows she's here, and I guarantee Elias Washington is not the leak."

"William, I know you're still capable of handling trouble, but I don't want to leave you here alone."

"I wasn't planning on being alone," William said. "How would you feel about being our inside man?"

"You want me to stay here?"

He nodded. "I already spoke to Elias about it. Neither of us likes the idea of your being in the field on this one since you've been linked to Summer."

Ethan let the implications of William's comment sink in. "You're afraid Valo's men might identify me and trace me back here."

"Yes."

"Do you have another spare bedroom?"

"It just so happens that I do."

CHAPTER 6

SUMMER TRIED TO ROLL OVER in bed, but received an instant reminder of her injuries. The pain that shot through her side and ankle paled in comparison to the ripping of her soul when she remembered. Henry was gone.

The deep ache that had settled in her chest intensified as she became fully awake. Two days ago, life had been normal. She had been making it as a single mom. Her job as a technical writer for an electronics company allowed her to work from home and provided enough income that she didn't have to rely on Lanny for support.

Wyatt's baby babble sounded from the portable crib beside her. Summer tried to push herself up in bed but only cried out in pain instead.

A knock sounded on her door a moment later, followed by Ethan's voice. "Summer?"

She took a second to catch her breath. "I'm okay."

"May I come in?"

"Yeah."

The door opened. His gaze lingered on her before focusing on Wyatt. "Hey, big guy. You ready to get out of that wet diaper?"

"Where's Hannah?"

"She's fixing breakfast."

Summer braced herself against the pain and tried to sit up again.

"Let me help you." Ethan hurried to her side. He put his hand on her back and helped her sit up.

Sweat beaded on her forehead, a result of pain and exertion. She took a second to catch her breath. "Can you help me into the wheelchair?"

Ethan's response was to push the wheelchair closer. Gently, he put one arm around her back and the other under her knees. Again, she braced against the pain. He lifted her from the bed and settled her into the chair.

Summer waited for the worst of the throbbing in her ribs to subside before she said, "Thanks."

"No problem." Ethan retrieved a diaper and the baby wipes off the top of the dresser and set them on the floor, along with the changing pad.

With apparent ease, he lifted Wyatt out of the crib, laid him down, changed his diaper, and dressed him in clean clothes.

"I can go get Hannah so she can help you feed him," he said.

"It's okay. Just hand me that baby blanket."

Ethan gave her the thin blanket and waited for her to drape it over her shoulder before he settled Wyatt onto her lap. He turned his back while she positioned the baby.

Finding his respect of her modesty endearing, she covered herself, Wyatt's legs sticking out from beneath the blanket. "I'm decent," Summer said. "What do you know about Henry and Lanny?"

Ethan turned to face her. "We checked out the three addresses we had for Lanny in the Phoenix area and two in Tucson. No sign of anyone at any of those locations."

"What were the addresses?" Summer asked.

Ethan retrieved a small notebook from his pocket. He read them one by one.

"You're missing at least four here in the valley," Summer said. "There's one in Paradise Valley, one in Glendale, and two in east Mesa."

"Do you have the addresses?"

"I know some of the street names," Summer said.

"I'll take whatever you've got."

Summer proceeded to describe the various houses she had visited with Lanny during their marriage. Of course, at the time, she'd thought he was buying houses to rent them out for his real estate business. Little did she know he was using several to create meth labs and distribution centers for the various drugs he smuggled in from Mexico.

When she finished giving him the list, Ethan held up his notebook. "This will at least give us a start."

"If we can get on Google Maps and Google Earth, I can probably identify the houses."

"That would be great."

Hannah poked her head inside the door. "Breakfast is ready whenever you are." She looked at Summer. "Do you need some help getting dressed?"

"I'll give you some privacy." Ethan deserted the room.

"Is he always this polite?" Summer asked.

"Ethan?" Hannah asked. "Always."

"I didn't know men like him really existed."

"They do." Her expression warmed. "I married one of them."

* * *

Ethan sat beside Summer at the kitchen table, scrolling through street-view images on the internet. They had already identified the two houses in Mesa. Now they were searching for addresses for the other two she had mentioned.

"I'm sorry, but I'm not sure where this one is. I know it's off of Glendale Avenue, but I can't remember the actual street name," Summer said.

"Let's go at this a different way," Ethan said. "Do you remember if you took the freeway to get there?"

"Yeah. We were on the Seventeen and took the Glendale exit."

Ethan zoomed out until he reached the image of where the exit merged onto the main road. "Try to remember how you got there instead of where you ended up."

"It's worth a try."

Ethan guided the mouse so the image on the screen followed the street view of the exit off the freeway. "Which way?"

"Left."

He made the virtual turn and continued forward. "Do you remember how far you drove on this road?"

"I'm not sure." She watched one intersection pass by on the screen, followed by a second, and a third. When the fourth approached, she said, "Can you show me the whole intersection here?"

"Sure." Ethan adjusted the image and made a 360-degree sweep of the area.

"No, that's not it," Summer said. "I remember there was a gas station on the corner."

"Then we keep going." Ethan continued the process of viewing each intersection as they returned to their virtual journey.

On the fifth one, Summer pointed at the screen. "That's it. Turn left there."

"Then what?"

"I'm pretty sure it was a right on one of these side streets."

For the next fifteen minutes, they searched through one neighborhood after another.

"We're never going to find it," Summer said.

Ethan recognized her despair and frustration. He put his hand on hers and tried not to think about the softness of her skin. "We'll find it, and we'll find Henry."

Wyatt squeaked from Summer's room.

Summer put her hands on the wheels of her wheelchair, but before she could move, Hannah called from the kitchen. "Don't worry. I've got him."

Summer looked back at the screen and straightened. "Wait. Go forward a bit."

Ethan scrolled up.

Summer pointed at the mouse. "Can I try?"

"Of course." Ethan handed it to her, along with a clipboard so she would have a hard surface for the mouse without having to reach the table.

"Thanks." She moved forward two blocks, then back a block. After circling once, she stopped and went through another 360 view. "That's it."

Ethan pointed at a two-story house with a wide front yard. "This one?"

She nodded excitedly. "Yes."

"I'll call it in." Ethan retrieved the disposable cell phone William had given him. "Do you need a break before we look for the last one?"

Even though Ethan suspected her medication was only taking the edge off her pain, she said, "I want to keep going."

"Okay." Ethan dialed Elias's number.

"Do you have anything?" Elias asked by way of greeting.

"I have another address for us to check out." Ethan peeked over Summer's shoulder to read it off the screen.

"I'll have Ray check it out."

Ethan crossed to the refrigerator. "Anything on the first two I gave you?"

"Nothing," Elias said. "We searched both, but there wasn't any sign anyone had been living there recently."

Ethan poured two glasses of water and carried them to the table. "Hopefully we'll have better luck with this one."

"We did have one development on our end."

"What's that?" Ethan asked.

"We found the missing social worker," Elias said, his voice grave. "A couple out walking their dogs by South Mountain found her body."

"These people are ruthless."

"I'm afraid so. Keep your head down. I'll keep you posted."

"Thanks." Ethan hung up the phone and plucked an apple and a banana out of the fruit bowl in the center of the table. "Pick one. You need to keep up your strength," he said to Summer.

She chose the banana. "Thanks."

"You're welcome." Ethan bit into the apple and sat beside her. "You ready to start again?"

"I'm ready to have Henry back."

"In that case, let's take a drive through Paradise Valley."

CHAPTER 7

LANNY WALKED DOWN THE HALL toward the sound of whimpering. He reached Henry's room, where his oldest son was curled into a ball, tears rolling down his chubby cheeks.

"Hey, Henry." Lanny sat on the side of the twin bed. "What's wrong?"

"I want Mommy."

Lanny fought his annoyance. "I'm here. You've got me."

"But I want Mommy."

"Mommy can't be with us right now." He ran a hand over Henry's mop of thick hair. "You go back to sleep."

"I'm thirsty."

Impatience replaced Lanny's annoyance. For the past three nights, Henry had woken crying, always demanding something to eat or drink before he would settle back down. Inevitably, he'd wet his bed before morning came, no matter how many times Lanny made him go to the bathroom.

"Get to sleep," Lanny said.

"But, Daddy . . ."

"You heard me," he snapped.

Henry's sob filled the room, and he curled back under the covers.

Unwilling to deal with his son's late-night demands any longer, Lanny rose and left the room.

Nigel walked down the hall toward him. "Is he okay?"

"He's fine." Lanny motioned Nigel into the living room, where they wouldn't have to listen to Henry crying. "Anything?"

"Nothing."

"How is that possible? You said yourself the FBI took her into custody."

"Yes, but our contact with the bureau checked all their safe houses in the area and came up empty."

"What about the agent who was with her at the hospital?"

"Ethan Flanagan," Nigel said. "He dropped off the radar too. Officially, he's on leave."

"He's got to be with Summer," Lanny said. "Who is this guy anyway?"

"No one knows much about him. He only transferred to the Phoenix office a few months ago."

"Do a deep dive into his background. See if we can squeeze this guy." Lanny poured himself a drink and downed it in one swallow. "If he has to choose between his family and Summer, he'll hand her and Wyatt over."

"His parents are dead. I know that much."

Lanny's jaw clenched. "There's got to be a way to find them."

"I wanted to talk to you about something else," Nigel said. "According to our source, your wife knows about Ruiz. If she's working with the feds, she can ruin everything."

"You know, I think there's a way to kill two birds with one stone."

"How's that?"

Lanny glanced at the hallway. "Sometimes to get what you want, you first have to let it go."

* * *

Summer lay Wyatt down in the portable crib in the living room, his body heavy with sleep. Over the past three days, the pain in her side had faded to a dull ache, but her anxiety over Henry's safety continued to escalate. Even though the Blakes had provided her with a set of crutches, she found it easier to rely on her wheelchair when holding Wyatt.

She lowered herself onto the padded seat as Ethan entered.

"Is he asleep?" he whispered.

"Yeah." Summer raked her fingers through her hair. "Ethan, I don't know how much longer I can do this. I don't know if Henry is scared or hungry or if he's even safe."

"I can't imagine how hard the last few days have been, but we're pulling in every possible resource." Ethan sat on the couch nearest her. "How are you feeling? You look like you're moving around a bit easier today."

"The pain isn't nearly as bad now as it was when I first got here."

William rushed into the room. "They found him."

Summer straightened. "You found Henry?"

"We're pretty sure we know where he is," William said. "Do you know if your ex-husband ever had dealings near the Mesa airport?"

"I'm pretty sure they were smuggling drugs through there," Summer said. "Before the divorce, Lanny and I were living a couple miles from the Mesa airport. He used to disappear in the middle of the night and not come back home for hours, sometimes days."

"That makes sense," Ethan said. "One of the shell companies we've identified as being Lanny's owns a jet that flies in and out of there regularly."

"Why do you ask?" Summer said.

"The bureau intercepted a call between Valo and Zacarias Chavez. They traced Lanny to a house near the Mesa airport."

"Do you know if he has Henry with him?" Ethan asked.

"Lanny mentioned leaving tomorrow to take his son to stay with family."

Dread filled her. "His mother lives in Mexico. If Lanny takes him out of the country—"

"We won't let that happen," Ethan assured her.

"What happens now?"

"Now we go arrest your ex-husband and bring your son home." Ethan stood and asked William, "Are you okay here without me? I'd like to be there when they go in."

"I figured as much. I already called a buddy on the police force. He's dispatching a unit to keep an eye on things here." William offered a wry smile. "The cops think they're looking for some burglars in the area."

"Whatever works to keep them close and alert." Ethan turned to Summer. "Does Henry have any drug allergies?"

"No, why?"

"It may be safest if we sedate him," Ethan said gently.

"You want to drug my son?" Summer asked incredulously.

"We want to make sure he doesn't end up in any crossfire," Ethan corrected. "Sedation will also protect him from possible emotional trauma in the future."

Summer's lips pressed together, and she forced herself to read between the lines. "You're afraid he'll see his father killed."

"No one should ever witness violence, especially a child," Ethan said. "With your permission, I'd prefer to take preventative measures."

Though it pained her to do so, Summer nodded. "When will you go?"

"I don't know yet."

"Bring him home safe." Summer reached up and took his hand. "Please."

"I'll do everything I can to do exactly that," Ethan said. "I promise."

* * *

Ethan gripped the gun in his hand, the weight of his bulletproof vest pressing on his shoulders. He really wished someone would invent body armor that didn't weigh so much.

The house in front of him was well lit, but with the exception of the gate at the entrance to the community, security didn't appear to be high on Valo's list of precautions. Thermal imaging gave them a relatively good idea of what was going on inside and where the boy was being held. A single heat spot in one of the upstairs rooms had been still since shortly after 8:00 p.m. The only other two heat spots had settled downstairs, both of them moving occasionally, either to do a security sweep of the house or to raid the kitchen.

Ethan didn't like that they had been forced to put this strike team together so quickly, but at least he was working with people he knew and trusted. Besides Ray, Charlie Whitmore and Brittany Moore had come down from the Flagstaff satellite office. Elias had specifically created this team to ensure they didn't have any possibility of a leak to Lanny Valo or his men.

"Ready?" Charlie asked through the communication headset he wore.

"Ready," Ethan confirmed, as did Ray and Brittany.

"Let's get this right the first time," Charlie said. "We'll secure the downstairs. Ethan, you go for the boy."

"Understood." The word was barely out of Ethan's mouth when he caught a glimpse of movement out of the corner of his eye. His voice low, he turned to see the shadow of a man disappear behind a eucalyptus tree. "Stand by."

"What's wrong?" Ray asked from his spot beside him.

"Movement. Northeast corner."

"Brittany, do you have anything?" Charlie asked.

"Checking." A moment passed before Brittany's voice came back over the headset. "Two new heat spots on the northeast corner. Looks like one is heading to the front of the house."

"Moving to intercept," Charlie said.

A new wave of adrenaline flowed through Ethan. "I'll take care of the other one."

"Keep it silent," Charlie warned.

"Understood." Ethan did understand. If they started shooting at suspects before they even got inside the house, there was no telling what would happen to Henry. "Ray, cover me."

"You got it."

Ethan holstered his pistol and drew his taser. His focus remained on the trees, his senses heightened. He took a step to the left and slipped behind the palm tree next to the back door.

He evaluated the span of yard between himself and his target. Only a narrow strip of grass separated the back of the house and the privacy wall, numerous trees and bushes filling the raised flowerbed that stretched the length of the yard.

Moving forward, he ducked behind the built-in grill, but his foot slipped on the rocks that surrounded the palm tree. He leaned down and picked up a rock the size of a baseball.

With the impromptu weapon in one hand and his taser in the other, he crept forward until the only thing between him and the shadow was fifteen feet of grass. The muscles in his left arm flexed, and he silently counted to three. He was between one and two when he heard a thump along the side of the house. Realizing Charlie must have engaged with the other suspect, Ethan sprang into action.

He hurled the rock at the eucalyptus tree and raced forward, angling so he could get a clear shot at the hidden figure. He raised the taser.

His voice low, Ethan issued his standard order. "Freeze. FBI."

The man didn't freeze. Instead, he took another step to keep the tree between them. Among the branches, the man's right hand came into view, his fingers gripping a pistol.

Ethan ducked.

Another thud sounded, this one accompanied by a cry of pain.

Ethan glanced behind him to see Ray holding a rock in his left hand. He switched it to his right and hurled it. This one clattered against the privacy wall.

Afraid the gunman would fire a warning shot or, worse, shoot Ray or him, Ethan reached down and grabbed a handful of mulch and dirt. The moment his opponent tried to circle the tree to get a clear shot, Ethan threw the earth into his face.

The man cried out and squeezed his eyes shut, but that didn't keep him from raising his weapon and aiming in Ethan's general direction. Ethan kicked his left leg out, his foot connecting with the other man's wrist.

The gun dropped to the ground, and the man followed, his hands feeling for the weapon.

"Freeze," Ethan demanded again. When the warning went unheeded, Ethan took aim and fired the taser. The buzz of electricity caused the man's body to vibrate on the ground.

Ethan retrieved his handcuffs. After he positioned the man's arms around the base of the tree trunk, he cuffed his hands so he couldn't get away once he regained consciousness.

Ethan spoke into his headset. "Target secured."

"That makes two," Charlie said. "Let's try this again."

Ethan moved back into position beside the back door, opposite of where Ray stood.

"Ten seconds." Charlie's countdown came across the headset in a quiet but firm voice.

Ray used finesse rather than strength to pick the lock on the door. He nodded at Ethan to indicate his success a fraction of a second before Charlie said, "Now!"

Ray shoved the door open and stepped inside. Ethan followed Ray into the kitchen, an open staircase visible to his right.

Charlie and Brittany's shouts carried toward them. "FBI! Freeze!"

"Go," Ray said, motioning Ethan to the staircase.

Ethan scanned the room and moved quickly to the stairs. He started up them two at a time, hoping to get to Henry before the commotion downstairs woke him up.

A child's cry met him as he hit the first landing. "Mommy!"

A gunshot sounded downstairs, followed by two others.

Ethan increased his pace, running up the last six steps. He reached for the syringe in the zipper pocket of his vest, but when he saw the little boy emerge in the hall, hair tousled and eyes heavy with sleep, Ethan reconsidered. He tucked his weapon into his waistband holster and approached the child.

Another round of gunshots echoed downstairs, and Henry startled. Ethan forced himself to focus on the boy. In a calm voice, he asked, "Are you Henry?"

Wide-eyed, Henry nodded.

"Your mommy sent me to find you," Ethan said. "Would you like to go see her?"

Hope bloomed on the angelic face. "Mommy?"

"Yes."

Another gunshot.

Henry startled again. "What's that?"

"My friends have the TV on too loud," Ethan said. "What do you think, Henry? Can I take you to see your mom?"

He nodded. "What about Daddy?"

"Where is your daddy?"

"I don't know."

"We'll find him for you, okay?"

"Okay."

"Come here." Ethan reached out his arms and scooped up the child. He spoke into his headset microphone. "Sit rep?"

"We're clear," Charlie said.

"Good." Ethan looked down at the little boy. "Henry wants to go see his mom."

"Come through the kitchen," Ray said.

"Brittany and I will take care of our suspects," Charlie said.

"We're on our way." Ethan carried Henry down the stairs, pleased that the child appeared to be in good health. Maybe once he was reunited with his mother, Summer too would be able to heal from this ordeal.

CHAPTER 8

HOURS HAD PASSED SINCE ETHAN had left the Blakes' house, each second feeling like an eternity. Logically, Summer knew the FBI wouldn't attempt to rescue Henry until well after his bedtime, but from the moment the grandfather clock in the hall had struck eight, she had convinced herself that a call would come any minute. "Any minute" had stretched into three hours.

"I thought we would have heard by now," Summer said from where she sat in the family room.

From his lounge chair, William looked up from his newspaper, a newspaper Summer was sure he had now read three times. "They'll take some time to observe the house before they decide how best to proceed. Sometimes waiting longer means less likelihood of a conflict."

"I don't know how you can be so calm," Summer said. "Didn't you say one of the agents with Ethan is your grandson?"

"Technically, he's married to my granddaughter, but I have to trust that Charlie can take care of himself. He and Ethan have been trained for situations like tonight."

"I hate the idea that they might have to drug Henry."

Summer tensed when William's phone rang. The older man snatched it up on the first ring. "Blake." William's gaze landed on her, and he nodded. "I'll tell her."

The instant he hung up, she asked, "Tell me what? Did they find him? Is Henry okay?"

"Henry is fine. Ethan is bringing him here now," William said.

Tears flooded her eyes, and her hand flew to her mouth as an indescribable relief poured through her. Just a little longer, and she would see for herself that Henry was safe. Now, if she could only make sure he stayed that way.

* * *

Ethan made it only half a block before he noticed a car pull out behind him. Taking evasive measures, he turned at the next corner. The headlights in the rearview mirror followed.

A left, a right, another left. Every turn Ethan made was matched by the other vehicle. Ethan pulled out his phone and called Ray. "I've got a tail."

"Where are you?"

Ethan relayed his location.

"I'll call in the locals."

"Roger that." Ethan kept the phone in his hand, waiting for Ray to give him further instructions.

"Head for the intersection of University and Higley," Ray said. "The police will be waiting."

"Got it." Ethan approached a stop sign at a main road. He paused only long enough to make sure it was safe before he pressed on the gas and turned toward his intended destination.

The car following him sped up and squealed around the corner, the back of the vehicle fishtailing.

The stoplight in front of him turned yellow, and Ethan increased his speed. He glanced in the rearview mirror to see that the car behind him didn't even tap his brakes before blowing through the red light.

From the car seat behind him, Henry whimpered.

"It's okay, buddy," Ethan said, trying to believe his own words. "I'm going to get you back to your mommy."

Henry sniffled but didn't speak.

"Status?" Ray asked.

Their pursuer closed the distance between them. Two miles and one left turn until they reached safety. Ethan pressed the gas pedal to the floor, but still, he couldn't gain an advantage.

"This guy must have one heck of an engine in his car," Ethan said. "He's closing on us."

"Can you make it?"

"I'll make it," Ethan insisted. Knowing his car wasn't going to be able to outrun the vehicle following him, he eased up on the gas. As soon as the other car changed lanes to pull beside him, Ethan slammed on the brakes and made a left turn a block earlier than intended.

Henry cried out. Ethan stomped on the gas. Tires squealed in the distance.

Ethan made it two blocks before the headlights reappeared. He slowed slightly, the trap laid by the police now only a quarter of a mile away.

"Approaching Higley," Ethan said.

"They're ready for you."

Ethan sped past two police cars. Immediately, the car behind him slowed. An instant later, it made a U-turn, and sirens rang out.

Not waiting to see if they caught their man, Ethan took a wrong turn before once again heading for the Blakes' home.

* * *

Summer gripped her hands together. Where were they? According to what William had said after speaking with Ethan, she'd expected Henry to arrive twenty minutes ago.

"Don't worry. I'm sure they're fine," William said.

Summer didn't answer. She wasn't going to believe her son was fine until he was standing in front of her. When she heard a car pull up outside, followed by the opening of the garage door, she pushed to a stand, grabbed her crutches, and started toward the door leading from the garage.

She was halfway there when it swung open and Ethan appeared holding her oldest son.

"Henry!" Summer closed the distance between them.

"Mommy!" He twisted in Ethan's arm to reach for her.

Ethan put him down, and Henry rushed to her, wrapping his arms around her leg.

Summer knelt and pulled him close, ignoring the pain that pulsed through her ribs. Joy and relief washed away the worst of her nightmares; Henry's presence a salve on the deepest of her wounds.

"I missed you," Henry said, squeezing his arms around her neck.

"I missed you too." Her gaze lifted to meet Ethan's. She mouthed the words, "Thank you."

His whispered response was barely audible. "You're welcome."

* * *

The mouthwatering scent of grilled meat filled the air, a flank steak sizzling on the grill. Ethan stood on the patio beside William and watched Summer through the sliding-glass door. She had abandoned her wheelchair to sit on the floor with her children, Wyatt lying on a blanket, chewing on a teething ring, and Henry sitting beside her, a book open on his lap. Summer pointed at the words, her melodic voice carrying through the glass that separated her from the warm spring air.

"That's a pretty impressive woman there," William said, following his gaze.

Ethan couldn't deny he'd had the same thought repeatedly over the past few days. The bruises on her face had faded, her natural beauty becoming more evident with each day. "I talked to Elias. Still no word on Lanny."

William used his tongs to rotate the foil-wrapped corn on the cob that occupied the top rack of the grill. "It would have been too convenient to have taken him into custody last night."

"I know," Ethan agreed. "I'm surprised he wasn't with Henry after he went to such lengths to kidnap him."

"He must have some business deal going down for him to leave Henry with one of his men."

"I had the same thought," Ethan admitted. "What I don't understand is why he didn't hire a nanny, especially if he expected to have Wyatt with him too."

"He could certainly afford one."

"I don't know if you've talked to Elias or Charlie lately, but Charlie is looking for someplace for Summer and the kids to stay," Ethan said. "We've imposed on your hospitality long enough."

"You know we've enjoyed having you, but . . ."

"We have to consider a possible backlash from Valo," Ethan finished for him.

"No luck in identifying who is leaking safe-house locations?" William asked.

"Not yet."

"Might be time to set some bait," William suggested. "If you put Summer in the system as being assigned to a safe house, Valo and his men might show up looking for her."

"Elias had the same idea. He wants to make sure we have Summer relocated before we dangle that carrot."

Ethan's phone rang, and he pulled it from his pocket. "It's Charlie." Ethan hit the talk button.

"Ethan, I've got a place for you," Charlie said.

"That's great. Where is it?"

"I'm going to meet you where you're staying now and guide you there," Charlie said.

"When?" Ethan asked.

"I'll be there in two hours."

"What about a protection detail?" Ethan asked. "Were you able to find a female agent Elias would approve? Our witness is going to need someone to help her get dressed and bathe for the next week or so."

"Brittany Moore is going to be your second agent," Charlie said. "I assume you know that Elias assigned you as lead agent on Summer's protection detail."

"I hoped that would be the case," Ethan admitted.

"Better start packing. I'll see you in a couple hours."

"Thanks, Charlie."

* * *

Summer watched Hannah and William sit in the living room with her sons, toys scattered on the carpet. The dinner dishes had already been cleared away, and the dishwasher was humming behind her. Ethan dried his hands on a dish towel and took the seat beside her at the kitchen table.

"What happens now?" Summer asked, her voice low.

"William and I were just discussing that." He glanced at his watch. "Another agent should be here in a half hour to take us to a safe house."

"I thought you said safe houses haven't exactly been safe lately."

"This one wasn't obtained through official channels."

"Where is it?"

"I don't know."

Panic bubbled inside her. "Wait. You're going to hand me over to an agent I've never met, let him take me to a place you've never heard of, and I'm supposed to be okay with that?"

"The other agent is showing us the way," Ethan corrected. "I'm coming with you."

An unexpected wave of relief washed over her. "Oh."

"I suspect the reason he didn't give me the location over the phone was to ensure no one could intercept the information."

Summer read the concern behind his words. "You think Lanny will come after the boys again."

"I think that with your help, we can find your ex-husband and eliminate any future threat against you."

"I've already told you everything I know."

"You know more than you think you do." Ethan put his hand on hers, the warmth of his touch seeping through her. "It's like when we were searching the internet for the houses you'd been to. You might not be able to tell me what I'm looking for, but together we have all the pieces of the puzzle."

"I hope you're right."

"Nothing wrong with a little optimism."

"Do you have some you can share?"

"Absolutely." Ethan hesitated a moment. "Can I ask you a personal question?"

"Of course," Summer said.

"How did you end up with Lanny?"

Summer had asked herself that same question hundreds of times. "I was young and naive. I let myself get swept up in believing fairy tales were real. By the time I realized Lanny was the opposite of Prince Charming, we were already married and I was pregnant with Henry."

"You didn't know what he did for a living?"

"Imports and exports," Summer said, the simplicity of Lanny's deception burning her tongue. "He left 'illegal' off his résumé."

"I'm sorry."

"Me too." Summer didn't think she could put into words the shock and embarrassment she had experienced when she'd stumbled onto a briefcase filled with cash. Or when Lanny had insisted she learn how to use a handgun in case she ever needed to protect herself and the boys. "Looking back, he made everything seem so routine. Meetings in the middle of the night. Taking me out to an old ranch to learn how to shoot. Installing surveillance systems in every house we owned."

"Did you move a lot?"

"About once a year," Summer said. "The first time, Lanny made it seem like a fun adventure. We were moving up to someplace better. By the next move, I realized we were running, trying to keep from being found by the authorities."

"I'm sorry you're running again." Ethan gave her hand a squeeze before he released it and stood. "Would you like me to have Hannah help you pack?"

"Yes, please." She glanced at her children. "I should probably bathe the boys and get them in their pajamas."

"Is it okay to bathe them together?"

"That's what I normally do."

"Great. You can sit in the doorway between the bedroom and bathroom. Hannah can help you pack, and I'll bathe the kids."

Summer pushed aside her irritation for needing help to do the things she wanted to do herself. "You're okay with giving my kids a bath?"

"As long as you don't mind."

"This should be entertaining."

Ethan gave her a puzzled look, which was quickly replaced with a spark of humor. "Your kids like to splash, don't they?"

"Oh yeah."

Summer's heart melted a little when Ethan simply pushed up his sleeves and started down the hall to fill the bathtub.

He glanced at Summer and must have seen the amusement in her expression. "What's so funny?"

Her response was to call to her oldest son. "Henry, time for your bath."

"Bath!" Like a bullet, Henry shot past his mother and headed for the tub.

"Hold on a minute, champ." Ethan caught him around the waist before he jumped in fully clothed. "You need to take your clothes off first."

Obediently, Henry stripped off his clothes and climbed into the tub. Ethan undressed Wyatt and set him in beside his brother. Immediately, the splashing began, Ethan's shirt absorbing a significant amount of the water that flew out of the tub.

In the bedroom, Hannah had entered and begun loading Summer's few possessions into canvas grocery bags.

Giggles and splashes continued in the bathroom, Ethan's shirt now plastered to him. At his waistband, Summer could see the outline of his holster, a reminder that he wasn't truly part of their lives but, rather, had crossed into them because of Lanny's actions.

"Ethan, thank you for your help."

Another tidal wave poured out of the tub and onto Ethan, only this one went high enough to soak his head.

He ran his fingers through his hair and scattered drops of water onto the floor. "Anytime."

CHAPTER 9

ETHAN FOLLOWED CHARLIE THROUGH A roundabout and turned onto Black Hills Drive. Cottonwood, Arizona. This wasn't where he'd expected to spend the next few days hiding out. The growing town was a hundred miles north of Phoenix, and the only airport couldn't handle anything beyond private planes.

With Summer seated beside him and two kids in the backseat, he could almost pretend they were a family going on holiday instead of an agent with a woman and her children, who needed protection. The tug of loss and his desire for a family of his own rose within him, and he pushed it aside. He had a job to do, and his personal needs and desires had to come second for now.

Charlie pulled up in front of a large fenced yard that held several structures, including two houses, a long storage building with multiple doors, and a detached garage. Porch lights from both houses illuminated the yard, and lights glowed through the windows.

Charlie climbed out of his vehicle and opened the gate on the right side of the property before waving Ethan through.

Ethan drove his borrowed car past the gate and parked beside the smaller of the two houses.

As soon as he turned off the engine, Wyatt began to fuss.

"He's probably hungry." Summer winced when she twisted in her seat to look at her boys.

"I'll get him."

"Are you sure it's safe here?"

"Yes. Another agent came early and secured the area." Ethan got out of the car and opened Summer's door before unbuckling Henry and retrieving Wyatt from his car seat.

Henry scampered out of the car and pointed excitedly at the yard. "Look! Swings!"

"Maybe we can play on those tomorrow," Ethan said. "If your mom says it's okay."

"Please, Mama?"

"We'll talk about it in the morning."

The front door of the little house opened, and Ethan's new partner emerged. "You must be Summer. I'm Special Agent Brittany Moore."

"Nice to meet you."

Ethan noted the flash of skepticism on Summer's face. Brittany stood only five feet five and couldn't have been more than a hundred fifteen pounds. Thankfully, Ethan knew firsthand the woman could handle herself in a crisis.

"You and your kids will be staying with me in here," Brittany said, apparently choosing to ignore Summer's lack of confidence. "Ethan, you'll have the big house to yourself."

"There are more of you. Why aren't you taking the big house?" Ethan asked.

"This one is set up for kids." Brittany held her hand out to Henry. "Do you want to see your room?"

Henry shied away from Brittany, grabbing onto his mother's leg.

"It's okay, honey. I'm right here," Summer said.

"I'll get your wheelchair," Ethan said.

"It's okay. I can use the crutches for now." Summer patted the top of Henry's head. "Come on, honey. Can you follow Agent Moore inside?"

Henry still hesitated.

Ethan settled Wyatt on his hip so he would have a free hand. He offered it to Henry. "Come on, kiddo. Let's go inside and see if they have any toys."

Henry took his hand, and together they walked through the door.

"The boys' room is the first one on the right. Summer, you have the one in the back."

Ethan glanced at the hallway. "How many bedrooms are there?"

"Two, but I planned to take the night shift and sleep in the other house during the day." She motioned to the couch. "Or I can take a nap there if I need to."

"I think I'd rather sleep in the same room as the boys," Summer said.

"There's an extra twin bed in there if you want it."

"Thank you."

Wyatt twisted in Ethan's arms and reached for Summer.

"I'd better feed him," Summer said.

"There's a rocking chair in the bedroom."

"Thanks."

Ethan followed Summer into the bedroom. A full-sized crib was pushed against the wall beside the door, and two twin beds occupied the space on either side of the single window. He spotted some toys in the corner. He pulled out a bucket of Duplo blocks and set them in front of Henry.

"Henry, can you play here while your mom feeds your brother?" Ethan asked. "I need to talk to my friends."

"Okay."

Ethan handed Wyatt to Summer. "I'll be right back."

He returned to the living room, where Brittany was talking to Charlie.

"I'm going to head home," Charlie said. "Give me a call if you need anything."

"Whose house is this?" Ethan asked. "It looks like someone really lives here."

"The property belongs to some friends of mine. They live in the main house during the school year, but they work in Paris during the summers."

"And this house?"

"Two of their employees lived here until a few months ago. They left the crib and some toys here so the mom could bring her kids when she was working here."

"Talk about a perfect set up," Ethan said.

"Yeah. I did let Mr. and Mrs. Peterson next door know that you're here. They tend to get protective of the property."

"Thanks for that."

Charlie handed Ethan an old-fashioned key. "This will get you into the main house. I'll see you later."

"Thanks again."

After Charlie left, Ethan turned to Brittany. "Are you sure you want to take the night shift? I don't mind trading off with you."

"It's fine. The kids already have an attachment to you, and I'm a night owl anyway," Brittany said. "I'll take ten at night until ten in the morning. That will give me time to help Summer if she needs assistance bathing and getting dressed, and you can help with the kids during the day."

Ethan caught an undertone running through her words. "Why do I get the feeling you don't want babysitting duty?"

"Because you're very astute." Brittany lowered her voice. "Kids are okay in small doses . . ."

"I get it." Ethan couldn't say he blamed Brittany. He usually shared her sentiment, especially when he was dealing with kids he wasn't related to. He didn't know why he had formed an attachment to Summer's children so quickly. Focusing on the task at hand, he asked, "What do we have for surveillance?"

"We're completely off grid here, but to be safe, Charlie and I set up surveillance cameras and motion detectors outside the two houses and on the shed," she said. "If someone tries to come for them, we'll know it."

"I'm hoping we can find Valo long before he has a chance to look for his family."

"We're all hoping for that."

* * *

Summer woke a dozen times throughout the night to check on her sons. They were here. They were safe.

Light streamed through the window as Wyatt gurgled happily. The clock on the side table read 8:23. Summer couldn't remember the last time she had slept so late. Of course, she had been up later than usual last night, taking a shower and doing a load of laundry so she would have something clean to wear today.

Henry had climbed in bed with her after Wyatt's midnight feeding, his little body snuggled against hers.

She slipped out of bed, tucking the covers around Henry, who flopped over onto his stomach. Summer put a hand on the bedside table to steady herself while she reached for her crutches.

Wyatt's babbles increased in volume.

"Just a minute, sweetie. Let me go to the bathroom before I feed you." Summer opened the bedroom door and hesitated. Did she dare walk the few feet to the bathroom and leave her children alone?

Brittany appeared at the end of the hall. "I thought I heard someone moving around in there."

Summer studied the other woman and had to remind herself that the brunette who appeared to be about the same size as her was a trained federal agent. Forcing herself to trust the protection she had been given, Summer asked, "Would you mind watching the kids while I go to the bathroom?"

"No problem." Brittany waited for Summer to come out of the bedroom and then took position in the doorway. "Do you need help getting dressed?"

"I think I can manage." She motioned toward the hangers holding the T-shirt and jeans she had laundered last night. "Could you hand me those?"

"I'll hang them in the bathroom for you."

"Thanks."

As soon as Brittany completed the task, Summer went into the bathroom. When she emerged a few minutes later, Brittany was nowhere in sight.

A flutter of unease surfaced, and Summer used her crutches to cross the few feet to her room. Ethan stood inside, holding Wyatt while Henry struggled to put his shirt on by himself. Relief and something else flowed through her.

Ethan looked up, his lips slowly curving into a smile. "Good morning."

"Morning." She glanced down the hall. "I didn't realize you were already here."

"Henry said he wanted to play on the swing set," Ethan said. "I thought I would take him outside to play after breakfast."

"I'm sure he would like that."

"Do you need help with anything?" Ethan asked.

"Would you mind getting something to eat for Henry? I need to feed Wyatt."

"No problem." Ethan waited for her to settle into the rocking chair and handed Wyatt to her. "Brittany will stay in the house until you're all set. Holler when you're ready to come into the living room."

"Thanks."

"Come on, champ. Let's go find you something to eat."

"Can I have arepas?"

"I don't think we have that," Ethan said. "How about some pancakes?"

Henry nodded and took Ethan's hand.

"Let's go." Ethan glanced at Summer. "See you in a bit."

"Henry, be good for Ethan."

"Okay."

Summer watched in amazement as her son trotted along beside Ethan as though he didn't have a care in the world. Was he really that resilient? Or perhaps the few days with his father hadn't been as traumatizing as she had thought they would be.

CHAPTER 10

ETHAN SAT AT SUMMER'S KITCHEN table, reviewing the file on Lanny Valo for the sixth time this week. Something wasn't adding up, and he couldn't relax until he figured out what it was.

Summer made her way down the hall.

"Are the boys asleep?"

"Yes. Playing outside this morning wore them out. With any luck, they'll nap for a couple hours." She propped her crutches against the wall and lowered herself into the chair beside him.

Ethan didn't miss the pain that accompanied her efforts. "You know, I can push you in the wheelchair if using crutches is too painful."

"I'm okay. The pain gets a little better every day." She slid the second laptop closer and turned on the video feed from the nanny cam in the bedroom. Once the image of the boys sleeping filled the screen, she turned her attention to Ethan. "What are you working on?"

"I was looking over Lanny's file again." Ethan leaned back in his chair and studied her, a flutter of attraction taking flight in his stomach. He fought against it, reminding himself that he was working. His personal life, or lack thereof, had to take a backseat until Lanny Valo was no longer at large. Trying to refocus on his task, he motioned to his computer. "I still can't figure out why Lanny let Henry out of his sight."

"He wasn't exactly the best father, even before we split up."

"What do you mean?"

"Lanny saw raising kids as women's work," Summer said. "He barely acknowledged Henry unless he wanted to show him off to his friends."

"What about Wyatt?"

"We split up before Wyatt was born. Lanny's only seen him twice."

"I forgot that you divorced while you were pregnant." Ethan tapped a finger on the table. "Why do you think Lanny wanted his kids? Why now?"

"I don't know. It's not like they're old enough to have anything to do with his business."

"When was the last time Lanny saw the kids?"

"Three months ago, right before I moved." Summer stared at the image of her children on the screen for a moment before raising her eyes to meet Ethan's. "I knew he was expanding his business, and it scared me to have anything to do with the Mexican cartels. When I moved, I was supposed to stay at a house Lanny bought for us in Scottsdale."

"But I found you in Phoenix."

"I know. I had some money saved up. My sister helped me rent the house in Phoenix under a fake name so Lanny couldn't find me."

"So you've been in Phoenix for the past three months?"

"I stayed in the house in Scottsdale for a couple days so Lanny wouldn't get suspicious," Summer said. "I don't know when he realized I moved a second time, but I doubt it took him long."

"He came after the kids because you cut him off from seeing them," Ethan said. "He probably started searching for you right after he realized you were gone."

"That's my guess."

Ethan rested his forearms on his thighs and leaned forward. "How do you think he found you?"

"I have no idea. I've been so good about always using cash for groceries, and my utilities are included in my rent. My sister takes care of paying for that every month."

"Where does your sister live?"

"In the Netherlands. Rotterdam," Summer said. "She does business in Switzerland a couple times a month, so she arranged to send the rent from a bank in Zurich."

"If Lanny knew you had family overseas, he might have figured out a way to trace the payments."

"Maybe. I was so sure he wouldn't find us. I honestly wasn't sure if he would care to."

"Something has to have changed in the past three months that made him want to find you," Ethan said. "Unless it took him this long to track you down."

Summer pressed her lips together. "I don't know how he could have found out."

"Found out what?"

"I'm not supposed to talk about it."

"Summer, I can't help you if you don't tell me everything."

"Three weeks ago, an agent with the CIA showed up at my house. She said the government wanted my help." Summer's voice lowered to a whisper. "She said no one would have to know I helped convict my husband. She promised I would never have to worry about hiding again."

Alarm bells went off inside his head. "This agent was going to arrest Lanny?"

"Yeah."

"And you said she was with the CIA?" Ethan asked.

"That's right."

"Do you remember her name?"

"Bridget Whitefield."

His sense of uneasiness growing, Ethan picked up his phone and dialed. "William, do you still have any contacts with the agency?"

"A few. Why?"

"Can you have them run a check on an agent named Bridget Whitefield?"

"Yeah. What's this all about?"

"Apparently, she approached Summer about building a case against Valo. Said she was going to arrest him."

"I'll make the call right now," William said, clearly sharing his concern.

"Thanks."

"What was that all about?" Summer asked after he hung up. "Why are you having William check Bridget out?"

"I think she wasn't really an agency employee," Ethan said. "The CIA doesn't make arrests, and they don't have jurisdiction in the United States."

"Then who was she, and what did she want?"

"That's what we need to find out."

* * *

Summer replayed the conversation with the fake CIA agent over and over in her mind. Why would someone pretend to want her help, even go to great lengths to assure her she would be protected if she cooperated?

Through the sliding-glass door, she could see Ethan holding a phone to his ear and pacing the small yard that spanned the area between the little house and the storage building Charlie had referred to as a shed. He lowered the phone and walked inside.

"I checked with my boss to see if anyone from the FBI or any other agency sent someone out to talk to you."

"And?"

"Nothing so far. He confirmed the bureau wasn't involved."

"And you don't think the CIA was either."

"It would be highly unlikely for them to conduct themselves the way you described." Ethan retrieved a notepad from his pocket. "Can you tell me what the woman asked you?"

"She wanted to know when I had seen Lanny last, and she asked about who he worked with."

"Tell me everything you told her."

"I said I hadn't seen Lanny since February, and she knew he didn't know where I was living." Summer lifted her leg and propped it on the ottoman. "I gave her the registration information on the cars Lanny and I owned together before the divorce and the cell phone numbers I had for him. I also gave her names of the men who used to come over and the kinds of cars they drive."

"Did she ask about any specific criminal activity?"

"Now that you mention it, she did. She wanted to know about a meeting Lanny had with a man from Venezuela."

"Venezuela?"

"Yeah. I overheard them talking about a weapons shipment. That was the last straw for me," Summer said. "The next day, after Lanny went to work, I loaded Henry in the car and drove to my attorney's office to file for divorce."

"How did Lanny take it?"

"I have no idea. I've only seen him in family court."

"I'm surprised he showed up. Court isn't exactly somewhere he wants to be."

"I'm pretty sure he was only coming to make it clear that if I talked to anyone about his business, he would kill me."

"He said that?"

"Yeah." Summer shuddered. "I believed him. That's why I was so hesitant to talk to the woman who came to my house asking about him."

"And three weeks later, Henry was kidnapped and you were nearly killed," Ethan said. "We'll get to the bottom of this, but for now, let's go over the names of your husband's employees. Maybe we can find him through one of them."

"You're going to need a bigger notebook."

"I'll use my laptop."

"Good idea."

* * *

Ethan emailed the list of Lanny's known associates to Elias before he walked the perimeter of the property. He was nearly to the front corner of the yard when the next-door neighbor walked outside with a rifle in his hand.

"Who are you?" he asked.

"Ethan. You must be Mr. Peterson."

"Ah, you're Charlie's friend." He propped the rifle against the side of the house and crossed the yard until he reached the fence that separated the two properties. "He mentioned someone would be visiting here for a bit. How long are you staying?"

"I'm not sure yet. Probably about two weeks." He motioned to the rifle. "Do you always carry a weapon with you?"

"I have a couple pesky rabbits who think my pepper plants make a nice snack," Mr. Peterson said. "Thought I might use them for some target practice."

"Isn't there an ordinance here about firing a weapon in town?"

"Yep." Mr. Peterson pointed at the road. "And that ordinance ends when you get to Airport Road."

"Good to know."

Mr. Peterson took a step back. "If you need anything, you let me know. My wife, Lucy, and I are home most of the time. If we don't answer, we're probably around back in the garden."

"Thanks. I appreciate that." Ethan lifted a hand in farewell before continuing along the front fence.

The door to the main house opened. Brittany stepped onto the porch and bounded down the steps with energy that belied the fact that she'd been up all night. "I'm going to pick up a few things from the store. Do you need anything?"

"Not that I can think of, but we should probably check with Summer," Ethan said. "Henry said something about wanting arepas for breakfast yesterday. I have no idea what ingredients we need to make those."

"I was heading to the house now," Brittany said. "She probably needs diapers and some extra clothes for the kids."

"I'll come with you." Ethan walked with her through the main yard, opting to enter the front door on the far side of the little house so he could once again make sure no one was in the area.

They walked in to find Henry sprawled on his stomach, a race car in his hand, his imitation engine noises filling the air.

Summer sat beside him, her hair curtaining the fading bruises on her cheek. Ethan had the fleeting wish that he could paint so he could capture the sweet, simple moment of a mother playing with her child.

Wyatt let out a squeal of delight from the small bouncy seat where he was playing a few feet away from his brother.

"Hey, Summer. I'm on my way out to the store," Brittany said. "Do you need anything?"

"Oh, I started a list." She waved toward the kitchen. "It's on the counter."

"I'll get it." Ethan retrieved the narrow strip of paper and read it. "Did you want Brittany to pick up the stuff to make arepas? I know Henry wanted one for breakfast yesterday."

"I don't know how to make those," Summer said. "Maybe we can get the recipe from Hannah."

"Hannah didn't make arepas for Henry," Ethan said.

"I just assumed . . ."

Ethan squatted down next to Henry. "Hey, buddy. Where did you eat arepas?"

Henry's only response was to run the race car across the floor in front of him again.

Summer put her hand on her son's arm. "Henry." She waited for him to look at her. "Honey, who made you arepas?"

"The lady with Daddy." The race car made another run across the carpet. "The one in the castle house."

"What did the lady look like?" Ethan asked.

Henry's little shoulders lifted. "I dunno."

"Was her hair the same color as your mom's or dark like mine or was it red?"

"Like yours." Henry's revving noises ended the conversation.

Summer straightened, and she and Ethan took a few steps away from where the boys were playing.

"Do you know what he meant when he said the castle house?" Ethan asked.

"I'm sorry. I don't."

"Can you think of anywhere Henry might have eaten arepas before Lanny took him?"

"No. I'm not exactly sure what they are."

"They're Venezuelan. They look like an English muffin, but they're made of white corn meal." When he noticed her surprise, he added, "There used to be a Venezuelan restaurant about a mile from my apartment when I lived in Virginia."

"I only know one person from Venezuela," Summer said, her wariness evident.

"The one who met with your ex-husband about running weapons?"

"That's right."

"I think your son may have just given us a huge clue as to who Lanny is working with."

"Knowing who you're looking for is one thing," Summer said. "The question is if you can find them. Lanny is quite adept at staying out of sight."

"Give us time. We'll find him."

* * *

Summer sat beside Ethan on the couch, the laptop on his legs angled so they could both see the screen. After Summer and Ethan had put the boys to bed, Brittany had come over to sit in the room with them. Summer knew she was being paranoid, but she also knew she would never be able to concentrate unless her boys were protected. She hoped an armed federal agent was protection enough.

"What about him?" Ethan flashed a headshot onto the screen.

"I don't think so," Summer said. "I'm sorry."

"I'm surprised you've remembered as many as you have." Ethan opened a spreadsheet and typed a note before retrieving another image, this one a casual shot of several men getting into a black SUV. "What about any of these?"

"Can you enlarge the image?" Summer asked.

"Sure." He zoomed in on the man to the right.

"No. I don't know him."

He dragged his finger across the mouse pad to frame the next one.

"Nope."

He moved to the next.

Summer leaned closer. "He looks familiar, but it's hard to see his face. Do you have any other pictures of him?"

"I think so, but let's finish with this one first." Ethan showed her the last two people in the photo, a man she didn't recognize and a woman with long, dark hair, her face hidden.

"I have no idea about the woman," Summer said.

"Let me get another photo of the one you said looked familiar." Again, he made notes in his spreadsheet before changing back to a photo.

Her hand came up, and she pointed at the screen. "That's the guy Lanny met with right before I left him. I don't remember his name, but I think it started with an A."

"Are you sure?"

"I think so."

Ethan brought up two more images, this time side by side. One appeared to be a driver's license or passport photo and the other a candid shot of a man and a woman.

She looked at the ID photo first. "This is the same guy."

"And that one?"

Summer's gaze skimmed over the man, landing on another familiar face. She put her hand on Ethan's arm. "Oh my gosh. That's Bridget Whitefield, the CIA agent."

"This woman?" Ethan pointed to the screen.

"Yes. I'm sure of it."

"And the man?"

"He's the same person in the last two pictures you showed me," Summer said. "Who is he?"

"Adrian Ruiz. He's the number-two man in the Ruiz smuggling operation, second only to his father. Their group is responsible for keeping Venezuelan crime bosses armed, as well as funneling cocaine into the US from Colombia."

"And the woman?"

"Ana Lobo."

Summer's jaw dropped. "Lobo? As in the Lobo drug cartel?"

"That's the one," Ethan said. "So, you've heard of them."

"Lanny didn't talk business much in front of me, but I would have had to be deaf to not know the Lobo crime family was his biggest competitor in Arizona," Summer said. "Why would she come to my house and pretend she wanted me to testify against Lanny and Adrian Ruiz? I thought the Lobo family had done business with Ruiz before."

"That was my understanding as well," Ethan said. "Maybe she didn't like the idea of Ruiz doing business with your ex-husband."

"But why come looking for me?" Summer asked.

"I don't know, but as careful as you were to hide your location, Ana has to be the one who told Lanny where you were."

"How do you think she found me?"

"I'm not sure." Ethan leaned back in his chair. "You said your utilities were included in your rent?"

"That's right, and my rent was paid through a Swiss bank account."

"Have you used any credit cards since you moved?"

"No. I use cash for everything: shopping, groceries, doctor visits," Summer said.

A new light appeared in Ethan's eyes. "When was the last time you took either of the boys to the doctor?"

"Last month. Wyatt was due for his shots."

"Did you use his real name?" he asked.

Summer rubbed her forehead. "Yes. The health department tracks the immunizations. I couldn't get him the right shots without proving what he'd already had."

"I think she probably tracked you somehow from that. Shots are at regular intervals so it wouldn't have been hard to watch for the record to come through if she had someone working in the health department."

"But why bother? What does she have to gain from finding me?"

"Distraction?" Ethan suggested. "Word is that Lanny has a big deal going down, bigger than anything he's ever handled before."

"That would make sense. The timing would be right from what I heard him and Adrian saying."

"If the Lobo family somehow got the information to Lanny that you were going to testify against him, he would be forced to deal with you now instead of waiting until after his business with Ruiz is complete."

"You think she came here to set me up."

"It's the only thing that makes sense to me."

Summer looked at the screen again. "I don't suppose you know where she is now, do you?"

"No, but I'll put an alert on her passport, and we'll see if the real CIA can locate her for us," Ethan said. "With any luck, finding her will be another avenue to finding Lanny."

"I guess if you travel enough crossroads, you eventually get where you want to go."

"Exactly, and we will get there."

Summer's eyes met his. "Thank you."

* * *

Ethan watched Summer use her crutches to go into her bedroom, worry gnawing at him. He didn't want her to know how dangerous Lanny's association with Adrian Ruiz could be or what it could possibly mean to her and her children. Danger was no longer a word with a capital D. It had bloomed into a word in flashing neon lights.

Brittany emerged from the bedroom. "She's settling in for the night. Can you do another perimeter search before you go to the other house?"

"Yeah, but first, come look at this." Ethan waved at his computer.

Brittany's mouth dropped open. "Adrian Ruiz? How does he fit into all of this?"

"I don't know, but Summer identified three separate pictures of him, never wavering that she was looking at the same person."

"I'd call that a positive ID."

"Me too."

"Do you realize what kind of havoc Ruiz could cause if he had access to Valo's distribution network? The drug traffic into Arizona could triple overnight."

"I'm more worried about the weapons he's known for dealing." Ethan closed his laptop and gathered his things. "I'm going to call Elias to give him an update."

"I'll let Charlie know what's going on," Brittany said. "If we're dealing with Ruiz's group, he may want us to relocate. No way he's going to chance that group finding us here at his friend's house."

"No one knows we're here," Ethan countered. The last thing he wanted was to upset the balance for the kids again.

"Charlie should know anyway."

"You're right." Ethan slid his laptop into his computer bag. "As soon as I drop this off, I'll walk the perimeter. Stay alert tonight, and call if you need me."

"You know I will."

"Thanks." Ethan went to the main house, stored his gear, and walked the fence line. As soon as he completed that task, he searched the outbuildings, circling the little house and then proceeding to do the same for the main house.

He was walking along the far side of the main house when he saw the twitch of the curtains in what appeared to be the kitchen window next door. He suspected the curious neighbor was Mr. Peterson rather than his wife. Sure enough, when he reached the front corner of the house, he glimpsed the older man pass by the side window in the living room.

Ethan went inside and made the call to Elias. After giving him the latest updates, he said, "Do you know of the Ruiz family owning property in the valley?"

"No. What are you thinking?"

"Henry mentioned something about a castle house."

"And if the house wasn't Valo's, it might have belonged to Adrian Ruiz," Elias said.

"That was my thought." Ethan wandered into the kitchen and opened the refrigerator, looking for a snack. "I don't know about you, but I'm not thrilled to find out anyone from the Ruiz family has been in the Phoenix area."

"I'm with you on that one. I'll have Ray search for any property owned by any of Valo's and Ruiz's associates."

"Might also be worth checking with a local Realtor. The description of a castle house might ring a bell." He took out a piece of string cheese and slid onto a stool at the kitchen counter.

"Not a bad idea. Ray's lived here long enough to know who he can ask about that," Elias said. "How are you holding up?"

"We're doing okay, but I have to admit, I'm feeling undermanned knowing that Ruiz is involved."

"You're off the radar," Elias reminded him.

"I know, but I've got a bad feeling about this. I can't see any obvious connection with Valo and Ruiz outside the potential deal we heard about, and I don't have any idea why Ana Lobo would have approached Summer other than to see if she could undermine Valo's business interests."

"Could she have been trying to see if Summer was willing to testify against Valo?" Elias asked. "If her main competitor was in jail, she'd have free rein over the drug traffic in the area."

"That thought crossed my mind, but Ana never tipped the FBI off. Maybe she thought we would uncover information against Ruiz . . ."

"And that would interrupt her business alliance with him," Elias finished for him. "Knowing we've got so many most-wanted types involved in whatever is going down, I think I'll have Charlie come down Monday to give you some extra support."

"I would appreciate that. Any progress on finding the leak?"

"Nothing yet," Elias said, his frustration evident. "Officially, Summer and her children are residing in a safe house in Cave Creek, but we haven't seen anyone come looking for them."

"Can you see who might have accessed the information?"

"That's the odd thing. I can't see any evidence that anyone has tried."

"That is odd," Ethan said. "Every time we've had a witness against Valo's organization, someone has shown up by now."

"My suspect list has been shrinking to nonexistent today," Elias said.

"How many people were on that suspect list?"

"More than I'd like to admit, but I had narrowed my top candidates down to two. One is an admin person, and the other is an agent."

"Any evidence of money transfers or sudden wealth for either of them?"

"Nothing that can't be explained," Elias said. "Maria Chase inherited a sizable amount when her mother passed away last year, and Joel Gavril won a quarter million dollars playing the lottery."

"But they're both still working?"

"Yes. They also both have access to the safe house locations."

"Is there anyone else who also has access to everything?"

"The only other person who knows where all of them are is Libby Webber, but we haven't found any indication that she is receiving any extra money or anything else that would raise any red flags."

"Is it possible that whoever it is realized we were setting a trap?"

"I don't know how, but that would make the most sense," Elias said. "I'll keep you updated."

"Thanks." Ethan ended the call and ate a bite of string cheese. He checked all the windows and doors to ensure they were locked, finally settling at the kitchen table with his laptop. Elias would get Ray to work on the search for the castle house on Monday, but that was still a full day away. No reason not to do a little research tonight.

Ethan spent two hours reading up on Ruiz's organization before heading to bed. He looked out the bedroom window, his view of the little house obstructed by the storage building between them. If he and Brittany could keep Summer and her boys off the radar, this was the perfect place to hide, but if someone found them, two agents would never be enough to establish a reasonable defensive position.

He dropped down onto the bed. Maybe Brittany was right. Maybe it was time to move Summer and her children again. As much as he wanted to let them remain in one place and find a sense of normalcy, he knew this was all an illusion. The only way Summer would ever be able to stop running would be to put Lanny Valo behind bars.

CHAPTER 11

Lanny loaded his pistol and tucked it in the front of his waistband. Time to end this. He studied the Google Earth images of the buildings on the three-acre property in Cottonwood, Arizona. A main house next to a long building that appeared to be too narrow to be a garage. Another building that was either another house or an oversized garage. A new building on the middle part of the property that appeared to be another garage. A small barn on the back part of the lot between two pastures.

A lot of places to hide, a lot of places to take cover.

Lanny looked up when Nigel walked into the kitchen. "Is everyone ready?"

"Yes. Are you sure you want to do this right now?"

He had asked himself this question a dozen times over the past two days. He wasn't sure what was more important to him right now: recapturing the legacy he hoped to build through his sons or protecting himself from Summer's potential testimony against him. He had kept her in the dark, but from the recording he had received from his FBI contact, Summer knew more than he'd realized.

He debated for a brief moment before making his decision yet again. "We can't wait. If someone realizes we're tracking Henry, we may never find them again."

"Yes, but even if we can't find them, the feds won't be able to find you either."

"We've built this empire on the ability to move freely in society when so many of our competitors can't. If I go into hiding, our operations will crumble a little at a time."

"I'll give you that." Nigel tapped his fingers on his thigh. "There's something else you should know."

"What's that?"

"Libby Webber."

Lanny recognized the name as his key FBI informant. "What about her?"

"She wants our help. Says someone at the bureau has been digging into her finances."

"What does she want from us?"

"Money. Relocation. Protection . . ." Nigel trailed off.

"Why do I get the feeling you aren't telling me something?"

"Does it strike you as odd that she was the only person at the FBI who knew about the recording of that CIA agent and your ex-wife?"

"It was pretty coincidental," Lanny said. "What are you thinking?"

"I think I recognized the other woman's voice on the tape," Nigel said. "Have you ever met Ana Lobo?"

"Xavier's sister?"

"One and the same. I had some dealings with her and her brother before I came to work with you," Nigel said. "I swear the woman on the tape is Ana."

"You think Libby is working with us and the Lobo family?"

"It would explain why no one else seems to know anything about an investigation into you by the CIA." Nigel shrugged. "Ana sets up Summer, gets her to say what she wants you to hear, and then has Libby pass it on to you."

"Why?"

"The Lobos weren't happy when they found out you were working with Ruiz."

"And our FBI friend helped Ana set me up, delivering Summer right into the feds' hands so she really would testify." Anger boiled inside him. "What did Libby want from us again?"

"She said if we don't give her enough money to help her disappear, she'll make sure the feds know everything about our operation," Nigel said. "If you're right, she's already started working against you."

"She wants to disappear, does she?" Lanny's eyebrows lifted. "Make it happen."

"When?"

"No time like the present."

"I'll send Antonio to take care of it," Nigel said. "In the meantime, we need to look at your plan for tonight. Do you really need this many men? Ten is a lot to commit when we're only two days away from making our biggest deal ever."

"Summer had help at the hospital. We have to assume the feds are involved."

"All right. You're the boss." He tapped the photos on the counter. "How do you want to play this?"

"Five groups of two men each. Two groups will block off the roads leading to the property to make sure reinforcements can't get there. Two men on each house, and the last team on the outbuildings. As soon as they clear their area, they move on to help whoever encounters resistance," Lanny said. "I will wait in the car down the street. As soon as you have my boys, bring them out to me, and I'll get them out of there. Everyone else will follow." He paused, his jaw clenching before he added, "Everyone dies except my boys."

"Even Summer?"

"Everyone."

* * *

Kneeling beside the bathtub, Summer strained to lift Wyatt.

"Let me take him," Ethan said, walking in behind her. He grabbed a towel, wrapped it around her smiling baby, and lifted him from her arms. "Come on, champ. Let's get you dressed."

"Thanks. His diaper and clothes are on the bed." Summer let herself enjoy the normalcy of the moment. She had no idea what it was like to have a spouse who helped with children, but she liked to think that if she ever married again, it would be to someone like Ethan. His innate kindness was such a contrast to the consistently neglectful behavior she had endured while married to Lanny.

"Come on, Henry. Your turn." She held his hand while he climbed out of the tub. When he was firmly on the bathmat, she dried him off. "Can you go get dressed?"

"Yes!" He raced out of the bathroom, and Summer braced one hand on the side of the tub as she stood. By the time she adjusted her crutches and made her way into the bedroom, Henry had his pants on.

Wyatt lay in his crib, his hands holding his toes as he gurgled happily.

Summer sat on the edge of Henry's bed. "Henry, come here. Let me help you."

Henry bounced across the bed and plopped down beside her.

"Put your arms up, and I'll put your shirt on." She picked up his pajama top.

Henry lifted his arms, and Summer noted a Band-Aid under his left arm that had peeled halfway off. Her stomach lurched when she saw stitches beneath it.

"Ethan, did you see this?"

"What?" Ethan left Wyatt in his crib and crossed to her.

"He has a Band-Aid on his arm." Gently, Summer pulled the Band-Aid all the way off. "It's covering stitches."

"What?" Ethan moved closer.

"He has three stitches in his arm. Looks like he sliced it on a knife or something." Summer took Henry's arm and held it still so Ethan could see the wound, a straight line with three neat stitches keeping the skin closed.

"Henry, how did you hurt yourself?" Ethan asked.

Henry's shoulders lifted. "I dunno."

Summer took her son's arm with the intent of putting a fresh bandage over his stitches. She pressed one side of the Band-Aid down, her thumb rubbing over a bump under his skin that she hadn't noticed before. Her brow furrowed. "Ethan, look at this." Summer pulled the Band-Aid off again.

"What is it?"

"A bump of some sort. It's right next to his stitches."

Ethan leaned closer and ran his finger over Henry's skin. A look of concern and curiosity quickly morphed into one of alarm. He motioned to the bedside lamp. "Turn that off."

"What's wrong?" Summer took Henry's hand in hers to keep him close and reached with her other hand to turn off the lamp.

Ethan turned off the bedroom light. "Wait here."

Ethan disappeared into the hall, and Summer could see the lights go off one at a time. Henry whimpered.

"It's okay, sweetie. I think Ethan wants to play hide and seek."

"I don't like the dark," Henry whined.

"I know." Her hand tightened on Henry's. "I'm right here." She looked up as footsteps approached, the only light now coming from the moonlight shining through the sheer curtains covering the windows.

Ethan walked in, his frame filling the doorway.

Summer stood. "What's going on?"

Ethan crossed to her and leaned down so his lips were beside her ear, his voice a soft whisper. "I think that bump on Henry's arm might be a tracking device."

Panic erupted. "What?"

"I'm going to call Brittany and have her set up a dampening field, but until I do, we need to make it look like no one is here."

"You think he knows where we are?" Summer asked, the panic streaking through her.

"It's possible."

"Who, Mommy?" Henry asked.

"No one, sweetie."

The light of Ethan's cell phone screen cast a soft glow on them, his fingers tapping the screen.

"Do we need to leave?"

Rapid footsteps approached, Summer's heartbeat quickening with every sound.

Brittany rushed into the bedroom. "Grab the kids. We have a security breach."

"Where?" Ethan demanded.

"Looks like at least two people heading for the main house." Her phone buzzed, and she looked down. "Two more heading up the driveway."

"Call for backup," Ethan ordered. "Summer, get into the bathroom."

Ethan scooped Wyatt out of his crib. Tucking the baby against his hip, he grabbed Summer's arm and helped her up. "Come on, Henry. You come too."

Terror clawed at Summer's throat as she hobbled forward, using one hand to brace herself against the bed and the other hand to nudge Henry in the right direction.

They crossed the hall and entered the small bathroom.

"Stay down, and keep the door closed until you hear Brittany or me on the other side." Ethan handed Wyatt to her. He lowered his voice. "This will go easier on them if they aren't awake for it."

Summer understood the unspoken question. Did he have her permission to drug her children? The trauma of Henry being dragged into a car, of her fighting to protect Wyatt, overwhelmed her thoughts. She looked down at her sons and nodded. She couldn't avoid reality, but she could at least make sure her sons didn't experience it yet.

Ethan opened the medicine cabinet and pulled two prefilled syringes from the shelf. His movements were deliberate as he unwrapped one, squatted down, and put his hand on Henry's arm. "Be good for your mama."

Henry didn't get the chance to respond before Ethan slid the needle into his arm and pressed the plunger. Henry's body went limp, and Ethan gently lowered him onto the bath mat. He repeated the process with Wyatt.

"I'll be back." Ethan locked the bathroom door and closed it between them.

Her baby in her arms, Summer leaned against the wall and slid down to sit on the floor. Something crashed outside, and she closed her eyes, wishing she too could sleep and pretend her world was at peace.

CHAPTER 12

His weapon already in his hand, Ethan rushed down the hall to find Brittany positioned at the edge of the kitchen, out of sight in case someone could see movement through the glass door leading into the side yard but with a full view of the front door and the mudroom, where the back door was located.

"Status?" Ethan asked.

"Police are on their way."

"Charlie is coming too, but he's a good hour from here."

"This will be over long before then."

"Have you had a visual?"

"No, but the motion detector on the shed also tripped."

"Three teams," Ethan summarized.

"At least two each," Brittany added. "How do you want to play this? They won't know which house the boys are in until they search."

"Not necessarily," Ethan said. "I think Valo implanted a tracking device in Henry's arm."

"You've got to be kidding."

"Wish I were," Ethan said. Though he could see only the front corner of the main house, the lights from the living room and front porch spilled into the front yard.

"Any idea how accurate the tracker is?"

"It's small. Probably gives them the location within fifty meters."

"Which would include the big house," Brittany pointed out.

"True. Hopefully, they didn't see me turn off the lights over here, and they're targeting the main house," Ethan said, reviewing in his mind the many hiding places between the two residences. He then looked up and down the narrow hall. Summer and the boys were locked in a windowless room, with the hallway as its only access.

"Maybe I should go out there and try to even the odds," Brittany said. "From here, you can guard both the front and back entrances."

Ethan glanced at her white T-shirt and then his own dark-blue one. As much as he wanted to be the last line of defense for Summer, logic won out. "Let me go," he said. "You'll be too easy to spot wearing that."

"Be careful."

"Let the cops know I'm out there," Ethan said. "I don't want to go down as a victim of friendly fire."

"You got it."

Ethan crouched down and made his way through the kitchen and to the sliding-glass door. Positioning himself beside it, he searched the darkness for any movement. A figure slipped from the far side of the shed and headed for the back door of the main house.

Ethan reached for the handle of the sliding door when the front door on the opposite side of the living room burst open. Ethan turned and took aim, taking a split second to verify the man wasn't in uniform, that he held a weapon in his hand. "FBI. Freeze!"

The scene unfolded exactly as an old training exercise at the academy. The man's gun hand came up and swung toward Ethan. Ethan squeezed his trigger twice in rapid succession, and the man dropped to the floor.

Ethan rushed across the room, kicked the man's gun out of reach, and quickly closed the front door to prevent any of the gunman's friends from entering without warning.

The fallen man moaned, but Ethan didn't dare turn on the lights to check the seriousness of his injuries. Instead, he holstered his gun, rolled the man onto his stomach, and cuffed his hands behind his back.

Ethan drew his weapon again and scooped the other man's gun up off the floor. He moved back toward the hall. "It's me."

He was only one step past the kitchen when the sound of wood splintering filled the air. Like a scene on repeat, a gunman entered through the mudroom and emerged on the far side of the hall.

Brittany called out. "FBI. Drop it!"

Two gunshots, the thump of a body hitting the floor. Brittany cleared the man's weapon. She was in the process of cuffing him when another shot sounded.

Brittany fell to the ground, and Ethan reached down and dragged her out of the line of fire.

"Where are you hit?"

She winced as she sat up and took two shallow breaths before she answered. "My leg."

Ethan pulled out his cell phone and called 911. "This is Ethan Flanagan, FBI. I need an ambulance at 197 S. Airport Road, and I need an ETA on police backup."

"The police are engaged with armed suspects at the two intersections accessing your location."

"Great," Ethan muttered. "Have ambulances standing by. I have multiple gunshot victims and an agent down."

"Can you give me the condition of the wounded?"

The newest gunman poked his head into the hall, leading with his weapon. Ethan ducked as a shot fired. He dropped the phone, raised his gun, and fired.

Behind him, Brittany scooped up his cell. "Special Agent Flanagan is a little busy right now. Just get us some backup." She paused. "I don't care if you have to send them up on horseback. We think we still have four more gunmen out there."

Ethan shot again to keep the man at bay.

Brittany dropped his phone to the ground, trading it for her fallen weapon. She took aim at where the gunman had been a moment before. Using hand signals, she motioned for Ethan to go out the other exit and circle around.

Ethan hesitated. The gunman's hand appeared from the mudroom again. He fired. The hand disappeared.

Options played through Ethan's mind. If another gunman came in from the living area, they would be pinned down. Brittany was right. He needed to eliminate the current threat, or eventually, the man in the mudroom was going to pick them off one by one.

Ethan gave Brittany a quick nod of acknowledgment and moved back into the living room. Another shot sounded behind him, and Ethan quickened his step.

He exited through the sliding-glass door, his eyes scanning the area to see he was alone in the side yard. He sprinted to the open back door, slowing three steps before he reached the doorway.

He ducked before peeking into the mudroom. The man before him was completely dressed in black, his back to the wall beside the hallway entrance. He immediately spotted Ethan and changed his focus. The man's gun came up, as did Ethan's.

"Drop it!" Ethan demanded, only to be ignored.

Ethan ducked behind the wall as the other man's bullet whizzed past him. A second shot sounded, followed by a third.

Ethan heard the click of a magazine being ejected from an automatic pistol and knew his opposition was reloading. He glanced into the room again, once more leading with his gun.

The man slid a new ammunition clip into place, but instead of lowering the weapon, he once again took aim. Ethan fired and hit his target.

He secured the man's weapon and retrieved one of his spare clips from his holster. He reloaded his own gun.

Three down. Three to go.

CHAPTER 13

SCREAMS ECHOED IN SUMMER'S HEAD, screams she stifled for fear that someone would find her and her children. The darkness pressed in on her, footsteps sounding in the hall again.

She cuddled Wyatt against her, his little body heavy with sleep, and kept one hand on Henry to reassure herself that he was indeed sleeping beside her.

Ethan's whispered voice carried through the closed door. "Three down. How's the leg?"

"I'm not going to be running any marathons any time soon, but I can still handle a gun," Brittany said.

"I'll stay here. Help should be here soon."

"You know better than that," Brittany countered. "If Lanny was smart enough to block off the entrances to this neighborhood, you have to figure he knows Summer has federal agents protecting her."

"No one can get to Summer and the boys as long as we keep this hallway secure."

"Ethan, if even two of them come at us at the same time, we aren't going to be able to hold them off. Having three extra guns doesn't help much if we don't have three extra shooters on our side," Brittany said. "You need to go out there and even the odds."

The whispered voices softened, the words becoming difficult to make out. Summer leaned closer to the door, pressing her ear against it in time to hear Ethan whisper, "Keep pressure on that. I'll be close by."

Muted footsteps retreated down the hall.

Summer drew a deep breath, fighting against her fear. Brittany was clearly injured, and her protectors were outnumbered. Knowing Lanny, he probably had more men waiting out of sight in case the first wave didn't succeed.

If Lanny and his men made it past Ethan and Brittany, she was as good as dead. Deep down, she knew it. She also knew her boys' futures would crumble if they fell into her ex-husband's hands.

Her chest tight, her stomach in knots, she groped in the darkness above her until she found the two oversized bath towels hanging on the rack. Still holding Wyatt, she pulled both towels down and draped them over her shoulder. She then scooted to the side of the bathtub. Laying Wyatt on the bath mat beside his brother, she rolled onto her knees and leaned over the edge of the tub. The water had all drained, her fingers brushing against the remaining moisture, a rubber duck, and the plastic cup she had used to rinse the boys' hair.

She moved the duck and cup to the side of the tub, used one towel to wipe away as much excess moisture as she could, and then lay the other towel on the bottom of the tub.

She lifted Wyatt over the edge and laid him inside. Straining, she repeated the process with Henry, positioning him next to Wyatt.

Satisfied that her sons were as safe as she could make them in this moment, she crawled to the door. She listened for a minute but didn't hear anything but silence.

Mustering her courage, she unlocked the door and pulled it open a crack.

"What can I do to help?" Summer whispered.

"Go back inside and lock the door."

"You told Ethan you were outnumbered," Summer said. "I know how to handle a gun. Lanny taught me well."

Brittany hesitated long enough to give Summer courage. Summer crawled into the hall and closed the bathroom door behind her.

"You have a spare weapon?" Summer asked.

"Yeah." Brittany handed her a pistol, handle first. "The safety is on, but the clip on this one is full."

"Can you light up your cell phone screen for a second? I'd like to make sure I'm familiar with the gun in case I have to use it."

Brittany complied by turning on the phone's flashlight and aiming it at the weapon Summer now held.

Summer did a quick inspection of the 9mm pistol. "I'm good now. Thanks."

"Ethan's going to have my head for letting you stay out here."

"As long as my boys are both still breathing when all this is over, I don't care who he yells at."

"Yeah, I like that about you." Brittany motioned toward the back of the house. "I'm going to move down a few feet so no one can pin us down from the back door. You watch for anyone coming in the front."

Summer drew a deep breath. "Okay."

"And, Summer?"

"Yes?"

"Don't shoot anyone on our side."

Summer nodded in the darkness. "I'll do my best."

* * *

Ethan skirted along the edge of the long building that served as a shed and spanned the back portion of the main yard. He sensed rather than heard someone's presence but couldn't identify the location.

He stopped and listened, scanning the shadows. Seconds ticked by, and Ethan edged another step forward. He caught a whiff of something human: body odor, deodorant, or a combination of the two.

In the distance, he heard glass break. He noted the open shed door three feet in front of him. Had it been closed when he'd walked by earlier tonight?

His hand tightened on the rubber grip of his pistol as he took another step forward. A figure emerged in a blur of movement, the shadow of a weapon visible in the man's hand. Too close to take aim, Ethan grabbed the man's forearm with his free hand. A shot fired into the air as the man's gun went off before the weapon fell to the ground.

Ethan ducked to avoid a fist that barely missed him. He released the man and took a step back, lifting his weapon. He opened his mouth to identify himself, but before he could get the words out, the man opposite him kicked out his leg, his foot connecting with Ethan's hand.

Ethan's gun dropped into the darkness.

The man lunged forward before Ethan could lean down and recover his weapon. A fist to his jaw knocked him back several steps, and Ethan's own fists lifted to block the next punch. He regained his balance, now keeping his weight on the balls of his feet.

The two men squared off, fists raised, weapons lost in the shadows. Though Ethan's instinct was to locate his weapon, at the moment, he was more concerned about his opponent doing the same.

The man jabbed with his right hand. Ethan ducked and threw two quick punches of his own into the man's midsection. The man circled back to where he had started, and Ethan caught a glimpse of the man's weapon lying two feet from the man's shoe.

Apparently, the man was well aware of where his gun had landed because he leaned down to pick it up. Ethan's heartbeat picked up speed, his sense of self-preservation kicking into high gear. He dove forward, wrapping his hands around the man's waist right as his adversary gripped the fallen weapon. The man rolled free of Ethan, but Ethan managed to grab his arm and pin his wrist to the ground.

The gun fired again; this time the shot was accompanied by the splinter of wood. A fist connected with Ethan's jaw, causing his grip to loosen.

Then suddenly, the gun aimed toward him. Ethan grabbed the man's wrist with one hand and the gun with the other. In the process of Ethan's turning the weapon toward his assailant, the gun went off again.

Ethan stiffened, his brain trying to wrap around what had happened. In the same instant, the man grappling with him went limp. Ethan's hand tightened on the gun, ensuring he had sole possession of it. He rolled backward. It took him a moment to realize the bullet had struck the man he had been fighting with. He checked for a pulse and found none.

Retreating back to where his weapon had fallen, he glanced around in the splash of light spilling through the windows from the main house. He spotted his gun beside a pecan tree and leaned down as another shot sounded, the bark of the tree splintering over his head.

Ethan grabbed his weapon, now with a gun in each hand, and dove behind a nearby pomegranate bush. Another shot impacted the ground behind his left foot an instant after he moved it.

Ethan took a moment to engage the safety on the confiscated weapon and tuck it into his waistband. He drew a deep breath and replayed the last few seconds in his mind to determine where the shots had originated. Back of the house? Or the front? He couldn't be sure.

The thick foliage kept him hidden, but it also prevented him from seeing any movement on the other side of the yard. He glanced behind him to the space between the little house and the shed. No movement.

Satisfied that he was still between Summer and the gunmen, he positioned himself on the side of the bush and called out. "FBI! Drop your weapons and come out with your hands up!"

Gunfire sounded in the distance, but it was too far away for Ethan to locate. Apparently, Lanny's friends were still keeping the local authorities at bay.

A creak of wood, muted footsteps, a door opening. Ethan couldn't wait. These men had certainly had enough time to search the main house and learn Summer and the boys weren't there. Two against two wouldn't be bad odds if it weren't for Brittany's being wounded and obligated to hold her position to protect Summer and the boys.

Afraid one of the men would circle past him, Ethan sprang into action. He popped up and fired off a shot toward the back of the house, then sprinted for the open shed door.

Bullets punctuated the ground behind him, the sound of an automatic weapon filling the air. Ethan crashed into the side of the shed and grappled to find the entrance, finally falling through and grabbing a shelf to steady himself as he came to a sudden stop inside the dark storage room. He breathed heavily as he took a brief moment to regain his composure before he peered into the yard. More gunfire sparked from beside the rose bushes lining the front corner of the house.

Ethan jumped back and pressed against the shelves at his back. His hand loosened on his gun grip before tightening again. He counted to three in his head, dropped to the ground, and rolled to the other side of the open doorway.

The movement invited more gunfire, but the man across from him didn't manage to adjust his aim before Ethan straightened and fired off two shots of his own.

The man jerked a step to his left and lifted his weapon again. Before he could squeeze off another round, Ethan fired again. This time, the weapon fell to the ground and the man dropped beside it.

Ethan looked outside in time to see someone disappear around the corner of the main house, heading toward the yard separating the house and the Petersons' property.

Ethan took a brief moment to make sure no one else was hiding in the bushes before he moved along the wall of the shed again and followed the last of Lanny's men into the yard.

CHAPTER 14

SUMMER STARTLED WITH EACH GUNSHOT that echoed through the night. She prayed the drug Ethan used on her children would keep them sleeping until after this whole ordeal was over, assuming it ever ended.

She looked down the hall to where Brittany sat. The wounded agent leaned against the wall, her fingers loosely wrapped around the gun that rested on the carpet beside her.

"Are you okay?" Summer whispered.

Brittany's chin lifted as though she was starting to nod, but the second half of the motion ended with her slumping to her side.

Summer crawled to where Brittany now lay on her side, her feet stretched out in front of her. She checked the downed woman for a pulse and found one, though it didn't seem as strong as it should be.

In the darkness, she couldn't see Brittany's wound, nor did she have any idea how to treat such an injury, even if she could identify it.

Not sure she could do anything for Brittany at the moment, she picked up the weapon Brittany had dropped when she'd slumped over and carried it and the one Brittany had given her a few minutes earlier back down the hall so she was opposite the bathroom door.

Silence stretched out for a minute before she realized the gunfire had stopped outside. Had Ethan been successful in stopping Lanny and his men, or had they stopped Ethan?

Three to one odds. Or worse. She prayed Ethan could survive the odds against him and that the ambulance would arrive soon.

She set the spare weapon behind her back and held on to the other with both hands, the gun barrel pointed at the ground.

Three to one, she thought again. She had survived those odds before, and so help her, she would do it again. She looked down at the weapon she held. Make that three to two.

* * *

Lanny gripped his hands on the steering wheel, the engine off, the key still in the ignition. What was taking so long?

From where he had parked, he could see the outline of the smaller of the two houses, no movement evident in the yard.

His men should have finished by now. The inconsistent gunfire made him think the altercations with the feds were happening in different areas of the property, but he hadn't received an update since Nigel had texted to say the outbuildings were clear.

His boys had to be in one of the two houses.

A text message buzzed, and he looked down to read it. *Main house is clear. Ricky and Valero are down. Leading the fed away from the little house.*

If Nigel knew two of his men were down, it was possible they weren't the only ones. If the men who were assigned to clear the smaller house hadn't brought the boys out yet, he had to assume they'd run into more trouble than they could handle. Incompetents. Six men should have been more than enough, especially with the road blocked off to protect them from reinforcements.

Not trusting his men to complete the task on their own, Lanny climbed out of the car. He drew his weapon and jogged forward until he reached the gate at the corner of the property. He slipped through and walked toward what appeared to be the front door of the house closest to him. Time to get his boys and make sure his ex-wife could no longer cause him grief.

* * *

Ethan reached the far side of the house. Light from the front windows combined with the light coming from the Petersons' home to illuminate the narrow yard, several trees lining the fence between the two properties.

Ethan scanned the area by the apricot tree and the deck beyond it. No sign of anyone else.

He padded forward, taking cover behind the grill on the deck. He stopped, listening once more for any sign of life. Nothing.

The thought surfaced that he was being led away from the little house deliberately. He debated whether to double back the way he had come or press forward.

Knowing that the man he was chasing wouldn't be able to clear the large front yard quickly, he circumvented the porch and jogged to the front corner of the main house.

Following his training, he paused before looking around the corner.

"Behind you!" Mr. Peterson's voice rang out.

Ethan dove to the ground, a gunshot sounding. Ethan scampered around the corner of the house and pressed his back against the brick.

Next door, Peterson stood at the edge of his porch, rifle in hand, and was using the wall of his house for cover.

"How many?" Ethan called out.

"Only saw one." Peterson nodded toward the door leading to the deck. "He cut through the house when you came around the corner."

Peterson's gaze left Ethan, and he jutted his chin toward the main yard. "You've got another one coming through the gate. Any chance he's a friend of yours?"

"Not likely." Two against one again unless he let Peterson and his rifle even out the odds. Not thrilled with involving a civilian, Ethan weighed his options. Concern for Summer won out. "Can you cover me?"

"You got it."

"Now," Ethan said.

Peterson shot a round. Ethan took a quick look around the corner, saw the figure in the distance, and started forward.

He made it four steps before the man he had been chasing a moment ago poked his hand around the corner, gun first.

Ethan took cover behind the front porch steps and returned fire. The man across the lawn picked up his pace. Using the trees lining the driveway as cover, he sprinted toward the little house.

Peterson shot twice, both times hitting right in front of the man. Unfortunately, the neighbor's efforts didn't slow him down.

Ethan sent off another two shots at the man closest to him but couldn't get the angle to hit anything besides the brick at the corner of the house.

With the other man closing in on Brittany, Ethan opted for a new tactic. He shot once, dropped, and rolled on the ground three feet to his right. He came up shooting, this time able to see his opponent clearly. His first shot went wide, but before the man could take aim, Ethan adjusted and fired again. This time his shot was on target, and the man collapsed on the grass.

Ethan kicked the man's weapon clear. He hesitated long enough to lean down and grab the gun but didn't stop to check the man's injuries. All Ethan could think about was the man who had disappeared behind the little house. Could Brittany protect Summer and her children long enough for Ethan to get there?

Sprinting forward, Ethan prayed he wasn't too late.

* * *

Summer heard the door open, saw the living room light switch on. The use of the light and the lack of gunfire outside gave her hope that Ethan had survived and that she and her children were truly safe.

That hope vanished the instant Lanny stepped into view. His gaze dropped to where Brittany lay before settling on Summer. His lack of expression when he looked at her chilled her blood.

Sirens sounded in the distance, but Summer already knew they were still too far away.

"Where are they?"

Summer still sat on the floor opposite the bathroom, her right hand out of Lanny's sight, her fingers still wrapped around the gun handle. "Why are you doing this?"

"They're my children."

"But why do you want them now?"

"It's not about them," Lanny said. "I'm afraid this is about you."

"I don't understand."

"You never should have talked to the feds." He shook his head. "I would have let you live, but . . ." Lanny's voice trailed off, and he glanced down at the gun he held.

Before last week, Summer had never before shot a living thing, had never considered that she would be capable of attempting such an act. Now, for the second time, she was the only thing between her children and a life of crime. She had killed once to protect her sons. Would she have to do it again? The cold blank stare that faced her pushed the possibility into reality.

His gun hand lifted slowly, as though he truly didn't want to go through with his threat. "I'm sorry, Summer. I really am."

Summer didn't dare wait to find out if he would experience a change of heart. She sucked in a deep breath and, in a quick motion, lifted the gun and fired a single shot.

Lanny stared at her in shock, and for a moment, Summer thought she had missed, despite the close range. Then Lanny's knees buckled, and his gun fell from his hand. He fell forward, his body sprawling at the entrance to the hall.

"I'm sorry too, Lanny," she whispered. "I'm sorry too."

CHAPTER 15

ETHAN WAS A FEW YARDS from the sliding-glass door when he heard the shot. His heart froze for an instant and then picked up speed. He rushed into the well-lit living room to find two bodies sprawled on the floor. It took him only an instant to realize Brittany was one of the fallen.

"Summer? Are you okay?" Ethan called out, rushing to Brittany's side. He checked her for a pulse, relieved to find she still had one. He looked up at Summer. "Are you okay?" he asked again.

She pressed her lips together as though fighting back tears, but she nodded.

Ethan secured the gun that lay next to the man. A closer inspection revealed the man was breathing but barely. Ethan also recognized him now. Lanny Valo.

After ensuring that no other weapons remained in the unconscious man's reach, Ethan took a step toward Summer. Lights from an emergency vehicle flashed through the window.

"I'll be right back." Ethan walked out the front door and yelled, "Over here!"

As soon as he was certain the paramedics were heading his way, he went back into the hall and made his way to Summer's side. The moment he knelt beside her, she threw her arms around his neck.

"He was going to kill me."

"It's okay." Ethan whispered the words, his hand cradling the back of her head and drawing her against his chest. "I'm here. You're okay now."

Summer held on for a moment before she abruptly pulled away. She patted his arms and his chest, her eyes meeting his. "Are you okay? I heard so many shots out there."

"I'm fine."

Two paramedics entered and split up to evaluate the gunshot victims.

Ethan turned and motioned to Brittany. "Is she going to be all right?"

"How many gunshots did she take?" one paramedic asked.

"I only know about one to her leg," Ethan said.

"That's the only one," Summer said. "She passed out a few minutes ago."

"She's in shock," one paramedic said.

Ethan motioned to Lanny. "What about him?"

The second paramedic shook his head. "Bullet to the heart."

"I really killed him," Summer said softly. "I killed my children's father."

"No. You protected your children from a man who had already proven he wasn't fit to be a father," Ethan said. "I'm so sorry I wasn't here for you."

"You were." Summer put her hand on his. She looked at the closed bathroom door. "And you made sure my boys didn't live this nightmare."

Ethan patted his free hand over hers. His chest tightened at the knowledge that Summer hadn't been given the same gift. "I'm so sorry, Summer."

"I know." She nodded at the bathroom door. "They're the ones who matter most. Will you make sure they're okay?"

"Of course." Ethan opened the bathroom door, his stomach clutching when he didn't see Henry on the floor where he'd left him, and Wyatt wasn't in sight. He took a step farther into the room, relief sweeping over him when he saw the boys sleeping in the bathtub.

He knelt and checked both children; they were unharmed. His protective instincts flared again as warmth flooded through him. Henry and Wyatt were safe, and so was their mother.

* * *

Both blockades Valo's men had erected must have fallen at the same time Lanny was shot because within a minute of the ambulance arriving, the property was swarming with emergency personnel.

From what Ethan overheard from the local police, several people had been wounded in their firefight as well, one police officer and four gunmen. What a night.

Ethan had moved Henry and Wyatt into the bedroom with Summer until he could take them to the hospital himself. Ambulances were in short supply tonight, and he doubted that was going to change any time soon.

Charlie entered the house right behind the coroner. "Hey, I heard about Brittany. Any news on her condition?"

"The paramedics said she was in shock, but they seemed to think she would pull through," Ethan said. "Can you coordinate with the police and make sure we get their crime-scene photos? I'd like to take Summer and her kids to the hospital. If there really is a tracking device in Henry's arm, I want to get it removed before we have any other uninvited guests."

"Not a problem," Charlie said. "Have you talked to Elias yet?"

"No. I sent him a text to let him know Brittany was down and that Valo was killed, but I haven't had time to make a call."

"I'm sure he'll have more details, but he thinks he found the leak in the bureau."

"What happened? Last I talked to him, he had three names he was looking into, but he didn't have any idea which one it might be."

"One of them ended up dead."

"What?"

"Shot at her home, execution style. Elias thinks she found out he was looking into her finances and got spooked," Charlie said. "Probably went to Valo for protection."

"And got a bullet instead." Ethan shook his head. "Not exactly the bonus one would expect. Any word on Adrian Ruiz or Ana Lobo?"

"Elias said he has a unit in place for some big deal that's supposed to be going down," Charlie said.

"Then Elias thinks it's safe for Summer to go back home?"

"If that's what she wants, but he recommended that she find another place to live since the Lobo family knows where she's living."

The idea that Summer had been so close to a woman suspected of murder sent shivers down Ethan's spine. "What do you think the chances are that the Lobo family would go after Summer?"

"I doubt they would waste their time," Charlie said. "Summer doesn't have anything on them that could put anyone in prison. A move for her would be more for her peace of mind than for her protection."

"You're probably right, but for now, do you have any suggestions for a good hotel around here?"

"You're booked in the Pines Motel. It's a couple miles down the road," Charlie said. "I figured it would be easiest to stay close to here so you can come back and pack everything up tomorrow."

"Thanks." Ethan started toward Summer's bedroom. Time to get her and her kids out of here before the boys woke up and saw the result of their father's actions.

CHAPTER 16

Summer sat in the examination room, unable to watch while the doctor cut open the stitches on Henry's arm and removed the object that had been inserted beneath his skin.

Wyatt lay in the stroller Ethan had found in the mudroom of the little house, both boys still sedated. At least Henry was able to sleep through this latest medical procedure.

All the way to the hospital, Ethan had assured her that everything would be okay, that Lanny could no longer hurt her or the boys. His words did little to take away the image of Lanny collapsing in front of her. Summer's pulse picked up rhythm every time she thought of what she had done, what she had been forced to do. The father of her children was dead, and he had died at her hand.

Her mind on overload, she reached down and ran a hand along Wyatt's leg. He twitched beneath her touch, but his eyes remained closed, and he quickly settled back into a deep sleep.

"This is a first for me," the doctor said. Using some sort of oversized tweezers, he dropped the metallic sphere into the plastic bag Ethan held.

"Is it really a tracking device?" Summer asked.

"I'm afraid so." Ethan walked to the door. "I'll be right back."

He left the room, and Summer turned her attention back to the doctor. "Is he going to be okay?"

"He'll have a couple new stitches that will need to be removed in ten days, but he'll be fine." The doctor continued with his task of stitching and bandaging the wound. He was nearly finished when Henry's leg twitched. "Hey, buddy. It's okay," the doctor said.

Summer picked up her crutches from where they lay against the chair beside her, then stood and crossed the room. Henry's eyes flew open, his look of confusion quickly replaced with terror.

He cried out, and Summer put her hand on his shoulder. "It's okay, honey. I'm right here."

"I'm all done." The doctor eased back to give Summer better access to her son.

Henry threw his arms around her neck, nearly toppling her over, but she regained her balance, though one crutch dropped to the floor.

The doctor picked it up and leaned it against the examination table. "Here you go."

"Thank you."

"You know, crutches aren't the most convenient when you have little ones. Let me see if we can upgrade you."

"Upgrade me?"

"I'll be right back." He disappeared out of the room.

Henry's grip around her neck tightened.

"It's okay, sweetie. I've got you." Summer rubbed his back, his body gradually relaxing against her.

Behind her, Wyatt stirred.

She couldn't move across the room while holding Henry, so she tried to set her oldest son down only to have his grip tighten again.

The door opened behind her, and a nurse entered, pushing a scooter. "Here you go. This will be easier to use than your crutches." She pushed it closer and pointed to the padded section where she could rest her knee. "It will give you more mobility while letting you keep your weight off your ankle."

"Thank you."

"You're welcome." The nurse retrieved a paper from a file holder mounted to the wall. The nurse set the paper on Summer's empty chair. "Here are the care instructions for your son's stitches. You'll need to come back in ten days to have them removed."

Summer nodded, even though she doubted she would be in this town ten days from now. Or would she?

The idea that she might be able to go back to her little house in Phoenix surfaced, but after what had happened there, she already knew that wasn't possible. She needed to find someplace new, someplace she and her boys could start a new life and know that Lanny's past wasn't going to catch up to them. The question was, where?

Ethan walked in looking more relaxed than she'd ever seen him. "Are you ready to go?"

"I am," she said even as Henry's grip tightened around her again. "I'm not sure about Henry though."

"Hey, buddy. Want me to carry you out to the car?"

Henry craned his neck to look around Summer at Ethan. When Ethan crossed to them, Henry stood on the examination table and held his hands out to Ethan. Summer's heart squeezed in her chest. Henry would miss Ethan when they moved on to their new life.

Her son wasn't the only one.

* * *

Ethan carried Henry through the hospital lobby, one hand propping him on his hip while he used his other hand to push Wyatt's stroller. Wyatt had woken up when they were in the elevator but had fallen back to sleep once they'd started moving again.

Summer had opted to use the knee walker to move through the hospital, the borrowed crutches in her hand.

Ethan had to admit she was able to navigate her way much easier with the new device.

She hadn't said much since they'd arrived, and he honestly wasn't sure what to expect. She had her life back, but Ethan had no idea what she wanted to do with it. His curiosity was killing him, but he was afraid to ask.

Henry's head drooped and came to rest on Ethan's shoulder. The satisfaction of having a sleeping child in his arms resonated, and he couldn't deny that part of him wished he could have many more moments like this one. He'd always known he would want a family someday, but he never knew he could come to care so much for children who weren't his own.

They made their way into the parking lot, and Ethan settled Henry into his car seat. He repeated the process with Wyatt, both boys barely stirring as he strapped them in.

"They're exhausted," Ethan said. He looked at Summer and noticed the weariness in her movements. He opened her door and said, "They aren't the only ones."

Summer didn't move toward the car. Instead, she lifted her gaze. "I don't want to go home."

"You aren't. We're staying in a hotel tonight."

"I don't mean just tonight." Summer gripped the car door. "I can't go back there. I don't want to remember what started all of this." She swallowed hard. "I don't want to remember that I killed someone there."

"My boss suggested you relocate," Ethan said. "I can help you with that."

"Relocate where?"

"I don't know." Ethan knew moving out of the Phoenix area could give Summer the fresh start she wanted, but the idea of not seeing her again left him hollow. "How do you feel about Cave Creek?"

"Cave Creek? I don't know. Why there?"

"That's where I live." Ethan kept his eyes on hers. "I thought that since I won't be assigned to protect you anymore, maybe you would let me take you out to dinner."

"Like on a date?"

"Yes."

The sharpest edge of her despair appeared to chip away only to be replaced by a look of regret. "I'd like that, but after everything that's happened, it's going to be awhile before I'll be able to leave the boys with a babysitter."

"Do you like Chinese food?" Ethan asked.

"I love Chinese food."

"Great. We can order in."

Her eyebrows lifted. "You want to go on a date with me at my house?"

"Sure. Why not?" His hands skimmed down her arms, and he took her hands. "I want to spend time with you. I'll come over, we'll have dinner with the kids, and then we can watch a movie or something. I want to get to know you when you aren't worrying about making it through the next day."

"I hardly remember what that's like."

"Maybe it's time to find out." Ethan pressed a kiss to her forehead before he thought it through.

The casually intimate gesture sent a spurt of longing through him. This woman he had come to admire so deeply was one of a kind. A second passed as his mind caught up with his emotions. The trust that had developed between them over the past week had grown into something deeper, something worth pursuing. His eyes dropped to her lips before his gaze met hers again.

As though reading his thoughts, Summer tipped her chin as though in invitation.

Ethan couldn't resist. He leaned down and kissed her, his lips firm against hers.

The kiss had been meant to soothe, to satisfy his curiosity, but when she slipped her arms around his waist and leaned closer, he sank. He deepened the kiss, a burst of emotions erupting in him.

All the terrifying events that had transpired over the past week faded in his mind, his thoughts focused solely on her. No longer was she someone to protect but someone to cherish. The longing for home, for family faded—his desire not for the abstract idea of home but for the specific life he could make with someone special, someone like the woman in his arms.

He pulled back and watched her eyes flutter open. He ran a finger along her jaw, warmth seeping through him. This woman had demonstrated so much courage and sacrificed so much in the short time he had known her. "You truly are an amazing woman."

"I'm far from it," Summer countered. "You have seen me at my absolute worst this week."

"Maybe it's time to discover what we can be together when things are better." Tenderness rose within him, and his thumb rubbed the back of her hand. "What do you say, Summer? Are you willing to see what we can be after you find your new normal?"

"Tonight, when you were helping me bathe my kids, I kept wondering if that was what life was like for other people." Summer looked at him for several seconds before she added, "I wondered what woman would be lucky enough to have you be there for her day in and day out."

Relief and something else pulsed through him. "I'd like to see if I can be there for you. At least for as long as you'll let me."

"I can't think of anything I would like more." This time it was Summer who leaned in. Their lips met again, the kiss holding anticipation and promise.

Ethan pulled her closer and let himself fall for one delicious moment. Hope flowed through him, Summer and her children at the center of every thought. He pulled back, brushing one last kiss over her forehead. "Come on. Let's get you and the boys settled in at the hotel. Tomorrow, we'll figure out how to get started on our future."

"Our future," Summer said softly. "I like the sound of that."

"So do I."

ACKNOWLEDGMENTS

THANK YOU TO THE DEDICATED employees at Covenant Communications for making this project possible. A special thanks to Samantha Millburn. You're the best!

Thanks to Paige Edwards, Ellie Whitney, and Kyla Beecroft for helping me polish this piece, and to Coco Francois for your insight into the life of a paramedic.

As always, thanks to my family for sharing me with my computer, to the Central Intelligence Agency Publication Review Board for your continued support, and to the readers who allow me to continue doing what I love.

ABOUT THE AUTHOR

TRACI HUNTER ABRAMSON WAS BORN in Arizona, where she lived until moving to Venezuela for a study-abroad program. After graduating from Brigham Young University, she worked for the Central Intelligence Agency for several years, eventually resigning in order to raise her family. She credits the CIA with giving her a wealth of ideas as well as the skills needed to survive her children's teenage years. She has gone on to write more than twenty best-selling novels that have consistently been nominated as Whitney Award finalists, and she is a five-time Whitney Award winner. When she's not writing, Traci enjoys spending time with her husband and five children, preferably on a nice, quiet beach somewhere. She also enjoys sports, traveling, writing, and coaching high school swimming.

OTHER BOOKS AND AUDIOBOOKS
BY CLAIR M. POULSON:

I'll Find You
Relentless
Lost and Found
Conflict of Interest
Runaway
Cover Up
Mirror Image
Blind Side
Evidence
Don't Cry Wolf
Dead Wrong
Deadline
Vengeance
Hunted
Switchback
Accidental Private Eye
Framed
Checking Out
In Plain Sight
Falling
Murder at Tophouse
Portrait of Lies
Silent Sting
Outlawyered
Deadly Inheritance
The Search
Suspect
Short Investigations
Watch Your Back

CORRUPTED

CLAIR M. POULSON

CHAPTER ONE

THE RESTAURANT WAS CROWDED AND noisy when Lieutenant Jay Tanstall and his two teenage children—Jonas and Kinzington—entered. When they were ushered to a seat, a pretty girl from the table beside them said shyly, "Hi, Jonas."

Fourteen-year-old Jonas grinned broadly. "Hey, Ada, what are you guys doing here?"

"Eating dinner. Mom and I get hungry like everybody else," the girl said with a teasing grin.

Jonas laughed. "Hey Dad, this is a friend of mine from school, Ada Pedler. Ada, this is my sister, Kinzington, and my dad."

"Oh yeah, your dad, the *cop*," Ada said with an impressed nod. "This is my mother, Celeste. She's a paralegal. She works with lawyers."

Lieutenant Tanstall stepped to the table and offered a hand to Celeste. Jonas had mentioned Ada was in his group of friends, but Jay had never met Ada or her mother. As Celeste smiled at him and took his hand, he was struck by how pretty she was.

"Ada has mentioned Jonas several times," she said. "It's nice to meet you both."

At the suggestion of seventeen-year-old Kinzington, part-time matchmaker, they asked their server to pull the two tables together. Kinzington and Jonas grinned at each other as their father and Celeste began to get acquainted. Jay found his conversation with Celeste stimulating and was almost sad when they'd finished their meal and said their goodbyes.

"Dad, you should ask her out," Kinzington suggested on their way home.

"Who?" he inquired, his face deadpan.

"You know who. Ms. Pedler. She kept looking at you and smiling all through dinner."

"At me?" Jay asked, feigning surprise.

Both kids laughed. "Yes, at you," Kinzington said.

"You just won't give up, will you? Aren't I doing just fine raising you kids by myself?"

"Yes, Dad, but I still think you should ask her out. She's pretty, or didn't you notice?" Kinzington teased.

"She's young," Jay protested.

"Not that young, Dad," Jonas said. "I agree with Kinzington. Ask her out. Ada and our friends would all think that's cool."

"I don't think so," he finally said, and both of them booed him.

In reality, he did think so. The following Saturday night, he pulled up in front of the modest Pedler home, just a dozen blocks from his own house, and shut his car off. He was as nervous as a teenager on a first date. All week long he'd thought about Celeste. Something about her had struck a chord, and he simply could not get her off his mind. But it wasn't until Thursday evening that he'd finally made the call. He'd shivered with adolescent excitement when she had readily agreed to go out with him.

***

In the words of Kinzington, Jay and Celeste had been an *item* ever since their first date, and Jay had not denied it. If he wasn't in love, he was sure close to it. And he felt like Celeste was feeling the same. He sure hoped so. They just seemed suited to each other. It was easy talking to her about any subject. She made him laugh. He made her laugh. They simply had fun whenever they were together.

They'd already been dating for a few months, but Jay was in no hurry. He was content to let their relationship develop slowly. He tried not to let his work as a detective interfere, although he knew that at any time, he could get a troubling case that would keep him so busy that he would see very little of her. But if she was truly interested in him, she would need to get used to that. He was in a dangerous profession.

CHAPTER TWO

IT WAS LATE AFTERNOON WHEN Celeste Pedler heard the loud but short-lived scream. Celeste knew that voice. She had heard Ada scream thousands of times during her fourteen-year-old daughter's life, but never had it been a scream like the one she had just heard. Ada's had always been screams of delight or of anger, or even of fear, but never a scream of sheer terror. It froze Celeste's heart.

She fled her kitchen, dropping the bowl she had been mixing meatloaf in on the floor. She reached the front door just in time to see a white panel van speeding up the street and turning south.

"Ada!" She ran outside, leaving the door swinging wildly. "Ada, are you all right?"

Silence. Her head felt like it would explode. A door opened across the street, and elderly Josie Jamison came out.

"Celeste," she called across the street while running in a waddle. "I heard the scream."

"It was Ada!" Celeste responded. "Did you see her?"

"Not when she screamed," Josie said, huffing for breath as she carried her squat, round body into the street as fast as her short legs would carry her.

Celeste ran into the street, and the two women met in the center. "When did you see her?" Celeste asked, fear spilling from her voice.

"I was reading in the living room when I heard the scream," Josie responded. "When I looked out the window, I saw her getting forced into a white van."

Celeste's world stood still. She had not recognized the van she'd seen only moments before. "She was being forced?" She trembled with fear. "Are you sure? I just saw a van driving away from here."

"Yes. She was thrown in by two men dressed in black." Josie caught a quick breath. "They picked her up and literally threw her through the back door."

She wheezed and took another breath. "The van took off after they jumped in after her. I didn't see the driver very well, but he was in an awful hurry."

"I saw the van," Celeste said. "I've got to call the police." She tried to corral her fear and do what she had to in order to save her daughter.

She ran back to her house, Josie waddling behind her. Celeste grabbed her cell phone from where it had been lying on the counter in the kitchen, but before she could make a call to her boyfriend, Lieutenant Jay Tanstall, she stepped in the spilled bowl of meat and raw eggs that she had dropped earlier. Her feet flew out from under her. Her head slammed into the counter and everything went black.

***

Josie found Celeste on the kitchen floor. "Celeste! Wake up, dear!" she shouted as she knelt beside her on the floor. "We've got to call 911."

Celeste did not respond. Josie could see that her chest was rising and falling, which was a small relief. She had to do something. Panicked, the elderly woman slowly got back to her feet and looked around the kitchen for a landline phone. She didn't see one. She did see Celeste's cell phone where it had landed when she fell. Josie picked it up, looked at it helplessly, and then laid it on the counter.

"I've never used one of these things," she said to Celeste's unconscious face. "I will hurry home and call 911 from there. I'll be right back."

When Josie returned, Celeste was still unconscious.

Josie awkwardly knelt beside her until she heard a police siren. She got to her feet, using the counter to hoist herself up, then scurried to the door, where she met an officer who looked to be in his fifties: his brown hair was mixed with gray. His uniform, wrinkled in places and slightly untucked, gave the impression that he didn't care overly much about his appearance.

"What seems to be the problem?" he asked.

"My neighbor, she's unconscious! Her daughter has been kidnapped! It's so horrible," Josie said.

"You need to calm down. I'm Officer Casper Spurr. Let's begin with Ms. Pedler, the unconscious woman. Do we need an ambulance?"

"I asked for one to come," Josie said as she led Officer Spurr to the kitchen.

"Okay, let's take a look." He squatted down beside Celeste. "Pretty bad bump."

Another siren sounded outside, coming closer.

In another minute that felt like an eternity, paramedics rushed inside the house and started taking care of Celeste. Officer Spurr oversaw the ordeal, but Josie needed his attention more. "Officer. About Celeste's daughter," she said. "You've got to find her."

"Let's take care of this woman first," he said.

"But they're getting away with Ada!" Tears formed in Josie's eyes. "Please. Someone has got to find Ada. She needs help *now*."

Officer Spurr ignored the old lady until the paramedics had safely carried Celeste into the ambulance. "All right. Tell me about this person, this girl who ran away. You say it was a girl?"

"She didn't run away!" Josie shouted, shaking her fists. "Celeste's daughter has been kidnapped. Two masked men in a van took her."

"Now don't get alarmed, lady. Usually in cases like this, young girls run away, but they sometimes fake it to look like a kidnapping. She's probably with her boyfriend right now. She'll come home soon, I'm sure."

Mrs. Jamison was beside herself. "Officer, listen to me! Ada was kidnapped just before I called 911. Two men in black grabbed her right from the sidewalk in front of this house. She screamed, then they gagged her and threw her in the back of a white van."

"Okay, let's assume for a moment that she really was kidnapped. I'll need a more detailed description of the gray van. Did you get a make?" Officer Spurr asked.

"Did I say gray?" Josie asked. "If I did, I was wrong. I'm pretty sure it was white."

"But you said gray. Which is it, Mrs. . . . . I didn't get your name."

"I'm Josie Jamison. I live right across the street. I heard a terrible scream and looked out the window just as they dragged Ada from the sidewalk."

"The van," he insisted. "You said it was gray. Tell me more about it."

"Let's see. It didn't have windows," she said. "It was a utility van, I think. You know, the kind workers carry tools and things in. Officer, aren't you going to call it in? Other officers could be looking for Ada right now."

"I need to be sure she didn't just run away. We need to wait twenty-four hours before we put runaways on the air. Kidnappers don't take people off the sidewalks in front of their houses in broad daylight. Does her boyfriend have a gray van?"

Josie's head spun. "She's fourteen. She doesn't have a boyfriend. Please, you've got to believe me. She's been kidnapped! Call it in right now. *Please*."

"In a moment, if you insist," Spurr said. "First, however, I need a description of the runaway."

"She didn't . . ." Josie began. "Oh, never mind. Ada is fourteen years old. Her last name is Pedler. Her mother is Celeste Pedler. Ada is about five feet tall and is a slender thing. She has long blonde hair, which was in a ponytail today. She's very pretty, like her mother. She was wearing blue jeans and a light-blue shirt. Is that enough? Please, officer, call that in."

"Okay," he finally agreed and pulled the mic from its holder on his shirt and called his dispatcher. "We have a runaway girl. Ada Pedler. Age fourteen. She has long brown hair and is dressed in green. She was last seen leaving in a gray van. License number and make of van is unknown."

Josie listened with her mouth hanging open. The officer had barely finished speaking when she said, "No, she has *blonde* hair. It was a white van. She was wearing blue. She didn't run away!"

"Mrs. Jamison, you're confused," Spurr said gently. "Let me walk you back to your house. You need to lie down."

"It was a white van. Ada has blonde hair," Josie insisted and then began to cry.

"I reported exactly what you told me," Officer Spurr said. "Now come on. You're all shaken up. We'll take care of things from here. Don't you go worrying yourself to death over a little girl who is just running off with her boyfriend."

***

In the hospital, Celeste Pedler finally regained consciousness. She tried to recall what had happened, but her mind was fuzzy. The nurse told her she had fallen in her house, which Celeste didn't remember at all. She did, however, remember Ada. Ada always came home around four in the afternoon, shortly after Celeste came home from her work as a paralegal at the law firm. That meant Ada would be home alone now. Celeste needed to call her, to let her know where she was, to tell her not to worry.

She asked the nurse to call Ada's cell phone. "Sure, honey. I'll need to use the phone at the nurses' desk," Nurse White said while retrieving a pen and paper to write on. "Okay. What's the number?"

"Oh no. I can't remember," Celeste said, willing the fog in her head to clear. "Maybe you can call my neighbor across the street, Mrs. Josie Jamison. She'll check on Ada."

"What's her number?" Nurse White asked.

"I . . . Let's see . . . I can't remember that one either." Tears of frustration formed in her eyes.

"Let me look it up."

"It's a home phone. Josie doesn't have a cell phone. She's a little over eighty and says she can't learn to use any new kind of phone. Her number and Ada's are stored in my cell phone, so I don't usually have to remember them."

"I'll find her number," the nurse said. "What do you want me to tell her?"

"Thank you so much," Celeste said. "Ask her if she would check on Ada and find someone to bring Ada here."

Nurse White stepped from the room to make the call. When she came back a minute or two later, she looked concerned.

"Is Josie going to call you back?" Celeste asked.

"I think you need to go back to sleep. Let me get you something."

"What aren't you telling me?" Celeste asked.

Nurse White hesitated. "I need to call the doctor, then I'll be right back." She left the room again.

Celeste was torn. She wanted to climb out of that bed and go home, but her head hurt terribly and she was having such a hard time remembering things. Ada needed her. Celeste had to find a way to reach her, and the nurse wasn't helping. Maybe she could get her to call Jay. He would listen to her. But she was so very tired. She closed her eyes, and even though she fought it, she fell asleep.

CHAPTER THREE

It was Lieutenant Jay Tanstall's job to uncover police corruption at whatever level it occurred. It was not a job he had asked for, and he most definitely had not wanted it. But when his police chief asked him to head a two-officer internal affairs unit in the department, he reluctantly accepted.

Chief Jerry Thurley believed that at least two officers in the department were involved in serious illegal activities. He didn't say who he thought they were or exactly what they were suspected of doing, but it concerned him enough that he had given this new assignment to his top detectives—Sergeant Vallie Salmon and Lieutenant Jay Tanstall.

When asked why he didn't have someone from another department conduct the investigation like he'd done on past events—shootings and so on—the chief had simply replied, "I want this kept in-house and I want my department cleaned. I think we have a problem. I'm not sure, so I won't say what or why, but I want my best and most trustworthy investigators on it. The two of them are my watch dogs, so to speak. They'll find out where the problem is, if there is one, and solve it."

A memo from Chief Thurley went out to the entire department. It stated that Sergeant Salmon and Lieutenant Tanstall would continue to handle regular investigations as their time permitted, but when concerns were raised about anyone in the department not following department regulations and procedures, Salmon and Tanstall would make investigating those concerns their first priority.

The other officer, Sergeant Vallie Salmon, was younger than Jay by about five years, but she had been with the department for twelve years. Both were experienced detectives. Vallie was an attractive woman, but more importantly, she was honest, trustworthy, and dedicated to her career. She was also not a timid woman. She had courage, which Jay admired. He felt honored to work with her despite not being happy about the assignment itself.

Sergeant Salmon had said something interesting on their first day together. "Lieutenant, it looks like you and I have been shoved into a different world. The first thought that came to my mind when the chief told me I was assigned to IA was that instead of being one of the men and women in blue, I was now their *enemy*."

Life at the station after the chief's memo was sent proved Sergeant Salmon's words to be true. They felt like they had become enemies of their friends, which was not a comfortable feeling for either of them. Rather than the friendly greetings they usually got in the station, officers looked the other way, failed to say hello, and hurried away from them.

That had hit Jay like a punch in the gut. He didn't want to be the enemy of the police officers he worked with and respected. He was one of them and wanted to remain that way. However, as he thought about Vallie's words, he realized how true it was. Even the most honest cops on their force of just over two hundred would fear being investigated by the newly formed internal affairs office.

Of course, they were not the enemies of honest, hardworking, dedicated police officers. But Jay supposed they could be considered the enemy to those who were crooked and did not honor their oaths or their badges. In a way, he was okay with that.

***

Shortly after noon on the second day of their new assignment, the chief asked them to speak with Celeste Pedler. "She was injured in a fall at her home yesterday, but she has no memory of the incident. Her neighbor Josie Jamison said Celeste's daughter has been kidnapped, but it seems that Officer Spurr, who was called to the scene, believes the girl simply ran away. Look into it, you two."

Jay felt like he'd just been slammed upside the head with an iron bar. *Not Celeste and Ada!*

Sergeant Salmon must have noticed the anguished look on his face. "Do you know this woman?"

Jay kept his voice steady as he said, "I've been dating her. Ada is friends with my children." Even as he spoke, he realized just how much he loved Celeste.

"Oh, Lieutenant, are you sure you can handle this?" his partner asked.

"I have the same question, Lieutenant," Chief Thurley said, looking at Jay sternly.

"Of course I can," Jay answered, making his voice strong.

"If you change your mind, let me know," the chief said. "Otherwise, get on it."

"May we take a look at Officer Spurr's report?" Sergeant Salmon asked when Jay simply nodded at the chief.

Thurley, who had been holding a folder while they talked, handed it to her. "Read it, but then start fresh, you two. What Ms. Pedler told me is not consistent with the report. Bear in mind that she had a concussion and doesn't remember the incident. Also, I am not suggesting any wrongdoing by Officer Spurr, but I want to be sure. Find out the facts and act on them as it seems appropriate. Keep me posted." He fixed his eyes on Jay. "And be objective, Lieutenant."

"I will," Jay said. "You can count on both of us."

Vallie and Jay looked at each other as the chief walked away, both of them shaking their heads. They went to their new office and each read the report before filing it away. They said nothing about it until they were in their assigned squad car. When they finally spoke, Vallie stated what Jay also had on his mind. "Lieutenant, did you get the feeling I did that even though Chief Thurley said he wasn't accusing Officer Spurr of any wrongdoing that he has serious suspicions about him?"

"First, we're partners. You can call me Jay and I'll call you Vallie when it's just the two of us."

"Whatever you think is best," Vallie said with a smile and a nod of her head.

"And yes, I do wonder what the chief is thinking in regard to Officer Spurr. Do you know Spurr?"

"I suppose we've met, but I haven't worked with him," she replied as she brushed a lock of her long black hair from her face. "I can't place him right now."

"I've had a little to do with him," the lieutenant said. "He's been on the department for many years. I think he's about fifty or so. He's never had a promotion, and I'm not sure why—maybe he just isn't a leader. But he hasn't struck me as a bad guy."

"What does he look like? Maybe I'll remember him."

"As I recall, he has brown hair, is probably about five eight, and doesn't look like he takes care of himself physically." He shrugged. "He's a sloppy dresser and a bit overweight."

Vallie thought for a moment. "I still can't place him."

"I'm going to be optimistic here and assume he's a good officer, an honest one. If we find that we need to speak to him, then we'll pull up his picture on the department roster. For now, I guess we'll see what Celeste has to say. I suppose it's possible that she's in denial over her daughter running away." Although he knew her well enough that he didn't actually believe that. Celeste was a strong, honest, and decent woman. The very thought of her having such a terrible worry on her mind tied his stomach in knots.

"You have children, and you know Ms. Pedler, Jay. You'd be able to assess that more accurately than I would." Vallie glanced at him. She'd never been married. She was a good person, and he wondered why some decent man hadn't stolen her heart. Though he hadn't known her for very long, she would be a good wife and mother in his estimation. That thought brought back an old, familiar ache.

Cancer had robbed Jay of the love of his life ten years ago. He had struggled ever since then to be both a mother and a father to his children. Kinzington had been seven at the time and Jonas four. They were both great kids, but he felt like they had missed out on so much, not having a mother for all those years. He was grateful for his widowed mother, who lived nearby. She had been a great help to them. And recently he had been grateful to the very woman he and Vallie were going to see right now. His kids had already come to adore Celeste, and Ada and his own children got along extremely well . . .

He forced his mind back to the matter at hand. Tragedy had struck. He only hoped and prayed that he could do something about it.

It was a warm September day in the Denver suburb where Celeste lived, only a few blocks from his own neighborhood. Hers was a fairly nice, tree-lined street that he had become very familiar with. Most of the yards, including hers, were well kept, but the houses were modest and older. It was clearly not an affluent neighborhood but one where most of the residents took pride in what they had.

Jay pulled their cruiser up to the curb in front of Celeste's house. It stood in stark contrast to the small and rundown one directly across the street. Celeste's house was white with blue shutters. It was small, and the yard, though neatly cared for, was not as large as some of the other places on the street even though none of them were very big.

Feeling awkward coming to Celeste's home as a police detective instead of as a boyfriend, Jay pressed the doorbell. A moment later, Celeste opened it, but she didn't look at all like her normally radiant self. Jay had to catch a breath. Her eyes were red and puffy, and her shoulder-length blonde hair was mussed. She wore no makeup. He knew her to be a very attractive woman, but the despair that emanated from her was shocking.

"Jay," she said.

Jay stepped inside, hugged Celeste, and gently kissed her lips. "Celeste, this is my partner, Sergeant Vallie Salmon."

"Oh, so Chief Thurley must have sent you. He didn't tell me who was coming, but I'm sure glad it's you. I've been beside myself."

"Why didn't you call me when this happened?" Jay asked. "I'd have come right then. You know I would've."

"I couldn't. Apparently I fell and slammed my head into the cupboard. My neighbor found me. I woke up in the hospital, and I didn't find out about Ada until later. When I did, I immediately called the police department and talked to the chief of police. When I was released from the hospital, I was too embarrassed to call you. I knew the police were taking care of Ada's case, but I didn't want you to see me like this."

"Celeste, I like to see you no matter what," he said earnestly.

"I know that, Jay. I'm sorry, but you have no idea how glad I am to see you now."

"Celeste, is this a good time to speak with you about Ada?"

"As good as any," she said sadly. "Please, come in, both of you." As they stepped past her, Celeste grabbed his hand and held it. He made no effort to remove it.

"I like your house," Vallie said as she looked at the neatly arranged and very clean living room. Attractive pictures hung on the wall. A vase of bright artificial flowers, a mix of blue, yellow, and red, sat on an end table. The furniture appeared to be old but was clean and well cared for.

When Celeste asked the officers to be seated, Sergeant Salmon sat on a recliner, and Lieutenant Tanstall sat on the sofa, very close to Celeste. He continued to hold her hand. What he really wanted was to take her in his arms and hold her close and comfort her, but now was not the time for that.

"Thanks for coming," Celeste said. "Jay, since your chief sent you, you must know what it's about. I know Ada would never run away. You know what a good girl she is." She looked at Sergeant Salmon. "I suppose Jay has told you this, but Ada is fourteen and a really special girl. She would never run away like that other officer claims." She looked back at Jay and snuggled close. "You know she would never do that."

"Yes, I do know that," he said. "She's an angel of a girl. So, Celeste, tell us what happened."

"I'm sorry, but I don't remember much. The fall I took caused a concussion, and I'm not able to recall everything clearly. Apparently, I was working in the kitchen, making dinner, when I heard Ada scream. I vaguely remember the scream, but that's about it. It was a scream of terror, according to my neighbor. I'm not sure what happened after that until I woke up in the hospital, worrying about Ada."

"Why were you worried about her?" Vallie asked.

"I was afraid that she was home alone wondering where I was," she said. "Would you officers be willing to speak to my neighbor? You know her, Jay. She's old but she is mentally very sharp. She can tell you more about what happened."

"We'll do that in a moment," Jay said gently. "But for Sergeant Salmon's benefit, please talk more about Ada. I know the kind of girl she is, but I want my partner to hear it from you."

"Okay, so let's see. First, she is a loving daughter and very responsible. Not the kind of girl who would leave without so much as a word to me," Celeste said, struggling to keep from crying. "She always comes home when she says she will. She has good grades in school. She doesn't have a lot of friends, but those she does have are good kids. Jay's son, Jonas, is one of them. Now, so is Kinzington."

"Speaking of friends, tell us about her boyfriend," Vallie said after briefly catching Jay's eye, knowing there wasn't one.

"I don't know where that other officer came up with that. She doesn't have a boyfriend. Jay knows that. The group she hangs out with consists of both boys and girls, but they are all just a group of good friends." Celeste had sparks in her eyes as she spoke.

"Okay, so tell us about your ex-husband," Vallie said.

Celeste shook her head.

"He walked out on us when Ada was about three. I was served with divorce papers shortly after that. Since our divorce, I haven't heard from him. He didn't even ask for visiting privileges with Ada. Like I've told Jay before, I have no idea where he is or what he's doing. And frankly, I don't care."

"He wouldn't have come back and—" Jay began as a terrible thought occurred to him.

"No," Celeste interrupted. "He doesn't care about us, Jay. Ada wouldn't even know him if she saw him. For that matter, he wouldn't know her. We don't have any pictures of him. I threw what I had of him away after the divorce, and we never talk about him. I know I've mentioned him to you, but only because you asked and because you're very dear to me. He no longer exists as far as I'm concerned."

"Sorry," Jay said. "I had to ask. So there's no way he would have forcibly taken her?"

That caused a look of concern to cross Celeste's face. She slowly shook her head. "Ada was kidnapped. I have no idea who took her or why."

"But it could have been him?" Jay pressed, knowing his questions were hard for Celeste. But he had to ask them.

"I suppose so, but I can't imagine why he would do that after all these years," she responded. "He doesn't even know her."

"Just to be thorough, would you tell us about your ex-husband? We need his name and a description," Vallie said in a kindly voice.

"His name is Royce Spear." She looked at Jay and added, "I never mentioned his name to you before, did I?"

"No," Jay said gently, "and I never asked. I didn't need to know before, but now we do."

Before Jay could ask the obvious question about his last name, noticing that it was different from hers, she turned to Vallie. "Jay knows this, Sergeant, but I work for a law firm; I'm a paralegal. What I never told you, Jay, is that my boss helped me change Ada's last name to my maiden name, and of course, I took that name back as well."

"What kind of work did Royce do when you were together?" the sergeant asked.

"He was a traveling salesman," she said. "He could have gone anywhere after he ran out on Ada and me. For all I know he met someone somewhere. As much as I hate to say anything good about him, I will say that he was very good at what he did. In other words, he made good money." She paused for a moment, and a cloud passed across her face. "I've wondered sometimes if it was all honest money."

"What kinds of things did he sell?" Jay asked as a dark suspicion entered his mind.

"Everything you can think of, possibly even some things he may have stolen," she said with a touch of fire in her voice.

Celeste gave them a description of Royce as he had looked the last time she saw him. She told them a little more about him: where he was from and any education he'd had. Finally, anxious to speak with her neighbor about the events that had occurred when Ada vanished, Jay said, "Should we have your neighbor come here, or should we go to her house and talk to her? I know she has a bit of a hard time getting around."

"I'll call her. Josie isn't able to take care of her home like she used to," Celeste said. "I think it might embarrass her if we went over there. Ada and I have tried to help her, as you know Jay, but we haven't done as much as we should, and no one else seems to care. But she is a good woman, an honest woman and a good friend. Her mind is very clear, contrary to what Officer Spurr seems to think." She shook her head at that.

"We wouldn't want to embarrass her," Vallie said. "Let's have her meet us here."

"My cell phone is in the kitchen. I'll go grab it and call her. She very much wants to speak to you. And I want her to."

CHAPTER FOUR

Josie Jamison was out of breath and red-faced after walking across the street to Celeste's house. Celeste gave her a drink of cold water, which she sipped. It was a couple of minutes before she was able to speak to the two detectives. Vallie had a small recording device, which she turned on when Mrs. Jamison was ready to speak. Mrs. Jamison's story concerned Jay; her account of what happened to Ada and the report that Officer Spurr had written differed in several crucial ways.

Vallie addressed one of them with Josie as soon as she finished speaking. "In Officer Spurr's report he says that you told him it was a gray van that she left in. Now you say it was a white one. Can you explain that?"

Josie's eyes narrowed. "Yes, I most certainly can!" she snapped. "It was *white*. He kept telling me that I first said gray. He was confusing me, or at least he was trying to, but I know it was a white panel van. You know, like the ones some guys carry their tools in. They tossed her into the van through a door in the back."

"You're sure of that description?" Jay asked.

"I'm positive." She punctuated her answer with an angry grunt. "That's what I saw and that's what I told him." She took another sip of her ice water.

"In the report," Vallie continued, "it says you told the officer that it looked like Ada was not fighting the two men in black, that she appeared to go willingly."

"He lied!" Josie said with a red face. "Why did he lie? Officers, I know what I saw and what I heard. Ada screamed, a most horrible, terror-filled scream, until they shoved something in her mouth. I saw them do that, and Celeste heard the scream. If only she could remember."

Yes, Jay thought. *If only.* "In the report it says she didn't make any noise. You were surprised at how willingly she climbed into the back of the van."

"That's three lies!" Josie said, her face red and her eyes bulging. She took another sip of water. "Why did that awful officer write such things? I told him exactly what I heard and saw. It was the scream that drew me to my window. From there I saw one of the men shove a piece of cloth or something in that poor girl's mouth." Jay could tell her anger was building, and she wasn't finished. "Three lies, I tell you. The van was white, Ada screamed, and that girl was kicking and struggling for all she was worth. Three men in masks took her, the two in black and a driver that I only got a glimpse of. He was never out of the van. But I am telling you; she—did—not—run—away!"

Josie ran out of steam, slumped back in her chair, and sipped her ice water again. Celeste jumped toward her and grabbed the glass as it began slipping from Josie's hand, spilling a little bit of the water. Josie's eyes closed. Vallie ran to her and caught her just as she began to slide sideways in her seat in a brief fainting spell. Jay was angry, and by the time Mrs. Jamison regained consciousness, he had his next moves planned.

Jay and Vallie stayed long enough to ensure Mrs. Jamison was all right. Jay kissed Celeste goodbye and assured her they would do whatever it took to find Ada and bring her home, and then they returned to their car.

"Celeste is very fond of you, and you are of her," his partner observed.

He did not deny it, but he also did not acknowledge it. Instead he said to his partner, "Someone is lying, Vallie."

"That someone is Officer Casper Spurr," she said with a touch of anger. "I don't believe for one minute that Mrs. Jamison lied to us. Spurr made three false statements in his report, and they were intentional."

"Three that we know of," Jay said snidely. "The one thing he does report the same way Josie Jamison did had to do with what the abductors were wearing. He did not contest her account of them wearing black."

"Besides the three direct lies, he also *omitted* an important fact. She said the two that grabbed Ada were masked, but he doesn't mention that in his report. I suppose that could have been just sloppy report writing. But I doubt it. So what do we do next?"

"First, we put an attempt to locate on the white van and distribute it to police departments all over the state and beyond, for whatever good that will do at this late date; we've already lost twenty-four hours. Second, we make sure everyone is looking for a girl who was abducted by force, not one who willingly ran away."

Their eyes briefly met as Jay pulled into the street.

"Then what?" Vallie asked.

Jay knew what he planned to do, but he wanted to make sure Sergeant Salmon felt the same way he did. So he put the question right back to her. "What do you think?"

"We should put on our internal-affairs-investigator hats and go after Officer Spurr," she responded firmly.

"My thoughts exactly," Jay said. He thought for a moment, and Vallie seemed to be doing the same. "Vallie, I can't help but wonder why Spurr would falsify his report. It's a stretch, but I have an idea."

"I'll bet you're wondering what I am," Vallie said. "Are you wondering if Spurr somehow had something to gain from Ada's abduction?"

"That's exactly what I'm thinking," he responded. "We're going to make a good team, Vallie. We think a lot alike."

"We do, don't we? So are you considering the fact that there has been no ransom demand?"

"Yes, I am." He glanced at her. "Even if there was, Celeste wouldn't be able to pay it. She doesn't make that much money. Not that we've ever talked about what she makes, because we haven't, but I know she is very frugal. I remember her saying that they didn't eat out very often. So as I think about it, I'd say she may have a modest savings account and possibly an IRA at most." He glanced at his partner before going on. "There has to be a reason someone took Ada. Let me throw three possibilities out to you."

"Okay. I'm listening, Jay."

"First, could it be Ada's father who has decided he wants his daughter after all these years?"

"What would that have to do with Officer Spurr?"

"I'm not sure. Maybe nothing, or maybe there was a bribe of some kind. I don't know, but we need to keep that possibility in mind until we can figure out where Royce Spear is living and check for an alibi. That brings me to my second theory. Celeste works for a law firm. Could this be a way to target one or more of the lawyers there? Could the firm get a ransom demand instead of her? And if they do, or even if they already have, would they tell us?"

"Okay. So we need to speak with the people at the firm and learn all we can about them."

"A lot of work there, but yes, we need to do that," Jay agreed. "Now, for my final theory. Could she have been kidnapped for the sole purpose of selling her?" His stomach revolted at the very thought, but it had to be considered.

"Human trafficking?" Vallie asked, slowly nodding her head even as her eyes grew wide with alarm. "We need to get Spurr in as soon as we can."

"He was the closest officer when the incident went down. How could he fake that?" Jay asked.

"Consider this, Jay. He could have known when and where the snatch was to occur and made sure he would be close so he would be the responding officer."

"That's horrible, but I suppose it's possible," Jay said angrily. "Could the chief have heard something about human trafficking involving one of our officers?"

"Or more than one," she added.

"As soon as we get this kidnapping information corrected and out there, let's have a talk with Chief Thurley," Jay said. "Now that we have these suspicions, maybe he will tell us more about what he's heard."

***

Following a short but enlightening visit with the chief of police, Vallie and Jay returned to their office feeling more worried than before. They'd both been aware that there had been several reports of missing girls in the Denver area over the past few weeks. Now they knew it was the very thing that had caused the chief to give them this assignment. He'd only heard rumblings, but he had decided that they couldn't be ignored.

"You officers may have very quickly gotten to the core of the problem I've been worried about," the chief said wearily. "I can't help but think you've already found the first link in what I am afraid involves officers in this department. I can't stress enough the need to be vigilant. If what we suspect is true, then Officer Spurr—if he is involved—and others will want to silence the two of you."

Jay's stomach did an uncomfortable little roll, but he and Vallie nodded in understanding.

"Jay," Vallie said when they returned to their office, "I'm afraid for Ada. She could already be headed out of the country."

"Let's see if any of the cases involving the disappearance of young girls in the area, even in the entire state of Colorado, are similar to what happened to Ada," Jay suggested as his stomach continued to pitch and roll.

"Or boys," Vallie interjected.

"Yes, or boys." Jay's own son and daughter came to his mind. He shuddered. "There must be similar cases, or the chief wouldn't have been approached by his unnamed sources and told that we could have officers involved in this sort of crime right here in our department. Vallie, it looks like we have some hard work ahead, and we've got to do it as fast as we can."

For the rest of the day, they worked feverishly. While Jay stayed in the office and searched the internet for information on the ex-husband of Celeste Pedler, Vallie made a visit to the law firm of Samuels and Jensen, where Celeste was employed.

After compiling what information he could find on Royce Spear, Jay called his home.

"Hi, Dad," his daughter, Kinzington, said as soon as he identified himself. "Jonas and I are both home. Are you going to be late?"

"I'm afraid so. My new partner and I are on a very serious investigation. I assume neither of you have plans to go out tonight." He was prepared to cancel those plans if they did.

"No, why do you ask, Dad?"

"I just need to know that both of you are home. Please, lock the doors and don't answer them for anyone. Call me if someone comes to the house."

"Okay. Dad, you just scared the pants off me," Kinzington said. "What's going on?"

"I hope nothing. I will fill the two of you in with what I can when I get home, but it will be late." Jay knew this call would frighten his children, but he thought it would be for the best. The chief's warning echoed in his ears. Once others learned that Vallie and Jay were looking at members of the department for something as serious as human trafficking, anything could happen. He wanted his family safe. If he had to scare them to make them more alert, then so be it.

He and Kinzington talked for a moment longer, and then he spoke briefly with his fourteen-year-old son, Jonas. As with his daughter, Jay tried to impress upon Jonas the need to be especially careful.

"Dad, is the job you're doing now more dangerous than your normal job?" Jonas asked.

Jay was honest with him—he had to be. "Yes," he said. "I'm afraid it is."

"What if someone comes to the door while you aren't here? Should we let them in?"

"No, Jonas. Don't let anyone in the house. And I do mean *anyone*. If someone comes to the door and they don't leave after a reasonable time, call me. No matter what I'm doing, I'll take your call."

"What if it's a police officer?" he asked as if reading Jay's mind. "We should let officers in, right?"

"No!" Jay said in alarm. "Don't let any officers in. If an officer comes, you call me immediately."

"Dad, I don't understand. You're an officer. They're your friends."

"Not all of them, Jonas. I'm working on a really bad case right now, and officers could be among the bad guys. I'll explain more to you when I get home. But don't let anyone in the house."

"Okay. I got it," Jonas said, but his voice was trembling. "I'm scared now."

"You'll be okay. Just do as I say, all right?"

"Yes, Dad. Please don't be too late," he begged.

He had Jonas put the phone on speaker so that Kinzington could hear him too. "Do both of you promise you'll keep the doors locked and not let anyone in the house?" They promised. "Keep a handgun where you can get to it in the unlikely event anyone tries to get in. I've taught you how to use guns. I hope you won't need to use it, but keep one loaded and where you can quickly get to it just in case anyone tries to force their way in."

"Dad," Kinzington said, "now we're really scared."

"I'm sorry, kids. So am I. When I get home we'll figure out what to do so you don't have to worry like this. Just stay safe until I get there."

"Dad," Jonas said, "Ada didn't go to school today. She must be sick. Is it okay if I call to see if she's feeling better?"

"No, I don't want either of you using the phone unless you need to call me," he said lamely. He wanted his kids to be nervous and careful, but he didn't want them to be petrified, and if he told them what had happened to Ada, they could be worse than petrified.

Vallie walked in a few moments after Jay finished the call to his kids. "You look stressed," she said to Jay. "What have you learned?"

"One important thing, which I'll explain in a moment. I just called my children and scared them. I worry about them being home alone; I want them to be safe."

Vallie, to her credit, did not try to tell him that they would be fine. She knew, as he knew, that if there was serious corruption in the department, guilty officers could and probably would do anything to stop her and Jay from doing their job, to stop them from uncovering evidence against them. "You're a wise father," she said. "I'm assuming you didn't tell them about their friend Ada."

"I did not. They don't need to worry about that too," Jay said.

"What have you learned about Celeste's husband?" Vallie asked.

"Royce Spear is dead," Jay said. "It took a while to confirm that, but it's true. He died in a car crash five years ago."

"You're sure it was him?" she asked. "Not that I doubt you."

"It was him. He wasn't a good man, I'm afraid. He has a long criminal record, some from before he met Celeste and some after he left her. It seems that he managed to stay out of trouble during their marriage."

"Or he was simply lucky enough to not get caught," Vallie added.

"Yeah, that's probably it. He's been in and out of prisons in California and in Nebraska since he left Celeste."

"Where was he killed?" she asked.

"In Kansas. He'd stolen a car, and when the cops spotted him, he fled. Long story short, he left the highway at an extremely high speed and died in the crash. I used the pictures of the crash to confirm it was him. Believe it or not, he had a well-worn photograph of Celeste in his wallet when he died."

As Jay spoke, he pulled up that same picture on his computer screen.

"Looks like Celeste all right," Vallie agreed after studying it closely.

"I texted a copy of the picture on his latest driver's license, one from Nebraska, to Celeste. She confirmed that it was him."

"Was she at all relieved to know he couldn't be involved?" Vallie asked.

Jay shook his head. "I couldn't tell. She's really shaken up. I wish I could help her. So, how did it go at the law firm?"

"Celeste is loved and respected there, Jay," Vallie said. "The people she works with are distraught about Ada's disappearance. They all knew the girl since she often came in with her mother to the office."

"Have there been any ransom demands? And did you get the sense that they wouldn't tell you if there were?" Jay asked.

"I believe they would. And no, they haven't had any calls about Ada, ransom or otherwise."

"Could any of the attorneys think of any clients, present or past, who might try something like this to get back at the firm for any reason?"

"They all told me they can't think of any."

Jay closed his eyes and held the bridge of his nose between his fingers. "So, I guess this means that we need to concentrate on Officer Spurr for now. That should be fun. Let's see if we can find him and have him come in."

CHAPTER FIVE

THE WINDS SHIFTED WITH EVERY word Casper Spurr spoke after he was finally located and brought into the station that night. He was surly and told Sergeant Salmon and Lieutenant Tanstall that the chief's idea to have an internal affairs office was an insult to the honor and integrity of every member of the force.

"I have a spotless record," he said when he was first asked to explain the differences between his report and what Mrs. Jamison had told them. "I tell you, that old lady is looney. She didn't have any idea what she saw. My report was as accurate as I could make it under the circumstances."

"Let's take these inconsistencies one at a time," Jay said, trying to be patient. "She said she told you the van was white and you kept telling her that she told you gray the first time you asked."

"That's right," he affirmed. "She said gray. It seems like she's not only looney, but she's a liar. And if you say you believe her, then you're a liar too."

Jay could feel Officer Spurr's anger quickly developing against him. But that was okay. It wasn't his job to be loved. It was his job to get to the truth. He moved on to the next inconsistency that he and Vallie had noted earlier. "Mrs. Jamison said a terrible scream drew her to the window, at which point she saw the girl being taken by force."

"Not a word of that to me. She said that girl went willingly. I'm sure one of the guys was a boyfriend."

"She mentioned nothing about a scream? That's interesting because she also said that scream drew the girl's mother from the house."

Spurr sneered. "If that were the case, perhaps Ms. Pedler should've said so."

"She's unable to remember due to the concussion she suffered from a bad fall when she ran into the kitchen to get her cell phone," Jay reminded him.

"How convenient. That leaves us with a lying old looney and her erratic tales," Spurr said. He was not making this easy.

With a glance, Jay shifted the questioning to Vallie.

"Mrs. Jamison told us that the girl was fighting those men for all she was worth," Vallie said, "even after they stuffed something in her mouth to stifle the screaming."

Officer Spurr shook his head. "Another lie by the old lady, or a faulty memory. She told me the girl went willingly. And don't ask me why she's changed her story because I don't know except that her head is messed up."

"So you're sticking to your report?" Vallie asked.

"Of course I am. It's accurate. The girl is a runaway, whether you want to believe it or not. You should be looking for the boyfriend. That's where you'll find her."

"Officer Spurr, there is no boyfriend," Jay said.

"Says who, the looney lady or the one without a memory?" Spurr asked.

"Officer Spurr," Vallie said, "Ms. Pedler's memory of events from before the incident is unaffected. She knows there was not a boyfriend. Don't try that stunt."

"It's no stunt. Either Ms. Pedler isn't willing to admit it, or she didn't know about him," the officer suggested. "The woman is probably in denial."

Both detectives took a deep breath while exchanging exasperated glances. "Moving on," Jay said. "Let's assume for the purpose of this interview that it was a kidnapping."

"It wasn't," Spurr spat angrily.

"Says you. But if it was, let's talk about why there has not been a ransom demand."

"There's your proof, Lieutenant. There isn't a demand because there isn't a kidnapping." Spurr looked triumphant.

"Or else it was a kidnapping for the purpose of selling the girl to human traffickers," Jay said quickly.

A look of fear crossed the officer's face. It was fleeting, but Jay was sure he hadn't imagined it. "You can go now. We may have more questions for you later. Sergeant Salmon and I may have a late night. We need to talk to some other officers."

Spurr left, strutting as he went.

"Jay," Sergeant Salmon asked when he was gone, "did you see the look on his face when you suggested human trafficking?"

"It was hard to miss," he agreed. "We have a problem here. A serious one. We need to find out which officers in the department Spurr hangs out with and bring them in." He looked at his watch. "It's getting late and I need to check on my kids. Let's start again at seven in the morning."

"I thought you said we had more officers to see tonight," she said.

"That was just for Spurr to stew over. I'm going home."

Vallie forced a smile. "Okay, see you in the morning then."

***

Jay found his kids safe but frightened when he got home a few minutes later. "Dad, tell us what's going on. You scared us," Kinzington said after he'd hugged them both.

"Let me grab a bite to eat first, and then we'll talk," he said as he felt exhaustion threatening to overcome him.

A few minutes later, he sat with his kids in the living room. "I've got to take some extra steps to keep you two safe," he began. "There are some kidnappings occurring in the metropolitan area, and I don't want to risk you two getting caught up in what's going on."

"Don't be silly," Kinzington said. "Why would anyone kidnap us? You don't have much money. If you did you'd buy me a newer car. My old clunker barely gets me to school and back."

"Not all kidnappings are about money," Jay said somberly. "My new assignment puts me in a difficult position. Not all cops are totally honest, and that's why Sergeant Salmon and I have been assigned as internal affairs officers. That means it's our job to locate dirty cops and turn them over to the police chief or to the prosecutors and the courts, whichever is appropriate."

"I don't see what that has to do with us," Jonas said. "It's not like we're doing it."

"No, but I am, and if a corrupt cop's job, or even his freedom, is in jeopardy, there's no way of telling how he or she will react. But revenge against Sergeant Salmon and me is a very real possibility."

The kids' faces were white. "Okay. Now I see why you said not to answer the door, *even if it's another cop*," Jonas said.

Jay nodded as Kinzington spoke up. "You barely started this new job. Surely you haven't made anyone mad yet."

"Actually, I have," he said. "But I'm home now, and we'll figure out what to do in the morning. Right now, it's late, so off to bed with the two of you."

They exchanged hugs and expressions of love, and the kids headed upstairs to their bedrooms. Jay sat and sipped at his coffee, which was now quite cool. He made no effort to freshen it up. He just sat on the sofa, deep in thought.

***

Celeste Pedler wandered through her house late that night. Sleep was next to impossible. All she could think of was Ada and what horrible things she might be suffering. She'd tried to watch a movie, but she couldn't concentrate. She tried reading, but her mind was not on the words on the page. She was falling apart with worry, and there was nothing she could do about it.

She wandered over to her window and pulled the blinds up. She'd kept herself shut in and had not stepped outside since Sergeant Salmon and Jay had been here. She thought about Jay, her lieutenant boyfriend. She wished he could stay with her for a while. He was so steady and strong. But he had to work, and really, that's what she wanted him to do. She wanted him to find Ada.

She stared across the street at Josie Jamison's house. Tears wet her eyes as she thought about the way Officer Spurr had refused to believe that sweet lady and basically labeled her a liar and a crazy old woman. She was neither. If Josie said Ada had screamed, then she'd screamed. Celeste also knew that her elderly friend was not lying about Ada's struggles to get away. Nor did she lie about Ada not sneaking away with her boyfriend.

Ada was a sweet, pure, innocent girl. She did not even hang out alone with boys. Celeste's relationship with her daughter was such that they could talk about anything. And they did. Never had the girl mentioned a boyfriend.

Celeste started to turn away from the window when she saw a shadowy figure running from the side of Josie's house before turning and heading around the back. She tensed. Should she call the police? No—unless she called the detectives working the case, she was afraid she would not be believed. She knew Jay would take her word for what she was seeing, but the figure might not be threatening, and she didn't want to distract Jay from his investigation. She watched for a moment longer, wondering if the man in black would reappear.

Suddenly, a powerful explosion rattled Celeste's windows. Huge flames shot through the roof of Josie's house. Horrified, Celeste heard herself scream. Then she ran to find her cell phone.

She had a 911 dispatcher on the phone by the time she'd reached her window again. Josie's house was engulfed in flames. Then to her horror, a figure stumbled through the front door. The fire that was consuming Josie's house was also consuming the figure.

Celeste dropped her phone, ran for a blanket, and then crossed the street as fast as her legs would carry her. Mrs. Jamison screamed, then plunged forward.

Celeste threw the blanket over her and attempted to snuff out the flames. Mrs. Jamison stopped screaming, and in moments her body became very still. The blanket Celeste had used burst into flames, and the searing heat forced her back. She was vaguely aware of others running toward her, shouting and screaming.

She looked around her as tears of helplessness flooded her face and anger filled her mind. Everyone else, clad as she was in night clothes, did what she was doing: nothing. There was not a thing any of them could do. After a couple of minutes, she heard sirens wailing in the distance. The sound of the sirens made her feel like she was in a bad dream. Sirens had always frightened her, and that was truer than ever right now. She suddenly felt faint, and the ground rushed up at her. Merciful blackness claimed her as her head thudded hard against the concrete sidewalk.

CHAPTER SIX

Lieutenant Tanstall awoke to the incessant ringing of his cell phone. He was surprised to find that he'd fallen asleep on his sofa. He was still in his slacks and sport coat, and his service weapon was still in his shoulder holster. The phone lay on the floor, where it must have slipped from his hands when he fell asleep. He retrieved it and answered.

It was the dispatcher telling Jay that he was needed at the home of Mrs. Josie Jamison. He was shocked to hear that her house was burning and she lay scorched to death a few yards from the front door. His heartbeat quickened when he heard that a neighbor, Ms. Celeste Pedler, had fallen unconscious in front of the burning house and so far had not responded to efforts to awaken her.

He headed for the garage where his cars were parked. He'd driven a department vehicle home after dropping his partner off at her apartment, so he started backing this car out of the garage when he remembered his kids sleeping in their beds. After slamming on the brakes and parking the car again, he ran back in and up the stairs to their rooms.

He woke them up and told them that he had an emergency and needed to leave. "Keep the doors locked and keep a gun close," he told them.

"And don't let anyone in the house, including other cops," Kinzington said, rubbing her eyes. "We got it."

"That's right. I'm sorry I have to leave. But I will get back as soon as I can." Jay's phone began to ring again. "Hello, Sergeant Salmon." He gave a little wave to his kids and hurried back to the cruiser.

"Are you picking me up?" she asked. "I can drive my personal car if you need me to."

"I'll pick you up," he said. "I'm assuming you know what's happened."

"Yes, someone murdered poor Mrs. Jamison," she said angrily.

"We don't know that, Vallie. She may have had a gas explosion or something."

"Yes, and the earth will quit orbiting around the sun one of these days," she said sarcastically.

"I know the timing is bad. See you in about five minutes."

Vallie was waiting in front of her apartment complex when he pulled to a stop. He leaned over and opened the passenger door, then sat back as she jumped in. "This is no coincidence, Jay," she said as soon as she'd shut her door. "I'm very skeptical about coincidences. I'm thinking about Office Spurr, and they aren't good thoughts."

"Yeah, same here."

They raced through the relatively quiet Colorado night. When they reached the street that Celeste lived on, it was alive with cop cars, an ambulance, fire trucks, and to Jay's dismay, a couple of news vans.

He double-parked, and the two of them jumped out and raced toward the burning house. He spotted the covered body of what had to be Mrs. Jamison on the ground. Near her, paramedics were working on someone else. It didn't take long before he confirmed what he had feared; it was Celeste. They had her on a stretcher. She wasn't moving, but it appeared that she had not been burned. His heart constricted. One of the paramedics waved the gawking crowd of news people and pajama-clad onlookers back as the paramedics pushed the gurney toward the street and the awaiting ambulance. Jay rushed over. He touched Celeste's face, then watched sadly as she was loaded into the ambulance.

Jay and Sergeant Salmon spent several minutes speaking with some of the crowd. No one had seen anything prior to hearing the explosion, but a couple of neighbors had witnessed Mrs. Jamison stumbling from her house following the explosion and had seen Celeste throw a blanket over Josie after she fell. When asked what happened to Celeste, the witnesses said she had collapsed, slamming her head on the sidewalk.

"I suspect she was overcome with grief," Sergeant Salmon suggested.

"That and maybe suffering an increase of concern for her missing daughter," Jay added. "I can't even imagine what she must be going through. For her to see her good friend die such a horrible death so soon after Ada's abduction had to be more than she could bear."

"So much for us being able to use Mrs. Jamison's testimony against Officer Spurr," Vallie said, her face dark. "This just doesn't seem like it could be a coincidence."

Jay agreed with her, but he was torn over his next move. Should he stay here and help other officers with the investigation, or should he head to the hospital in the hopes that Celeste would wake up and could talk? His partner made the decision easy when she said, "Jay, let's go to the hospital and see if we can speak with Celeste as soon as she wakes up. Maybe she saw something more that could help us."

"That's a great idea," he agreed with relief. "Let's go. We can stop back here later."

Jay had barely put the car in gear when his phone rang.

"Dad, we need you!" Kinzington said, her voice trembling.

"I'm coming," he said as his heart leaped with concern. "What's going on? Are you and Jonas okay?"

"I guess so," his daughter responded. "But we're scared. Someone knocked on the front door and rang the bell. We were both still awake, so Jonas came into my room. I had the gun. We sat on my bed and waited. Whoever it was wouldn't quit ringing for a long time. Finally, we went downstairs so we could watch the front door. We were afraid whoever was out there might try to break in."

"Have they left?" Jay asked urgently. He drove as fast as he could toward his home.

Vallie watched him with concern, but she said nothing.

"They're at the backdoor now!" Kinzington said suddenly.

Jay coaxed more speed from his police cruiser. "Stay where you are. We're coming as fast as we can."

Jay listened to his daughter's heavy breathing. She was saying nothing now, but he could hear his son's voice as he said, "Some guy is shouting at us!"

"Kinzington, can you tell what he's saying?" Jay asked.

"I think he said they brought us a special delivery package. We heard a bump on the deck." Kinzington was near hysteria.

"Stay put. We'll be there soon," Jay said. "And stay on the phone with me."

"Okay, Dad," she said in a voice that squeaked.

Jay and his partner leaped from the vehicle as soon as it rolled to a stop in front of his house a couple of minutes later. "Check the back," Jay instructed. "I'm going in."

"Hey, kids, it's me," Jay shouted as he opened the door. The two of them were huddled together on the sofa. They jumped up and ran to him, throwing their arms around him, sobbing. "It's okay now. I'm here." He comforted his two teenagers, holding them close.

After a moment, they broke apart, and Sergeant Salmon, her face somber, walked through the front door, which Jay had left open in his hurry to reach his children.

"What did you find back there?" Jay asked, nodding toward the back of the house.

"I'm not sure. I didn't see anyone back there, but there's something wrapped in a blue tarp and tied with cords."

"Could it be a bomb?" he asked in alarm.

"No." Vallie had an odd warning look on her face as if she knew what the strange package was but didn't want to explain in front of the children. "We'd better check it out. Oh, and there's a paper taped to the door. It was dark, and I didn't attempt to read what was written on it."

"You kids stay here," Jay instructed. He took a moment to shut and lock the front door before moving down the hall, toward the back door.

"Dad, please, can we just follow you?" Kinzington asked with a tremor in her voice as they trailed him back through the house.

Jay felt like screaming when he looked at his normally happy-go-lucky daughter's face. She was anything but that now. He'd never seen her so terrified. And her little brother was every bit as shaken up as she was. "Okay, but you stay back a little ways while Vallie and I check it out."

He and Vallie pulled on latex gloves before going out. He flipped on the deck light and immediately saw the blue tarp bundle lying against the door. Jay swept the dark yard with his eyes. "I don't see anyone. Keep an eye out while I check this, Vallie."

They stepped over the bundle, and Jay knelt down on the far side of it. He felt the bundle carefully, and when he did, he began to tremble. He looked up and saw the note taped to the center of the door. He stood, pulled the note off, and read it. Cold chills ran up his spine.

He stumbled back. "Kids," he said in a hoarse voice, "shut the door and stay inside." Once they did as they were told, he turned to the sergeant. "Call for backup. I think we have a body here."

Without a word, Vallie did as instructed. As soon as she'd finished, she said, "May I see the note?" She read aloud. *"Lieutenant Tanstall, we brought her back. Now all you cops back off."*

They looked at each other. "Could it be?" Vallie asked.

Jay nodded, his mind in turmoil. "I hope not. I guess we'd better see, but before we do, let's get some pictures. This is still a crime scene, even if it is my own home."

Vallie retrieved the camera from the cruiser. Before she'd finished taking pictures, two uniformed officers showed up. Jay explained what had occurred, and then, with his partner snapping pictures, he and one of the officers cut away the tape and cords holding the tarp in place. Finally, they unwrapped the body of a teenage girl.

Vallie and Jay stepped back, looking at each other in horror. The girl's face was mutilated beyond recognition. It appeared that she had been beaten badly. Her long blonde hair was tangled and bloody. She was dressed in a plain white gown, which was also bloody, and the girl had nothing else on. Never in his career had Jay seen anything more disturbing than this.

It was Sergeant Salmon who finally broke their stupefied silence. "It's Ada Pedler, isn't it?"

Jay shook his head, turned back to the body of the dead girl, and studied it for a moment. "I don't know. The face is unrecognizable, but Ada has hair this color, and the body is the right size for her."

"There's no jewelry to help identify her. Perhaps Celeste will be able to identify her gown," Vallie suggested.

"That's not Ada's," Jay said. "In Josie's report, she said Ada was wearing jeans and a light-blue shirt when she was taken."

"I guess you're right," Vallie said.

"I hate to think what this will do to Celeste," Jay said as he pictured the face of the woman he had come to adore. "Perhaps we should start with dental records and fingerprints. We'll even do DNA if we need to, but that's a slow process. We must confirm that it's Ada, if it is."

"Who else could it be?" Vallie asked sensibly.

"Who knows? We're dealing with people who have no consciences. I suppose they could try to fool us, but if so, someone else's daughter is dead." He paused and studied the dead girl a moment longer. "I'm afraid that it is Ada. But we've got to be sure before we say anything to Celeste."

Jay noticed one of the uniformed officers walk a short distance away and make a call on his cell phone. He was on the phone for only a few seconds, and then he rejoined the others, whispering something to his partner that Jay couldn't hear. Something about the officers bothered Jay, but he couldn't put his finger on it. He noted the names of both officers, making a mental reminder to do a background check on them later. Perkins and Alvarez. He would remember them. It was probably nothing, but he wasn't taking any chances.

Jay turned back to his partner. "Vallie, I need to go inside and talk to my kids. They can't be allowed to see this girl's body, but I have to let them know what we found. I hope it doesn't . . ." Jay let the thought linger. Anger built inside of him as he thought about someone doing this in such a cruel way. They had to have known it would be terribly damaging to his children.

He had to keep them safe. He could not let them stay here alone while he continued his investigation into the death of Mrs. Jamison.

CHAPTER SEVEN

By the time Lieutenant Tanstall and Sergeant Salmon were finally able to visit the hospital to check on Celeste, both were exhausted. It had taken several hours before the body of the teenage girl could be removed from Jay's back porch. The dead girl's fingerprints had been taken, but no match was made, which wasn't surprising. Celeste probably never had a reason to have her daughter's prints taken.

Dental records were now the best choice. The records would need to be located to determine if the body was in fact that of Ada Pedler. The officers needed to learn from Celeste who her daughter's dentist was without revealing that her daughter may have been found dead.

It had also taken some time to calm Jay's teenage children. They were traumatized, and there was no way they were willing to stay home alone after what had happened. Nor was Jay willing to let them. His mother, who had been such a help to them since Jay's wife died ten years ago, was visiting his sister in California, and he wasn't sure he would have wanted to leave them with her anyway. That was why, with no other family nearby, Jay had arranged for them to stay at a hotel until he could figure something else out. He and Vallie had left them there with the same instructions he had given them at the house; they were not to allow anyone into the room or even answer the door.

It was extremely unlikely that anyone could figure out where they were, but extreme caution was necessary anyway. He had left them with a pistol for their protection, knowing that it probably wouldn't be needed; but it added some sense of comfort to the kids. He had also registered the room under a fabricated name.

The two detectives walked into the hospital just as the sun was coming up. The day it awoke was a gloomy one—cloudy, chilly, and drizzling. It matched

Jay's mood. He was as gloomy as he'd ever been since the death of his wife ten years ago.

They found Celeste sleeping, but they were assured she'd regained consciousness earlier and could be woken up and spoken with. The officers asked the nurse to gently wake her.

Tears instantly filled Celeste's pretty green eyes when she recognized Jay and Vallie. "I'm sorry I'm such an idiot," she said softly. "I guess I passed out and fell on the sidewalk when I realized that Josie was probably dead. It was horrible. It was just one more thing than I could handle."

"You are not an idiot," Vallie said gently. "How are you feeling now?"

"Numb," Celeste responded. "The doctor told me I got another concussion when my head hit the sidewalk. He said I can't leave the hospital until he sees some substantial improvement."

"You're looking quite good after what you've been through," Jay told her as he gently stroked her hair.

"Yeah, well, the nurse brushed my hair and helped me brush my teeth," she said with an attempt at a smile.

"You look nice, Celeste. And your teeth are so white. You must have an amazing dentist." Jay continued to tenderly stroke her hair.

"Dr. Cook," she said, somewhat comforted by Jay's touch. "She's really good. Ada and I have both gone to her since Ada was a toddler."

He was surprised at how easily he had discovered who Ada's dentist was, but he made no comment about it and didn't ask for more information. He and his partner could easily find Ada's dentist now that they knew her last name.

"I'm just glad to see you looking as well as you are. You have been through way too much," Jay said. "Now, let me ask you this. Has Mrs. Jamison ever said anything to you about anyone who might dislike her?"

Celeste shook her head. "No, never." She looked up at Jay. "Are you sure it wasn't just an accident? You know, like maybe she left the stove on and there was a gas explosion. She does have a gas stove."

"There are arson investigators there. They'll let us know what they find," Vallie assured her.

"I hope they can. I don't know if this will help, but this latest bump on my head has done something strange. The doctor said it's rare, but it happens sometimes."

"Oh, what is that?" Jay asked.

"I can remember now what happened when Ada was kidnapped."

"You mean you can remember hearing Ada scream and seeing her being taken?" he asked, incredulous.

"Yes. Can I tell you now? It may not help you find my dear Ada, but it will at least prove that Officer Spurr lied about what Josie told him." She began to sob. "Why would he do that? Oh, Josie, I'm so sorry." She covered her eyes with her hands.

"We will find out why the officer lied. And yes, please tell us what you remember," Jay said, glancing at Vallie, who was already preparing her phone to record what Celeste had to say.

There wasn't a lot of new information to be learned from Celeste, but what she remembered was almost exactly as Josie Jamison had told them and was radically different than what Officer Spurr had put in his report. As soon as they finished, Celeste asked, choking on her words, "Have you seen any clues about where my sweet little Ada might be?"

"We and a lot of other officers are working on finding her," Jay said in a non-answer to her question. "Finding her is our department's top priority."

She accepted what he said as if it were a complete answer. "Please keep trying. She must be terribly scared." Tears erupted from her eyes in torrents. Jay and Vallie offered consoling words, but soon they needed to leave.

"We need to find that dentist," Vallie said as soon as they were back in the cruiser. "As hard as it will be on Celeste if the dead girl is her daughter, at least she will know, and she can try to find a way to get on with her life."

Three hours later, Jay and Vallie were waiting in the parking lot of the building where the office of Dr. Donalee Cook was located. It was still morning, and they figured she should be in soon. When she arrived, they would present her with a court order to turn over all of Ada Pedler's dental records, if she was in fact Ada's dentist. They were pretty sure this was true since she was the only female Dr. Cook in the area.

Soon a woman in white pants and a blue blouse stepped out of a silver Mercedes and strode purposefully toward the building.

Her office was already open, other employees having arrived earlier. Jay and Vallie followed Dr. Cook into the office, where they were greeted by a receptionist who asked them what they needed.

Jay held out his shield. "I'm Lieutenant Jay Tanstall, and this is my partner, Sergeant Vallie Salmon. We need to speak with Dr. Donalee Cook for a moment."

They were told that Dr. Cook had a patient coming to an appointment very soon, but Jay protested. "We have a court order here for the dental records of Ada Pedler. It is very urgent that we get them as quickly as possible."

A minute later, they were seated in Dr. Cook's office. They introduced themselves, and Jay explained what they needed as he presented the order to the dentist. She glanced at it and then looked back up. "Ada and her mother are very good people," she said. "I heard about Ada running away. It's shocking. She never seemed like that kind of girl."

Vallie spoke up. "Ada did not run away."

"But the news said she did," Dr. Cook responded, looking puzzled.

"Unfortunately, that isn't correct. She was abducted, and we're trying to find her," Sergeant Salmon said firmly.

"Why would she be abducted?" Dr. Cook asked.

"We intend to figure that out, but our first priority is to get Ada's records from you," Sergeant Salmon said.

"What good will dental records do at this point?" the dentist asked.

"This is very confidential," Lieutenant Tanstall said. "What we tell you must be kept in strict confidence. You mustn't tell even your employees."

"Okay. You have my word."

"Thank you," Jay said. "We have recovered a body." He did not tell her that it was sent to his home *special delivery* in the middle of the night. "We believe the body might be that of Ada Pedler."

Dr. Cook's eyes grew wide with horror and she gasped. "Did you check her fingerprints? Did you have Celeste look at the body? Surely there is an easier way to identify Ada than from my records."

"Yes, we did check the fingerprints," Vallie explained, "but it doesn't look like Ada ever had her prints taken anywhere. Also, the face had been badly beaten, making it unrecognizable. We could use DNA, but that would take much longer than the dental records will."

"But even if the face is damaged, I'm sure her mother would recognize her."

"Possibly, but her mother is in the hospital," Jay said.

"Oh," Dr. Cook said, her face pasty. "This is atrocious. We will get you the records you need. It will take us a few minutes to download them to a thumb drive."

They were still waiting a few minutes later when Jay got a call from an unknown number. "Our trade is complete," a muffled voice said. "Quit investigating what you've been investigating, or I'll go one up on you."

"Who are you? What trade?" Jay demanded, but the call was terminated.

A sick feeling erupted in his stomach as he opened his phone and hit Kinzington's number. The call went to voicemail.

"Vallie, we've got to go!" he said in a strangled voice. "We'll send someone for the dental records, doctor."

He hit the door at a run, his partner right behind him. He didn't stop running until he was at the car. He unlocked the door and leaped in, Sergeant Salmon doing the same. He tore out of the parking lot, turned on the siren, activated the red lights mounted in the grill, and gunned the engine.

"Jay, what's going on?" Vallie asked as his speed leveled out on the street a moment later.

"That call I had was from an unknown number, and the voice was muffled. I'm pretty sure it was a man. He told me if we continue investigating, he would go *one up on me*."

"Quit investigating what?" his partner asked.

"What we're investigating," he said.

It was silent for a moment as Jay continued his mad dash across the city.

"Jay, are you heading for the hotel where we left your kids?" Sergeant Salmon said suddenly.

"Yes," he answered, choking on the word.

"Oh no," Vallie said weakly. "What have they done now?"

They reached the hotel in record time, parked in front of the main entrance and charged into the hotel. As they passed the desk, Jay flashed his badge and shouted to the attendant standing behind the counter. "Follow me and bring a master key. Now!"

Apparently he was convincing because the fellow did exactly as he was told. They reached the elevator and rode it up to the third floor, then ran to the room where Jay had left his son and daughter. He pounded on the door, praying that all would be well.

There was no response. He took the key from the hotel employee's hand and jammed it in. He opened the door and, gun drawn, entered. Sergeant Salmon shouted to the attendant, who stood to one side, mouth agape. "Wait out here. Don't go anywhere." She followed Jay inside, her weapon also drawn.

Jay's son, Jonas, was tied to a hard-backed chair, a cloth stuffed in his mouth, terror in his eyes. Jay jerked the cloth from his son's mouth. "Where is your sister?" Jay demanded.

"They took her, Dad!" Jonas wailed.

"Who took her?"

"I don't know. Three guys in suits just walked in. I guess they had a key. They didn't even knock. They had black cloths over their heads. I never got a chance to see their faces." Jonas sobbed in anguish.

"What did they do?" Jay asked.

"One of them grabbed me and one grabbed Kinzington. Two of them tied me to this chair. Kinzington tried to scream, and she kicked the guy in the face, but one of the other guys, a big guy, pinned her down and stuffed a rag in her mouth." Jonas's words came fast and frantic. "As soon as I was tied, the one who pinned Kinzington down told me to tell you that if you don't do exactly what he tells you to do when he calls that something very bad will happen to Kinzington. He also said that they would find me again and take me too. Then they jerked Kinzington to her feet and told her they would kill me if she didn't go with them quietly. Then they walked out. After their backs were to me, they pulled the black things from their heads, but I never saw their faces."

"One of them called me a few minutes ago," Jay said. "That's why we came here."

"Dad, how did they find us?" Jonas asked.

"I don't know," Jay said, but then he remembered the officer at his house who had walked off and made a phone call. He had been whispering with his partner right afterward.

"Other officers are on the way here," Sergeant Salmon said. "I wonder if that officer who made the call is corrupted and if he followed us after we left your house."

"Or if both of them are. Somehow they *must* have followed us," Jay said as he fought the panic he was feeling over his daughter being so cruelly snatched away. "Could cops be part of this whole kidnapping/human trafficking thing?" He shuddered as tears pricked his eyes. "Oh, Kinzington."

"We'll find her," Vallie said, pumping her fist. "I think I know right where to start."

CHAPTER EIGHT

"You take care of your son, Jay. I'll work on this alone for now," Vallie said.

"No, Dad, you go with Sergeant Salmon," Jonas said. "Take me to your office at the police station, and let me stay there where I'll be safe."

Jay and Vallie glanced meaningfully at one another. "No, I don't think that's the best place right now," Jay said. In fact, it was the last place he wanted his son to be. "There are some cops we can't trust. We'll figure something out. For now, you're not leaving my sight."

After making sure Jonas would be safe, they did go to the police station. There they had Officers Alvarez and Perkins, who had been the first to respond to Jay's house when the body had been found on his back porch, escorted in. They chose to speak with them one at a time, and the first one was to be Officer Cortez Alvarez. The officer that was on his phone at Jay's house was Vincent Perkins. They would talk to him second.

As they waited for the two of them to be brought in by other officers, they did some background searches on both suspects. "Ah, this is interesting," Jay said as he peered closely at his monitor. "Perkins was given his field training by Officer Spurr. So they're probably friends."

"This is equally interesting," Vallie said, looking up from her computer. "Alvarez and Spurr were partners before he and Perkins were paired."

"Which makes me wonder where Officer Spurr's current partner was the night of Ada Pedler's abduction." Jay rubbed his head. It was aching from loss of sleep and from worry over the welfare of his daughter.

He also worried about Jonas, but for now, his son was safe. He was on a bus to Kansas City, where Jay's late wife's parents lived. As a precaution, Jay had sent a burner phone with his son. He didn't know how much the kidnappers knew, but he didn't want them tracing Jonas by the GPS in his iPhone.

By the time the two officers arrived, Jay had learned that Spurr's partner was on an extended sick leave and that Spurr had volunteered to work alone until he came back.

"That's very suspicious," Sergeant Salmon said. Jay had to agree.

Officer Alvarez walked in with a cocky tilt of his head. He was a small man, about five six and maybe one hundred forty pounds. "Have a seat, Officer," Jay said as politely as he could. "We have a few questions for you."

"Whatever you say. But I have one first," Alvarez said. "To what do I owe the honor of having some other officers escort me here to meet with the distinguished internal affairs officers? And why are we meeting in the middle of the day when you know very well I worked all night and was home sleeping, getting ready for tonight's shift? Surely it doesn't have anything to do with that dead girl you found on your back porch."

Jay had to hold his tongue. His emotions were high, and so was his anger level. He was afraid that when the chief found out about his daughter having been taken that he would pull him off this assignment, and Jay would not allow that to happen any sooner than need be. In the meantime, he was going to work every minute trying to figure out if cops were involved and, if so, which ones. He didn't know where else to start in his desperate search for Kinzington.

He looked at his partner and nodded. Vallie knew what to do—it was all prearranged. Sergeant Salmon focused on the officer's face. "Let's see, Officer Alvarez, you are thirty-two years old?"

"You know I am," he snarled. "I've been on the force for ten years. So I know my job, and I have done nothing wrong. Why am I being treated like this?"

Vallie caught him off balance when she said, "Tell me about Officer Perkins, your partner."

"Oh, so he's crooked? Is that what you're saying?"

"I'm not suggesting anything. Just tell me about him."

"He's a good guy. I'll tell you that much," Alvarez said. "He and I get along really well. We have each other's backs. And I'll tell you this: I've never known him to do anything wrong."

"Nothing?" she asked even as Jay wondered if having each other's backs was true of any corruption they might be involved in.

"That's right. So I guess I'll go now," he said, getting to his feet.

"Sit down!" Jay ordered, his temper barely in control.

Vallie glanced at Jay and mouthed, *I've got this.*

He nodded and focused again on Officer Alvarez's face.

"Last night," Vallie started, "while you were at Lieutenant Tanstall's house, Officer Perkins walked away for a minute and was talking on his phone. What was that about?"

"How would I know? Maybe his wife was calling him. It was probably none of my business."

"You didn't ask him?" Vallie pressed.

"No, why should I?"

"You two were whispering about something right after he made the call," Vallie reminded him.

"We were? I don't remember that. You must be wrong," Alvarez said.

Jay and Vallie exchanged glances. Jay knew the man was hiding something, or he would have told them what they were talking about.

Next, Sergeant Salmon asked something that she and Jay had decided on earlier as a bluff. "What were you and Officer Perkins doing at the Hilton Hotel last night? It's outside of our jurisdiction."

Officer Alvarez's eyes flickered, and for a moment his cocky grin faded. Even as she asked the question, Jay mentally kicked himself for not asking to see the surveillance video at the hotel. He made a mental note to see that mistake rectified very soon. Alvarez stammered for a moment. When he finally opened his mouth, Jay knew a lie was about to spew forth.

Alvarez was a smart man. And in that brief, guilty pause, he came up with a story. "We were chasing a speeder. He tried to get away from us, and we followed him. Going outside of the city limits is legal in a hot pursuit like that, you know."

"Yes, it is. Who wrote the citation?" Vallie asked. "Was it you, or was it Officer Perkins?"

Jay was impressed at how seamlessly Vallie continued to call Alvarez's bluff.

Again, there was a guilty hesitation and then an answer. "The guy had an emergency. It was legit, so we let him go."

"What was the emergency?" Vallie pressed quickly.

Once again, a telling hesitation, but then he said, "His mother had just been taken to the hospital, and she was not expected to live. We both believed him, so he got off with a verbal warning."

"That sounds reasonable," Vallie said as Jay rose to his feet and headed for the door. "What was the guy's name, and what hospital?"

Alvarez was sweating and squirming in his chair, and Jay was quite certain the officer was lying. His hunch that he'd been followed to the hotel had been proven valid. He waited for a moment to see how Alvarez would respond. "I can't remember. We didn't write him up."

"Come on, you know his name."

Alvarez rubbed his chin for a moment, appearing to be thinking. "Wait, I remember now. It was a common name. His name was Jones."

Another lie. The question was why he was lying. "You keep questioning him, Sergeant," Jay said. "I'll be back in a few minutes."

Jay jogged to his office and began to do some checking. The first thing he learned was that there had been no call made to the dispatcher by either officer regarding a traffic stop. That was against departmental regulations if there had been a traffic stop, which was most unlikely. *Strike one.* He also made several calls to local hospitals. No one by the last name of Jones had been admitted at any of them the night before. *Strike two.*

The next call was to the Hilton Hotel where Jay had left his children, *thinking they were safe.* It took a few minutes for someone there to check their cameras. But as he suspected, a marked police car from his jurisdiction had driven by the front of the hotel last night. And the license number on the car had shown up clearly on the video. He soon learned that it was the car assigned to Alvarez and Perkins. *Strike three.*

Jay hurried back to the interrogation room and watched through the one-way glass for a moment. He could see that Sergeant Salmon was winding down. It was time to get Officer Perkins across the table from her. Jay stepped into the room.

"I think we're finished here, Lieutenant," Vallie said. "I told him he would not be allowed to leave the building until we say he can go."

"That's right," Jay said. "Oh, Officer Alvarez, I need your cell phone."

"You can't have it," the officer growled. If there was such a thing as *strike four,* Alvarez had just taken another bad swing.

"Now," Jay said as he felt his temper rise, knowing he had to control it.

Officer Alvarez shook his head and stood up. He stepped to the door. Sergeant Salmon blocked his way, firmly shoving Jay to the side, a move for which he was grateful—it made sure he didn't get physical with the officer.

"Give it to me," Vallie ordered.

"It's mine. Get a search warrant," the cocky officer said.

"We will before we open it, but you will give it to us now, or you will be leaving this room in handcuffs," Sergeant Salmon said in a tone that seemed to convince the officer that he'd better comply.

He finally pulled it out and handed it over to Vallie, who gave it to Jay. Then Alvarez left, accompanied by another officer. "Get Perkins, Vallie, and don't let the two of them say anything to each other," Jay said.

"You've got it, Lieutenant." She hurried out after Alvarez and his escort.

While he waited for her to come back with Officer Perkins, Jay sat down and put his head in his hands. He'd never been a very religious man, but he found himself praying on the off chance that God could hear him. He had to get Kinzington back, and it had to be very soon.

He stood up when he heard the door begin to open. A very unhappy Officer Vincent Perkins stepped in ahead of Sergeant Salmon. Jay said nothing. His partner got Perkins seated and started the recording device before Jay sat back down. He pushed a note toward Vallie that he'd penned while he was in his office making the calls a few minutes earlier. The three strikes against Officer Alvarez were all written there in detail.

Vallie smiled at Jay. "Would you like me to begin, Lieutenant?"

She knew he wanted her to, but of course, Officer Perkins did not.

"Yes, please do, Sergeant."

"Okay. I just wanted to make sure. Chief Thurley is listening in," she revealed.

That was not what Jay wanted to hear. Even better, then, that Vallie ask the questions. Jay was afraid he was about to be pulled off the case. Although, his partner must have said something to the chief that had at least convinced him to let them finish this interrogation first.

Sergeant Salmon wasted no time getting into the matter of the telephone call made in Jay's back yard.

"It was to my wife," Perkins said. "I was afraid that I was going to be late getting home, and she needed to know."

Vallie left it at that. She said nothing about the whispered conversation between him and Alvarez. They would be seizing Perkins's phone, which meant they would know if he was lying soon enough, although Jay was almost certain that he was. Vallie continued. "Tell us what you were doing driving by the Hilton Hotel last night."

"I don't know what you're talking about," Perkins said. "That hotel is outside the city limits."

"That's right. So you're saying you weren't there?" Vallie pressed.

"Of course I wasn't there."

"What would you say if I told you that your partner, Officer Alvarez, admitted that you were?"

Since the two officers had not been given the chance to speak to each other since they had been picked up, Perkins was caught totally off guard. For a moment, he didn't answer, but finally he said, "Maybe we did. Yeah. We did. I forgot."

"And why did you leave your jurisdiction?" she pressed firmly.

"I can't remember. I was busy typing on my laptop, making notes from the investigation at Lieutenant Tanstall's house," he said, his face turning red. "You'll have to ask Alvarez."

"I already did," she said. Alvarez's lie had already been confirmed.

"What did he say?" Officer Perkins asked.

She ignored his question and asked another of her own. "You and Officer Casper Spurr are good friends, right?"

"He trained me, so I guess you could say we are," he said, his face flaming now.

"And Officer Spurr and your partner, Officer Alvarez, are also good friends. Right?"

"I suppose. They were partners at one time."

Sergeant Salmon looked at Jay. He knew what she was thinking. It was time to get tough. He nodded at her, and she turned back to Officer Perkins just as Jay's phone buzzed in his pocket.

CHAPTER NINE

"This is Lieutenant Tanstall speaking," he said quickly after stepping out of the interrogation room and nodding an acknowledgment to Chief Thurley. He listened for a moment, having a hard time believing what he was hearing. "Are you sure?" he asked, even though he couldn't imagine the medical examiner telling him what he just had unless he was certain of his facts.

When Jay was told that the results were absolutely beyond question, he thanked the medical examiner and ended the call. He turned to Chief Thurley. "That was the medical examiner. The girl whose body was dumped on my back porch is not Ada Pedler. As of yet, he doesn't know who it is, but he's working on that. It may take a while."

"Several girls have been kidnapped in the greater Denver area lately," Chief Thurley acknowledged. "I'm sorry that your daughter is one of them."

Jay felt his throat tighten up. "I've got to find her," he said, knowing he sounded desperate.

"Lieutenant, there's your son to think about too."

"He's on a bus headed to his grandparents' home out of state. They will meet him at the bus depot. He's safe for now."

"Does he have a phone with him?" Chief Thurley asked.

"Not the one he usually uses. I have that one, and he has a cheap burner phone," Jay explained.

"That's good to hear," the chief said. "Lieutenant, you are emotionally involved now. I need to have officers on this that can be totally objective."

"Chief, please, if you pull me off the case, I'll go nuts and I'll have nothing to do. Please, let me keep working it," Jay begged. "No one has more incentive than me to find my daughter and to bring down the people who are doing this."

Without a response, the chief turned back to the window. They could see and hear the interrogation on the other side of the glass. Sergeant Salmon was saying, "Officer Perkins, were you and Officer Alvarez on duty the night that Ada Pedler was kidnapped?"

"What night was that?" he asked.

"She has him rattled," Chief Thurley said without looking at Jay.

"She's good, Chief. She'll make sure I stay focused on this investigation."

Chief Thurley again did not respond. On the other side of the glass, Sergeant Salmon was telling Perkins the date. Perkins thought for a moment, and then he said, "No, it was our day off."

"Where were you that night?" Vallie asked.

Perkins did not hesitate before saying, "Home in bed. Where else would I be?"

"I'm asking you," Sergeant Salmon said, looking fiercely at him.

"Go back in there, Lieutenant," Chief Thurley said. "For now, you're still on the case."

"Thank you, sir," Jay said as he stepped to the door.

"*For now*, Lieutenant, that's all I can promise."

"I understand."

"Oh, and I'm going to have Officer Spurr picked up. He'll be your next interrogation."

Jay nodded before rejoining his partner.

"You're back," Vallie said, sounding a little surprised.

"I am. Keep going, Sergeant. Chief Thurley is sending someone to pick up Officer Spurr."

Perkins's face, which had been quite red for the past few minutes, suddenly went pasty white. Jay held back a smile. "On second thought, Sergeant, let's let Officer Perkins have a moment to gather his thoughts. Maybe he will realize it is best to stop lying to us when we come back in."

"Whatever you say, Lieutenant," Vallie agreed. She spoke into the recorder for a moment before shutting it off and picking it up.

As soon as the door was shut behind them, they looked through the one-way glass at the badly shaken officer on the other side. Chief Thurley was no longer in the room. "So the chief is letting you continue to work on this?" Vallie asked.

"For now," Jay said. "We've got to make some progress very quickly before he changes his mind."

"Jay, we're onto something with these officers. I can feel it." Vallie pointed a finger at the one-way glass. "Those guys are lying through their teeth."

"That's for sure," Jay acknowledged. "I think if we keep the pressure on, one of them is going to crack and admit something. I'm just not too sure what that admission might be."

"I think you're right," Vallie said. "Okay, Jay, the phone call you received. What was it about?"

"The girl's body on my porch was not that of Ada Pedler."

Sergeant Salmon was not an easy person to shock, but Jay had just succeeded in doing so. For a long moment, he let her think about it. "Who was it?"

"We don't know," he responded. "But the medical examiner is working on finding out. Celeste Pedler will be no better off and no worse at this point. I'm glad we didn't tell her about the dead girl. But some other parents will be devastated when we learn who the body is."

"We've got to bring Celeste up to date," Vallie said. "Not that she needs to know about a dead girl, but she needs to know we're working hard and might be making progress."

"I agree." He thought about Celeste and how very much she had come to mean to him over these past few weeks.

"Jay, she likes you," Vallie said as if reading his mind. "Did you notice how she blushed when you told her she looked good?"

He had noticed. "Don't get silly on me, Vallie." Despite his best efforts, he felt his cheeks redden. "We're just dating."

She shook her head, keeping her face serious. "I will continue to work on Officer Perkins. You go see Celeste. It will be good for her to see you and to know that we're working hard to find Ada. I won't start questioning Officer Spurr until you return."

Jay took a deep breath. "Okay. I'll hurry."

"And Jay, we'll find her daughter and yours. These officers know something. I can feel it. I'll see you when you get back."

He nodded and left the room. Whether there was a future between him and Celeste Pedler was not important at this moment. Their children were what mattered. Right now, she needed to know that there was still a chance, albeit slim, that they would get her daughter back.

A few minutes later, Jay entered Celeste Pedler's hospital room. She was awake, but her eyes were red and puffy. He could tell that she'd been crying a lot. When she saw him, she said with a broken voice, "Jay, do you have any leads on where Ada is yet?"

Jay reached out, took her hand, and looked tenderly into her eyes. "Let me tell you what I just learned, Celeste. There are officers involved, and we know who they are. We're questioning them. We'll break one of them before long, and then we'll have more to go on."

She smiled a very thin but attractive smile. "You will find her for me, won't you, Jay?"

"I will do everything in my power to find her. I promise you that."

She squeezed his hand. Their eyes locked. Something passed between them, something even deeper than he had felt before. Jay had no desire to deny it; this woman was special.

"Jay, you look like you are extremely upset. I can see it in your eyes. Is there something else I need to know?" Celeste asked. "Please tell me if there is."

Despite his best effort, Jay couldn't hold back the tears. He let go of Celeste's hand and rubbed his eyes. He couldn't find his voice. A look of alarm crossed Celeste's face. "Jay, what is it? What aren't you telling me? Is Ada dead?"

"No," Jay managed to say. "I'm pretty sure she's not."

"Jay, please, what is going on?" she asked as she held her hand out to him. He took it again, and she squeezed. "Please tell me, if you can."

Jay took a very deep breath. "They took Kinzington," he choked.

For the next few minutes, two grieving parents shared a lot of tears and a few emotional words.

***

Sergeant Salmon had continued to hammer away at Officer Perkins. "Give me your cell phone," she said in frustration. "Then I'll let you go for now."

"You can't have my cell phone," he said hotly.

She held out her hand and locked her determined eyes on his. He finally relented and handed it over. "There, I let you have it in good faith," he said. "But I will report this. You don't have a warrant."

She did not comment on that. She knew that he knew better. She let him leave the room in custody of another officer with instructions that he was to be kept separate from both Officer Spurr and Officer Alvarez and that none of those three officers was to be allowed to contact anyone in any way until she gave her permission. After thinking about what she had learned and what she had not learned from the two officers, she decided to take another crack at Alvarez.

If anything, Alvarez was cockier than ever when he was ushered back into the interrogation room. "I don't know why you brought me back in here," he started. "I have nothing more to say. It's pretty clear that you and Tanstall are trying to make a name for yourselves at the expense of innocent officers. It's little wonder you asked to be given this assignment. You're both power hungry."

She leaned toward him. "Nothing could be further from the truth, Officer Alvarez. Neither of us sought this assignment. But we were assigned anyway. All we're doing is what we have been ordered to do. Now, let's go over what we talked about earlier."

Officer Alvarez crossed his arms tightly, clamped his lips together, and said nothing. She tried several questions, but he had made it clear that he was not answering any more questions. "Okay, that will do for now," she said finally in exasperation.

She was told that Officer Spurr had been located and was waiting with another officer to be called into the interrogation room. She didn't want to start on him again until her partner returned. So she took a break in the office she and the lieutenant shared. She was deep in thought about what Perkins and Alvarez had told them and was considering the best way to handle Officer Spurr when Lieutenant Tanstall came back in.

"How did it go with Celeste?" Salmon asked. "Is she hanging in there?"

"She's trying. She's very worried."

"You told her about your daughter?"

"I did," he said sadly. "She could tell that I was more upset than ever, so she pressed me on it. I guess the two of us have something more in common now. Anything new from Perkins?"

"No. He's got his story, and he's sticking to it. I brought Alvarez back in, but he clammed up and wouldn't say anything."

"Okay. Then let's go have another round with Officer Spurr," the lieutenant said. "It's time to ratchet up the pressure on him."

CHAPTER TEN

KINZINGTON TANSTALL WAS FRIGHTENED BUT determined. She was her father's girl, one of both intelligence and courage. She knew she was in serious trouble, and that scared her, but she also knew that she would not give up, no matter what these men did to her.

She'd been ushered from the hotel without anyone noticing anything out of order. She had gone peaceably, knowing that if she didn't, they would go back and hurt or even kill her little brother. She was placed in a white van, blindfolded, gagged, her hands tied, and driven to a location she estimated to be about fifteen to thirty minutes from the hotel. From the echoes she could hear as she was dragged from the van, she thought they must be in a large room in a very large building. She was taken to a door that led to a stairway and was forced to walk down. Finally, she was unceremoniously shoved into a room, and she heard a door slam behind her, followed by the loud click of some kind of lock.

It had only taken her a moment to realize she was not alone. The smell of the place had been enough to tell her that others were in the room. It smelled like an appalling restroom, one that hadn't been cleaned in ages.

She'd heard moans and occasional sounds of sniffling. She'd stood still for a moment, and then someone had thrown two arms around her and, while hugging her tightly, cried in a hoarse, emotional voice, "Kinzington. It's Ada!"

For a moment, Kinzington had stood there in shock.

"I'll help untie you," Ada had finally said.

She'd sensed others moving closer and felt someone tugging at the gag that was in her mouth. It had finally popped out.

"Thank you. Is that really you, Ada?" Kinzington had asked as the blindfold was also removed and her eyes fell on the girl, who was dirty, with bloodshot eyes.

"Yes. I can't believe they got you too."

"Oh my goodness, Ada! We were all so worried when you didn't show up at school, but we just thought you were sick. Are you okay?"

"I guess so," Ada had answered. "I'll see if I can get your hands untied."

It wasn't totally dark in the room, but the only light came from a rather dim light bulb that was in a porcelain fixture in the ceiling at the center of the room.

As Ada had worked at the knot that bound Kinzington's hands, Kinzington had looked around the room. There was no furniture of any kind. All she could see were girls. She didn't think any of them were as old as she. A second girl had stepped close and helped Ada untie the knot. Finally, the rope had come loose and they let it drop to the floor. Instantly, Kinzington had hugged Ada tightly. The younger girl had hugged back. Both had shed tears.

They had finally stepped apart. "How many of you are there in here?" Kinzington had asked as she'd massaged her sore wrists.

"Eight," was Ada's answer. "You make nine. One more, then they're going to take us somewhere else." She'd spoken with very little emotion after the shock of seeing Kinzington had worn off. It seemed that she'd accepted her fate and no longer cried a lot about it.

"So is ten a magic number?" Kinzington had asked.

"Yes," another girl had answered. "My name is Nicole."

Kinzington had studied her for a moment. She looked about twelve or thirteen. She was a pretty girl, as was Ada. One by one, the girls had introduced themselves, giving only first names.

"Like Ada just said, my name is Kinzington," she'd finally said.

"You look older than the rest of us," a girl who had introduced herself as Aimee had said.

"I'm seventeen. How old are each of you?" she'd asked.

One by one, they'd each stated their ages. The last one to speak, whose name was Sue, had said, "I'm sixteen. I was the oldest until they brought you here."

That had been a couple of hours ago. Not much had been said during that time, but Ada had stayed close to Kinzington, touching her often, as if relishing her presence and perhaps sensing security having her older friend here with her now. Kinzington had spent those hours thinking and scheming. She was not going to stay here or be moved somewhere else without a fight. She was determined to try to escape.

She looked at the girls, who were all sitting on the bare cement floor, leaning against a wall, or lying on thin mattresses on the floor. The youngest was eleven.

The others ranged in ages from twelve through sixteen. "Hey, let's talk. Is that okay?"

No one objected, and they all slowly gathered around Kinzington. "How long have you each been here?" Kinzington asked. "Of course, I already know Ada and how long she's been here. But I want to hear from the rest of you, and please tell me where you're from."

"You sort of talk like a cop," Sue said.

"Her dad is a cop," Ada revealed.

All the girls stared at Kinzington for a minute or two. "That won't help us," Sue finally said with a helpless shrug. "I've been here the longest. They took me from my home in Aurora when I was alone one night. That was about four weeks ago. The other girls have come in one at a time every few days since."

"Earlier, you said they wanted ten of us. So there will be one more, and then they want to take us somewhere?" Kinzington asked. She peered closely at the other girls in the dim light, and it suddenly occurred to her that there was one thing every girl had in common; they were all very pretty.

"One of the guys talks to us when he brings food. He says that we'll be sold to people in foreign countries," Ada revealed.

Despite her determination to stay strong, Kinzington's fear broke through, and she let the tears flow. Then the others followed suit.

It didn't last long, though. These girls had all clearly cried plenty already, and Kinzington had to be positive. She had to be the strong one, no matter how hard it was. For the next few minutes, each of them related where they were from and how they'd been taken. Every one of them referred to three men in black and a white van. They were from all over the Denver metropolitan area.

They grew quiet, and Kinzington began to concentrate. She didn't know how yet, but she was determined to somehow get out of this place before they were sent off to buyers somewhere to become slaves—or something worse.

"You're all dirty, but you don't look like you're starving," Kinzington observed.

"Oh, they feed us okay, I guess," Sue said. "That one guy said they want us to stay pretty so that we will bring lots of money. But they don't care that we're dirty. He said they'll let us clean ourselves up when it's time."

"It smells like a dirty restroom in here," Kinzington observed. "I need to use the toilet. Where do I do that?"

"We have to use the bathroom over in that corner," Sue said. "There's a bucket and toilet paper and a little water to wash our hands in. Once a day, a guy comes in—not the one that feeds us, but a different guy—to take the bucket and the dirty water, and he leaves a new bucket and more water. He never says a word to us."

"But he looks at us in a way that's really scary," the girl named Aimee said.

"I hate the way he looks at us," Sue said with a frown. "But the other guy, the one who brings food, he actually seems sort of friendly. I mean, he tells us not to try to get away, but at least he always says hello to us and asks us if we're all feeling okay."

"Are you all feeling okay physically?" Kinzington asked.

"Pretty much," Sue said. "But Missy—she was sick. She told the guy that brings the food every day, but he didn't seem to think there was anything he could do."

"Which one of you is Missy?" Kinzington asked as she glanced at the girls who surrounded her. "I don't remember one of you telling me that name."

"That's because she's gone. She told us she needed medicine or she would die," Sue said. "We told the guy who feeds us that, and he finally said he would tell the boss."

"How did she leave?" Kinzington asked with growing dread.

"The guy who empties the bucket and some other guy came in and told her they were tired of her complaints," Sue said. "Then they grabbed her and carried her out. We could hear her screaming after they locked us in again. It sounded like they were beating her just on the other side of the door."

"Could she be dead?" Kinzington asked as she thought about the girl that had been left on her back deck.

"Probably," Ada said. "There's no way they'd take her home, and she was no good to them anymore when she was sick and all."

Kinzington took a breath, carefully looked at her fellow captives, and finally, mustering her courage, said, "Girls, we have to get away."

"We can't," Aimee said. The others agreed with her.

"Would you be willing to try if I could figure something out?" Kinzington asked.

"Maybe, but they might kill us if we try," Sue said, her voice cracking.

"Listen, I don't want to die. But I would prefer that to becoming some dirty old man's slave or . . . or . . . never mind. Just think about it. Isn't it worth trying to get away?"

"We're just girls. These guys are strong," Aimee whined.

"Like Ada told you, my dad is a cop. He taught me self-defense, and he also had my brother and me study martial arts in a studio. I can fight. I can fight really well if I get a chance. If I fight, will you help me?" she asked.

For the first time, Kinzington saw hope in the eyes of the pretty, dirty girls that surrounded her. It was a dim hope, but at least it was a start. She had them thinking. She really could fight. She'd hurt one of the men who took her from the hotel, but she hadn't really had a chance then, and they'd hurt her for fighting. She'd been taken totally by surprise. But she had her mind made up that it wouldn't happen again. She would be ready when an opportunity presented itself.

She wanted to help these girls get ready too. She stood and walked to the corner where the toilet bucket was located. It was disgusting. She did what she had to do, noticing that all the other girls looked away the entire time she was there. After she was done and had washed her hands the best she could, she rejoined the other girls.

"When do the men who feed you and change the bucket and water come in here?" she asked.

"We don't know. We don't have watches. Do you?" Ada asked. She was still staying very close to Kinzington most of the time. And she looked at her with hope in her eyes.

"No, they took that while I was in the van," Kinzington replied. It seemed that the same had happened to the others.

"If it wasn't for that one little light, it would be dark in here. We've lost track of time," Sue explained. "But I think the guy who changes the water and the bucket will be coming in an hour or two. The other guy usually comes a little while after him. He brings a few sandwiches and bottles of water that have to last us for a day."

"Okay. Let me think for a minute." Kinzington paused, thoughtful, and then she said, "Okay, listen up, you guys. Are you all with me if I try to escape and help you escape too?"

They slowly, one by one, agreed.

"Then here's what we need to do," she began.

CHAPTER ELEVEN

At Sergeant Salmon's suggestion, they'd postponed the next session with Officer Spurr while they did some research into his background and his history with the police department. They'd learned he was married for the second time and had a teenage daughter with his second wife, a woman much younger than him. The daughter's name was Missy Spurr, age fifteen, and she was diabetic.

Spurr's wife worked as a secretary for an ad agency. She had a clean record, but a call to her place of employment was concerning to them. She had not been at work for several days. She had continually called in sick, and her boss told them he was not happy with her.

Until the issue of falsifying the report on the abduction of Ada Pedler, Officer Spurr had not had any serious problems as an officer. He had been passed over for promotion several times, but it was never for anything other than his not being someone the chief and others considered good leadership material.

Finally, they did some checking on his recent patrol assignments and found that he had requested the area he had worked the night Ada Pedler was abducted. Jay and Vallie agreed that was troubling.

They finally brought Spurr into the room. Once again, Sergeant Salmon began the questioning. The first thing she asked was if he had his cell phone with him.

"Of course," he said.

Vallie reached out a hand. "I'll take that, please."

"I don't think so," he said as he stared at her. "I don't see why you need it. Just because I disagree with you over Mrs. Jamison's statements is no reason to take my phone. Anyway, I don't think you have that authority."

"Actually, we do," Sergeant Salmon said firmly. "Hand it over and we can get on with things here."

He looked from her to Jay and back again.

"Officer, you have been given an order by a superior officer," Jay said, fighting to control his temper. "Hand it over right now."

Spurr's eyes again came to Jay's face. A look of defeat entered his gaze, and without another word, he pulled his cell phone from a pocket and handed it to the sergeant.

"Thank you," she said, giving the phone to Jay. "We have a few questions. First, tell us why you were working the area of the city you were in the night of Ada Pedler's abduction."

Officer Spurr's eyes jerked back and forth between Jay and Vallie, and his hands trembled ever so slightly. He hesitated before finally saying, "It was because my sergeant told me to work that area." *Strike one.*

"I see," Sergeant Salmon said. "Do you have a close personal relationship with Officer Vincent Perkins and Officer Cortez Alvarez?"

"Not really," Spurr said, his darting eyes failing to meet those of his interrogator. "They're okay guys, but we really don't see a lot of each other." *Strike two.*

Vallie and Jay had yet to examine Officer Perkins's cell phone since they needed to get a search warrant first. But they had agreed that they might try bluffing Spurr if it looked like it could help move him along in the interrogation. After all, the bluff they'd used on Alvarez had worked well. Vallie caught Jay's eyes, and he nodded almost imperceptibly.

"Officer Spurr," Vallie said, "what did Officer Perkins discuss with you when he called you last night?"

Spurr was looking more defeated with each question. But he took a sweeping *strike three* when he said, "He didn't call me."

Sergeant Salmon looked at him, shaking her head. "Do you really think I would have asked you that question if I didn't already know the answer?"

Officer Spurr simply shook his head. He was beginning to perspire. Jay thought there was something bothering the guy, something more than just their questioning. He decided to poke a question at him. "Why is your wife not going to work? She could lose her job."

Spurr stared at his trembling hands on the table in front of him for a good minute or longer.

Vallie and Jay let the silence stream on.

"She's not well," Spurr said finally, again failing to lift his eyes.

"I'm sorry to hear that," Vallie said. "What exactly is wrong with her?"

"That's private. She doesn't want me to talk about it, so I won't," he said, more assertively now, with a touch of anger.

There was a gentle knock on the door. Jay stepped over and opened it. Chief Thurley signaled for him to come out, and he did so with a terrible sinking feeling in his stomach. He was about to get pulled off of the case, and then what would he do to find his daughter? He had to find her.

"I think we're going to have to cut Perkins and Alvarez loose before too long," the chief said. "Unless you need to talk to them again."

"Can you give us just a few minutes? We have a few more questions for Officer Spurr and then we want to grill the others for a little bit before working on Spurr some more."

"It's your call, Lieutenant. Some of the other officers are sensing that you and Sergeant Salmon are up to something, and I don't want those suspicions to get too serious. I don't want others thinking we may be getting close to something here until you're ready to make some arrests."

"I understand. But please, just give us a few more minutes," Jay said.

"Okay. I'll do that. I've been observing here for a couple of minutes," the chief said. "There's something gnawing at Officer Spurr. You need to find out what it is before I let the others go home and rest."

"We'll do our best," Jay said. The chief thanked him, and Jay reentered the interrogation room. He was relieved that he was still on the case, but he was also feeling a lot of additional pressure.

***

The door to the small room where the nine girls were being held captive opened. A man entered carrying a large jug of water. Kinzington glanced at Sue, who nodded, acknowledging that this was the one they needed to overpower.

Kinzington stepped in front of him as the other girls cowered together a few steps back. "Sir, I really need to get out of here and go home," she said bravely.

The guy laughed and spat at her feet. "You ain't going nowhere, girly." He looked her up and down, a terrible look on his face.

"You're wrong," she said as she suddenly gave him a karate kick that literally dropped him to the floor. Before he could get up, she kicked again, catching him on the side of the head. He moaned and collapsed.

"Let me check him for a weapon and a cell phone," she said, "and then we'll tie him up the best we can with his belt. Then we'll get out of here and lock him in. But be watchful; there could be more men outside the door."

The girls moved quickly, encouraged by how easily Kinzington had knocked the guy down. He had a gun on him—a small 38-caliber Chief revolver.

Kinzington took it and stuck in inside her waistband, but she did not find a phone. Disappointed over that, she led the way to the door. She didn't see anyone, so she signaled the other girls to follow. Sue locked the door behind them.

They hurried up the stairway to the large room above. It appeared to be empty, so Kinzington led the girls across the room to a small outside door just to the left of a much bigger door, one large enough to drive a truck through. She opened the door a crack and groaned softly. Two men stood outside with their backs to the door. They were armed and looked very dangerous. Kinzington silently closed the door when one of them started to turn toward it. She looked around her desperately and noticed a stack of crates to their right.

"Quick. We need to hide behind those crates," she whispered. "Then we'll have to wait. There are two guys out there. Be patient. We'll get away."

The girls did as she instructed, and they were all soon behind the crates, huddled like a herd of frightened sheep.

***

Celeste lay in her hospital bed, her head aching terribly but her heart aching far worse. She glanced occasionally at the door, hoping to see Jay come in. His strong, confident presence was comforting to her. He was a wonderful man whom she wished she'd met a long time ago.

Tears occasionally filled her eyes, and she wiped them away each time. Ada just had to be okay. She couldn't stand the thought of losing her permanently. Nor could she stand the thought of the terrible things Ada could be going through now and what could await her in the future.

There was a light knock on the door and hope filled her. She watched as it opened, expecting to see Jay, but she was disappointed. It was only the nurse. Celeste answered the woman's questions and listened to her positive voice as she checked vital signs. The nurse told her she was improving, but until the doctor felt like her concussion was a lot better, she would have to stay in the hospital.

After a few minutes, the nurse left, leaving Celeste with a few words of encouragement. She hadn't been gone long before the landline phone on the little table by her bed began to ring. Celeste answered it, wondering who could possibly be calling her on it. Her boss maybe? But he'd come in earlier, encouraged her, promised that her job was secure, and left.

She reached for the phone and lifted the receiver to her ear. She did not recognize the voice that spoke.

"Listen, lady, and listen carefully. Your daughter will not be coming back to you, but she is safe and in good hands. She will not be hurt unless . . ." the caller let that ominous word drag out. Then he finished by saying, "Unless you don't make sure that Lieutenant Tanstall and Sergeant Salmon stop poking their noses into things that are none of their business. You tell him I said that."

"Who are you?" she asked, her voice weak and almost breaking.

"It doesn't matter who I am. You can just think of me as Boss. You better use all your womanly charms on that lieutenant friend of yours to make sure he quits searching for his daughter and yours, or they will *not* be okay. Their lives are in your hands."

Before Celeste could make another response, the call ended. She was shaking so badly she couldn't hang up the phone. She dropped the receiver and let it dangle as she searched for the call button and pressed it. Moments later, the nurse rushed in. "I need to make a phone call," Celeste said with a shaky voice. "Will you dial for me?"

The nurse asked her what the matter was, but she simply said, "Please, dial the number I tell you."

The nurse grabbed the dangling receiver. Looking at Celeste with concern, she punched in the number that Celeste recited. Then she handed the phone to Celeste. "I need to be alone for this call," Celeste said.

The nurse protested, but Celeste insisted. So she finally left but didn't close the door behind her. The phone was ringing.

"Lieutenant Tanstall speaking."

"It's Celeste. I just had a terrible call. I'm so frightened for Ada and Kinzington."

"I'm on the verge of what could be a breakthrough. Can you tell me about the call and then I'll call you back shortly?"

"Okay." Celeste told him everything.

"You know we can't drop this, Celeste."

"I know that. But please, find my . . . find our daughters fast. Please. He might hurt them."

"Hang in there, sweetheart," he said soothingly. "I'll get back to you as soon as I can."

"Thank you," she said.

CHAPTER TWELVE

As Lieutenant Jay Tanstall slowly put his phone back in his pocket, he watched through the one-way glass. His partner was still asking Officer Spurr questions, but she wasn't learning anything of value. However, Jay couldn't help but think that a breakthrough was imminent, as he had just told Celeste. His heart ached for her. She was a wonderful woman. What he wouldn't give to be able to return her daughter to her unharmed. But it sounded like the captors were feeling pressure as a result of what he and Vallie were doing, and that meant they needed to break Spurr down and quickly. Spurr was the key.

Jay was certain of one thing now: cops were involved in the kidnappings. Otherwise, why would the kidnappers be feeling pressure? The only people they were putting pressure on were police officers in their department.

He was about to rejoin his partner when the chief came back in. "How close are you to letting me release these officers?" Chief Thurley asked. "I'm getting pressure from a union attorney now. Apparently someone made a call and told him we were harassing three of their colleagues. The attorney says we either need to charge them with something or let them go. If we don't, he says he will take a court action against the department."

Jay took a deep breath. "We have nothing to charge them with except lying to us. Spurr is a different matter; we could charge him with falsifying a report. Please, give us a few more minutes. I think we can break Spurr pretty quick."

"Do that, if you can, but unless you can give me something more than your suspicion that they're lying, I'll have to let Perkins and Alvarez go, as much as I hate to."

Jay stared at his hands for a moment. "I know they're lying. But let them go if you have to. We haven't gotten anything more from Spurr so far that will help us in questioning either of them again. Just let them know that if we need them, we'll come after them."

"Oh, I'll do that," the chief agreed.

"I'll go back in and see if we can get any further with Spurr. He knows something but won't say what."

"He looks like a whipped pup in there right now," the chief acknowledged. "But if you can't get something from him in the next ten minutes, you will need to let him go too. I don't think it would be helpful to your investigation to charge him over the false report at this point."

"I understand. We really need to examine their cell phones, Chief. I know we'll make progress when we do that."

"All right, Lieutenant. Finish up here with Spurr and then get the search warrants ready and approved. We'll bring them back in if we find enough evidence to justify it."

The chief left, and Jay returned to the interrogation room. For several minutes, he and Vallie continued to pressure Spurr, but he did not admit to anything.

Jay's phone buzzed again. Thinking it was probably Celeste, he stepped from the room and answered without looking at the screen. But it was the medical examiner, who told him they had identified the girl whose mutilated body had been dumped on his back porch. He reeled when he heard the name. He reeled again when he was told that she had died as a result of not having insulin for a prolonged period—that and a severe beating.

Jay was stunned. He finally thanked the medical examiner, opened the door to the interrogation room, and signaled for Vallie to come out.

"The chief has cut the other guys loose. But now I know why Spurr is so upset and uncooperative," Jay said as soon as Vallie joined him and shut the door. "The medical examiner just called and told me that the girl whose body was on my porch is a girl by the name of Missy Spurr."

"Oh . . . my . . ." Vallie started. "She's probably his daughter. Did he say the cause of death was the beating she had?"

"Not entirely. She was diabetic and had been without insulin for quite a while."

"Let's get back in there. Jay, why don't you take the lead for now? Are you okay doing that?" Vallie asked.

"You'd better believe I am," he said fiercely. "Between this Missy Spurr thing and what Celeste just called me about, I'm ready to start tearing people apart."

"Wait. What happened with Celeste?"

Jay told her about the threatening call. "We've got to get these guys fast. I wish the chief hadn't turned Perkins and Alvarez loose, but he was getting intense pressure from the union. Someone told them we're harassing these guys. The union attorney is threatening to take legal action against us."

"Like I told you, Jay, we are the enemy now."

"At least we can probably eliminate our three guys from being Celeste's caller—the guy who called himself Boss—because they haven't had access to a phone." Jay grabbed the handle to the door and jerked it open.

The detectives entered and sat down. Vallie started the recorder, spoke into it for a moment, and then looked at Jay.

"Officer Spurr, tell us about Missy," he said.

Spurr, whose head had been in his hands, practically jumped from his seat.

"Settle down," Jay said. "Tell us about her."

Spurr began to sob, but he didn't say a word. Jay pressed him. "Officer, we're waiting, and I'm running out of patience."

"Okay, okay," he said. "She's my daughter. But you knew that, didn't you?"

"We assumed it. It's time you told us everything you know," Jay said roughly. "We're not playing games with you anymore."

The officer shook his head slowly and rubbed his eyes. "I can't talk about it, or she could be hurt."

"Casper," Jay said loudly. "They have my daughter! You'd better help us here."

"Your daughter?" Spurr asked. The way his eyes opened wide made Jay think he hadn't known that.

"Yes, my daughter! And I know they took yours as well. So tell us, when did they take Missy, and why haven't you reported it?"

Spurr hung his head. "It's been a couple of weeks. But if they find out I told anyone, they'll let her die."

"What do you mean?" Jay asked, knowing full well what he meant.

"She's diabetic. She had some insulin on her when they took her, but it won't have lasted this long. That's for sure. And they knew it. They said if I didn't keep all of this to myself and do whatever else I could to help them that they'd let her die. Lieutenant, I couldn't do that. She's my little girl."

"So you've been helping them?" Jay asked, intentionally keeping the deep sympathy he was feeling from showing on his face or in his voice.

"Please, you probably just condemned my daughter to death," Spurr said.

Jay and Vallie glanced at each other. She answered his unspoken question with a nod of her head. He turned back to Officer Spurr. "Casper, I have some really bad news. Your daughter is already dead."

"What?! That can't be! They promised. I did what they asked. They promised," he repeated. "They said they'd given her more insulin."

"She died from a lack of insulin," Jay said. "It was her body they dumped on my back porch."

Officer Spurr's face was white. "That can't be true. He told me it was Ada Pedler."

"Perkins told you that?" Jay asked darkly.

Spurr didn't answer directly. "You're lying to me. You're trying to get me to tell you who's doing this, but I can't tell you. They'll kill my daughter."

"Listen to me. *They already have.* And I'm sorry about that. But I intend to save mine, so you'd better come clean right now." Jay's anger overcame any sympathy he'd felt.

***

The two men from outside the warehouse entered and headed down the stairs to where the girls had locked up the other man.

"Let's go," Kinzington whispered.

They all scrambled for the door to the outside. Sue jerked it open just as they heard steps coming up the stairs behind them.

"Run!" Kinzington shouted. All the girls made it outside and a short distance from the door before a shot rang out. Kinzington fell when the bullet struck her leg. Ada stopped to help her up. "No, go!"

"I can't leave you," Ada cried as the two men stepped out of the door and advanced on them.

"Go!" Kinzington screamed again.

Another shot rang out as a second bullet struck Kinzington. Ada finally ran for all she was worth. A third shot hit Ada, but it did not knock her down, and she followed the others around the edge of the building and out of sight.

Kinzington, who lay face down, managed to pull the pistol from her pants. She raised it and fired once. The man in the lead plunged headlong to the ground, his pistol flying from his hand. Kinzington expected another bullet at any second. She knew she was about to die. She lay still and waited for death to overtake her, but no other shots came.

The man she had not shot stepped right to her, and she could hear him breathing hard above her. She tried to lie totally motionless, even stilling her breathing the best she could. She heard the man speak into what she assumed was a cell phone. He told someone he called Boss that the girls had gotten away, all but one.

"I'm pretty sure she's dead," he said.

The man called Boss shouted so loudly over the phone at the kidnapper that Kinzington could hear him as he yelled. "Find them! Do it now. I'll send help. If you fail me, you're a dead man."

"You got it, Boss," the kidnapper said as he stepped over Kinzington and then ran to the edge of the building where the other girls had disappeared.

Kinzington could barely move. The excruciating pain told her she was close to death, but she didn't want to die. She wanted to live. She wanted to help her father bring all these men to justice.

With that thought coursing through her pain-filled mind, she passed out.

***

Lieutenant Tanstall had finally convinced Officer Spurr that his daughter was dead, but it took a call to the medical examiner to do it. A lot of time had been wasted, and neither he nor Sergeant Salmon were in any mood to allow Spurr to stall anymore. Lives were in jeopardy.

Spurr stubbornly insisted that he wouldn't speak again until he knew his wife was safe. So the chief was notified, and he sent a pair of officers to pick up Mrs. Spurr. Then he joined Lieutenant Tanstall and Sergeant Salmon in the interrogation room. The chief was, to say the least, highly agitated.

"Spurr, I'm very sorry about your daughter. But you must tell us all you know, and you'd better do it right now," Chief Thurley said.

Spurr's eyes were red and puffy. "Not until my wife is safe."

"I have officers going to pick her up," the chief assured him.

"When I hear her voice, then I'll talk, and I'll do it without a lawyer."

Jay had taken all he could. "So help me, Casper, if my daughter dies because of you, I will hold you personally responsible!"

"I haven't done anything but try to protect my daughter's life," Spurr said. "And now I'm trying to protect my wife's life. Don't blame me."

"I do blame you. You can prevent further deaths. Now start talking."

Spurr shook his head.

Jay stood up and signaled to the chief that he needed to leave the room. Chief Thurley followed him out.

"You've got to find Perkins and Alvarez and get them back here," Jay said.

"I already have officers looking for them," Chief Thurley responded. "Neither one is at home. I don't know where they went when they left here." The chief gave an exasperated sigh. "I could kick that union attorney in the teeth . . . don't repeat that."

Jay's phone buzzed, and he pulled it from his pocket.

"Jay, it's Celeste. Have you found Ada and Kinzington yet?"

The sorrow and worry in her voice were almost more than he could bear. He choked up. "We're working on it, Celeste."

"Please, don't let them kill my Ada . . . or your Kinzington," she pleaded.

"Believe me, I'm doing everything I can. I'll let you know as soon as I know more."

"Promise?" she asked softly.

"Yes, I promise," he said and ended the call.

CHAPTER THIRTEEN

Officer Spurr's wife finally spoke with Spurr on the phone as she was being transported to the police station. Only after talking with her for a minute did the distraught officer agree to speak. By then, another pair of policemen had been dispatched to the home of Officer Perkins with orders to pick up his wife and bring her in for questioning. Officer Alvarez was not married, but he had a girlfriend, and a search was underway for her.

Jay sat down across from Casper Spurr and next to Sergeant Salmon. Chief Thurley and another command-level officer watched through the one-way glass. "Okay, Casper, tell us all you know: names, addresses, everything."

Spurr was clearly a defeated man. "Well, you asked if I was friends with Officer Perkins. The answer is no! I hate that man! He's the one who told me my daughter was being held. He wouldn't say by whom, but it was clear that he knew. He promised me that if I would do whatever he asked, Missy would be given insulin, her life would be spared, and she would be given back to me. He lied!" Spurr slammed his hands down on the table. "He let her die!"

"What did he say when he called you on the phone from my backyard?" Jay asked.

"He said that the Pedler girl had caused a problem and had to be eliminated and that she had been delivered to your home." Spurr had to stop for a minute as he fought to control his emotions. "My wife said she was with an officer when I talked to her a minute ago. Where is she now?"

"We'll keep your wife safe," Sergeant Salmon said. "Now please, tell us where Perkins and the others are keeping the girls."

"I don't know where," he said helplessly. "If I knew, I'd have gotten Missy back myself."

"How is Officer Alvarez involved?" Jay asked.

"I don't know. I just know that he and Perkins are tight. So I'm sure he's part of this."

"You don't have any idea where the girls are being held?" Jay pressed.

"I'm not lying to you, Lieutenant," Spurr said as he rubbed his swollen eyes. "I should have killed Perkins. If I had known that nothing was being done to save my little Missy, I would have killed him. I still will if I ever get my hands on him."

Jay had no doubt Spurr would do exactly that. That could not be allowed to happen, but deep down, Jay understood how he felt. He pressed on. "Okay, Casper. Give me some more names. Are there other police officers involved in this besides Perkins and Alvarez?"

"Not that I know of," Spurr said.

"If not more officers, who else is? Give me some names, please," Jay pleaded.

Spurr was thoughtful for a moment, and Jay, as uptight, angry, and worried as he was, gave him time to think. "They call the head man Boss," Spurr said finally. "I'm not sure about this, but I got the feeling he's related to Vincent Perkins. But I don't know in what way."

Sergeant Salmon left the room in a hurry, saying, "I'll get to work on this."

After his partner had stepped out, Jay said to Officer Spurr, "The report you did on the kidnapping of Ada Pedler contradicted what our witness, the late Josie Jamison, told me. Can you explain that?"

Spurr hung his head and said very softly, "I lied. I had to make it look more like a runaway than a kidnapping."

"You were told to do that?" Jay asked.

"Yes! I had no choice!"

"Casper, tell me exactly how Officer Perkins was involved."

Spurr rubbed his eyes. "Okay, but you guys have to lock him up if I tell you what I know. He's a dangerous man."

After a short pause, Jay pressed, "Go on, Casper."

"Well, he knew my Missy . . ." Tears flowed down his face, and Jay had to wait for him to compose himself. Finally, he wiped his eyes, blew his nose, and then said, "He knew Missy had been taken."

"Could he be the one who took Missy?" the lieutenant asked.

Spurr didn't even hesitate. "I tried to tell myself that he wouldn't have done that, but yes, now I think he was one of the men who did."

"Casper," Jay said, still using his first name in an attempt to keep his confidence, "who kidnapped Ada Pedler? I want the truth. You volunteered to work that area that night, which tells me you knew who was in the white van."

"I have no idea who the driver was, but one of the ones in black who grabbed her was Perkins. He never told me who the other one was, but both he and Alvarez had that night off, so I expect it was Alvarez that helped him."

"Okay, let's talk about when Mrs. Jamison's house was burned. Was that you who did that?" Lieutenant Tanstall asked, his head as close to Officer Spurr's as he could get with the table between them.

Spurr's eyes went wide. "What! No! I would never do anything like that."

"You allowed Ada Pedler to be kidnapped," Jay reminded him. "That's *like that*."

"I had to! But I swear I had nothing to do with that old lady's house being torched."

"Casper," Jay said, exercising all the patience he could muster, "her statements, which were contrary to your report, made her a danger to you and Perkins. Isn't that right?"

"Yes, but I didn't do it."

"Maybe you didn't torch it, but you knew it was going to happen, didn't you?"

Spurr shook his head. "Okay, yeah, I knew. Perkins did it. He tried to get me to, but I just couldn't make myself do it. I told him I wouldn't. And that's probably why he let my little girl die. So I guess in a way, I killed my little Missy."

In that context, Spurr was right. But at least that one time, the guy made the right choice. Jay was about to ask another question when his phone buzzed. He was tempted to ignore it, but when it continued, he finally pulled it from his pocket and looked at the screen. The call was from Vallie.

He answered and had barely said hello when Vallie said urgently, "Leave Spurr there. Someone will take him into custody. I'll meet you at our car. We need to go. The girls have escaped. They flagged down a passing car and asked the driver to call the police."

"Don't move," Jay said to Spurr, and he sprinted for the door. A uniformed officer met him at the door that led from the observation room. "Cuff him and hold him." Jay pointed at Officer Spurr through the one-way glass.

As soon as he reached the car, he jumped in. Vallie was right behind him. "Let me drive," she said.

"I've got it," he said and pointed to the passenger side. She hurried around, and as soon as her door was closed, they sped off. "Tell me where to go."

She gave him an address. "That's where they were being held. It's an old abandoned building, probably a warehouse."

"I know the area," he said, concentrating on his driving.

"Jay, nine girls were being held there. Ada is one of them. She's been shot, but it's a superficial wound. They're safe now. I just spoke with one of the officers who responded to the call to let us know they had escaped."

Jay's chest constricted. He knew from the tone of his partner's voice that something more was going on, something bad. "Sergeant," he said, his voice low and full of emotion, "what about my daughter?"

Vallie looked down at her hands. "Ada told the officers that Kinzington made Ada leave her. She said it's because of her that the others were able to escape."

"Vallie! What else aren't you telling me?" Jay demanded as he flew through a red light. "Are we going to where Ada left Kinzington?"

"Yes. She was just a little ways beyond the building when Ada left her," she said. "Ada couldn't say how far. Jay, I'm so sorry. Kinzington was shot too. But she was alive when Ada finally ran."

Jay was unable to respond to that news. The shock was too great. He could only pray that his girl was still alive and that they would get to her in time.

Sergeant Salmon's phone rang. She answered, listened for a moment, and then said, "Okay, I understand." She ended the call. "Jay, they can't find Perkins or Alvarez. Why don't you stop long enough to let me change places with you? You're too worked up to drive."

"I'm okay. We can't afford to lose any time. Who knows, Perkins and Alvarez may either be there or headed there. We've got to save my girl."

CHAPTER FOURTEEN

KINZINGTON HAD REGAINED CONSCIOUSNESS, BUT she had not moved other than to turn her head just enough to see the corner of the building where the other girls had gone. She prayed that they were all safe, that they had managed to escape. She knew she had to move, to find a way to escape before someone found her. But to her alarm, the man who had left her there and run after the other girls, came into sight around the corner. He was talking on his phone, making broad gestures with his free hand.

"I'm pretty sure she's dead," he said.

He meant Kinzington. Since it was too late to attempt to crawl away, Kinzington decided she'd better pretend she really was dead so he wouldn't shoot her again. She thought about God and tried to pray. He was the only one who could help her now.

"I'm telling you, she's dead already," the man said.

The man stood directly over her, and she could hear a voice coming from the phone. "Jonesy, shoot her now!"

"I can't," Jonesy said.

"Coward!" the voice on the phone exploded.

"No, you know I'm not. I'd shoot her, but I lost my gun chasing after those other girls." He almost seemed to whimper.

"You let them get away?" the angry voice screamed. "Do you know what that means?"

"It wasn't my fault," Jonesy said.

Kinzington felt a flood of relief flow through her in knowing her efforts were not in vain. Maybe God had heard her. The others had gotten away, and maybe she still had a chance if this guy really couldn't shoot her. She had to get up and get away—if she could.

"You're an idiot, Jonesy. You'll wish you hadn't lost your gun."

"Sorry, Perkins, but I stumbled, and my gun must have fallen out of my pocket. Those girls were fast, and I don't know where they went. They just disappeared. I'll find my pistol," Jonesy promised. "When I do, I'll shoot this girl again, but I know she's already dead. I mean, I saw Ignacio shoot her twice."

"Boss is going to be furious with you, Jonesy. You know how he feels about guys who mess up. And you've messed up big time."

Perkins. Kinzington was fairly certain that was the last name of one of the officers who had responded to their home when the body was dumped on the back deck. Could an officer be a part of this horrible thing that was happening? She remembered her father mentioning an Officer Vincent Perkins. Or maybe it was a Victor Perkins? Could that really be who was screaming and cursing on the phone?

"Please, Vincent, don't tell him. I'll find the gun." Jonesy was almost crying now.

Kinzington was shocked. She'd guessed right. The officer that came to their house must have been Vincent Perkins—the same man on the phone. A policeman wanted her dead!

"You stay right there with that girl," Perkins ordered. "I'll be there shortly, and I'll make sure she's dead. After I make a phone call, of course."

"Please, don't call your brother. He'll kill me," Jonesy begged.

"No, I can promise you right now that he won't," Perkins said. "Now, I tried to call Ignacio earlier, but he's not answering. Where is he?"

"The girl shot him. It was just before she died," Jonesy reported.

"Where—is—he?" Perkins asked, the anger in his voice so intense that it was a wonder the phone didn't burn Jonesy's hand.

"He's just a few feet away from where the girl is."

"Let me talk to him," Perkins said. "He can talk, can't he?"

"I don't think so. He might be dead too."

Perkins said a few horrible words that Kinzington tried to block out. "Get his gun and shoot her, you idiot. Do it now."

"All right, Vincent. I'll do it."

"One more thing before I make my call, Jonesy. Which girl is it?"

"The dead one?"

"Yes, you idiot, the one you're going to *make sure* is dead."

"It's the one you guys brought in this morning."

"Are you serious? Lieutenant Tanstall's daughter?" Kinzington could hear Perkins as he laughed hysterically. "That couldn't be better. Now get Ignacio's gun and take care of business."

Kinzington hadn't even thought about the other man's gun. She had to do something now, or she would die. They knew who she was, and clearly, Perkins hated her dad. Was he one of the reasons her dad had told them not to even let a cop in the house if someone knocked or rang the bell? Probably. She tried to push herself up, but her body wasn't cooperating, and the floor was slick. It took her a moment to realize she was lying in her own blood. However, the hand she still held the little Chief in felt dry, and she was able to move. But it took a lot of painful effort. Shooting Jonesy before he got that other gun was her only chance.

She was too slow. Jonesy was back.

"Wait a minute here," he said softly to himself. Kinzington held as still as possible, but she could sense him waiting, watching as he shifted on the asphalt. "You just moved your hand. You aren't dead, are you, girl?"

Kinzington could not get her hand to where she could take a shot up at him, and she knew then that she was about to die. She let her body relax in resignation. She expected the bullet any moment now.

She heard a short *click*, and Jonesy used some choice language. "The gun's messed up. Something must have happened to it when Ignacio dropped it."

She could hear him slamming his hand on the gun. Then she could hear more clicking as he tried again. Suddenly, he threw the gun to the ground in anger. For a moment, Jonesy tromped around, swearing and carrying on something awful. Kinzington was still alive, but that wouldn't last long after Perkins got here. She had to ignore the intense pain and weakness and make her body work.

With a monumental effort, she managed to turn slightly. Then, to her absolute terror, Jonesy said, "Wait a minute. You have a gun, don't you, girly? You won't need it where you're going."

In a moment, Jonesy came into view in front of her. "You're a bloody mess, girly," he said. "How could you still be alive? Well, don't worry your pretty little head. I'll take that gun now." He leaned down, but Kinzington had the gun tucked slightly beneath her body, concealing it from him. "Where is it?" He leaned down closer.

In desperation, Kinzington adjusted her hand a little and pulled the trigger. Blood spurted from Jonesy's foot. He screamed and fell over backward, swearing up a storm. Just then a car drove squealing around the corner. It slid to a stop a few feet from her, and a man jumped out of it. He had the largest pistol she'd ever seen.

"Vincent, I'm hurt," Jonesy cried out.

For a moment, Officer Vincent Perkins said nothing. Then he began to laugh. "You shot yourself in the foot. What an idiot. Well, I just talked to my brother. Remember how I told you that he wouldn't kill you? I wasn't lying. He won't. He said that would be my job. Of course, I sort of volunteered for it."

"Perkins! No!" Jonesy screamed in terror.

There was a shot. From the corner of her eye, Kinzington saw a shower of blood, and then Jonesy fell back and lay still. From somewhere deep within her, Kinzington found the strength she thought was gone and was able to push herself to her knees as Perkins walked over to the man he had just killed.

"Too bad, Jonesy, old boy. But I had to do that. Now I'll make sure the lieutenant's daughter really is dead."

***

"There!" Vallie shouted. "It's Perkins! He's going to shoot Kinzington again!" She stuck her gun out the window and tried to take aim.

Jay let out a hoarse scream and pushed the accelerator to the floor. Vallie fell back, barely keeping hold of her handgun. She heard a gunshot above the roar of the big police cruiser's engine and groaned in defeat as Jay continued his mad drive toward the gunman.

***

Kinzington could no longer hold onto the pistol. It fell from her hands, and she slid to the ground again. But she was able to follow Perkins with her eyes as he stumbled back, clutching his bleeding stomach. Then, out of nowhere, a car roared past, hitting Perkins. He was tossed high into the air before dropping to the ground.

Kinzington's body had taken all it could take, as had her mind. She felt herself slowly fading away, her mind numb, pain gone, fear no longer existent. God could take her now if that was what He wanted. At least the other girls were okay. Her death wouldn't be for nothing.

***

Jay slid the speeding patrol cruiser to a stop and leaped out. He ran toward his daughter, who was lying so very still upon the hard, bloody ground. "Kinzington!" As he dropped to his knees beside her, his tears spilled onto her long blonde hair.

CHAPTER FIFTEEN

Vallie jumped out of the cruiser as well. She forced herself not to watch her partner but slowly approached the man their car had rammed into.

Before she could reach him, another car approached from the distance at a high speed. She moved to a spot where she couldn't be easily seen, crouched in a shooter's stance, and watched the car.

It stopped in a cloud of dust, and the driver ran to where Officer Perkins was lying on the ground. "Vincent," the man cried in anguish. "We were so close to being rich. Someone's going to die for causing this. Who did this to you?"

Sergeant Salmon figured out who the man was as she watched him mourning over the body of his brother. He had to be the man Spurr referred to as Boss. He looked strikingly similar to Officer Perkins.

The man slowly turned, just as he seemed to notice her partner crying over his daughter. He pulled a gun from his shoulder holster and approached Jay.

"Drop the gun, Perkins!" Vallie shouted.

He did not, and Vallie fired.

Boss Perkins joined his brother, and without another thought for the dead man, Sergeant Salmon joined her partner.

*****

The job was not yet finished. Despite the pain in his heart and the anguish in his soul, Lieutenant Tanstall refused to take the rest of the day off. There was nothing more he could do for Kinzington. He'd watched the paramedics take his daughter away, and it almost tore him apart, but he had to finish the job for her sake. While others attended to the multiple crime scenes outside and inside the large building, he and his partner went in search of Officer Cortez Alvarez.

A short while later, armed with an arrest warrant, a search warrant, and additional officers as backup, they knocked on Alvarez's door. There was no answer, so they forced the door open and went in. A quick search of the apartment for the officer was negative; he was not at home. A more thorough search found a number of incriminating items, such as two sets of black clothing, which included black masks.

A subsequent search at the home of Officer Perkins turned up no significant items. However, his angry wife gave them the address of a man she referred to as Andy Perkins, Officer Perkins's older brother. She told them that he liked to be called Boss, so other officers were dispatched to his home to conduct a search.

Lieutenant Tanstall and Sergeant Salmon headed for the hospital, but before they arrived, they received a call from Officer Spurr, who had been suspended by the chief but allowed to go home with instructions that he was not to leave town.

"Alvarez is at my door," Spurr barked. "If he comes in, I'm going to shoot him."

"Stall him," Jay ordered. And with that, another high-speed drive ensued. Due to the terrible strain Jay was under, Sergeant Salmon now drove.

As they neared Spurr's home, Officer Alvarez's car sped past them, going the other way. Vallie flipped a screeching U-turn and pursued him.

They caught up with him as he roared onto a major highway. In an effort to avoid his pursuers, Alvarez cut into the path of a semi. The big truck swerved and managed to avoid directly hitting the car Alvarez drove, but it did strike a glancing blow. The sedan spun off the road. It tipped onto its side with a resounding *thud*.

Alvarez climbed out of the passenger door, which was now facing the sky. Then he must have seen Jay and Vallie running toward him from their police cruiser since he climbed faster and tumbled to the ground, dropping the pistol he had in his hand. Before he could pick it up again, Jay tackled him.

***

Jay and Vallie finally made it to the hospital, and as they ran for the entrance, Jay's phone began to ring. He pulled it out and looked at the screen. The call was from the burner phone he'd given to Jonas.

"Dad, I'm at Grandpa and Grandma's now," he said as soon as Jay answered.

Jay and his partner slowed to a walk. "Thanks for letting me know," Jay responded. "You stay there with them until I tell you it's okay for them to put you back on a bus to come home."

"Okay, but Dad, have you found Kinzington yet?" Jonas asked.

***

Sergeant Salmon walked ahead and let her partner talk to his son in private—if it could be called talking. Jay's suppressed emotions had finally burst, and he was crying like a baby.

Vallie found Ada Pedler seated beside her mother when she entered Celeste's room. The girl's left shoulder was bandaged, but despite her injuries, she looked okay. When Sergeant Salmon stepped in, however, the look of peace and relief vanished.

"Where's Kinzington?" Ada cried. "She saved my life."

"Please tell us you got to her in time," Celeste said. "She's got to be okay. What she did was so brave and selfless."

"I'm sorry, but Kinzington is not okay," Vallie said. "Let me explain—"

"Where's Jay?" Celeste asked.

"He's talking to Jonas on the phone. He'll be in shortly."

***

Jay did not go to Celeste's room after his gut-wrenching talk with his son. Instead he went to the main desk, where he was told his daughter was still in surgery, as he had suspected. When he asked how much longer it would be, the nurse told him she didn't know.

Jay thanked her after being promised that he would be notified when Kinzington came out of surgery. Then he went to Celeste's room.

He found the woman he'd fallen in love with sitting on the side of her bed with her daughter next to her. Sergeant Salmon stepped back and ushered Jay toward them. Celeste threw her arms around Jay and sobbed into his chest.

"I'm so sorry about Kinzington," she finally managed to say. "Your partner has been telling us what happened."

"Jay," Vallie interrupted. "Were you able to see her?"

"No, Kinzington is still in surgery. But what matters is that she's still alive. And I pray that she will come out of the surgery okay."

"It must have been horrible," Celeste said, still clinging to Jay.

For a moment Jay couldn't speak. When he did, his words were filled with pain and weariness. "When I saw her lying on the ground, I thought she was dead. I'm so grateful I was wrong. I sent her off on an ambulance by herself when they said I couldn't go with her."

"Jay, why don't you stay here now with Celeste and Ada?" Vallie said. "I'll go back to the office and see if Alvarez will talk to me."

"Thanks," he said. "I'll do that. I want to be here when Kinzington comes out of surgery."

***

A week later, Kinzington was allowed to go home to finish recovering there. Jonas, who had returned from his bus trip to his grandparents' house just two days before, was waiting with Ada when Jay carried Kinzington in. Celeste followed them.

After putting Kinzington to bed, Celeste and Jay stood beside her.

The first words out of Kinzington's mouth as Ada and Jonas also entered her bedroom were, "Are you and Celeste going to get married, Dad? I've told you all along that you needed to get married again. And now you've found the perfect lady!"

"We'll talk about it," Jay said, looking fondly at Celeste. "You kids just need to give us a little time."

"Okay, you guys, we'll do that, but it can't be very long. You need each other, and Jonas, Ada, and I need the two of you."

"You'll have us," Celeste promised.

Jay did not disagree.

ABOUT THE AUTHOR

CLAIR M. POULSON WAS BORN and raised in Duchesne, Utah. His father was a rancher and farmer, his mother, a librarian. Clair has always been an avid reader, having found his love for books as a very young boy.

He has served for more than forty years in the criminal justice system. He spent twenty years in law enforcement, ending his police career with eight years as the Duchesne County Sheriff. For the past twenty-plus years, Clair has worked as a justice court judge for Duchesne County. He is also a veteran of the U.S. Army, where he was a military policeman. In law enforcement, he has been personally involved in the investigation of murders and other violent crimes. Clair has also served on various boards and councils during his professional career, including the Justice Court Board of Judges, the Utah Commission on Criminal and Juvenile Justice, the Utah Judicial Council, the Utah Peace Officer Standards and Training Council, an FBI advisory board, and others.

In addition to his criminal justice work, Clair has farmed and ranched all his life. He has raised many kinds of animals, but his greatest interests are horses and cattle. He's also involved in the grocery store business with his oldest son and other family members.

Clair has served in many capacities in The Church of Jesus Christ of Latter-day Saints, including full-time missionary (California Mission), bishop, counselor to two bishops, Young Men president, high councilor, stake mission president, Scoutmaster, high priest group leader, and Gospel Doctrine teacher. He currently serves as a ward missionary.

Clair is married to Ruth, and they have five children, all of whom are married: Alan (Vicena) Poulson, Kelly Ann (Wade) Hatch, Amanda (Ben) Semadeni, Wade (Brooke) Poulson, and Mary (Tyler) Hicken.

They also have twenty-five wonderful grandchildren and a great-granddaughter.

Clair and Ruth met while both were students at Snow College and were married in the Manti Utah Temple.

Clair has always loved telling his children, and later his grandchildren, made-up stories. His vast experience in life and his love of literature have contributed to both his telling stories to his children and his writing of adventure and suspense novels.

Clair has published more than thirty novels. He would love to hear from his fans, who can contact him by going to his website, clairmpoulson.com.

INSIDIOUS

GREGG LUKE

To the Reader:
All the disease states and medicines in this story are real.
No exaggerations were made.

CHAPTER ONE

Friday, July 14, 2000

ANDREW MINER HELD HIS FAVORITE Altius vaulting pole in a firm grip, left hand atop the pole in front of him, right hand gripping the pole at his waist. The resin-impregnated, carbon-fiber shaft held precisely the flex and tension required to propel his 167-pound frame twenty feet into the air. Currently, the vaulting cross bar was set at 5.35 meters—roughly seventeen and a half feet. As an Olympic hopeful, he'd cleared that height many times before. For many world-class vaulters, a height of seventeen feet was still within their warm-up routine.

A steady din rose from the large crowd in Hornet stadium at Cal State, Sacramento. Andrew blocked out the noise as he rocked back and forth, preparing to sprint down the 130-foot runway. Despite his attempts to remain calm, his nerves ran wild. He felt strangely out of balance. His arms and legs quivered wildly—not with nervous anticipation but from some strange ailment he'd been experiencing over the past few weeks.

Not now, he pleaded, trying to control the uncontrollable trembling. The team physician had said it was nothing to be concerned about. Probably just overexertion from the intense training he'd pushed himself to do for the Olympic trials. The doctor had given Andrew some muscle relaxants and anxiety meds, but he hated taking them. The meds calmed his nerves but did little to halt the trembling. And they did nothing for his balance issues.

He stepped back from the takeoff line to shake out his legs and reestablish his grip. This was probably his last chance to make the US Olympic team. At twenty-seven years old, he was edging past his prime. He doubted he'd be able to compete as well in four more years—if at all.

Closing his eyes, he tried to focus. *You can do this*, he coached himself. *It's all about speed and placement. Six, eight, ten. Kinetics is your friend. Six, eight, ten. Kinetics is your friend.* This was the mantra he said before each vault attempt. It was stupid, yes, but it helped him soar.

As if reading his mind, his wife, Taryn, called from the sidelines, "Come on, Birdman! Show them you can fly!"

With a determined frown, Andrew zeroed in on the pocket at the end of the runway and rocked back and forth to establish a rhythm. He held his pole pointing skyward, slightly less than vertical. *Six, eight, ten. Kinetics is your friend.* At six steps his pole would begin to dip forward; at eight steps he'd extend his arms over his head; at ten steps he'd drop the end of the pole into the pocket. He'd then put all his force into bending the pole while lifting his feet over his head. At that point, kinetic energy would take over and launch him nearly twenty feet into the air.

Drawing a deep breath, Andrew took off in a loping gate. All seemed well until his eighth step. He tried to lift the pole, but his arms wouldn't obey, nor could he make himself slow down. His vision suddenly twisted out of focus, angling him slightly off course. He tried dropping his pole but couldn't. Locked into a head-on collision with the landing pad, the tip of his pole bounced once off the runway, then somehow found the pocket. But because of his awkward angle, the pole bent sideways, lifting Andrew six feet off the track, disastrously off center. His knees were only halfway raised when he collided with the right-side standard. Inertia folded his body around the standard, cracking three ribs before he spun off. He heard the crowd draw a uniform gasp as he missed the landing pad entirely and slammed onto the grass. His head repeatedly jolted against the turf as he flop-rolled to a halt.

The crowd was now shrieking in panic. Chaos erupted.

Try as he might, Andrew couldn't draw a breath. He felt himself convulsing, each paroxysm sending a fresh jolt of pain though his body. A dark fog began to encroach his thoughts. He heard people running toward him, calling out his name, but he couldn't respond. As the cerebral fog thickened, the frightened cry of the crowd quickly faded. Several sets of legs surrounded him. His vision dimmed. His hearing deadened. The last thing he sensed was Taryn kneeling beside him, shouting his name as he slipped into the smothering black void.

CHAPTER TWO

Saturday, July 15, 2000

"Mr. Miner? Mr. Miner, can you hear me?" The female voice wasn't one Andrew recognized. She sounded young—maybe twentyish.

Andrew struggled to open his eyes, struggled to crawl out of the foamy gloom swishing through his head. He moved his mouth, but no words formed. All he could manage was a thin, wheezy garble. His mind felt strangely disconnected. He knew what he wanted to say; he just couldn't make it happen. It was as if his body didn't know how to respond to prompts from his brain.

"I'm sorry, Mr. Miner. I can't understand you. Can you speak clearer?"

I'm trying! he wanted to shout. He had no idea where he was. The room— if he was in a room—smelled strangely antiseptic. He heard the low hum of electronic equipment. He felt some discomfort across his torso but no real pain. As he fought to gain perception, a sudden clarity enlightened his mind, like someone had flipped a switch, dissolving the murk. He remembered every detail of his disastrous vault attempt: the tremors, the lack of muscle response, the uncontrolled flight, the collision, the crash landing, the screaming. With crushing finality, he knew his missed attempt meant he did not make the team. *All because of a stupid muscle twitch.*

Andrew had feared the rapidly worsening symptoms he'd been experiencing over the past few weeks would not go away on their own. But he kept hoping. Now, with his fears confirmed, his throat involuntarily seized. He found it very difficult to swallow. All-consuming panic surged against his ability to maintain a sense of composure. He felt his body begin to seize; his arms and legs convulsed wildly, yanking against some kind of restraint.

"You need to calm down, Mr. Miner. You're going to hurt yourself again. Just try to relax."

He *was* trying! He just couldn't coordinate the movement of any limb, couldn't even keep his thoughts on any one item for more than a few moments. It confused him as much as it scared him—and simultaneously made him angry. Focusing all his efforts on relaxing, he felt himself gradually mellow to a fidgety tremor. Wanting to be as coherent as possible, he deliberately released a lungful of air while shaping his mouth until it made the right sound.

"Whhhhhere?"

"You're at Mercy General Hospital here in Sacramento. My name is Sarah. I'm your floor nurse. Do you understand what I'm saying?"

He forced a jerky nod and raised his brows until his eyes peeled opened. The room's brightness made him wince.

"Well, hello there," Nurse Sarah said, smiling at him. She was indeed twenty-something; she was young but exuded confidence. "Welcome back. Do you remember why you're here?"

He pressed himself to take in his surroundings but couldn't keep his eyes fixed on any one object for very long. A bright hospital room—hence the antibacterial smell. A standard, two-bed suite—the second bed empty. No one present but the nurse and himself. Health monitors hummed on either side of his bed. Daylight glared from behind louvered blinds. He got it all, but the effort made his head pound.

"Mr. Miner? Andrew? Do you know why you're here?" Sarah repeated firmly.

His eyes snapped back to the persistent nurse. He wanted to say *duh!* but couldn't.

"You had an accident at the Olympic tryouts. You botched your pole vault attempt and cracked three ribs. It all happened so fast. You should see the replay. It's insane," she explained as if talking to someone other than the guy who experienced it. "You also bonked your noggin pretty hard and apparently have a concussion. Do you have a headache now?"

Andrew's gaze drifted from her face, but strangely, he couldn't do anything about it.

"Oops. Are you having trouble focusing, Andrew?"

Obviously! For some reason her happy-go-lucky nature deeply annoyed him. If he could, he'd verbally curse her lack of professionalism. *Botched* his vault? *Bonked* his *noggin*?

He waited for a moment to steady his emotions, feeling like at any second, he would either scream his head off or burst into tears. The feelings confused him. Why were his emotions so erratic? He'd never acted this way before or even felt like acting this way.

With great effort he again shaped his mouth and forced out, "Hhhoow lllonng?" But he wasn't sure if the words came out right. Even the timbre of his voice sounded strange.

"You've been in and out of consciousness since you got here yesterday afternoon. But this is the first time you've been responsive. That's a good sign."

He felt something rubbing against his legs and arms before realizing they were still twitching under the sheets. He tried to hold them steady but failed. He endeavored to look at his legs but had difficulty getting his eyes to fix on them. He did, however, notice that his arms were loosely tethered to the bedframe.

As if reading his thoughts, Nurse Sarah explained. "You have perpetual spasms in your legs and arms. We've restricted your movements because of your seizures. You've yanked out your IV line twice. It's important to keep it in since that's how we're controlling your seizures and pain. And we don't want you to hurt yourself." She examined the line dripping fluids into a vein in the back of his left hand. She then looked closely into his eyes, as if determining the depth of his cognitive ability. "Andrew? Are you in any pain or discomfort?"

He mouthed the word, *no.* Not meaning to, the word came out in a yell: "No!"

"No need to shout, Mr. Miner. I'm just trying to help you," she responded in a matronly tone.

He wasn't in significant pain, and he didn't remember yanking out his IV line. He didn't even know that he was hooked to an IV. Now that he did, was it still necessary to tie him down? They shouldn't restrain him without his consent. And what did she mean when she said she didn't want him to hurt himself again? Did they think he was suicidal because he'd *botched* his vaulting run? Sure, he was devastated. Why wouldn't he be? *It was only the 2000 US Olympic track and field team!* he thought with unrestrained snark. Yes, he was sad. But he wasn't so depressed that he'd kill himself. Perhaps if he got out, he could convince Coach Chaplin to let him try again. He tugged violently against the restraint, unable to control the amount of force he used.

"No, no. Try not to do that, Andy. Just relax."

Andy? He hated that abbreviation of his name. That's what his mom called him.

He glared at the nurse and made the shaking of his head as intentional as possible but, instead, felt it roll sloppily from one side to the other. Why? Did he break his neck too? No. He'd be in a neck brace if he had. So what *had* happened to him? Was it a brain tumor? Is that why he'd been having coordination and focus issues? Worse, why did it have to strike full force during his vault run of all times? What in the world had happened—*was* happening—to him? He needed answers. Nurse Sarah wasn't giving any.

"Wwhhyy thiiis?" he managed to wheeze.

"This what?" Sarah asked.

This condition, you idiot! he felt like screaming. He focused as hard as he could through the foamy emptiness in his head. "Mmmee thiiis waayy?" he forced through his constricted throat.

"I told you. You're still having seizures, perhaps from hitting your head on the ground so hard."

"Nnooo!" That's not what he meant. Why had he been having these symptoms even before the accident?

Sarah patted his shoulder. "Don't you worry, Andy. You're awake now. We'll figure out what's wrong and get you better in no time. Oh, your wife is here, by the way. She sure is pretty. She stepped out to get something to eat, but she should be back soon. You just try to relax."

Andrew frowned, suddenly more confused. Had he heard the nurse correctly? He had a wife? His focus was so erratic. It was so difficult to keep his mind on any one topic. The past was a milky blur to him. He knew he was married, so of course he had a wife. She was his other half—his better half. He recalled acknowledging daily that meeting her was when his life had truly begun. But . . . when exactly was that? Worse . . . what was her name?

CHAPTER THREE

Sunday, July 16, 2000

ANDREW AWOKE TO THE SOUND of his wife's voice. He recognized the tone. She sounded perturbed, and that made him grin. He sounded exactly the same when he got irritated. It'd always amazed him how closely their temperaments matched. Just one of the many proofs that he was meant to be with . . . with . . . ? He frowned. Why couldn't he remember his wife's name?

He opened his eyes. The room wasn't nearly as bright anymore. He glanced toward the window and saw that darkness now framed the blinds. How had the time passed so quickly? He must have drifted off again. Was it even the same day?

His wife was talking to a man who appeared to be in his early sixties. The man had professionally styled gray hair and wore a white smock and a stethoscope. They stood at the foot of Andrew's bed, but neither of them was looking his way. His wife's arms were folded tightly. "I'm sorry, Doctor," she said brusquely, "but I don't see how any of that would help."

"I understand and appreciate your anxiety, Mrs. Miner. You've witnessed a horrible event involving your husband," the doctor said with a practiced air. "I'd simply like to discuss Andrew's medical history with you personally just to double-check all the facts. Oftentimes, reviewing things out loud brings more information to mind."

She huffed. "Fine. Andrew does not have a personal or family history of seizures, epilepsy, or MS. He's never had severe head trauma or unexplained fever. He's not diabetic or hypertensive. He's taken some muscle relaxants and anxiety meds, but nothing else. The only supplement he takes is glucosamine sulfate for his knees and a daily protein shake while training. We have an occasional glass of wine but otherwise don't drink. I honestly can't think of any other pertinent medical information about his past that would lead to uncontrolled tremors."

For some reason, both of their voices sounded echoey like they were speaking inside of a long, narrow tunnel. Andrew hoped it was just some side effect of whatever meds they had him on and nothing more.

"I've gone through our medicine cabinet at home just to be sure," she continued. "Believe me, there's nothing there that would cause these symptoms."

Andrew could tell his wife's irritation was leading to anger. He was familiar with the heated pitch in her voice. The receiving end of her ire was never a good place to be. But she also sounded . . . scared—an emotion he'd rarely heard from her.

Nurse Sarah entered the room. "Oh, hi, Taryn."

"Hey, Sarah."

Taryn! Mrs. Taryn Miner, Andrew suddenly recalled. *My beautiful wife.* He closed his eyes, feeling overwhelmingly grateful he finally remembered her name.

"Here's the summary you requested, Doctor," the nurse said.

"Thanks," he replied flatly.

There was a pause in the conversation. Andrew could hear the doctor—or someone—repeatedly clicking a ballpoint pen. Before long, the doctor spoke again. "Has Andrew experienced any recent changes besides his bouts of trembling?"

"Yeah," Taryn said with a hint of surprise. "He's had a lot of balance issues lately. You know—like needing to lean against something to stay standing."

"And how long has this been happening?"

"Perhaps six to eight weeks or so. It's been off and on, although it got worse the closer he got to the tryouts. We both assumed it was from his increased training. He'd get so tired he couldn't stand for very long, so he'd always lean against something."

"How about emotional changes?"

A moment of silence passed. When Taryn spoke, her voice was softer, less bitter. "Over the past two weeks or so he's developed some issues with anxiety and . . . and introversion."

"What do you mean by 'introversion'?"

"Well, it's a strange kind of . . . drawing into himself. There's been a couple of times when I'd leave for work that he'd be slumped in his office chair looking kind of like a ragdoll. He's a website designer and works from home. Anyway, I thought he was just being silly. He does stuff like that to make me laugh. But when I got home from work, about ten hours later, he was still there in the same position. I'm not sure he'd even moved. He hadn't eaten or bathed or . . ."

Taryn's tone slid from frustration to desperation. "One time he'd even . . . wet himself. Like I say, it's only happened a couple of times, but each time I had to shake him out of it—like waking him from a trance. He didn't remember being slumped in his chair all day. He said he was just 'feeling empty.' I asked what he meant, but he just shrugged off the question."

Really? Andrew thought. *I don't remember any of that.*

"Is it possible he was just having an off day?" the doctor asked.

"Andrew? He's never had an off day since I've known him. We've been married almost seven years. I've never seen him like this before, even before we got married."

"Well, I'll make a note of it. We'll get to the bottom of this, I promise," the doctor said in his practiced tone. "We specialize in neurologic disorders here. No need to worry."

"Is that what you think this is? A neurologic disorder?"

"It's one of many possibilities. The trouble is, there are several conditions that cause the symptoms Andrew has: tremors, seizures, loss of consciousness, eye rolling, inability to speak, and so on. They're almost always a pathology of the nervous system—predominantly the brain. But we're still in the early days. Don't be too concerned."

"Too *concerned?*" Taryn cried. "Dr. Winters, perhaps you don't know, but I'm a pharmacist. I consider myself pretty levelheaded. I don't jump to conclusions or give in to flighty emotions. I'm *concerned* because this is something I've never seen in my husband before. I'd like some logical, rational possibilities I can follow up on. So far all I've been told are things I can see for myself."

"A pharmacist, huh? That's admirable," Dr. Winters said in a tone that suggested anything but admiration. "Well, to be honest, we're still evaluating his symptoms."

"So what's your initial guess?"

There was a short silence punctuated with a few pen clicks. "I believe it *is* some kind of brain trauma. But don't let that alarm you. In medicine we often have to rule out what it *isn't* to find out what it *is*. Because of his seizures, we did an initial CT scan, but it didn't show any obvious signs of cerebral trauma. We also ran a preliminary tox screen, but it too came back clean. Electrolytes and blood glucose are all within normal parameters."

"What about a stroke?"

"Perhaps. The blood markers for stroke won't show up for forty-eight hours, so I've scheduled another CT and a comprehensive CBC tomorrow afternoon."

"And the Parkinsonian tremors? The inability to communicate?"

"As I said, that normally indicates brain pathology—either external or endogenous. It could be the introversion you mentioned was exacerbated by his accident. It could also be a kind of whiplash from hitting the standard. That doesn't always show up on a CT. That's why I've also ordered a full cranial and spinal MRI for nine a.m. Friday morning."

"Friday?" she cried. "So he just stays like this for five more days?"

"He's in no immediate danger," Dr. Winters assured her. "We're monitoring him round the clock. Your husband's vital signs are stable. His seizures and pain are well controlled."

"Yeah, I've noticed," she said in a huff. "You've got him on enough fentanyl, phenytoin, and promethazine to knock out a water buffalo. Throw a benzo like diazepam into the mix—like I see you did when he was first admitted— and it's a disaster waiting to happen."

"Um . . ." the doctor hedged. "How . . . ?"

"I read his med list," she said defiantly.

"That information is confidential, Mrs. Miner. You shouldn't—"

"Look, Dr. Winters. I'm his pharmacist and have a signed HIPAA release in my pharmacy, so there's no confidentiality concerns. Because I'm also his wife, I'd like to be involved in every aspect of his care and recovery."

Andrew was so proud listening to Taryn. She talked about pharmacology with the same passion 49ers fans talked about their football team.

The doctor was again silent for a moment. He was probably deciding how much to let Taryn in on. "All right," he conceded with a click of his pen. "It's standard practice in patients with unexplained seizures to keep them as seizure-free as we can. We call it 'breaking the seizure.' That often requires a heavy load of sedating and muscle-relaxing meds like diazepam. But at the same time, slowing his nerve response makes diagnoses more difficult, so we try to maintain the patient somewhere between harmless tremors and cognitive sedation."

"I agree. But I noticed his chart mentions a few apneic episodes. I wonder if he's getting too much narcotic."

"I am aware of those episodes. That's why I added theophylline to his meds. Normally it's very effective, but honestly, it hasn't helped much in Andrew's case."

"Um . . . you do know that phenytoin can decrease levels of theophylline, right? It's a cytochrome pathway interaction."

"Yes, of course," the doctor said as if he was caught off guard. "We've taken that into account, but like I said, we're getting minimal effect. His breathing is still very shallow and erratic. We may need to put him on a respirator."

"May I suggest you take him off the synthetic opioid?" Taryn asked. "The latest FDA guidelines recommend fentanyl is used only for chronic pain associated with cancer—which, as far as we know, he doesn't have. That'll significantly lessen the respiratory depression."

Another pause preceded the doctor's response. "Sure. I can do that. I'll give him Oxycontin instead. He has three cracked ribs and a possible whiplash, so controlling his pain is still a principal concern."

"Um, I wouldn't recommend that either. Oxycontin is a very potent *mu* agonist—the one known primarily for respiratory depression. There's a good chance high doses would stop his breathing. I suggest pentazocine or low-dose tramadol."

"Tramadol is just as bad as fentanyl in respiratory depression," Dr. Winters said as if correcting an obvious fallacy.

"Are you kidding?" she replied sharply. "Tramadol is only a partial *mu* agonist. Fentanyl is over a hundred times stronger than tramadol. It's right up there with heroin for causing opioid overdose."

"In those that abuse it," Dr. Winters amended.

"And in those who are prescribed too much." The bitterness had returned to Taryn's voice. "I'd really—" She paused, undoubtedly to calm her fervor. "Look. I don't mean to step on anyone's toes here or question your therapy, but this is my husband we're talking about. I apologize if I get a bit overzealous, but I know my meds extensively. I'd appreciate some professional courtesy in that regard."

"I suppose that's fair," Dr. Winters said with a fatherly chuckle. "For now, Andrew is stable. Let's give him another day, then we can reevaluate. In the meantime, if you want to be involved, try to recall anything he may have experienced in the last few months. Any business trips he may have taken, any competitions he attended out of the country, any additional changes in behavior or habit, any flu-like symptoms he may have had. Anything you can come up with will help. I suggest you carry a notepad and jot down items when they come to mind no matter how insignificant they may seem."

"Oh, I plan on it," she grumbled. Andrew again recognized her tone. She clearly felt the doctor was sidestepping her request—was perhaps even being condescending. Even without looking at her, he could tell she was seething.

"Good. Have a nice evening, Mrs. Miner. Try to get some rest."

The room quickly quieted. He sensed the lights being dimmed and tried to open his eyes but couldn't get his lids to comply. He then felt his bed sag on one side. A gentle hand brushed the hair from his forehead. He detected the fragrance Taryn wore. Warm lips affectionately lingered on his brow.

"I love you, Birdman," she whispered.

Andrew tried to respond but couldn't. Whatever was happening to his body and his mind was maddening. He focused on the things she and Dr. Winters had discussed. Were his tremors and confusion somehow connected to his past? Or was it some strange new illness? HIV was still a big concern in the Bay Area. Was it some unknown strain of that virus? Having no medical background, he could only guess.

Sometime later—it was difficult to keep track of time—Andrew smelled Taryn's fragrance again and felt her kiss his cheek. He tried to turn his face to her but instead felt it jerk to one side.

"Shh, it's okay," she whispered. "I hope you can hear me, Andrew. I have to go now. Don't worry about a thing. I've got this. You just focus on getting better. I love you."

I love you too, Taryn, Andrew desperately wanted to voice.

CHAPTER FOUR

Monday, July 17, 2000

DR. TARYN MINER WASN'T NORMALLY a clock watcher, but she couldn't stop glancing at the digital readout on her pharmacy computer. She'd just finished with the daily four-to-six rush at her CVS Pharmacy in Stockton, CA, and was catching up on filing prescription hard copies, preparing prior authorization requests, and wondering when Mr. Dempski was going to return to claim she had shorted his clonazepam again. He always came back soon after picking up his prescription, alleging he was shorted a random number of tablets. Taryn had recently taken to physically counting the pills right in front of him at the consultation window. This morning, however, she'd been stuck on the phone battling an insurance company rejection over a dosage increase while trying to keep up with prescription verification, medication consultations, questions about OTC products, and fielding doctor calls. It was simply one of those headless-chicken kind of Mondays. She'd verified Mr. Dempski's clonazepam as being the correct medication, double-counted the correct amount, and, after he declined consultation, let the clerk ring him up. She realized a few minutes later that she hadn't physically counted the pills in front of him. He'd be back.

Despite the hectic nature of the day, it was very hard not to constantly worry about Andrew. She hadn't really minded returning to work that morning. It was better than sitting at Andrew's bedside watching his health deteriorate while not understanding why. Besides, there was no one available to cover her shift, and the pharmacy could not open without a licensed pharmacist on site. Not showing up was not an option. She went in determined to make it a good day.

Taryn was intensely professional when it came to her career. She didn't want to end up being just a pill counter. She took all prescription orders seriously—

checking for dosing anomalies, redundancies, interactions, and mistakes—and made sure her patients understood the optimum way to take their meds. It was rare for her to let personal distractions disrupt her focus. Yet every time she thought about her husband, her feelings of inadequacy and helplessness roiled in her gut. It was beginning to make her queasy. It was all she could do not to cry.

Taryn had begun compiling a chronological list of Andrew's symptoms the previous evening. As far back as she could remember, Andrew had rarely been sick. It had only been in the past two, maybe three months that she'd noticed anything that could be considered a symptom. Andrew was pretty much a health nut, especially when he was in training. He was up at five a.m. six days a week. He'd run three miles, then go to the track and train. His workouts alternated between weight lifting, running sprints, and working the vault. He even did weekly yoga and tai chi to improve his coordination and balance. At home he *did* spend a lot of time at his computer job, but he'd set up his monitor and keyboard on a flat drafting table with a tall stool, so he could alternate sitting and standing. The one thing he wasn't totally compliant with was his diet. The man adored hamburgers. Of all things to have a passion for! Even so, his rigorous exercise kept his weight exactly where it needed to be to compete.

Over the past ten weeks, Andrew had mentioned having sporadic bouts of anxiety and challenges with balance—but those could be explained by his intense training schedule. When resting, he'd have occasional twitches and trembling in certain muscle groups. *Myoclonus*, her medical references called it. Again, that could simply be from hard exercise.

Was there anything else? He'd had headaches and occasional lapses of memory—but who didn't? More recently, he'd had uncalled-for bursts of anger and laughter. The laughter she could understand. He loved comedies and would often laugh out loud when recalling a particular scene or seeing something funny on the internet. But the anger . . . ? Andrew was one of those people who held his temper like a saint. Still, none of those things seemed extreme enough to be considered a medical red flag. Everyone had an occasional bad day.

"Taryn, there's a new script on line one," her technician Melissa said, bringing her back to the present.

Taryn answered the phone and wrote down the information as it was recited by the doctor's assistant: patient Edith Fawson. Aricept 5 mg at bedtime. Thirty count. Six refills. She took down the patient's date of birth, the prescriber's data, and other pertinent information. Aricept was a medication for dementia related to Alzheimer's disease. Taryn always smiled at the inherent irony of this class of drug. How was a medicine for forgetfulness supposed to work if the patient couldn't remember to take it? She hoped that wouldn't be an issue with Mrs. Fawson.

Taryn was grateful the doctor's office had called. She'd been expecting this prescription. Edith Fawson had just turned eighty-nine and still lived at home. About five months ago, her daughter Beverly had come in to pick up Edith's medications and had mentioned her mother was getting very forgetful—even more so than normal.

"It's more than just misplacing things," Beverly had explained. "Two weeks ago, when I went to visit, I found her in her underwear."

Taryn had chuckled. "Well it *was* almost a hundred degrees; humidity in the nineties. It was insufferable," she'd said, trying to keep the mood light.

"She was out front watering a flowerbed."

"Oh my," Taryn had gasped, struggling to suppress a smile.

Beverly had ranted on, growing more and more emotional. "And then last week she made some tea just after I'd left that morning and she forgot to turn off the stovetop. It was still burning when I got there that evening. And that's just *one* of the potentially dangerous things that've happened. I can't be there all the time and I can't afford a live-in assistant. And she refuses to even talk about an assisted living center." She'd paused to dab her eyes with a tissue. "I'm afraid she's going to hurt herself, or worse."

Taryn had suggested having Edith examined for dementia and her daughter agreed. Apparently, her doctor did too.

As Taryn filled the Aricept prescription, she rehearsed in her mind what Beverly should expect from the medication, including how soon she should see an effect on Edith's dementia symptoms.

Dementia symptoms!

What were the classic signs of dementia onset—or *predementia*? Memory loss, trouble focusing, random bursts of unwarranted emotion, even occasional blurry vision. There were others, but she couldn't immediately recall them. Andrew had experienced those same symptoms. But Edith Fawson was almost ninety; Andrew was twenty-seven. It was highly unlikely that a man his age would have Alzheimer's. Taryn tried to recall all she'd learned in pharmacy school about the disease. Did dementia ever strike at such an early age? How fast was its onset? Were there any triggers besides old age? She knew numerous medications caused various forms of memory loss, but Andrew wasn't taking any. Even so, would a dementia medication help Andrew even if he didn't have the condition? She pulled a small spiral-bound notepad from her pocket and scribbled a few possibilities to follow up on when she got home. She also made herself promise to call Andrew's mother. Perhaps there was a clue she could identify.

When Edith's daughter showed up an hour later, Taryn met her at the dispensing window.

"Here you go, Bev," she said, showing her Edith's prescription bottle. "But before I explain this med to you, let me ask: does Edith have a daily pill minder?"

"Yes and no. It's a dual kind for day-and-night dosing, but it doesn't really help. Mom often forgets what day the week it is, and she'll take Monday's dose with breakfast and Tuesday's dose a few hours later, thinking she'd forgotten to take it that morning. So now *I* use the minder to load up her meds, then I bring it when I visit every morning and evening to give her the correct dose. Thank goodness she doesn't have to take anything in the afternoon, or I'd be sunk."

"I'm sure you'd find a way, Bev," Taryn said with a kind smile. "You're just that kind of daughter." She opened the prescription vial to show Beverly the flat, white tablets. "Now. Let's talk about this medicine and what kind of pluses and minuses you and Edith can expect from it. A little nausea and diarrhea are quite common initially, but they shouldn't be incapacitating and should only last until her system gets used to the drug—a few days at most. Make sure you dose it with food . . ."

Even though Taryn felt true empathy for the woman, it was difficult talking to Beverly because many of Edith's dementia indicators mirrored what Andrew was experiencing. When she talked about Edith, an image of Andrew came to her mind. And yet, Andrew had a number of contradictions to the disease. Most glaringly, he was simply too young for dementia. Plus, the *onset* of Alzheimer's rarely caused Parkinsonian tremors. Could he have progressed to an advanced stage in just ten weeks?

As Taryn bagged the prescription, Dallin, a pharmacy technician, approached her. "Excuse me, Taryn, but you have a call on line two."

"Okay, thanks."

She told Beverly to call her if she had any questions or concerns that came up later and then bid her goodbye. Stepping back to her workstation, she picked up the line.

"Hi, this is Pharmacist Taryn. How can I help you?"

"This is Vince Dempski," a gruff male voice nearly yelled. "You shorted me on my clonazepam again!"

CHAPTER FIVE

Tuesday, July 18, 2000

"Why do you want to try Aricept?" Dr. Winters asked as he scanned Andrew's chart. "I'm more concerned about diagnosing his Parkinson's symptoms than enhancing his memory. Besides, he hasn't been lucid enough to determine if his memory's been affected."

Taryn was sitting on the edge of Andrew's hospital bed, holding his hand. Andrew occasionally turned his eyes to her, but they held a vacancy she'd never seen before. It was as if he recognized she was *there*, but he didn't recognize *her*. She felt helpless, and it took everything she had not to let Andrew see her sorrow.

She had tried conversing with him all morning but never got more than a few unintelligible grunts in response. Perhaps it was the nasogastric tube they'd inserted that made it hard to speak. *No, that can't be it. An NG tube goes down the esophagus, not the trachea,* she argued with herself.

She shrugged. "It's just a theory I have. I was hoping a cholinesterase inhibitor would enhance his lucidity, not just his memory," she explained, watching the doctor read the chart, wondering if he was even listening to her answer. "Andrew clearly has trouble concentrating. Because Aricept—donepezil—is a centrally acting acetylcholinesterase inhibitor, it blocks the breakdown of the primary neurotransmitter in the brain. So if we can increase Andrew's cortical acetylcholine by slowing its breakdown, he might become lucid enough to tell us what he's experiencing."

"But increasing acetylcholine levels could also increase his seizures," Dr. Winters said, rapidly clicking his pen twice as if adding an exclamation point to his rebuttal.

"That's true, but if we start with a low dose, we can easily monitor its effects. Besides, you're doing a great job keeping his seizures under control," she said, putting on her most appreciative smile.

Dr. Winters stared at her with a discerning eye. Taryn couldn't tell if he was judging her or her suggestion. There was a definite sense that he didn't appreciate being lectured to or second-guessed. But she wasn't trying to do either. She was hoping her expertise in medicine could help with Andrew's symptoms and diagnosis. She was trying to corroborate, not correct or contradict. Or . . . maybe she was. Seeing her husband in such a helpless state made it undeniably difficult not to let her emotions override her decorum.

Dr. Winters briefly referenced Andrew's chart and clicked his pen a few more times. "I can appreciate your interest in your husband's therapy, Mrs. Miner. I'll be sure to give every medical suggestion the consideration it's due."

She nodded, hoping his comment wasn't simply a brush-off—and yet suspecting it was. "Please don't misunderstand my motives, Dr. Winters. I don't mean to come across as a know-it-all, and I'm certainly not questioning your expertise. I'm just throwing out ideas here, looking at every alternative, you know?"

"As am I."

"I appreciate that. So, what *is* your latest prognosis?"

Dr. Winters paused a moment, tapping his pen against his lips. "I'm wondering if Andrew might have a rare form of meningitis."

"Is that possible? I mean, he's never had it before. And I don't think he's ever been around someone who *has* had it," she said, gently caressing Andrew's hand while holding it firmly enough to prevent him from jerking it away. "His temperature has been stable ever since he got here, hasn't it?"

"Yes, but meningococcal infection doesn't always have an accompanying fever."

"Perhaps not. But every form of infection causes a lymphocyte bloom. Was there any indication of white blood cell increase in his follow-up CBC?"

Dr. Winters flipped to a page in the chart. "No. All inflammatory parameters on his white count look normal."

"Did you notice any brain swelling on the second CT scan?"

The doctor's eyes jerked up to meet hers, then jerked back to the chart. The reaction confused Taryn. He then hung the chart on the end of the bedframe and cleared his throat. "No. But we're still awaiting a reading on it from radiology."

Taryn thought she detected a note of frustration in his manner. The physician clearly did not like being stumped. Perhaps it'd be best for her to back off a bit and not be so assertive. She brushed an errant strand of hair off Andrew's forehead and wiped some spittle from the corner of his mouth. "Thank you for answering my incessant questions, doctor. I don't mean to be a pest."

"Overly concerned perhaps, but not a pest," Winters said kindly.

Just as Taryn was going to ask another question, Andrew broke into a coughing fit. The barking paroxysms sounded deep and wet. Taryn rubbed his chest while softly shushing him. When the fit subsided, a large amount of sputum had run down his jaw. She gently wiped it away. "That doesn't sound good. Have his apneic episodes gotten worse?"

"Actually, they've improved."

"So taking him off the fentanyl was the right choice," she said, trying not to sound cocky.

"It appears to have helped, yes."

"That's good. Any thoughts on why this cough is so productive?" she asked, continuing to dab Andrew's face. "If his white count is normal, it can't be an infection."

"Coughs like his often come when a patient is supine for extended periods. Bronchial fluid pools and is not cleared."

"What do you consider an extended period? Andrew's only been here for four days."

Dr. Winters clicked his pen and made a notation in the chart. "I'll include a chest x-ray on his itinerary tomorrow and do another white count," he said, ignoring her question. "Have you started that health journal yet?"

"Yes, but I haven't found anything that could lead to whatever is causing these symptoms."

"Well, keep at it. Are his parents still alive? Perhaps they can recall something you're unaware of."

"His mom lives in El Cerrito. She owns a curio shop there. But they've never been very close. He never got into her granola lifestyle. I've been updating her regularly on his condition over the phone. When I asked about his past, she said she'd bring over a scrapbook she's kept on him since childhood. His dad passed away a few years ago from prostate cancer. But they were divorced long before that."

"Prostate cancer? Was that listed on his admissions paperwork?"

"Of course. But I've never heard of prostate cancer causing these kinds of symptoms."

Dr. Winters cleared his throat again. "Please don't jump to any conclusions, but cancer can spread in unexpected ways. A brain tumor can cause Parkinson's-like tremors and seizures. We'll address that possibility in his MRI. For now, I think it's very unlikely. I'll include a tumor marker panel in his blood analysis and a fecal occult blood check just in case."

"I appreciate the extra efforts and for humoring me this way," she said, standing to shake his hand. "You're an excellent physician. I mean that. I trust your expertise."

Dr. Winters smiled as he clasped hands with her, clearly warmed by her sentiment. "Truth be told, Taryn, I admit I don't like being second-guessed. The only reason I hesitate on atypical therapies and tests is because it's my name on the chart. I am ultimately responsible for Andrew's outcome. But so far everything you've suggested has made sense." He clicked his pen and began scribbling on the chart. "Aricept really isn't a bad idea. I'll get the changes on Andrew's IV implemented right away." He turned to leave, then paused and turned back to face her. "I hope you believe me when I say I want to get to the bottom of this as much as you do and *not* simply because my name is on the chart."

The sincerity in his voice touched Taryn. "Thank you, Dr. Winters."

He considered her for a moment. "Are you feeling okay? You look very tired. Kind of drawn and pallid."

"I haven't slept well lately," she confessed. "Maybe three or four hours a night since this began. I admit this whole mystery has made me sick to my stomach."

"Would you like a prescription for some Restoril or Xanax?"

"No thanks," she said, rubbing her eyes. "I'm not a fan of benzos."

"Oh yeah. I remember," he said with the hint of a chuckle. He gestured toward the adjacent bed. "Well, if you'd like to spend the night here, I'll authorize it."

Taryn's heart swelled. She knew that wasn't typically allowed. "Thanks, doc, but I have to work tomorrow. I might take you up on it later in the week though."

Dr. Winters clicked his pen again. "I'll see that the bed remains empty. Until then, I want Sarah to take your temperature, take your blood pressure, and draw a CBC."

Taryn frowned. "Honestly, doctor, I'm just tired. As soon as I get some sleep, I'll feel better."

"Humor me just this once," he said with a stern smile. "It'll make it easier for me to authorize the bed for you, and it'll make me feel better knowing you're not coming down with anything Andrew might catch."

That made sense. "Okay. As long as she draws the blood from my right arm. I'm left-handed and I hate wearing Coban wrap on my dominant arm."

"Of course. Get some rest, Taryn," he said before walking out the door.

CHAPTER SIX

Wednesday, July 19, 2000

WEDNESDAYS WEREN'T AS HECTIC AS Mondays, but Taryn couldn't determine if that was good or bad. Keeping busy kept her mind off her husband's mysterious condition. Having slow times at work allowed her mind to wander to places best left unvisited. Thinking about not being with him made her physically ill.

Several of her coworkers—and even a few patients—inquired about Andrew's progress. She did her best to remain upbeat but doing so sapped her strength. By lunchtime, she felt drained and was near collapse.

"Taryn, there's a call on line three for you," Technician Melissa told her.

She sighed heavily and picked up the line. "Hi, this is Pharmacist Taryn. How can I help you?"

"Hi, Taryn. This is Coach Chaplin. How're you holdin' up?"

"Oh hi, John," she answered with a touch of confusion. "Why didn't you call me on my cell phone?"

John Chaplin was the head coach of the US Olympic track and field team.

"I tried. Kept going to voicemail and you know me: I don't quit. I just wanted to call and say how sorry I am for Andrew's accident and all. How's he doing, anyway?"

Taryn sighed. "Not good, Coach. His condition hasn't gotten any better. The doctors still aren't sure what's wrong with him."

"How about you? What do you think is wrong?"

"My expertise is in medicines, not diagnostics. I wouldn't know how—"

"Don't give me that nonsense," he cut across her. "You're as smart as they come, kid. Drew always said his brain was half the size of yours, and Drew wasn't just some dumb jock either. Kid knows computers like he was part cyborg himself."

That made Taryn laugh. Andrew *would* say something like that. And while Andrew disliked any abbreviation of his name, he allowed the coach to call him Drew. At least it wasn't "Andy."

"I honestly don't know, John. Something is affecting the brain functions that control his muscles. It also seems to be blocking his ability to focus and communicate." She stopped to suppress the mournful pressure welling in her chest. She hated when anyone saw her when she was vulnerable, especially Coach Chaplin. He was a nice man, but he abhorred any show of weakness.

"Well, the guys at Mercy are top-notch in my book. Drew's in good hands—theirs and yours."

"Thanks, John. I appreciate that. Who made the team, by the way?"

"Some good men. Lawrence Johnson got first at 5.83 meters. Nick Hysong took second at 5.73 meters. The three-way tie for third was surprising: Harting, Miles, and Manson all cleared 5.62."

Taryn closed her eyes and commanded herself not to cry. Andrew had cleared 5.73 meters before. He'd yet to reach the elusive nineteen-foot mark, but he was so close. There was a good chance he would have made the 2000 Olympic team if only . . . she shook her head to stop the negative thought.

"Anyway," Chaplin continued, "you tell Drew for me the guys are rootin' for him, and so am I. You tell him I want to see him in four years clearing 5.9. That's orders from the coach. You tell him that, okay?"

Taryn could hear the suppressed emotion in Chaplin's voice. It touched her deeply. "Thank you, Coach. I will. It'll mean the world to him."

"I mean it. *We* mean it. Drew was always the guy on the sideline rootin' for his teammates. Didn't matter who was vaulting higher. He was there to cheer them on. Not many guys like him, I can tell you."

"I know. I'm a very lucky girl."

"Ha! He always said *he* was the lucky one." The coach chuckled. "Man, there wasn't a day go by that he didn't have some story to tell about you and him—about how smart you are and how he was always tryin' to keep up. The guys teased him about you calling him Birdman and all, but inwardly they was all jealous. And Drew knew it. He used to do a Lou Gehrig impersonation saying he was 'the luckiest man on the face of the earth.' That was all because of you, kid. So you hang in there, you hear?"

That did it. She couldn't stop the tears from pooling and falling. "Thank you, John. Really. Thank you."

Coach Chaplin bid Taryn good-bye and hung up. She leaned against a shelf of drugs and rested her face in the crook of her elbow.

"You okay, Taryn?" Melissa asked worriedly. It was so like her to exhibit such compassion.

"Yeah. Thanks, Melissa," she said into her sleeve. "Just give me a minute."

Taryn walked quickly to the pharmacy bathroom and washed her face. Coach Chaplin hadn't needed to make that call, but she was profoundly grateful that he had. As she was freshening her makeup, something the coach said replayed in her mind. She capped her mascara and stared at the slender tube in her fingers. *Lou Gehrig.* Gehrig was a well-known Yankees baseball player in the 1930s. His "luckiest man" line from his farewell address was famous. But even more famous—or infamous—was the mysterious disease that was later tagged with his name. Amyotrophic lateral sclerosis. ALS. Lou Gehrig's disease.

Taryn scribbled the three telling initials on her note pad, then returned to work. Throughout the rest of her shift, she kept thinking about the disease. Admittedly, she knew only the basics about it. When she got a break in the workflow, she referenced Lou Gehrig's disease on her computer.

ALS: A slow, degenerative disease that destroys nerve cells in the brain and spinal cord, particularly those that control skeletal muscle function throughout the body. As many as 30,000 Americans have the disease at any given time.

So it's common enough that Andrew could have it, she determined.

She referenced the onset of symptoms: *No specific muscle is the first to show signs of the disease. It can attack muscles singularly or in concert with full muscle groups.* The medical text listed a few examples. The first two were telling: *a patient may experience twitching and weakness of the muscles of the hands or lower legs. If the muscles of the face or throat are affected, the problem at onset would be difficulty with chewing, swallowing, or with movements of the tongue and face that affect speech.*

Andrew's symptoms!

Taryn felt her nerves begin to rapid fire. She clenched her fists to control her hands from trembling. A few paragraphs down, even more similarities came up: *If the muscles of the chest are affected, the patient may have difficulty breathing. In many instances, the first symptoms may be involuntary weeping or laughing.*

Her lungs suddenly felt empty. She drew a chest-full of air and let it out slowly, while rehearsing in her mind Andrew's latest chart notes. Had Dr. Winters tested Andrew for ALS?

She immediately called Mercy General Neurology and asked to speak to Dr. Winters. She was transferred twice before she got through to his receptionist, Cecelia. "I'm sorry, Taryn, but Dr. Winters is in surgery right now. Can I take a message?"

"Yes, please. Ask him if he's tested Andrew for ALS. I think it might be what he has."

"I sure can the minute he gets out. How are you holding up?"

Taryn let out a huff. "I don't know, Cece. Mornings are the worst knowing I have to tackle the day on just a couple hours' sleep. Sometimes I feel like I just can't go on."

"But you always do," Cecelia countered. "That's what Dr. Winters says. He's says that you don't give up and that you are very tenacious about your husband's therapy."

Taryn smile fleetingly. "I'm sure there was another meaning behind that comment, but thanks. Please give him the message and have him contact me as soon as possible."

"I will. The nursing staff is very impressed with you, so you hang in there, okay? We're all rooting for your husband."

"Thanks, Cece. That means a lot."

She hung up and took a moment to gather her thoughts and emotions before returning to work. She popped open a Mountain Dew and took a large sip. Then another. Normally, she shied away from sugary, caffeinated sodas, but today she considered the fizzy beverage medicinal. She needed the boost.

She still wanted to research more about ALS. There was a ton of material to cover. She knew there was no real cure for the disease, but there were some good treatment options. For now, however, she needed to focus on being a good pharmacist for her patients.

CHAPTER SEVEN

Wednesday, July 19, 2000

TARYN WENT STRAIGHT HOME AFTER work to change her clothes and freshen up. Dr. Winters's nurse had returned Taryn's call with the message that the doctor would include an ALS panel in his review. It irked Taryn that the man didn't tell her that himself, but she understood. In healthcare, an unforeseen complication or a patient that demanded an undue portion of the provider's time could disrupt even the best-planned schedule.

Glancing at her watch, she determined she had about twenty minutes before she had to leave. She made a quick sandwich and some lemonade and booted up her computer while she ate. She pulled up the Mayo Clinic's webpage and searched for possible causes of ALS. What she found was informative, but she had a hard time accrediting any specific cause to Andrew's condition. Four main possibilities were listed:

Gene mutation: There were both inherited and noninheritable forms of ALS. Since Andrew didn't have a family history of the disease, it'd have to be a gene mutation. But the likelihood of that was miniscule.

Chemical imbalances: People with ALS generally had higher levels of glutamate in their central nervous system. So a glutamate inhibitor was one of the treatment options. She made a note to have that tested along with all the other tests her poor husband was being subjected to.

Disorganized immune response: In recent years, autoimmune disorders had become more identifiable—lupus, rheumatoid arthritis, certain forms of psoriasis, and many others. Were there autoimmune disorders that attacked only nerve cells? She'd have to look into it.

Protein mishandling: Mishandled proteins within nerve cells led to a gradual accumulation of abnormal forms of those proteins, which disrupted the normal function of cells. "Mishandling" was the operative word. She'd have to look into that too. Right now, she had to get to the hospital.

* * *

The lights were dimmed down in Andrew's room. The low hum of medical equipment—normally a pleasant white noise—scraped at Taryn's tender nerves. She hoped Andrew was oblivious to the noise.

He looked even worse than he did yesterday. His hair clung to his scalp in a greasy mat. *When was the last time they'd washed it?* His face was drawn and ashen. His subdued, rhythmic tremor was still there, but it didn't seem to bother him. His head was turned, facing the window, his eyes open and wandering. The sunset painted the sill with muted, blood-red hues that softened its angular edges with a macabre radiance.

Taryn moved to the end of Andrew's bed. "Hey, Birdman," she said softly, not wanting to startle him.

He continued looking at the window without acknowledging her presence. The blinds were slightly raised, revealing some city lights beyond.

"Andrew?" she said a bit louder, moving to his bedside.

He still did not respond to her. Taryn wondered if his hearing had also fallen prey to whatever heartless disease held him captive. She tenderly touched his arm with her fingertips and stroked it back and forth.

"Andrew," she repeated. "It's me, Taryn."

His body stopped shaking momentarily, as if her touch had short-circuited something, then gradually continued its Parkinsonian tremors as if nothing had changed. His head turned toward her, his eyes seeking focus. They locked onto the hand touching his arm, then deliberately followed her arm up to her shoulder, then over to her face. His eyes met hers and held them.

Taryn ceased breathing. She couldn't believe it. There hadn't been this much connection since the accident. Her heart pounded loudly in her chest.

"Hey there, Birdman," she said, not caring that she was grinning like a fool or that her eyes pooled with tears.

Andrew's face filled with a sluggish smile. He opened his mouth as if to speak. His lips moved without creating a sound, but it was clear he was trying to communicate.

"Can you hear me?" Taryn asked, placing a hand on her chest to dampen her thundering heartbeat.

His eyes cleared slightly more. His head flopped forward as if to nod, but it did not come back up. He struggled to right it. Taryn tenderly took his face in her hands and tipped it up to meet her eyes.

"Are you there, my love?" she asked in a hoarse, hopeful whisper. She rarely used such sappy endearments, but this one came unbidden from deep within.

With some difficulty, he mouthed more words. Taryn couldn't read lips, but she knew the shapes that formed "I love you."

His sluggish smile inched higher just before a fit of coughing broke their fragile connection. Taryn stood and cradled his head against her chest as he wretched with paroxysms. She shushed him tenderly, fighting unsuccessfully against overwhelming emotions. As much as she longed for it, desperately pled for it, she knew the connection was lost.

* * *

Taryn felt a hand tap her shoulder. She hadn't realized she'd fallen asleep on Andrew's chest. The feel of him, his scent and form, had lulled her into a sense of comfort she hadn't felt since the accident. It was as if they were at home in bed without a care in the world, snuggling close to each other, their souls melding as one. The hand tapping her shoulder yanked her from that perfect dream.

"Taryn? Sorry to wake you." It was Dr. Winters's whispered voice.

She sat up and wiped her eyes. "Oh, hi. Sorry. I didn't realize I'd fallen asleep."

"Why don't you move to the other bed," he suggested. "You'd be a lot more comfortable there."

She looked back at Andrew's sleeping form and smiled. "I doubt that," she said warmly.

"It'd be safer for Andrew," he kindly persisted.

She nodded and moved to the other bed. Sitting cross-legged and wiping the sleep from her eyes, she asked, "Did you have a chance to consider my message?"

"I did," he said, sitting on the edge of Andrew's bed so they could speak in low tones face to face. "We haven't run the tests yet, but I don't think we'll find the appropriate markers."

She opened her mouth to protest, but he held up his hand.

"We'll still check, I promise. It's just that Andrew doesn't fit the typical ALS profile. The most common age is forty or older. I have never heard of someone Andrew's age getting it. And we've already ruled out familial ALS. There may be some environmental triggers that we haven't addressed, but even those are iffy."

"But if it's environmental, shouldn't I have it too? We've pretty much been together since high school."

"Not likely. ALS is predominately a male disease. Female cases are very rare. Smoking various substances can increase the risk, but that's only been seen in postmenopausal women. There's some evidence that exposure to lead or other substances may increase risk, but no single agent or chemical has been consistently linked."

"So it's not Lou Gehrig's," Taryn said, feeling a strange mix of elation that it wasn't ALS and dejection because it still left them in the dark.

"I won't make that call until after the test results are in. Andrew's MRI is still set for Friday. I've talked to Dr. Nassir Panju in radiology. He's promised to do a complete workup, no corners cut. I've also scheduled an electromyogram, a spinal lumbar puncture, and a muscle biopsy for tomorrow. Those are usually spot-on for identifying ALS."

"An EMG and a spinal tap," Taryn said, grimacing.

"He'll be fully sedated," Dr. Winters said assuredly. "There's very little danger."

"I know," she said, again rubbing her face. "My emotions are just all out of whack."

"Then get some more sleep. Do you need a change of clothes or a toothbrush or anything?"

The caring in his voice touched her. "Maybe a toothbrush," she whispered. "Thank you."

He looked at her with a critical eye. "You sure you're okay? You still look a little gaunt. Are you eating?"

"Not really. I can't keep anything down. But I'm fine, really. Just exhausted. This ordeal has sapped my endurance."

Dr. Winters nodded and stood to go, then paused. "Oh. Did you get that scrapbook from Andrew's mother yet?"

"No. She was supposed to bring it by my pharmacy since it's closer to her place than our house. She said she doesn't want to drive all the way here just to bring it."

Dr. Winters frowned. He looked both confused and angry. "You mean she hasn't come here yet—to the hospital—to see her son?"

"Nope," Taryn said with slumped shoulders. "She claims to love everyone with all her heart until you ask something of her. Andrew says they've never really gotten along. I'll call her again tomorrow morning. I'll try to persuade her to come here if you think it'll help."

"I do. I don't want to leave any stone unturned until we get a definitive angle on your husband's condition."

Taryn smiled at him sideways. "And you say *I'm* the tenacious one."

The doctor's eyes widened slightly as if he were shocked that she knew he'd said that. The lights were low in the room, but Taryn could swear his face reddened.

"It's okay," she said with a soft smile. "I'm very glad you're as tenacious as I am."

Dr. Winters pointed at the pillow on her bed. "Get some sleep, Taryn. I need you fresh in the morning so *we*—" he paused to emphasize the pronoun— "can figure this out."

CHAPTER EIGHT

Thursday, July 20, 2000

MARY JANE STARR (SHE'D DROPPED the name Miner even before the divorce) was a quintessential flower child of the sixties. She still wore her hair long and straight, preferred loose-fitting tie-dyed tees to silk blouses, and even sported an occasional braided headband and a pair of Birkenstock sandals. She allegedly ate only organic produce, abhorred the eating of red meat, and drank only rainwater. She proudly claimed to have tried every form of drug available to young adults in the Hippie era and continued to sell bongs, pipes, and other drug-related items in her curio shop despite California's paraphernalia laws. To say Mary Jane Starr lived a life without boundaries was an understatement.

She'd named her shop "Sweet Chariot" in honor of her son, claiming to have conceived Andrew during Joan Baez's rendition of *Swing Low, Sweet Chariot* at Woodstock. Her given name was Marjean, but she felt Mary Jane more accurately personified her inner essence while still maintaining elements of her birth name. Taryn didn't dare call her Marjean because it sent her into a rant about how controlling her parents had been. Yet she also refused to call her mother-in-law by her chosen name because it was a common street name for marijuana.

Taryn had lost count of the number of times she had argued the pros and cons of marijuana use with Mary, and she was in no mood to do so again—especially not in the hospital. Quite surprisingly, Mary had shown up at Mercy General unannounced, but when she pulled a baggie of homemade brownies from her large crocheted purse, Taryn couldn't hold back.

"Mary, you know that's not allowed in here," she said firmly. "Not to mention it's illegal."

"What? I can't bring my own son a get-well-soon treat?" she replied innocently.

"No, you cannot. He's on a strict diet. Besides, he can't even chew anymore because of his condition. You see that tube running up his nose? That's how he's being fed. *Plus*," she went on knowingly, "I suspect those aren't merely Betty Crocker brownies."

"Of course they're not," Mary huffed. "They're *my* brownies. It's a secret recipe I created years ago. It was Andy's favorite."

"I highly doubt he knew what he was eating back then," Taryn scoffed.

Mary set the baggie of brownies on the bed and stroked the side of Andrew's face with a hand adorned with natural crystal-and-stone jewelry. "He was always such a happy boy. Always so full of adventure and imagination."

"I'm sure he had a memorable childhood," Taryn said, trying not to sound cynical.

In high school, Andrew had told Taryn that his home life was one of isolation and disorientation. He was an only child, and he had few friends because his family moved every three months or so, being evicted from one low-rent apartment to another. His dad said it was to make him more accessible to his work and his fans. His dad was a rhythm guitarist in a band. He also did stand-in work for other bands throughout the Bay Area. To Andrew, his dad was a ghost, gone every night, sleeping in until after Andrew had left for school, and often not being there when he got home. Sometimes Andrew didn't see him for days. The rare times he did were at dinner where his parents would regularly argue. Such a lifestyle was rough on a young family and rougher on a marriage. By the time Andrew was fourteen, his parents had divorced. His mom coped with the separation through a network of stoner friends and binge parties. It was a lifestyle she'd followed since her teenage years.

Mary Jane moved to look out the window. "Oh, Andy had a fabulous childhood—no thanks to his father. And he adored the outdoors. He loved all nature, especially the birds down by the bay. He always dreamed of being able to fly. That's why he took up pole vaulting. Did you know that?"

Of course Taryn knew that. They were on their high school track team together. She ran the 1500 meter; he did long jump and pole vault. Andrew had frequently mentioned the reason he liked being outdoors was that the stench and second-hand smoke generated by his parents and their friends burned his eyes and gave him terrible headaches—not to mention it made his clothes and hair smell questionable.

"Yes. He's always preferred the outdoors," Taryn responded genially. "He's always loved the feeling of flying—*physically*. Did he tell you he's taking flight lessons? He wants to get his pilot's license."

"All the more reason to get all these fake chemicals out of his system," Mary growled. She returned to Andrew's bedside and donned rose-colored reading glasses that made her somewhat resemble John Lennon. Peering closely at the IV bags draining into the back of Andrew's arm, she huffed loudly. "Lactated Ringer's solution? Tramadol? Phenytoin sodium? Theophylline in dextrose? Donepezil hydrochloride? Promethazine?" she said, stumbling on the names. "No wonder he's not getting better."

"Those are standard medicines to treat his symptoms and keep him hydrated, Mary. There's nothing harmful about them in the right amounts."

"Nothing harmful? They're evil, brainwashing chemicals created by the government to enslave the masses."

Taryn rubbed her eyes, willing herself to not get sucked into debating Mary's accusatory diatribe. She'd had that debate several times before. It didn't matter if Taryn used solid empirical evidence or plain common sense; Mary Jane was a hard-core conspiracy theorist with a permanently jaded mind.

"Well, the doctor thinks the meds are necessary to control his pain and seizures, and I happen to agree," she said stiffly, feeling her temper rise.

"Well of course you do," Mary said tediously. "You've been indoctrinated into the system with your fancy degree. Didn't they teach you anything about natural herbs and crystallography in pharmacy school?"

"Yes, we studied quite a bit about herbs. Many modern medicines originally came from plant sources. I've studied those therapies and other complementary therapies since then on my own. I believe they—"

"Then why aren't you using your so-called learning to treat Andy naturally, without chemicals?" she demanded. "I put two full ounces of premium-grade reefer in these brownies. They're loaded with THC, the best seizure *and* pain medicine on the planet. Everybody knows that—including the drug companies. And it's 100 percent chemical free."

Taryn had had enough.

"Actually, nothing is chemical free because *everything* is made of chemicals: the food and water your body needs to survive, the air you breathe—even *you*, Mary, are made of chemicals. And believe it or not, your body treats tetrahydrocannabinol more like an artificial chemical than you'd think. The cannabinol receptors in your brain—the ones involved in pain and pleasure perception, mood, appetite, and memory—they don't really know what to do with THC. It supersaturates and overstimulates those receptors. They weren't made to handle such excessive stimulation. That's what gets you 'high.' And that's what invariably leads to addiction and withdrawal. *And* that's why it's considered a gateway drug because when the THC high doesn't bring enough pleasure, people seek out other means of euphoria."

"Blah, blah, blah. I've heard the same propaganda for decades. There's plenty of evidence that pot is very effective for both pain and seizures."

"The scientific, verifiable proof is that pain relief comes mostly from CBD: cannabidiol. That's the chemi—the natural ingredient that blocks pain, triggers the immune system, and stimulates the release of endorphins and other 'feel-good' hormones."

"Blah, blah, blah again. Don't get all hoity-toity with your big fancy words, Taryn. You know what I'm talking about. Pot is nature's miracle drug, plain and simple. Herbalists have known that for centuries."

Dr. Winters's voice sounded from the doorway. "The trouble is, Mrs. Miner, our understanding of medical marijuana is still in an infant stage. We simply don't know enough about what it does in the body to determine its safety and justify its use." He entered the room and set a chart book on an adjustable tray.

"It's Mary Jane *Starr*. The divorce was final. And you obviously learned from the same biased sources Taryn did," she said smugly, quickly stuffing her baggie of brownies into her purse.

Just then, Andrew wheezed, gagged, and started coughing. Dr. Winters quickly donned his stethoscope and listened to his lungs. Mary stepped back, covering her mouth and nose defensively. When Andrew had settled, his lips were again coated in sputum.

"I'm going to order some dexamethasone for the fluid production in his lungs," Dr. Winters said, looking at Taryn.

She nodded.

Mary Jane huffed and folded her arms. "You two are unbelievable. Andy's getting worse, not better. Anyone can see that. If you really wanted him to get better, you'd do more than fill him with unpronounceable chemicals."

Taryn rubbed her eyes and blew out a sigh. "Look, Mary. Bottom line is marijuana is still illegal, and Andrew is not going to be ingesting it or anything else you bring him."

"More Western medical manipulation and cover-up. The only reason it's illegal is because the big drug companies haven't figured out a way to capitalize on it without everyone just growing their own."

Dr. Winters patiently removed his stethoscope. "Actually, Ms. Starr, the FDA requires—"

"The FDA!" Mary snorted. "That stands for Fascist Devil-Worshiping Anarchists."

"Food and Drug Administration," he corrected.

"Funded top to bottom by American drug companies."

Taryn raised her palms to lessen the palpable tension. "Okay, let's all take it down a notch. Mary, we all know how you feel about modern medicine. Dr. Winters, don't bother. Her mind's made up."

"Because *I* know the truth," Mary said with conviction. She shouldered her purse and flipped back her hair. "And the truth has set me free."

Dr. Winters looked from Taryn to Mary and back again. Taryn gave him a subtle eye roll.

"Well, if you're not going to let me help my son, I've wasted my time coming here. I've got to get back to my shop," Mary announced, glaring at both of them. "If my son dies from all that theo-pheny-chemical crap you're pumping into him, you'll hear from my lawyer."

Dr. Winters and Taryn silently watched Mary Jane march out of the room. The moment she was gone, the doctor turned to Taryn and raised his eyebrows.

"Don't worry," she assured him. "Her lawyer makes all his money defending her and her friends in drug court. I can't tell you the number of times she's threatened to sue me simply because I work in a pharmacy that dispenses modern drugs."

He rubbed the back of his neck. "Well, her frustration is certainly warranted. I'm just as frustrated that Andrew's not getting better. But I haven't given up yet. I hope you believe that."

Taryn looked at the restless form of her husband and sighed. "I do."

CHAPTER NINE

Thursday, July 20, 2000

AFTER ANDREW WAS RESTING AGAIN, Dr. Winters pulled up a wheeled stool and sat in front of Taryn. The look on his face was a mix of disappointment and amusement. "You were right about his mother."

She nodded. "Welcome to my world."

He smiled, then retrieved the chart book and opened it. "I have the results of Andrew's intensive labs and lumbar puncture."

"That was fast," Taryn said, taking a seat on the bed. "You just drew those samples this morning."

"I put a rush on it. I wish I could say it helped."

"What do you mean?" Taryn asked, dreading that she already knew the answer.

"It means that everything still looks normal; that is, within normal ranges anyway. His urine shows a slight elevation in protein excretion. His blood urea nitrogen is also up, as is his serum creatinine. They're not critical, but they are high. Even so, those results are pretty much expected for a patient who's had constant tremors and seizures for five days. The good news is his spinal fluid shows no evidence of ALS or meningitis. What concerns me the most is this worsening cough." He donned his stethoscope again and listened to several places on Andrew's chest. "His lungs are definitely filling with fluid, but I think the dex should help."

"Is it a nosocomial infection?"

"I hope not. We run a very clean hospital here. And his white count still isn't elevated, so I don't believe it's an active infection. Even so, there is conspicuous fluid buildup, so I might put him on an antibiotic just in case." He quickly held up his hand as if to thwart any comment Taryn might make. "It won't be erythromycin. It *is* standard for respiratory infections, but I know it interacts significantly with both phenytoin and theophylline." He winked at Taryn. "See? Having you around has made me triple-check everything."

Taryn smiled. "I hope that's a good thing."

"It is."

"Then may I suggest we wait until we get the results of the MRI? Perhaps radiology can find the source of the fluid buildup in his lungs. I'd hate to create an antibiotic resistance if there isn't an identifiable infection."

Dr. Winters double clicked his pen and made a notation in Andrew's chart.

"Have you determined what's causing the seizures?"

"No, but I'm convinced it's a disorder in his nerve tissue. Several of my colleagues are looking over his charts. Maybe they'll see something we've missed." He checked the IV label. "Good. I see they've added the donepezil."

"I think it's helping, too," she said eagerly. "Yesterday evening, when I first got here, Andrew and I had a . . . a connection."

"A connection?"

"Yeah. Like he was momentarily more lucid. He looked at me with eyes that actually *saw* me, you know? There was no verbal communication, but there was a connection."

Dr. Winters removed his penlight and checked Andrew's pupils. "Have you noticed any other changes?"

"Maybe. I might be overly optimistic, but his eyes don't seem to wander quite as much anymore."

"But no talking yet?"

She shook her head. "Probably too early for that much effect. But I can sense he wants to tell me something." She sighed deeply. "I hope that's not just wishful thinking."

"As do I," Dr. Winters said in an encouraging tone. He pushed a call button and Nurse Sarah almost immediately entered the room. "Let's get him ready to move. The EMG lab is ready. Are you staying?" he asked Taryn.

"No. I need to take care of some things at home. I guess I need to call Mary too. She didn't leave the scrapbook and in all the excitement, I forgot to ask."

Dr. Winters rolled his eyes. "So did I. Oh and I forgot to tell you, we've rescheduled his MRI for six a.m. instead of nine. I know you wanted to be here, but there's really not much you could do anyway. And it'll take some time for radiology and me to interpret what we find. You may want to take the morning off."

Taryn nodded. "Maybe I'll go to El Cerrito for that scrapbook if you still think it'll do any good."

"I do. If I hear anything about Andrew's results sooner, I'll contact you. Do you have a cell phone?"

"Yes."

"Great. If you'll leave your number, I'll let you know when he's back in his room. That way you don't have to watch the clock."

She smiled. "Thank you, Dr. Winters."

* * *

Sitting at her kitchen counter with a cup of green tea and her notebook, Taryn dreaded making the call to Mary. Instead, she wrote down every aspect of Andrew's training, thinking it might reveal something she'd overlooked.

His workouts were intense and merciless, but that was only because he pushed himself for perfection. Throughout the last month, even Coach Chaplin had told him to back off and rest. Taryn had agreed. Andrew's body needed time to rejuvenate and heal. It actually did more damage not to give the body a chance to rebuild. He'd occasionally comply, but then he'd work himself much harder the next day. He claimed it was because he felt "out of focus." He said he couldn't get his body to respond the way it should. His headaches and balance issues were getting worse and—

She froze mid-thought and stared blankly ahead. *His coach!* Taryn had been so caught off guard by the man's phone call that she hadn't thought to ask him any questions. In the past eight weeks, Andrew had spent more time with Coach Chaplin than anyone else—even her. If anyone had seen telling clues, it'd be him.

Taryn immediately called the coach. He picked up on the first ring.

"Taryn. I sure hope you're calling with good news."

"I wish. Andrew is stabilized, but he's still not getting any better. Now he's got fluid in his lungs."

"Is it pneumonia?"

"Dr. Winters doesn't think it's an infection. We simply don't know yet. He's getting an MRI tomorrow. I'll let you know what we find out."

"Dean Winters? He's a good doctor. Crazy smart."

"Yes, he is," she chuckled. "Listen, John. I need to ask if you or anyone else on the team has been sick lately."

"Sick how?"

"You know, like a cold or flu. Or has anyone felt shaky or had constant headaches like Andrew's had?"

There was a pause on the other end of the line. "No, not that I can think of."

"Have you or any of your team ever had meningitis or any sort of fever lately?"

Another pause. "Remind me again what meningitis is."

"A very serious infection of the fluid surrounding the brain and spinal cord."

"No, not that I know of. Why do you ask?"

Taryn sighed. "Dr. Winters has a team of specialists looking at Andrew's condition, but they still aren't sure what's wrong with him. I'm just searching every possibility from my end in case he picked up something at home or on the track."

His third pause was even longer. "Is the team in any danger? I need to know because we leave for Sydney in just a few weeks."

"No. Whatever Andrew has, it's probably not contagious. At least not through water particles or casual contact." She cleared her throat and quickly added, "Or even intimate contact."

"I'll take your word for that, Taryn," Chaplin said. "And I'll watch my team and staff just the same."

"Thanks. Say, do you recall seeing any of Andrew's symptoms? I sent them to you in an email from work."

"Yeah, yeah, yeah," he said quickly. "I saw Andrew come in and out of focus a few times. Kinda weirded me out if you know what I mean. Like when I asked him to do some isometric stretches, he couldn't do 'em. Kept falling on his tush. I mean, the guy used to lead the exercises at the beginning of the year, remember? But by the time we started training in the Hornet, things weren't looking so hot, you know? But what was even stranger was that the weirdness wasn't consistent enough to cut him from the team. The next day he would shine even better and fly like a bird. He was clearing eighteen feet like it was nothin'. You just never knew when one of his attacks would happen. Guess he didn't either. What is it, doc? Some kind of seizure?"

"Yes. We just don't know what's causing it or why it's recently laid him out flat," she said, the last three words coming out in a sob.

"Woah, hey, Taryn. You're stronger than this. Things are always handled better on an even keel. You know what I'm saying? Don't get too worked up over somethin' you can't change."

"But what if I *can* change it, Coach? I know my meds pretty darn well. I should be able to come up with something that'll work, right?"

"Taryn, I already told you you're as smart as they come. Your brainpan holds three times what mine can. But there are some things in life we can't do nothin' about. So you do the best you can. Don't settle for second best. Do your best and then move on."

Wise council. Second best would put Andrew in a grave. That was unacceptable.

"Well, thanks for your help, Coach. You keep your eye on the team. If they start having similar symptoms, let Dr. Winters know. Okay? And best of luck in Sydney."

"Thanks, Taryn. Remember, you tell the Birdman I want him clearing 5.9 in four years. Okay?"

"Sure, Coach. I will."

She said good-bye and closed her phone. In her notebook, she wrote *coach* and *team*, then put a check mark next to each. She also drew a line through the letters *ASL* but left the words *dementia* and *Alzheimer's* with question marks.

She finished her tea and reopened her phone. The LCD clock read 4:21. Plenty of time for Mary to have returned to El Cerrito. Taryn brought up *Mary Starr* on her speed dial and placed her thumb over the call button. She closed her eyes and took a deep breath before pushing the button.

CHAPTER TEN

Thursday, July 20, 2000

MARY JANE STARR PICKED UP on the ninth ring. Taryn knew she should have hung up on the eighth. "I'm surprised you had the nerve to call," Mary snipped.

"Mary, I'm sorry about this morning. I didn't mean to go into lecture mode, but Andrew needs real medicine right now—"

"Marijuana *is* real medicine, *natural* medicine, the way benevolent Mother Earth created it for our unrestricted use."

"All right, all right. Look, I didn't call to continue the debate. We can look into using a medical form of cannabinol if it comes to that. In the meantime, we're still researching Andrew's past for any clue to his illness. Did you find the scrapbook?"

"Yes. It was in my car, but I didn't have a chance to give it to you before Dr. Wisenheimer shoved me out of the room."

"He didn't shove—" Taryn stopped, knowing it was futile to rehash the way the morning had actually played out. If Mary remembered it that way, then that's the way it really happened. "Actually, yeah, I'm sorry about that too. The hospital has rules in place for the health and safety of the patients, and I guess he—"

"Are you suggesting I'm a danger to my son?"

Taryn bit her lip so as not to answer too quickly. "Of course not, Mary," she said with great effort. "I know you want Andrew to get better as much as I do."

"Most likely more."

Taryn pulled the phone from her ear and used all her willpower *not* to throw it across the kitchen. She took a number of deep breaths before she spoke again.

"Mary, I would still like to look through Andrew's scrapbook. May I come over and get it?"

A long pause followed as Mary deliberated Taryn's request. *Why does she even need to mull it over?* Taryn grumbled in her head. *This could save her son!*

"Okay. But I'm at my shop, not my house."

"That's not a problem," she said and quickly hung up.

Taryn got ready in record time. Mary had agreed to a second favor, and Taryn didn't want to give her time to change her mind. The drive from Stockton to El Cerrito normally took about seventy minutes. She made it in fifty-five.

The Sweet Chariot curio shop occupied a small nook in a strip of derelict stores along old Main Street in downtown El Cerrito. Mature Indian Laurel trees lined the street, giving the neglected avenue a shadowy aura, and litter and refuse sullied the gutters and sidewalks to the point that the old town drew few tourists. Urban sprawl and big outlet chains had drawn the majority of consumers away from old, established mom and pop stores. As such, real estate in old town had plummeted, and Mary Jane was able to purchase her shop for a song.

Taryn parked in a stall a few spaces up from Sweet Chariot. She didn't want to give Mary a heads-up on her arrival. She pushed open the glass front and was instantly assaulted by a noxious mix of burning incense and THC. The incense, she guessed, was meant to cover up the marijuana odor, but it failed miserably. A decent sound system did little to make Bob Dylan sound like a vocalist that could hold a tune. While he bemoaned his life in song, Taryn approached a lean tattooed man reading a magazine behind the counter. His long, greasy hair was mostly gray. A hand-rolled cigarette dangled from his lips. The man quickly snubbed out whatever he was smoking and closed his magazine.

"How'ya doing today, baby?" he asked in a raspy yet friendly voice.

"Pretty good, I guess," Taryn answered, trying to sound uncaring as she glanced around for her mother-in-law.

"Something I can help you find?"

"Not really."

Taryn felt the man's eyes slither down and back up her tee shirt and blue jeans. She still ran regularly and liked her clothes to fit well, but at this moment, she wished she had worn a sleeping bag.

"Well, if we don't have what you need, I'll do whatever it takes to get it for you," he continued, rubbing his hand across a psychedelic, five-bladed leaf stenciled on his tank top. "Whatever you need. No questions asked."

"Actually, I'm here to see Ms. Starr," Taryn said with as much bravado as she could muster.

The man frowned. "Who?"

"Mary Jane Starr. The owner?"

"Oh, MJ. Yeah, sure. Just chill a sec." The man disappeared through a doorway curtained with strings of beads and seashells.

Taryn wandered through the small shop, trying to ascertain the uses of the various items displayed while listening to Bob Dylan glorify getting stoned pretty much wherever he went. *And people wonder what went wrong with that generation*, she scoffed.

"Hello, Taryn," Mary Jane said, looking out from behind the curtain of bangles.

"Hi, Mary. Sorry to interrupt you at work, but I really need to borrow that scrapbook."

Mary pushed through the beads and shells and put her hands on her hips. "Well, I don't know why you came here then."

Taryn blinked. "Excuse me?"

"I said I don't know why you came here."

"Because . . . you told me to?"

Mary Jane flipped her long hair back and frowned. "I did no such thing."

Shock kept Taryn from replying. She stood with her mouth agape, her brow knitted, feeling her temper build.

Mary moved to the counter and began straightening the clutter there. "You asked me if you could come look through Andy's scrapbook. And I said okay but that I'm at my shop."

"Yeah. So . . . ?"

"So the scrapbook is at home. I was trying to explain that on the phone, but you hung up on me." She pulled an emery board from a drawer and began filing her nails.

Taryn clenched her fists. "Mary . . ."

"Don't get angry with me, young lady. It's your fault you can't understand simple directions. The scrapbook isn't here. If you'd like to meet me at my house, I'll be happy to lend it to you."

Taryn looked down at the floor and fumed. She couldn't look at her mother-in-law without excoriating her with language that would make a dockworker blush. Through gritted teeth, she said, "Fine. Let's go to your house and get it."

"My pleasure," Mary said, switching hands to file the opposite nails. "The shop closes at seven. Sledge is taking me to dinner after we close and then maybe to a club, so I'll meet you there around midnight?"

"WHAT?" Taryn couldn't help but shout.

"Sweetie, you really need to get your hearing checked. I said I'll meet you at my house around midnight—"

"I heard what you said; I just can't believe it! I drove an hour to get that stupid scrapbook and you don't even have it like you said you would."

"Don't you dare raise your voice at me. It's *your* fault you came *here*. I clearly said I'm at my shop, *not* my home."

"That's bull and you know it!"

The tattooed man pushed through the curtain of beads. "Hey. I told you to chill," he growled.

"It's okay, Sledge," Mary cooed at the man. "The young lady was just leaving, weren't you, dear?"

Taryn couldn't talk, couldn't think straight. Her knuckles blanched white. Glaring at Mary, Taryn's vison narrowed to pinpoints shaded in red. The woman no longer registered as her mother-in-law. She was now a target.

"Careful, MJ. I don't like the look on her face," Sledge said, stepping next to Mary.

"It's okay, babe," Mary said, pocketing the emery board. "She's too professional to do anything rash. She's a *licensed* pharmacist."

Sledge's face quickly brightened. "Groovy. Hey, man, maybe you could hook me up with some Roxys. I've got the bread."

Taryn breathed heavily through her still-clenched teeth. Glaring at Mary from under furrowed brows, she spat out each word: "I'm—trying—to—save—my—husband's—life."

"He was my son before he was your husband."

Taryn screwed her eyes closed and forced herself to breathe slowly. "Then get me that scrapbook. Please. It may be the only thing that can save him."

"Oh? You mean your fancy medicines aren't actually helping?" Mary said in mock surprise. "Well, you know my feelings on *that* already." She walked to the curtain and regarded Taryn over her shoulder. "If you want the scrapbook, be at my house at midnight. If that's too late, then come by tomorrow morning."

CHAPTER ELEVEN

Thursday, July 20, 2000

IT WAS FIVE THIRTY IN the evening. Taryn had no intention of hanging around El Cerrito until midnight. She knew where Mary lived, but she also knew her mother-in-law would love to catch her trespassing in her home. It would give her debate ammunition for a decade. For all Taryn knew, Mary actually had the scrapbook with her at the curio shop. It'd be just like her to goad Taryn into doing something she'd later regret, like breaking and entering. And yet Taryn was sensible enough to know that if she stuck around El Cerrito, something—or someone—would get hurt.

Taryn was normally a very even-tempered person. As a retail pharmacist, she had to be. Every day she dealt with people who were ornery because they were sick and people who were ornery because they thought it would garner them better customer service. She'd come to appreciate the saying that some people weren't happy unless they were miserable. She was not going to be one of those people, but the suddenness and intensity of Andrew's crisis had stretched her good nature to the breaking point. Mary Jane seemed intent on making the final push.

Taryn could always get the scrapbook later. She wasn't altogether sure it would offer much information anyway. Mary was not known for her organizational skills since she was more of a fly-by-the-seat-of-your-pants kind of woman just this side of scatterbrained.

Taryn decided to return home.

The roads back to Stockton seemed to be plagued with stupid drivers. Stupid people going too slow in the fast lanes; stupid people changing two lanes at a time and without signaling; stupid people driving three abreast at the same speed so that no one could pass. Taryn knew it was her anger that was making the drivers appear worse than they were, but at that moment, even a freeway devoid of vehicles would irritate her. She tried turning on the radio but nothing she heard mollified her. She brought up the playlist on her iPod, but none of those selections interested her. Everything seemed to upset her. Maybe her hormones were just out of whack. Stress could do that. Resolving to simply languish in her ill temper, she switched off the music system and focused on not exceeding the speed limit by more than ten miles per hour.

How could Andrew's mother be so insensitive to her son's condition? Taryn knew they hadn't ever gotten along. But he was her son! Taryn shook her head, trying to clear that incomprehensible attitude. She had learned long ago that common logic and deduction were wasted on her mother-in-law. Mary lived and breathed conspiracy theories and shunned empirical science. She claimed truth had set her free, but it was *her* version of truth. *Truth jaded by PCP and Quaaludes*, Taryn scoffed inwardly.

Perhaps the reasoning centers in Mary's brain *had* been fried in the sixties. Taryn knew very well what recreational drugs did to brain tissue, nerve synapses and receptors, and cerebral neurotransmitters. It was not out of the realm of possibility that Mary could have done some irreparable brain damage. But why was Andrew experiencing symptoms of brain damage? He'd never experimented with illicit substances.

Taryn replayed many of the stories Andrew had shared about his childhood. Regrettably, not many were happy. He ate poorly because they rarely had grocery money. He'd grown used to being cold because their living quarters were rarely heated. He'd missed out on medical care because his mom didn't believe in Western practices. He didn't know the comfort of his own bed until he was almost ten. He hadn't owned a new pair of sneakers until he had saved enough to buy them himself. At thirteen, he got an off-the-records job cleaning floors at a small crab processing outfit on one of San Francisco's many piers. At sixteen, he was operating a fifty-foot boom crane to offload boats. He quickly learned the value of a dollar and learned even more quickly how to hide his money from his mother. By the time Taryn had met Andrew in high school, he was basically living on his own while still sharing an apartment with Mary and whatever guy she happened to be dating at the time. Andrew bought his own food and clothing and did his own cooking and laundry. He developed a love of meat because his mother despised it. Because he rode his bike everywhere, he stayed fit and his leg muscles thickened into steel springs. Not only could he run fast, but he could also leap like a kangaroo. He tried out for the long jump in his sophomore year and made varsity. The following year, the coach asked him if he'd like to try flying.

And fly he did. Just after the start of his senior year, he cleared sixteen feet three inches, shattering the old record of fifteen feet two inches.

Taryn remembered with perfect clarity the first time she saw Andrew vault. She was on the girl's track team running the 1500 meter. She never set any records, but she didn't mind. She ran because it kept her mind sharp enough to handle the science she loved. And it gave her more time to watch the cute, tall guy with the wavy brown hair and well-defined shoulders. He made flying through the air look easy. He had a natural grace to him that flowed like a ballet dancer. And he had amazing leg muscles. She felt like she could watch him for hours on end—and she often did.

Just one week into their senior year, she made it a point to do her warm-ups on the field at the same time he did. Taryn claimed that Andrew didn't notice her until the fourth week of practice. Andrew insisted it was the first day of track and field. They started dating and hit it off instantly. He was confident, thoughtful, and funny. Taryn's only heartbreak was that she wasn't able to accompany him and a few others to a ten-day, multi-school, invitational track meet in Oxford, England, at the end of their senior year.

Following graduation, Andrew went to Cal State Sacramento on a track-and-field scholarship while Taryn attended the University of the Pacific in Stockton. Andrew studied computer programming, Taryn biochemistry. The fifty-mile difference between universities was a strain on their relationship, but they both had goals in mind, and those goals included each other.

In 1994, they married and Andrew put his education on hold so he could put Taryn through the University of Pacific Thomas J. Long School of Pharmacy and Health Sciences.

It was then that she'd found out that Andrew had only had his primary immunizations at birth but no follow-up boosters. When they asked Mary why not, she said she'd refused it on the grounds that punching a syringe full of man-made chemicals into a small, unsuspecting child was not only cruel, but that it also gave children severe mental disorders. Refuting that falsehood was the first argument Taryn had had with Mary. She'd showed Mary that numerous studies confirmed there was no verifiable link between vaccinating children and cognitive disorders. She also showed how, mathematically, the number of vaccines given verses the rate of mental disorders in children made a link statistically impossible. Mary still didn't believe her; but in the end, it didn't matter. Andrew was now an adult, and Taryn had seen to it that he got caught up with all his inoculations in two sessions. They then moved to—

Taryn jolted as if she'd been physically yanked from her memories. *Could a large mix of adult-dose vaccines have caused Andrew's symptoms?*

Oh, Mary would love that!

In Andrew's case, the likelihood was so low it'd be considered a one-in-a-million chance. Even so, she would definitely look into it.

When Taryn got home, she sat at the kitchen table and called the hospital to check on Andrew.

"He's not good, Taryn," Nurse Sarah reported. "He couldn't stop coughing because of the fluid buildup in his lungs. Dr. Winters gave him a bolus of dexamethasone and put in a drain."

"A thoracentesis? For a cough?"

"Dr. Winters says Andrew's having abnormal heart rhythms too. He thinks it might be the onset of congestive heart failure."

Taryn held her stomach and swallowed hard. "No," she whispered.

"I'm so sorry, Taryn. The doctor's also added furosemide to his IV, so that should help eliminate excess fluids."

"Is he going to run an EKG?" she asked, trying to stay analytical.

"I don't see one ordered . . . but he did say something about adding a cardio emphasis on Andrew's MRI tomorrow."

"Good heavens. With all the other areas of focus, that stupid test is going to run all day."

"Probably so," Sarah said compassionately. "If you have errands to run or projects to do tomorrow, you might want to do them before you come in. It'd be better than just sitting around worrying."

"That's true. Thanks, Sarah. Let me know if anything changes."

"Will do, Taryn."

They said good evening and disconnected. Taryn took a moment to look around the dark, empty room, then put her forehead on the tabletop and tried not to weep. She no longer felt like doing anything other than curling up in bed and praying for sleep. She stood, intending to do just that—until she realized the only errand she had tomorrow was to go back to El Cerrito and get Mary's scrapbook. She barely made it to the bathroom before throwing up.

CHAPTER TWELVE

Friday, July 21, 2000

A BRIEF EARLY-MORNING RAIN GAVE a pleasant chill to the muggy air. Stepping out under their covered back porch, a steaming cup of fresh brew cradled in her hands, Taryn listened to the precipitation tap a soothing melody against the awning. She loved the sound of rain and the smell of it too, how it washed all the corruption from the air. Rain brought refreshing and renewal. It filled her with peace—something she desperately needed this morning.

She glanced at her watch. Since Mary went out on the town last night, it meant she would not wake up until around ten. That gave Taryn plenty of time to get cleaned up and drive to El Cerrito. She appreciated not feeling rushed, but Taryn was never one to take a gift of extra time for granted. She liked to stay busy no matter what her timetable allotted.

Going back inside, she booted up her computer and searched the latest on dosing multiple vaccinations simultaneously in adulthood. Not much had changed since the last time she looked into the topic. The new hepatitis B vaccine had been a hot item a few years back with the HIV outbreak in the Bay Area. She'd made sure Andrew had received that one after his first set of catch-up vaccines. But she found no contraindications for dosing several standard vaccines at once, other than local pain and swelling at the injection site and a mild fever from the antibody bloom. She accessed records from the World Health Organization's campaign to rid the planet of preventable diseases and found that over ninety percent of the world no longer contracted polio. Measles and smallpox eradication weren't far behind. But nowhere did she find any record of any vaccine recipient exhibiting the symptoms that now plagued her husband.

Another dead end.

Scribbling a note to ask Dr. Winters about the possibility of vaccine-induced dementia in adults, she headed to the bathroom to prepare for the day. She showered, combed her hair straight, and dressed in a manner Mary would approve of. She hated cowing to anything Mary preferred, but she needed to employ every advantage to get any information that might help Andrew. She put on a tie-dyed tee shirt Mary had given her and a denim skirt. Standing in front of a mirror instantly changed her mind. The garish shirt seemed to validate Mary's eccentricities while mocking everything Taryn was trying to do for her husband. All for a scrapbook she wasn't sure would reveal anything. Still, as Dr. Winters had said, she didn't want to leave any stone unturned. Exchanging the tee for a cotton blouse, she left their home with renewed determination.

The drive to El Cerrito was a blur. Her focus was single-minded: get the scrapbook, return to the hospital, and go through the pages while waiting for Andrew's MRI results. By the time she got to Mary's house, the sun had broken through the clouds and was sluggishly warming the bayside town.

Mary Starr's house was an ill-kept clapboard bungalow from the forties. The only curb appeal it had were the colorful wildflowers covering the entire front yard. A fine mist hovered just above the ground. Bees and humming birds were already out gathering pollen and nectar. It was a pleasant scene, and yet it did little to soften Taryn's mounting anxiety. She knew Mary was home; her VW Bug glistened with raindrops in the driveway. She prayed the imminent encounter would be brief.

Taryn knocked on the front door and waited. When no one answered, she tried the doorbell. Not hearing a ring from within, she knocked much louder. A man's voice shouted an obscenity from inside the house. A moment later the door yanked open.

"What the—oh, it's you."

Wearing only boxer shorts, Sledge stood tall and revolting in the doorway. His hair was disheveled, his eyes red and puffy. The tattoos on his sagging skin had morphed into images reminiscent of Salvador Dali. The tell-tale funk of alcohol and burnt THC wafted from inside.

"Good morning, Sledge," Taryn said, glancing at her watch. It was ten minutes past ten. "Is Mary up yet?"

"What do you think?" he snarled.

"No? Well, no need to wake her. I'm here for that scrapbook she promised."

The vile man scratched his flaccid belly and sneered. "I don't remember her promising you anything."

Taryn suppressed the urge to comment on his failing memory—and numerous other things about the man—and stood her ground. "She promised to bring it to the hospital but forgot to leave it. That's why I came to her shop yesterday, but as you may recall, it wasn't there. So now I'm here to get it. I'm heading to the hospital right now, so if you could just hand it to me, I'll let you get back to bed."

He huffed in disgust and rubbed his bloodshot eyes. "Fine. Come in."

"No, thanks. I'll wait right here."

He glared at her. "Suit yourself," he said, slamming the door.

Taryn waited patiently on the stoop. She heard clutter being shoved to the hardwood floor inside and more cursing. A few moments later the door opened again. Mary stood wearing a lacey bathrobe and nothing else. "So you've decided to stalk me now?"

Averting her eyes, Taryn said, "I'm not stalking you, Mary. You suggested I come by this morning, so I'm here now to borrow the scrapbook. May I have it, please? Andrew's doctor wants to look through it for clues. As I told your boyfriend, I'm heading to the hospital right now."

"My boyfriend? Oh, you mean Sledge? He's just a free spirit, as are we all. Surely you can't disapprove of that too."

Taryn was familiar with Mary's tactics for changing the subject, and she wasn't going to let herself be misdirected. "That's your choice, Mary, not mine. The scrapbook, please?"

Mary challenged Taryn with mascara-smudged eyes, then turned and reached for something beyond Taryn's view. She turned back with a three-ringed photo album—and the large baggie of brownies sitting atop it. "You can have it only if you promise to give Andy these brownies. They're medicinal, regardless of what your college books say. I insist."

Taryn sighed. "Mary, you know I can't do that. It's illegal."

"No brownies, no scrapbook."

She sighed again. "Fine."

"You promise?"

"Yes. I will give them to him just like you ask."

Mary handed over the two items with a smug grin. "I don't think you'll find anything in there," she said, indicating the binder. "It's just a bunch of pictures. There are no medical records. I have no idea where his birth certificate is. Most of that junk is made up anyway just to line the doctors' pockets."

Taryn quickly took the items from Mary's hands. "Yeah, birth weight, gender, bilirubin level, condition at delivery, and stuff like that is all made up. Thanks for the album."

Sledge stepped up behind Mary and slid his hands around her waist. He kissed her neck and oozed, "Come on, baby. Let's go back to bed."

Taryn turned without a word and walked quickly to her car, feeling like she needed to find a hazmat station for a chemical shower.

CHAPTER THIRTEEN

Friday, July 21, 2000

ANDREW'S HOSPITAL BED WAS NOT in his room. A brief surge of panic filled Taryn's chest before she remembered that the bed had wheels. It was basically a glorified gurney. It was much easier to transport non-ambulatory patients to and from appointments using their own beds.

Taryn moved to the extra bed and scooted onto it. The photo album sat on her lap. Knowing her husband was physically incapable of accepting the brownies, she'd tossed them into a dumpster. The room lights were low, but there was enough light to read by. She kept them dimmed on purpose; she needed some down time, some time to decompress.

Taryn wasn't normally the praying kind. She had a belief in God and even considered herself a Christian, but she'd never been much of a churchgoer. She kept her religious sentiments deep within her heart and expressed them through her actions. She participated in Goodwill charities. She loved going to retirement homes for brown-bag lunch events where she could counsel residents on their medications and health concerns or simply talk to those who were lonely and needed a friendly ear. She and Andrew even mentored summer youth fitness camps to encourage kids to develop healthy exercise habits. Andrew was always so great with the kids. They had planned to start a family right after the Olympics . . .

Taryn shook her head forcefully, trying to shake such thoughts from her mind. Such daydreaming would only bring heartache. She wrapped her arms around her stomach and doubled over on the bed. *Stop it, Taryn! You're not going to cry here in the hospital.* What if Andrew came back? She couldn't let him see her losing control. She needed to stay strong—for him and herself. She knew that life brought heartache as well as joy. She knew that was part of God's plan. You can't know the sweet without experiencing the bitter. But why was all the bitter happening at once?

Andrew was her everything. She had no problem admitting that. She had her career, yes, but that too was because Andrew had postponed his so she could finish pharmacy school. He'd never once complained about that. He supported her causes and even participated in several of them. On the days she worked, he cooked dinner and kept the house. On her off days, she did the chores so he could focus on his web-based business and his training. He thrilled in her successes and she reveled in his. It was as if their two persons shared the same soul. He was always there for her. So why couldn't she be here for him? Why couldn't she figure out what was happening so she could cure him?

With her body still folded in two, she saw the lights brighten and heard a soft gasp.

"Oh! Taryn, I didn't know you were here." It was Nurse Sarah.

Taryn sat up and grabbed a tissue from the bed stand. "Hi, Sarah. Sorry I frightened you," she said, wiping her face. Dang it, she *had* started crying.

Sarah sat and wrapped an arm around her shoulder. "Hey, sweetie. Don't you worry. We've got this. Mercy General just got the latest MRI available. It's twice as fast as the old models and takes higher resolution images from every angle without needing to adjust the patient. Whatever is making Andrew sick, they're going to figure it out."

Taryn truly appreciated the comfort Sarah tried to give her. She wished she could accept it fully. Her heart wanted to, but her analytic side kept those emotions just beyond reach. Sometimes she hated being a realist.

Sarah gave her another squeeze. "You go into the bathroom and wash your face now. I'm going to prep the room. Andrew should be back in about ten minutes, and you don't want to look like a banshee when he gets here."

Taryn gave a half sob, half laugh. "Thanks a lot, I think."

"Not that you ever *could* look bad," Sarah said, standing and opening the bathroom door for her. "You're a hottie and you know it."

"I feel significantly less than lukewarm right now," she said, standing. "But thanks."

Andrew was wheeled in as Taryn freshened up. She was grateful for the heads-up and for Sarah's endeavors to lift some emotional weight from her shoulders. The nurse was right; she wanted to look her best for Andrew—even if he didn't recognize her anymore.

Brushing that negative thought aside, she reentered the room and froze. The emotional reprieve came crashing back down. Andrew was now intubated.

"Has he stopped breathing on his own?" she asked Sarah in a constricted voice.

"No, I don't think so."

Dr. Winters came in at that moment. "You're wondering about the endotracheal tube? Andrew was struggling for breath so much the MRI tech couldn't get a clear image. It was necessary, I'm afraid."

Taryn exhaled heavily. "Sorry. I just wasn't expecting to see that." She moved to Andrew's side for a closer look. Along with the breathing tube, Andrew still had the NG feeding tube, the urinary catheter, and the thoracentesis drain. Having done several rotations through a hospital as part of her training, she was used to seeing such devices. But seeing all four tubes on her husband changed their logical necessity to something truly horrifying. Averting her eyes, she faced the doctor. "How did the scans go?"

"Quite well in the end. We had to sedate him fully with midazolam to keep him motionless." He held up his hand quickly to stop any comment. "I know midazolam is a benzodiazepine and that you're opposed to them, but this one is very short acting, as you undoubtedly know. We only use it for procedures where immobility is required along with sedation, never long-term."

Taryn smiled sheepishly. "Good heavens, am I that assertive?"

"Yes, you are," he said with a smirk. He glanced over at Sarah knowingly. "But the nurses love that you constantly dispute me."

"I don't mean to dispute," she said in a quick apology.

"Well, maybe not dispute. But you certainly challenge me enough to keep me on my toes."

Taryn felt herself blush but didn't hide it. "I'll take that as a good sentiment. Thank you, Doctor. Did you get a chance to look at the scans?"

"Some initial images," Winters said with a slight hesitancy. "But I'm not a radiologist. I'll leave it up to them for a detailed diagnosis."

"What about your preliminary thoughts?"

"Well, it's still too early to say . . ."

Taryn persisted. "Come on, Dr. Winters, please. You're the best neurologist here. I read your bio in my research. You have top marks from almost every neuroscience academy there is, so I know you know how to read an MRI."

He gestured toward the spare bed. "Sit down, Taryn, please." When she did, he pulled up the wheeled stool. "His spinal cord and meninges look good, as does his heart. His ribs are healing nicely in spite of his coughing. His lungs are markedly filled with fluid, but I couldn't find a definitive infusion point. The drain is working well, but his blood oxygenation is low, so I'd like to keep him intubated for now." He paused and stared at the floor.

"And his brain? What did the cranial scan show?"

He let out a breath. "There were some areas that . . . concern me. They didn't look right. But that might be the clarity of this new machine. I saw details I've never seen before. But then there were areas that didn't come through as well."

"What do you mean by that?"

He shook his head and looked up. "Areas in his cerebrum, particularly the cortex. I . . . I really don't know. It's certainly nothing I've ever seen in this hospital before. I'd like to get Dr. Panju's analysis first."

Taryn nodded, hoping it was just as he said—that it was a new imaging perspective he wasn't confident reading. "When will Dr. Panju do an analysis?"

"He's doing it right now. But we won't get results until tomorrow—perhaps Monday at the latest. He's very thorough."

Taryn's eyes dropped. Another delay. She nodded, unable to speak. Dr. Winters placed a caring hand on her knee. It was very uncharacteristic of him, but that made it all the more appreciated.

"Is there anything I can get for you?" he asked softly.

"A miracle," she whispered.

CHAPTER FOURTEEN

Friday, July 21, 2000

IT WAS LATE. NURSE SARAH brought a fresh salad from the cafeteria, but Taryn could only eat a few bites. Her appetite had diminished in proportion to her husband's health.

Andrew's sedative had worn off and his steady tremors had returned. A machine regulated his breathing, so it was hard to tell if the thoracentesis and the diuretics were keeping up with the fluid production in his lungs. But his blood oxygen level had risen, so the respirator was doing its main job. His eyes were open, languid, and wandering. His head flopped lazily to one side, clearly showing a lack of motor control. It broke Taryn's heart to watch him succumb to this dreadful malady. If his previous symptoms *were* precursors, they'd been deviously subtle. The disease in full force was merciless and catastrophic. Andrew had zero control over any muscle. He couldn't even breathe on his own. Even so, Taryn sensed somewhere deep inside his malfunctioning body, Andrew was still in there. He wasn't giving up.

Eventually Andrew dozed off. It was undoubtedly from exhaustion. A body simply could not maintain incessant skeletal muscle movement without total burnout. Grateful to see him finally relax, Taryn eagerly looked though the photo album and was appalled that she'd never seen the pictures before.

There were several shots of him as a baby. They were grainy, often burry images taken with cheap Kodak cameras or Polaroids. Many were yellowed or fading with age. She knew of a few electronics shops that offered to convert old photos to a digital format. The images would still be rough, but at least they would no longer fade. She scribbled a note to do that before returning the album to Mary. Strangely, a number of the photos had been cut in half.

It wasn't hard to guess that Mary had cropped out all images of Andrew's father. The next few sleeves had shots of Andrew as a toddler. He'd been an adorable towhead. He was always smiling, always happy. Taryn noticed that the background scenes changed about every third picture, confirming that they had moved a lot. Again, a number of the prints had been cut in two. Toward the time he was a preteen, his smile grew less ubiquitous. His face was more deadpan than filled with any emotion. It looked as if he was merely tolerating life. Those images spoke volumes.

How terrible, Taryn thought, feeling her heart clench. Those times in *her* life were some of her fondest memories.

The pictures grew less numerous as he got older. There were only a couple of him in front of Carlmont High School and one or two of him on the track team. He still looked young, but his shoulders were squared, and there was a cockiness in his eyes. An influx of testosterone, she reasoned. The onset of manhood. Taryn remembered how she had felt back then seeing his confident look that still maintained an innocence of boyhood. It was an irresistible mix.

Images clipped from newspapers filled the next sleeve with a few personal photographs sprinkled throughout. They showed track and field events from his sophomore and junior years. She hadn't seen the newsprint images in years, and looking at them again made her heart skip anew. She remembered clearly how his broad smile weakened her knees and set to flight a thousand butterflies in her tummy. Every once in a while, there was a picture of her standing next to him. There was even one of them racing each other in a distance match. She'd forgotten about that. She'd won, but not by much. He was a much better sprinter. Then there were the prom photos from junior and senior year. His borrowed suit and—*gah!*—her dresses! Good heavens, were those really the styles back then? And what was up with her hair?

After turning the page, she saw a bold newspaper article inserted in the sleeve:

Five Carlmont Track and Field Athletes Selected for International Goodwill Meet in Oxford, England

The article went on to list four Carlmont runners who would compete in the 4x100-meter relay, one of whom would also run in the 100-meter sprint. The fifth athlete would compete in the pole vault: Andrew Miner. It was his big break, his once-in-a-lifetime opportunity.

Taryn felt the hollow pang of disappointment at not being able to accompany the team return to her chest. She and Andrew had been dating regularly by then. Knowing he was going off on such an adventure didn't sit well at first.

But she wanted the best for him and encouraged him to go. Andrew had already gained the attention of local universities with his record-breaking vaults. He'd already been approached by scouts from Cal State, UCSF, and UCLA. Such an international event would certainly draw more attention to him. If he did well, it would guarantee him a full-ride scholarship to college. He needed that. There was no way his mom could afford to send him to a university, and his dad had vanished long ago. He'd have been stupid not to go.

Pictures of that trip filled the next three pages. Most were of track and field events and a number were of him out on the town with his buddies. She didn't recognize many of the faces. There were also a number of shots of cute British girls clinging to the tall, good-looking American athletes. Taryn chose not to dwell on those photos. However, she did pick up on the fact that every image of Andrew out on the town was at a local eatery with piles of heavy British food covering the tables. Andrew claimed that's why he only got the bronze medal at the meet. He was favored to get the gold, but the team was treated to mountains of English beef, sausage, mutton, and seafood every night. And of course, every meal came with a truckload of potatoes deep fried as chips—the British term for thick-cut french fries. Big meals were a rarity for him back home, so he indulged in the free excess. In the end, such gluttony cost him on the field. He'd gained five pounds even before it came time for him to compete. He admitted that he'd acted like a dumb kid back then and he deserved what he got, but he never forgave himself for letting everyone else down. When he got back from England, he made a personal vow to one day make it to the Olympics. He tried in 1996 but missed the cut.

Last Friday had been his final chance.

Taryn dabbed at her eyes and turned to the next page. A few photos showed Andrew at Cal State, Sacramento. A few more of him with Taryn on various outings. One photo of their wedding. *ONE!* (They had dozens of wedding photos in their albums.) Taryn gritted her teeth and continued. A shot of him standing next to Taryn at her graduation from the University of the Pacific. A couple of shots of him and Mary at scenic places around the Bay. And that was it.

Taryn looked though the album again, scrutinizing each photo, but didn't see anything telling. She felt strangely disappointed . . . and relieved. If there *had* been something glaring, she could tell Dr. Winters about it, and they could formulate a therapy. But she didn't see anything—dubious or otherwise. So why did Mary put up such a fuss?

Because she is Mary. Period.

Taryn closed the album and stepped to Andrew's side. She gently combed his hair off his forehead. His eyes remained closed. She held his face steady and leaned down to kiss his brow.

"Still not giving up on you, Birdman," she whispered hoarsely.

CHAPTER FIFTEEN

Saturday, July 22, 2000

IT WAS TARYN'S RESPONSIBILITY TO run a stack of pharmacy sales reports at the end of each week. She could have easily delegated the task to one of her technicians or the pharmacist on duty, but she needed the distraction. She stopped in Saturday morning and ran the report while the regular staff worked the pharmacy. Reading over the printout, she saw that their sales had been slightly lower. She was actually glad because it meant whoever had covered her shifts had an easier workflow. She felt horrible for having missed so much work. But she knew that everyone understood. In fact, a few members of the staff wondered why she'd shown up today at all.

"Heck, I don't even like my husband," a middle-aged clerk named Leisa spouted, "but I'd be weeping gallons of crocodile tears over him if it got me a day off with pay."

Taryn smiled at Leisa's attempt to cheer her up. "I want to be there for him, of course," she explained, "but it kills me to just sit there and do nothing."

"But what if there's an emergency?" Melissa joined in.

"They'll contact my cell phone, and the hospital is only forty-five minutes away. They've given me a VIP parking pass, so I can be inside in seconds." Taryn wanted to sound confident, but she wasn't sure how well she pulled it off. No one looked like they believed her.

"Girl, there are some great malls in Sacramento," Leisa said. "Just call in a family emergency, go shopping, and then if a true emergency happens, you can be there in a heartbeat."

"That's not being very principled," Taryn said with censure.

"No, but it *is* making the most of a bad situation," Melissa said, raising her eyebrows several times.

Taryn finished the reports, sent an email copy to headquarters, and filed the hardcopies in a cabinet. Just as she was about to leave, the pharmacist on duty asked, "Hey, Taryn, do you mind if I take a quick break to grab something before you go?"

"Sure, Kent," she said, not minding a brief delay. "Take your time." It felt good to help her colleague, even if it was for just a couple of minutes.

Taryn fielded calls and verified scripts, glad for the chance to focus on something else; glad for a chance to feel like she was truly helping someone. Kent came back ten minutes later with two 24-packs of Diet Coke.

"Geez, Kent, do we need to perform an intervention?" Taryn teased, pointing to the sodas.

He feigned shock. "Hey, I drink this purely for its diuretic properties. Don't want to get puffy ankles from standing all day, you know?"

"If you say so," she said, logging out of her computer. She turned to him and lightly touched his sleeve. "By the way, thanks again for covering the weekend for me."

He gave her a thumbs-up. "Any news on Andrew?"

"Same old, same old, I'm afraid. Still can't figure it out."

"Sorry to hear that. Hey, I was thinking—it's none of my business—but why don't you make a table?"

Taryn frowned and tilted her head to one side.

"You know, like a spreadsheet or a flowchart. On one axis you list Andrew's symptoms and on the other axis you list known illnesses."

"I've done that already," Taryn explained wearily. "It's a mess."

"Did you list all of them singly or as a group? All of the symptoms, I mean."

"Singly mostly. Dr. Winters said he did the same thing. He said there are too many illnesses that cause identical symptoms. That's what makes diagnosis so hard."

"That's what I'm saying. Change your parameters. Search several symptoms as a set. That way you're not getting bogged down looking at every individual possibility. You know, like in pharmacy. How many drugs have 'stomach upset' listed as a possible side effect?"

Taryn scoffed. "All of them."

"Exactly. Instead of searching 'stomach upset,' search 'stomach upset, headache, constipation, double vision, and hair turning green,' and see what comes up."

Taryn smiled faintly as her eyes dropped to her palms. "Kent, I've tried that too. From the top down, everything I tagged has some negating factor that makes it impossible for Andrew to have contracted it."

"Huh," Kent said, scratching the back of his head. "Have you tried working from the bottom up?"

"And slog through all the partial hits? No, thank you." Taryn did appreciate Kent's efforts. She was simply too worn out to think about tedious work that had an extremely low chance of success. "Thanks anyway, Kent. Enjoy the rest of your weekend."

"Yeah. You too, Taryn."

As Taryn walked out to her car, she reconsidered Kent's suggestion. Maybe he was on to something. Maybe she had offhandedly eliminated a clue because it didn't fit with the others or had discounted an illness because it sounded too far-fetched for Andrew to have contracted it. Perhaps she *should* go back and start over, grouping each symptom into sets and matching them with illnesses that, however remote, generated those symptoms. Then, instead of researching the results with the highest number of hits, start from the bottom and work up. It would be an exhaustive undertaking, but she didn't have anything else to do. And who knew what might turn up?

CHAPTER SIXTEEN

Saturday, July 22, 2000

AT HOME, TARYN MADE A spreadsheet listing each of Andrew's symptoms in sets of three. It was a long list with several redundancies. So she also included known time frames from first onset of symptoms to full manifestation. Entering those sets into a search engine, she hit send and got over 800 results.

"It's going to be a long afternoon," she said to her computer screen.

Taryn opened the first hit—and sat back in frustration. The list included many disease states she'd already looked into: Alzheimer's, ALS, multiple sclerosis, polio, Parkinson's, stroke in many forms, HIV, cancer, myasthenia gravis, multiple myeloma, and others. But there were just as many others that Dr. Winters had never brought up. Perhaps that was because the likelihood of Andrew having any of them defied logic.

She decided to follow through on Kent's suggestion and opened a hit from the bottom of the list. She clicked on each link and read until she found a factor that eliminated Andrew as a candidate. The first dozen excluded him by the second parameter. Most required subsets like gender specificity and family history of the disease. Others had age limitations, such as not manifesting until a person was in their fifties. A few were seen only in certain races and nationalities or were spread by vectors not found in the United States.

After three hours, she took a break and made herself a sandwich. She was tired but refused to give up. As she resumed her search, one disease on the list caught her eye because of its funny-sounding name: *Kuru*. Not having a clue what it was, she clicked the link. What she read made her laugh aloud.

KURU (variant): a very rare, neurodegenerative disease (spongiform disease) caused by an infectious protein (prion) found in contaminated human brain tissue.

Kuru was found among indigenous people from New Guinea (South Fore) who practiced a form of cannibalism in which they ate the brains of dead people as part of a funeral ritual. The ritual is no longer practiced. No cases have been reported in anyone born after 1959.

Well, that ruled Andrew out on several levels. She crossed Kuru off her list and moved on. The two diseases following Kuru were related to animals, not humans. Bovine encephalopathy and one called "scrapie" in sheep. Since Andrew was neither animal, she deleted them from her list.

Just then, her phone vibrated in her pocket. It was Mercy General Hospital. She answered the call with trepidation. "Hello?"

"Hi, Taryn. This is Dr. Winters. I just wanted to let you know radiology has finished reviewing Andrew's MRI. They were very thorough."

"Okay . . . ?" she asked, wondering why the doctor didn't immediately say what they found.

"As I mentioned yesterday, the preliminary spinal and thoracic scans looked very clean. Dr. Panju agreed; he saw nothing untoward, no evidence of nerve damage or infection. There is definitely fluid accumulation in his lungs but still no confirmation on whether it's caused by bacteria. Could be a virus we haven't pinpointed."

When Winters paused, Taryn's mind searched for options. "Could it be tuberculosis? Some latent strain, maybe, because he was vaccinated so late?"

"We actually checked that too. There was no evidence of mycobacterium anywhere."

When the doctor offered no further comment, she cleared her throat. "You still haven't mentioned the cranial scan."

"No. No, I haven't." He paused. She heard him draw a deep breath. "Taryn, do you remember me saying . . . well, claiming that I wasn't sure how to read the CT image and the MRI of the cerebral cortex? Well, that wasn't altogether true."

There was an unmistakable hesitancy in his voice. It coiled in Taryn's gut like a pit viper. With a suddenly dry throat, she asked, "What aren't you telling me?"

No immediate answer. This time, the empty pause over the line rang like a death knell.

Taryn forced herself to speak. "Dr. Winters, please."

"Yes, I'm still here," he said, as if also forcing himself to proceed. "I just . . . I thought I saw something that I haven't seen since med school. The MRI and Dr. Panju confirmed my suspicions. But it's . . . it's a bit hard to explain over the phone. Perhaps it'd be best if you come back to the hospital right away."

Grasping at straws, Taryn blurted, "It's not kuru, is it?"

She heard a sharp intake of breath over the line. "No, but . . ."

"But what?"

"Just please come as quickly as you can."

The line disconnected.

CHAPTER SEVENTEEN

Saturday, July 22, 2000

TARYN DROVE WAY TOO FAST. It was reckless, but she didn't care. Even if a highway patrol cruiser had been behind her with lights flashing and siren blaring, she wouldn't have noticed. All she could think about was her husband. What had Dr. Winters found? What had Dr. Panju confirmed? It couldn't be a disease caused by cannibalism. Andrew? Impossible.

She made it to Mercy General in under thirty minutes. Dr. Winters was waiting for her outside Andrew's room. The look on his face betrayed his feelings.

"I apologize for my hesitancy over the phone," he said as she approached. "It was highly unprofessional of me."

"You scared the tar out of me. What's going on? Is Andrew okay? Do you what it is—his condition?" she asked, rapid-fire.

"I believe we do. But I'm still very confused as to how he acquired it."

"Explain."

He gestured toward the elevators. "Let's go down to radiology and meet with Dr. Panju. He's got some questions about Andrew that may help us both understand."

Taryn held her ground, her fists clenched. "I'm not going anywhere until you tell me what it is."

"It's better if I let him explain."

"Is it a tumor? Some form of cancer?"

"No. This is something completely different."

She folded her arms. "Then what? Stop dodging the question, doctor. I'm not some plebe you need to handle with kid gloves. Stop trying to soften the blow and just tell me!"

Dr. Winters nodded shortly. "He has spongiform encephalopathy."

Taryn frowned. "I was just reading about that . . . but I thought it was very rare."

"It is. Extremely rare. But it *is*, in fact, related to kuru."

She scowled. "Are you saying Andrew practiced cannibalism? He ate infected brains?"

"Good heavens, no," he said, forcing a chuckle.

She swallowed hard and folded her arms even tighter. "Then can you explain to me exactly what spongiform encephalopathy is?"

"I will. Let's head to radiology so I can show you as Dr. Panju and I explain it." When Taryn refused to move, he added, "I'm not trying to stall or avoid the question, I promise. You deserve a complete answer because, frankly, Andrew's condition is grave."

Taryn felt everything come crashing around her—her nerves, her anger, her determination, her confusion, and her sense of helplessness. Dr. Winters hadn't said the word "fatal," but his tone told her there was no cure for Andrew's condition. She looked toward the elevators but couldn't get herself to take the first step. Moving in that direction, going to radiology, felt like a betrayal to her husband. An ardent voice inside told her that if she didn't go to radiology, Andrew might live. If she did go, he would die. Confirming his malady would seal his doom. It was a ridiculous notion, but part of her desperately wanted to believe it.

She looked at the dark doorway to Andrew's room. Her husband lay beyond the threshold; her best friend, the only man she'd ever been in love with. She felt an overwhelming need to be with him. Any distraction would rob her of whatever time they had left.

"Please, Taryn. This will only take a few minutes," Dr. Winters urged.

Taryn knew the doctor was right. She *needed* the details. Only a complete understanding of the disease would allow her to come to terms with it. What harm would a few minutes do anyway? And maybe, just maybe she might be able to supply a clue that would help the doctors find a cure for Andrew.

"May I see him first?" she asked timidly.

"Of course," he said with a nod.

Taryn entered the quiet room but stopped just beyond the threshold. The room felt like a tomb, unusually cold and devoid of spirit. The blinds were closed, but enough daylight crept around the edges to illuminate to the space. Andrew lay asleep in his bed. Something looked different; it took only a few seconds to realize he was no longer intubated. He also had a gauze patch on the top of his head. His body still shook with a slow Parkinsonian tremor, a steady rhythm that looked more peaceful than deleterious. Taryn wanted to run to Andrew, to embrace and comfort him. But she knew if she took a single step toward him, she'd never be able to leave.

She backed out of the room and turned to the doctor. "He's breathing on his own?"

"The chest drain and diuretic are keeping his lungs sufficiently cleared for now. It's better for his system to breathe on its own."

She nodded slowly. "Take me to radiology. I need to know everything."

* * *

Dr. Nassir Panju was a short, balding man with thick brows and dark circles around his eyes; but his ready smile and comforting demeanor gave a welcoming appeal to his overall appearance. He sat at a large desk with three large flat-screen monitors. Two displayed black-and-white MRI images showing various sections of a brain. The third had a 3D graphic of an entire brain.

He stood when Taryn and Dr. Winters walked in.

"You must be Taryn Miner," Dr. Panju said with a light accent. He extended his hand. "I am Dr. Nassir Panju. May I call you Taryn?"

"Sure," she said quietly, taking his hand.

"Dr. Winters has told me much about you. He is a man that does not impress easily, and yet you have made a great impression on him, both as an expert in medicine and as a human being."

Taryn looked at Dr. Winters. He gave a shy smile. "It's true."

"Thank you," she said to both men.

"Please, have a seat," Dr. Panju said, indicating a chair next to his. He spoke with an equal amount of confidence and tenderness. "I want you to know I am terribly sorry for this tragedy you are going through."

"My husband is going through it, not me."

"But are you not suffering too?" he asked in a way that showed he fully understood what this disease was doing to both of them.

She nodded, feeling her eyes burn.

He turned back and tapped a stylus to a pad on his desktop. The monitor in front of Taryn switched to a single, large image of a brain cross section. It did not look normal. Numerous empty dots riddled much of the image. "I have been studying your husband's MRI results with great interest. This is an image of a biopsy we took from his cortex. I have rarely seen this condition. It is both fascinating and disturbing."

"Spongiform encephalopathy," Taryn said.

"Indeed," he said, turning back to her. "I wish to ask you some questions about your husband that will help us formulate a plan to care for him."

A flash of hope burst through Taryn. "You mean it's treatable? There's a way to cure him?"

Dr. Panju shook his head. "I am terribly sorry if I misled you, Taryn. This type of encephalopathy has no cure we know of."

No cure we know of. The words crushed her soul. She took a steadying breath and pushed past the words to ask, "Can you explain it to me, please?"

"Certainly. Do you see these many empty spaces throughout the tissue?" he asked, drawing circles with the stylus around specific areas on the image. "It gives the tissue a sponge-like appearance. This is why it is called *spongiform* disease."

"How is it caused?"

Dr. Panju brought up a 3D image of a few rod-shaped objects on the adjacent monitor. "These are twisted strands of protein, short sequences of RNA called 'prions.' Are you familiar with them?"

"Sort of. Do I need to be?"

He smiled at her candid response. "Only inasmuch as it may help us determine the source of Andrew's infection. You see, all proteins within us are made for specific purposes. Kidney proteins filter urine from blood, muscle proteins form cells that can contract on a signal from the brain, and brain proteins create synapses and branching connections that regulate thought, emotion, memory, and all other bodily functions." He tapped the pad to bring up a picture showing how DNA opens to transcribe RNA, which in turn is used as a template to make protein.

"Basic biology," Taryn said in agreement.

"Precisely. Remember that when a protein coded for a specific body function— in this case, nerve function—is damaged, the function will take place improperly or not at all."

Taryn nodded. "Sure, but then why doesn't the body get rid of it like it does with other damaged cells?"

"Ah. This is where prions are both elegant and sinister," he said, not in delight but with admiration nonetheless. "Normally, a misfunctioning protein *is* destroyed and eliminated by the immune system. But to activate an immune response, a *trigger* must be present—something on the protein that the immune system recognizes as being wrong. In this case, however, because prions are made from the body's own RNA protein, no trigger is present and the immune response is not initiated. This is how prions hide in plain sight."

"That's why there was no white-blood-cell bloom," she said, looking at Dr. Winters.

He nodded. "Andrew's body did not know it was infected."

"But . . . how did he *get* infected?"

"Prions are typically ingested," Dr. Panju explained, "but a prion can also be passed by injection or by organ transplantation and perhaps even absorbed through the skin."

"Well, that can't be right," Taryn argued. "Andrew and I have been together for almost eight years. We do *everything* together. If he has it, then why don't I?"

"First, you must understand that all prion diseases are terribly insidious in nature. They do not manifest until years after infection. Perhaps there was a time your husband ate infected beef when you were not together?"

"Infected beef?"

"Yes. It is the primary source of this infection. Keep in mind that this episode most likely took place around eight to ten years ago. That is the typical incubation period for this type of encephalopathy to manifest."

"Andrew has been harboring this disease for ten years?" she asked in disbelief.

"As I said, it is terribly insidious."

Taryn's brow knit. Andrew had been a meat eater his entire life. His love of steaks, hamburgers, and all things beef was because he loved the taste and because his mother disapproved. It would be impossible to determine any one given day when—

Taryn froze. Her breath lodged in her throat. Several factors lined up in her mind, each one confirming the source of Andrew's infection. There'd been a devastating outbreak of mad cow disease in England roughly ten years ago. Mad cow disease is a type of spongiform encephalopathy. The US and European nations had banned the import of all British and Canadian beef during that time—the same time Andrew was in England. Mary Jane's scrapbook opened in her mind as she remembered pictures of Andrew and his teammates eating at various pubs around Oxford. She'd have to revisit the photos, but she was certain many showed hamburgers and roast beef sandwiches being consumed. He *had* eaten contaminated beef.

Despite her efforts to remain analytical, Taryn felt her stomach seize and all the blood drain from her face.

CHAPTER EIGHTEEN

Saturday, July 22, 2000

"ARE YOU ALL RIGHT, TARYN?" Dr. Panju asked, placing a hand on her shoulder.

Taryn stared blankly at the images before her: a brain with horrible damage, damage caused by tiny infectors called prions, folded proteins that the body didn't recognize as dangerous. Andrew's body. Andrew's brain. Unknowingly destroying itself each time a cell reproduced.

"Would you like to lie down?" Dr. Winters asked. "You're terribly pale."

She shook her head, forcing herself to refocus on the condition for the benefit of her husband. "Can I have some water, please?"

"Of course," Dr. Winters said, stepping away. "I'll check on your CBC we took the other day to see if your potassium is low."

She nodded, thinking only of her husband.

"Would you like me to continue?" Dr. Panju asked, giving her shoulder a tender squeeze.

"Andrew. He went to Oxford in 1990 for a track-and-field tournament. He said he ate lots of beef. He loves English beef."

"Oh dear."

"Yeah. So, this is bovine encephalopathy?" she asked, pointing at the monitors. "You're saying my husband has mad cow disease?"

"No, not exactly. Andrew has Creutzfeldt-Jakob disease. *Variant* Creutzfeldt-Jakob disease, to be precise: vCJD. It is spongiform in nature and is believed to be caused by ingesting the bovine variant prions."

Taryn thought about the diseases she'd reviewed before running to the hospital. Of the several listed, the ones she'd skipped over had been the true culprits. *Bovine encephalopathy*, BE, mad cow disease. *Scrapie*, the BE equivalent in sheep. Why had she discarded those so off-handedly? She closed her eyes and took a deep breath. Would it have done any good anyway?

"Tell me more," she asked softly, knowing the information would do nothing for Andrew but still needing to understand. "Andrew eats everything well done. Why aren't prions destroyed in cooking?"

"We're not sure," Dr. Panju admitted. "They're not 'alive' in the same way bacteria and viruses are, so you can't really 'kill' them. Even so, prions show no reduction in ability to transmit disease despite being subject to microfiltration, pressurization, superheated steam, hours of focused radiation, months of soaking in formaldehyde, or even being incinerated to ash."

Dr. Winters returned with a small bottle of water. He opened it and handed it to Taryn. She took a sip and sat back, feeling completely numb. Was there anything that could be done against these super organisms? Was it even an organism? No. It was just a piece of protein, a sloppy line of genetic code that caused the nervous system to self-destruct.

Nothing can be done for him. She tried to speak but couldn't get herself to say the words that would condemn her husband. Drs. Panju and Winters waited patiently for her to gain her composure.

"So there is no cure?"

Dr. Panju sighed and drew a random pattern on his desktop with the stylus. "Researchers are working on ways to combat prion replication, but as of now . . ." He sighed again. "I am terribly sorry."

"The hard answer is no, Taryn," Dr. Winters said. "There is no cure. All we can do is keep him comfortable and—"

"And wait for him to die," Taryn finished.

"He is not suffering, I promise," Dr. Winters continued. "We will keep him that way until he passes."

Taryn heard a thousand arguments flashing through her mind, but none of them were loud enough to break through the numbness inundating her. Strangely, what did pierce the emotional miasma were hundreds of unbidden sweet memories: seeing Andrew for the first time on the field, watching him jump impossible distances and launch to astounding heights; the first time he smiled at her and feeling her heart flutter inexplicably in response; an instant friendship without pretenses or games; his openness and feeling his desire for her happiness; his incessant efforts to make her laugh; his willingness to sacrifice his education so she could fulfill her dreams; their wedding, their plans for the future . . .

She screwed her eyes closed in an effort to stop the images.

They were tender and poignant but bittersweet. Their life together was over. They would never create any more memories. She would never again laugh at his jokes, feel his embrace, taste his kiss—

Stop it! She rubbed her eyes forcefully. *Stop being so selfish!* She needed to focus on how she could make Andrew his happiest right now in the little time they had left.

"How long?" she asked in a voice shaky with effort.

Dr. Panju brought up a screen with several brain scan images. "I have compared Andrew's current condition with scans from other patients with vCJD. His spongiform deterioration has been very rapid. I do not believe he has much time left."

She stiffened and braced herself. "How long?" she insisted.

"Days to mere hours, I'm afraid."

She nodded courageously, yet she felt anything but brave. "Is he cognizant? Can he sense anything?"

"We don't know," Dr. Winters answered. "He doesn't appear to respond to any stimuli. It could be the drugs, or it could be the condition."

"Can he hear?"

"Again, we don't know."

"May I try?"

"Of course you can," Dr. Winters said, gesturing toward the door.

Taryn stood shakily. She extended a hand that trembled uncontrollably to the radiologist. "Thank you, Dr. Panju. It helps to understand."

He stood and took her hand in both of his. "I wish I had better news for you."

"Me too."

CHAPTER NINETEEN

Saturday, July 22, 2000

Taryn stopped outside Andrew's room. The brightness beyond the blinds had lessened to the muted hues of evening. The interior was still somber, but it no longer held the foreboding it previously had.

"Can I get you anything?" Dr. Winters asked.

"No, thank you," she said with sincere appreciation. "But thank you for helping me understand what is happening. You should probably contact the other members of the track team that went with Andrew to Oxford."

"My staff is already looking into that. Carlmont High School is helping us get the word out. If there's anything else I can do for you—"

"I'll be sure to ask," she cut across gently. "Right now, I'd like to be alone with my husband."

The doctor nodded, smiled tenderly, then left.

Taryn took a moment to gather herself before entering the room. Andrew lay peacefully with his eyes closed. His body pulsed with a mildly controlled tremor. His breathing was deep and coarse but without struggle. She sat on the edge of his bed and placed her hand on his chest, then leaned forward and kissed his cheek.

Placing her lips next to his ear, she whispered, "I love you, Birdman. I wish I could do more for you, but I can't. I wish I could give you a particle of what you have given me, but anything I think of falls way short. I don't want you to go like this, and I don't want to be left alone. I . . . I wish I had a part of you to always be with me. We always talked about having a family. I don't know why we waited so long to start trying, but I regret waiting like we did. I had my career and you had your Olympic goals and—"

She stopped to wipe the tears from her face. Excuses were no good now. Why try to justify inaction that could never be rectified? It wouldn't do her any good and it certainly wouldn't help Andrew feel better. If he was still able to hear her, she shouldn't fill his head with regrets. She should do whatever she could to buoy him up in his last . . . hours? Minutes?

A soft rap on the door made her sit up.

Nurse Sarah poked her head inside. "Taryn, you doing okay?"

"Yes," she said, again wiping her face. "Come in."

"I heard the news. I am so sorry. How are you holding up?"

"Coming to grips." She looked back at Andrew's peaceful face. "The doctors aren't sure whether or not he can still hear or understand, so I thought I'd talk to him as if he can."

Sarah stepped over and extended her hand. In it was a folded sheet of paper. "Then you might want to tell him the good news."

Taryn frowned. How could there be any good news at a time like this?

"The blood panel we did on you came back with a bit of a surprise."

Taryn unfolded the paper and held it to the light. She gasped, bringing her hand to her mouth. She looked at Sarah through new tears. The nurse had tears in her eyes too. Sarah gave her a tight, lingering hug, then turned and left the room.

Taryn leaned back down to Andrew's ear. "Sweetheart," she said through her sobs. "I have great news. We aren't going to be separated. Part of you is in me now, creating a legacy for us. I will always have a part of you with me! We're going to have a baby, Andrew! A baby! I hope you're as happy as I am. Oh sweetheart, I love you so much." She tenderly held his face in both of her hands and kissed him.

Pulling back, she drew another gasp. His eyes were open. They wandered briefly before locking onto hers, then held them steady for a full minute. "Andrew?" she whispered fervently.

A faint hint of a smile tugged at one side of his mouth. Then slowly, his stare drifted off toward the window, breaking their brief connection. But Taryn had seen perception in his eyes. He understood what she had said. She was certain of it.

* * *

Early the next morning, Taryn lay by Andrew's side, nestled next to him as she loved to do. There was an overwhelming sensation of calm in the room.

She snuggled closer—and felt Andrew stop shaking. Her hand on his chest rose as he took a deep, prolonged breath, then fell as it slowly rattled out. She held him tightly, silently pleading for him to draw another breath. But none came. She lay motionless for a time, not wanting to ever leave, not wanting to accept what had just happened. But she knew she must.

She kissed his ear and quietly whispered, "Sleep well, Birdman. I will always love you." She buried her face in his shoulder and wept, both with sorrow and happiness—sorrow for the loss of her soulmate and happiness for the end to his suffering and for the continuation of his life growing within her.

ACKNOWLEDGMENTS

There are always several people I wish to thank upon completion of any novel. In the case of *Insidious*, my utmost gratitude goes to my good friend and colleague Dr. Jim Davis. His knowledge of emergency medicine and clinical diseases was of particular value to this story. If there are any procedural errors in the telling, the fault is mine. I would also like to thank Cecelia Andrade for her suggestion on how to rescue a tale with an unavoidably sad ending. And as ever, I wish to thank my beta readers, Erika Luke and Melissa Duce, for checking continuity, content, and ever-elusive typos. Last but never least, my sincere thanks to the wonderful, ever-vigilant, ever-encouraging staff at Covenant Communications. They are the best!

For those interested in learning more about prions, spongiform syndromes, and variant Creutzfeldt-Jakob disease, I strongly recommend the book *Deadly Feasts* by Richard Rhodes.

ABOUT THE AUTHOR

Gregg R. Luke, RPh, was born in Bakersfield, California, but spent the majority of his childhood and young-adult life in Santa Barbara, California.

He served a mission for The Church of Jesus Christ of Latter-day Saints in Wisconsin then pursued his education in natural sciences at SBCC, UCSB, and BYU. He completed his schooling at the University of Utah, College of Pharmacy, including a rotation with the Utah Poison Control Center.

Gregg currently practices pharmacy in Logan, Utah. He is a voracious reader and has been writing stories since childhood. He has been published in *Skin Diver* magazine, *The Oceanographic Letter*, *Destiny* magazine, and the *New Era* magazine. His fiction includes *The Survivors, Do No Harm, Altered State, Blink of an Eye, Bloodborne, Deadly Undertakings,* and *The Healer, Infected, The Hunter's Son,* and *Plague,* six of which were Whitney Award finalists. His novella "The Death House" was included in an anthology with Traci Hunter Abramson and Stephanie Black.

Find out more about Gregg's novels at www.greggluke.com.

SOMETHING BEAUTIFUL FOR SOMETHING EVIL

STEPHANIE BLACK

CHAPTER 1

HE'S A SMALL BUSINESS CONSULTANT, Kate told herself as she stared at the paper she'd found behind the shredder in Colby's home office. *She must be one of his clients, or he's hoping to take her on as a client.* He was always scouting for clients. It wasn't necessarily strange that he hadn't mentioned he was approaching her new boss.

Kate read the paper again, struggling to think of a reason why a business-related document would include notes of Jamie Stokes's habits. How could the fact that Jamie left home two hours before her husband on Tuesday and Thursday mornings and at the same time as her husband on Mondays, Wednesdays, and Fridays possibly be information Colby would need in order to advise her about the iconic town gift shop she owned? How could the facts that she parked near the west entrance to the grocery store when she shopped and carried a large blue-and-white polka-dot handbag be relevant to anything professional? Or the fact that she preferred gold jewelry to silver and particularly liked unique, handcrafted necklaces and earrings?

Jamie was young; she couldn't be much older than Kate's twenty-six. She was pretty, with a heart-shaped face, brown eyes, and chestnut-brown hair curving to her shoulders.

Grow up, Kate. You find a business paper you don't understand and you panic that your husband is cheating on you?

Kate realized she was clutching the vacuum hose while the vacuum hummed dutifully at her feet, waiting for her to finish the baseboards. She set the paper on Colby's desk and forced herself to resume vacuuming. She would not be clingy. She trusted Colby.

But Colby could be so stubbornly private. He'd refused to open a joint bank account with her or apply for joint credit cards. She never saw any of his financial statements. Did he not want Kate to have access to his accounts because she'd see purchases like jewelry he hadn't given to Kate? *Unique, handcrafted necklaces and earrings?*

"Hey, Katie." Colby's voice wafted over the growl of the vacuum. Kate looked up to see him standing in the doorway, holding a flat, white box.

She fumbled with the vacuum, searching in the wrong place for the power button. Finally, she managed to switch it off. "Hi, hon. How was your day?"

"Good. And you are the best. When I mentioned the baseboards in here needed vacuuming, I didn't mean for you to do it. I was planning to take care of it."

"After painting all afternoon, I wanted a break."

"Still working on the Berkshires landscape?"

"Yes, because I'm waiting for you to tell me what you want in here." She gestured at the blank wall above the desk. "Your birthday is next month, so hurry up."

"Everything from your paintbrush is beautiful, so it's hard to decide. Love you, babe." Colby rested his free hand against the doorframe, looking like he was modeling his striped shirt and silk tie for a men's clothing ad. Full lips, Roman nose, hair cut short on the sides and gelled upward on top, sculpted biceps—everything about Colby attracted Kate. Did it attract Jamie?

Shoving her insecurity away, she went to kiss him. He wrapped his arms around her and magnified her brief kiss into a long, silent greeting.

"What's on the stove?" he asked as he released her. "It smells great."

"It's . . . um . . ." Flushed and distracted, Kate couldn't remember what she'd cooked.

Colby grinned, obviously pleased that his kiss had left her wobbly.

"Soup," she said. "Minestrone. It's ready anytime we want to eat it."

"I won the jackpot on perfect wives." He offered her the box. "I got you something to celebrate your new job."

"You're the sweetest!" Kate opened the box. Inside, wrapped in tissue paper, lay a small notebook made of powder-blue leather. On the cover, sparkling teal and purple crystals formed a peacock.

"You said your boss suggested you carry a notebook," Colby said.

At the mention of Jamie, Kate's joy glitched. "I'm impressed you remembered," she said, trying to sound casual. "Thank you. This is gorgeous. Peacocks are my favorite."

"I know."

Kate glanced at the desk. She couldn't endure having her excitement about the gift tainted by ridiculous worries. She'd ask him about the paper straight out, like she would any business paper she found lying around—not that Colby usually left papers or anything else lying around. He was meticulously tidy. "Speaking of Jamie Stokes, I didn't know if this was something you still needed." She went to pick up the paper. "Is the Treasure Chest a new client?"

Colby took the paper from her hand and scanned it. "Where did you find this?"

"Behind the shredder, when I was vacuuming."

He folded the paper and jammed it into his pocket. "Did you mention this to Jamie or to anyone?"

"Why do you ask?"

He gripped her shoulders. Kate tried to shrug him off, but his fingers tightened. *"Did you mention this to anyone?"*

The stone-hard urgency in his manner smashed her hope that the paper was business-related. "No. I just found it."

"Okay." He released her. "Okay, Katie. That wasn't something for your eyes."

Kate stepped backward. "Then you should have made sure you shredded it."

"Yeah, I screwed up." Colby's face had a stoic blankness she'd never seen before. Beneath his tailored shirt, his ribcage moved with two deep breaths. "This needs to be a sit-down conversation."

Keeping her balance felt like attempting to walk during an earthquake as Kate followed him into the living room. One year into her marriage, and it was over. Colby was involved with Jamie—friendly Jamie, who'd enthusiastically welcomed Kate to Britteridge and assured her she'd love it here, who'd acted delighted to have Kate working at her store. Kate had thought Jamie and Colby had met for the first time when Colby had picked Kate up from her interview last week. Had he met Jamie earlier, on a business trip, before they'd moved here two months ago? Colby had been the one to tell Kate about the opening at the Treasure Chest and suggest she apply. Had Jamie hired her to give herself more excuses to see Colby?

"Sit down," Colby said. Kate thought about grabbing her purse and stalking out the front door, but she sat on the couch. She ought to give him a chance to explain. Maybe she was jumping to conclusions.

Colby closed the window Kate had opened earlier to welcome a fresh September breeze into their apartment. "I'm sorry, Katie." He closed the blinds. "I didn't mean to upset you. That report doesn't mean what you think. I'm not involved with Jamie Stokes."

Kate battled the urge to let her tears flow. "Why are you keeping a schedule of when she's home and her husband isn't?"

He sat next to her and reached for her hand. She withdrew it. The room was dim now, and though it was clean, it felt suddenly grimy to Kate. Why had he closed the blinds, blocking the early evening light?

"What a mess," he muttered. "I can't believe I missed that paper. I don't know what's wrong with me."

"Maybe keeping secrets is wearing on you."

"Yeah, actually, I think it is." He rubbed his eyes. "This is a secret I hated keeping. I'm not supposed to share it with you, or anyone. But I'm not going to leave you worrying I'm having an affair. The people I work for will have to deal."

"You work for yourself," Kate said, bewildered.

"I'm not talking about Durham Consulting. I . . . have a . . . side gig."

"A side gig?"

"I work for the . . ." He fidgeted with one of his onyx cufflinks. "Truth is, I've wanted to tell you ever since I met you. Maybe it's fortunate I got sloppy."

"What secrets are you keeping?"

"I work for the government," Colby said. "For a task force combating domestic terrorism."

She gaped at him.

"Yeah, I know, it doesn't sound like me, the straight-laced businessman, Mr. Wharton MBA. They recruited me right after I finished my undergrad. I can't give you details of who or how—that's all classified."

Thoughts swung and flipped and twirled through her brain. "Is . . . that why you travel so much?"

"My travel's been about three-fourths business related and one-fourth connected to the task force. Up until now, I haven't done much for them, but that's changing. I hope this doesn't make you angrier, but . . . they're the reason we moved to Massachusetts. My supervisor asked me to relocate." Colby smiled sheepishly. "When I told you a growing portion of my business was in the Boston area, it was mostly true. I just didn't clarify which business."

Kate tried to process this. She didn't mind the move itself. She'd been happy to leave Pittsburgh, since budget cuts had eliminated her part-time job as an elementary-school art teacher, and the only thing she'd liked about her other job at a home décor store was the fact that she'd met Colby there when he'd come in to order curtains for his apartment. But she *did* mind that Colby had moved them to Britteridge under false pretenses. "Why did he want you here?"

"We're keeping an eye on an anti-government group that's gotten more active lately."

"You're . . . CIA?"

"No. We operate under the direction of the Department of Homeland Security." Colby touched her cheek. "I'm really sorry. Every time I had to hide things from you, I hated it. I'll be in boiling water for telling you any of this, but I'll take any consequence over letting you think I'm chasing another woman."

"What does Jamie Stokes have to do with this?"

"I hope nothing, because I know you like her, but we've received information we have to explore. I've been assigned to learn everything I can about her."

"Did you know her before you got this assignment?"

"You met her before I did. The only time I've talked to her is when I picked you up from the Treasure Chest last week, but one of my Durham Consulting clients is her old high school English teacher. He's now running a private tutoring company."

"Is that relevant?" Kate asked, doubting it was. Colby was the master of small-world connections. He was perpetually linking people with each other and with himself.

"Right now, we don't know which details might be relevant, so there's a lot of clutter in my report. The page you found is one of about fifty."

"May I see the page again?"

"Why not? Makes no difference now." He slid it out of his pocket.

She unfolded it. As she read it in the context of Colby's explanations, crushing anger and fear lightened somewhat. The information did make sense as a list of facts about a person under investigation. Most of the information, at least. "Why would you care about her jewelry preferences?"

"I told you, we don't know what's important yet. I was looking for any hints of wealth that didn't match up with what she and her husband earn. Expensive jewelry could be a marker of that. Or expensive designer clothes. You can see where I noted—" He checked the paper. "Oh, the thing about clothes is on the next page. She doesn't wear pricy brands, by the way. I didn't spot anything suspicious in how she dresses."

Kate liked Jamie's colorful, comfortable style, but unlike Colby, she wasn't experienced at recognizing designer brands. She had no idea if Jamie's blouses and slacks were JCPenney or Prada. "What does her husband do?"

"He's a professor at Britteridge College. Teaches ballroom dance. So he's not raking in the big bucks."

Kate's gaze fixed on the watercolor hanging on the wall—her painting of the 40th Street Bridge viewed from Herrs Island. The reference photo she'd used was one she'd taken on the evening Colby had first kissed her. "It's . . . hard to imagine Jamie being involved with terrorists. Then again, I've only met her in person twice."

"I know what you're thinking, and I don't blame you. You're wondering if I'm making up crazy lies to hide my affair. I wish I could give you more information. More evidence. I'll try to get permission to do that. Can you trust me enough to wait?"

Kate attempted to sound teasing. "I don't suppose you have a badge, like a cop? Or an ID card?"

He jumped to his feet. "You know, babe, I do have an ID. Didn't even think of that—obviously, I don't carry it with me most of the time. I only use it when I'm at headquarters, in DC. It's in my safe. Hang on." He headed into his study. A couple minutes later, he returned and handed Kate an ID card on a blue lanyard.

She examined the card. It displayed Colby's name, picture, and several combinations of letters and numbers that meant nothing to Kate. A holographic overlay bearing the white-eagle seal of the U.S. Department of Homeland Security covered the front of the card. Colby's hair was longer in the picture and his face more boyish.

"You look about eighteen," Kate said.

"I was twenty-two. Told you, it was right after I got my bachelor's degree. Let me put that back in the safe."

Kate passed him the ID. He hurried to stow it, as though uncomfortable having the ID in the open air of the apartment, even with the blinds shut. When he returned, he sat next to her, closer than before. "I can't overemphasize how important it is that you tell no one about any of this. I'm trusting you with my life, Katie. If word leaks as to who I am and what I'm doing, I'm dead." He reached for her hand again, and she let him take it. "I feel horrible about blindsiding you. You thought you were signing up for a peaceful civilian life when you married me. Now I'm hitting you with something way out of your comfort zone."

At the moment, Kate was so relieved he wasn't cheating on her that nothing sounded outside her comfort zone. "I can handle things beyond a peaceful civilian life."

He smiled and kissed her forehead like a father amused by a daughter who'd declared herself Wonder Woman. Did he think she *couldn't* handle anything beyond quiet suburbia?

"I'm supposed to start work tomorrow." She pulled her hand free. "I'm shadowing Jamie for a few hours, then she's giving me the full orientation after the store closes. Why did you suggest I apply at the Treasure Chest if it puts me in the middle of a terrorist plot?"

"You won't be in the middle of anything except a gift shop. Whatever Jamie might have going on the side, the Treasure Chest is a legitimate business. It's been around for over fifty years. Jamie took over a few months ago. The original owner deeded it to her when he retired."

"She bought it?"

"No, he gave it to her. Quite the gift, right? As far as we can tell, it was on the up-and-up. He was a pillar of the town, a wealthy philanthropist type of guy— he's retired to Florida now—and we can't find evidence that he was ever involved in anything shady. Jamie's mother worked at the Treasure Chest for decades, and Jamie followed in her footsteps. The owner viewed her as a granddaughter."

Kate pictured the two-story Treasure Chest, with its gray clapboard siding and burgundy shutters, its black-and-gilt sign, its planter boxes filled with orange-and rust-colored chrysanthemums. She'd loved the smells of cinnamon and paint, the shelves of handcrafted merchandise, the antique wooden floors. That was quite a gift to give someone. Had Jamie manipulated the owner somehow? "Even if there's nothing unsavory taking place at the store itself, I don't understand why you'd want me working alongside a suspected terrorist."

Colby massaged the back of her neck. "We didn't get the tip about Jamie Stokes until she'd already hired you. When I found out she was under suspicion, I told my supervisor I'd ask you to withdraw your acceptance, that I'd claim I'd learned the Treasure Chest was a rotten, stressful place to work. He was adamant you shouldn't withdraw, that a change of heart risked compromising our mission."

"How?"

"Britteridge is too small of a town. It would be easy for Jamie to learn you were still job-hunting and get suspicious as to why you changed your mind about the Treasure Chest, especially since it would be a plum connection for you in establishing yourself as a local artist. He's been tracking this group for years, and he swears you won't be in danger working there. It took him a while, but he convinced me he was right. Trust me, if I didn't agree with him, I'd have moved us both to the South Pole before I'd have let you work for that woman."

"Your supervisor should have given you permission to tell me the truth and let me decide whether or not I wanted to work there."

"Classified stuff is maddening sometimes, but we have to be careful."

"What is this terrorist group up to?"

"I can't discuss that."

"Tell your supervisor I'm capable of keeping secrets. Especially when lives are at stake."

"I will. I will. I trust you, and he should too. Fact is, Katie . . . please don't punch me for this . . . they already ran a background check on you before we got married."

"They investigated *me*?"

"Not with my permission, but yeah. They wanted to make sure you weren't a security risk."

How extensive had the check been? The thought of Colby's superiors researching her mediocre academic history, her lack of savings, the boyfriends who'd dumped her, her inability to make any kind of a living from her artwork or to nail down a satisfying full-time job at all . . . They must have wondered what successful, handsome, sophisticated Colby saw in her. "What if I had been a security risk?"

He grinned. "Then I would have quit the task force and married you anyway. They'd have had to recruit some other sucker to take my place."

Kate leaned toward him and kissed him. "You'd be hard to replace."

"I agree, so thanks for passing the background check."

"Colby . . . if you think Jamie Stokes might have ties to a domestic terrorist group, can't I help you? Your boss doesn't want me to quit, so let me be useful there. I'll be working with Jamie almost every day. I could do a better job keeping an eye on her than any of your agents could, and she'd have no reason to suspect anything."

He slid forward on the couch and braced his elbows on his knees. "I knew that was coming. I knew you'd want to help."

New adrenaline glittered through her bloodstream. "It would be a waste for me not to help. I can look around and listen in a natural way."

"Babe, listen. You read spy novels. You love spy movies. In every Halloween picture I've seen of you, you're Carmen Sandiego, Agent 99, or some other glamorous save-the-world type. But real undercover work isn't like that."

Kate flushed. "I know that."

"You haven't trained for this. I'd worry about getting you involved."

"I'm not suggesting I scale the walls of the Treasure Chest and steal secret missile schematics or whatever you think my perception of your work is. I'm suggesting I keep my eyes and ears open and tell you what I observe."

His expression switched from frown to grin to frown. "I need to run it past my supervisor. The stakes are too high for any of us to go rogue."

"If you could get permission to tell me what type of things I should watch for, I could be even more of an asset to you."

His mouth stabilized in a grin. "It's a good idea, letting you gather intelligence. I'll talk to him, okay?"

"Thank you." Exhilaration flooded Kate at the thought of showing up to work tomorrow, pretending to focus on learning the business of the Treasure Chest while really focusing on uncovering and stopping terrorists.

That sounded far more exciting than selling harvest wreaths and ceramic pumpkins, and Jamie Stokes would never suspect that her smiley new clerk was reporting to the Department of Homeland Security.

CHAPTER 2

K EYS IN HER HAND FROM locking the front door at the end of the business day, Jamie watched her new employee flit between displays of autumn-themed handicrafts.

"Everything is so adorable!" Kate Durham picked up a porcelain black cat with yellow-jeweled eyes and made duck lips at it. "Sooooo cute. Meow, little kitty."

"I'm glad you like it." Jamie smiled—almost sincerely—at Kate, pleased that she was enthusiastic but less pleased that Kate seemed to have lost about a decade's worth of maturity since Jamie had made the decision to hire her. Kate was as adorable as the merchandise she was admiring: blush-pink, round cheeks; apple-cider-colored hair cut in a style Jamie figured would be the first hit if she googled "short, sassy hairstyles for women." At both the initial and follow-up interviews, Kate's cheerful demeanor, retail experience, artistic talent, and intelligent responses had convinced Jamie there was more than cuteness to Kate. Now, watching her bounce around the Treasure Chest's main room, squealing over silk sunflowers and nutmeg-scented candles, Jamie was starting to question her own judgment.

She was fine with customers while she was shadowing you today, Jamie reminded herself, watching Kate select town hall from a display of hand-carved Britteridge landmarks and study the underside of it with big eyes, as though checking for termites. *Now that she's alone with the owner, she's just nervous, wondering how she did today.*

The owner. *I'm the owner.* That fact still felt fresh, thrilling, and overwhelming. *You can do this. You'll be fine.*

Kate set town hall down and swished across the aisle to snatch a hickory-wood basket painted with red and green apples. "Thank you so much for giving me the opportunity to work here, Mrs. Stokes."

"Call me Jamie."

"Okay. Jamie. I want to post pictures of *everything*!"

"Please do. I run the Treasure Chest's official social media accounts, but we love it when employees and customers post pictures on their own accounts and tag us."

"Oh, for sure!" Kate hugged the basket. "My friends will *die* at how precious this stuff is."

"Handmade items should have gold 'Handcrafted by' stickers identifying the artist," Jamie said. "When business is slow and you're straightening merchandise, check for missing stickers. Sometimes they fall off, or we miss marking an item or two."

Kate set the basket on the display table. "Extra stickers are in the second drawer down under the register, right?"

"Yes," Jamie said, glad Kate was remembering instructions. A dud of a hiring decision would have given the town complainers new ammunition against the way Jamie was running the Treasure Chest, and they'd found enough to pick on already. "If we're out of stickers for a particular artist, make a note of it, and I'll print new ones."

"Got it."

"Take advantage of slow times to get familiar with our stock." Jamie walked to the front display window and picked up a few pieces of straw that had fallen to the floor. White and orange lights twinkled in the window, bright accents against the twilight sky outside. "Our customers love recommendations, and if you remember customers' tastes and make personalized suggestions, they feel flattered and cared for."

"I have my notebook." Kate joined Jamie at the window as Jamie straightened the scarecrow slouching in a distressed wood chair. "My husband gave it to me." Out of her apron pocket, Kate pulled a blue-leather journal with a jeweled peacock on the cover.

"It's beautiful." Jamie had met Colby Durham when he'd picked Kate up after her first interview. Handsome, young businessman, so perfectly groomed that Jamie had felt self-conscious about shaking his smooth hand when she'd had paint stains under her fingernails and a hot-glue-gun burn on her index finger.

"I love it." Kate opened the notebook and showed Jamie where she'd jotted notes on a regular customer she'd served under Jamie's supervision.

"Nice job." Jamie spotted red patches on the skin around the neckline of Kate's dress. The whimsical spikes of hair around her ears were damp with sweat.

The room wasn't hot—Kate *was* nervous, and apparently, bubble-headed overenthusiasm was her coping skill. "You're doing great, Kate. You're a natural with customers. Before we go upstairs, do you have any questions about the main room or the crystal room?"

Kate giggled. "Just how do I keep myself from buying one of those gorgeous vases with the dried flowers pressed inside the glass? I don't think my husband would appreciate me spending the rent money on a vase."

"It's a challenge. For years, I had to leave all cash and credit cards at home so I couldn't surrender to instant gratification." Jamie escorted Kate up the staircase to the second level.

"Everything is so homey," Kate said. "These wood floors!"

"The beauty of the wood is worth the creaking." Jamie decided not to admit that sometimes the creaking still made her jump when she was here alone. "This was originally a private residence, built in 1948. In the midsixties, Edward Allerton's father modified it into the Treasure Chest. It's been a Britteridge landmark ever since."

"It's so perfectly New England-y!"

"I think so." Jamie gestured Kate through the doorway of the linen room. "Any questions about the merchandise here?"

"Let's see." Kate darted from display rack to display rack. "All the fabric home goods are in this room. Handmade quilts are one of our signature items. Formal tablecloths are here"—she pointed—"informal tablecloths are here, and the red-and-white checked tablecloths embroidered with chickens are particularly popular. Place mats, embroidered dish towels, oven mitts, throw pillows . . . but we don't carry bed sheets or pillowcases."

"Good job," Jamie said.

"You told me some of the quilters will do special orders. Where is the information on that?"

"Right here." Jamie opened a drawer on a nineteenth-century cherrywood cabinet and took out a three-ring binder with a quilted cover displaying the logo her mother had designed thirty years ago: a treasure chest overflowing with gold coins, flowers, and knickknacks. "Each of our quilters has a section where it lists options and pricing. If a customer wants something not listed in the binder, give them the quilter's business card." Jamie showed Kate the inside front cover of the binder, where business cards were organized in clear-plastic compartments. "They can contact the quilter directly and do their own negotiations."

"Perfect. Oh, who knew pot holders could be so darling?" Kate held up an orange potholder embroidered with black bats.

"Every year, I'm excited to see the seasonal crafts our artists create," Jamie said. "Any other questions about the linen room?"

"I can't think of any right now."

"Let's have a look at the book room." Jamie headed into the hallway, with Kate following her. "The main responsibility you'll have there is checking regularly to make sure things are tidy. We want it to be a pleasant, relaxing spot for customers who'd like to linger and read for a while, enjoy the ambience. We have some regulars who'll read for hours in there—after spending plenty of money on the sales floor."

"You don't sell the books themselves, right? But people can borrow—oh, this is lovely!" Kate paused at a circular table near the entrance to the book room, where Jamie had placed a porcelain wishing well surrounded by miniature porcelain flowers.

"That was a gift from the committee that runs the town's annual spring gala," Jamie said. "We always help with the gala."

"I'd love to get involved." Kate leaned over the well and read aloud the brass plaque on the base of it. "'*To the Treasure Chest. It takes many sources of clear water to fill the well that nourishes our town. Thank you for being one of our springs. With gratitude, Glenda Sagramore and the Britteridge Spring Gala Committee.*' That's a sweet play on words. Oops, I don't think this belongs here." Kate reached into the well and pulled out a figurine. "A customer must have changed their mind and stashed it—eww, this is creepy. I like the cute Halloween stuff . . . oh . . . I'm sorry, I didn't mean to . . . I didn't realize . . ."

Jamie couldn't imagine what item among her inventory could earn a "creepy" rating, nor why Kate's whole face was now fiery crimson. She went to take the figurine.

It was a flat wooden doll of a woman, about eight inches tall. The doll's face was snowy white with eyes closed. Her lips and the skin around her lips were blotched with green. One hand held a bucket stained with rivulets of green and marked with a tiny skull and crossbones. Shallow carving added texture to the doll's features. Painted strands of chestnut-brown hair framed wide cheekbones and a pointed chin. The figurine wore a cranberry-red Treasure Chest apron over gray slacks and a navy ruffle-sleeved blouse Jamie recognized as one of her favorite shirts. The black loafers on the figurine's feet matched the comfortable loafers she wore at least once a week.

"That's so well done," Kate said, transparently worried she'd offended Jamie. "Did you paint it?"

"No." Jamie rotated the doll, scrutinizing all sides of it. "It's not part of my inventory. I definitely do not sell Jamie dolls. I have no idea what it's doing here." She smiled at Kate. "Must be an early Halloween prank from one of our artists. I'll plot my revenge." She tucked the doll into the pocket of her apron. "Come on and let me show you our book catalog system."

* * *

In the brisk evening breeze, Kate walked along the path that crossed the back lawn of the Treasure Chest. When Colby had dropped her off this afternoon, the grounds had been so breathtaking that she'd wanted to grab an easel and canvas and paint everything in sight—ruby and citrine leaves drifting onto emerald grass, the redbrick path lined by wrought-iron lampposts, the Treasure Chest itself. Now, in darkness, the illumination from the lamps seemed weak, leaves made a haunting rustle, and she feared if she looked back, she'd see Jamie watching her from a window.

Though she wanted to get to Colby as quickly as possible, Kate controlled her pace. Hurrying might appear suspicious. She reached the smaller building on the property, a hall Jamie had told her they rented out for parties and receptions, and turned left toward the graveled parking area located behind a low stone wall.

Colby's Dodge Charger waited in the lot, exhaust steaming from the tailpipe. The only other car was a green Subaru Outback that must be Jamie's.

Kate opened the passenger door on the Charger, grateful she'd let Colby chauffeur her on her first day. She'd have been skittish getting into her own dark, empty car, wondering if she should check underneath it for a bomb.

"Thanks for picking me up," she said, settling into her seat.

"Cranked the heat for you." Colby shifted into reverse. "Cold tonight, huh?"

"Thanks." She usually wanted the car warmer than Colby did, but despite the chilly walk, she remained hot from nervousness. She didn't want to admit that to Colby and turn the heat down.

"How did it go?" he asked.

"It was good." Casually, she adjusted a vent so it wasn't blasting her quite so directly. "I think Jamie likes me. She was impressed at how quickly I learned things."

"Nice! You impressed your boss a lot more than I impressed mine."

"Did you talk to . . . ?" Kate trailed off, not sure how frank she could be.

"Yeah, I talked to my supervisor." He grimaced. "I got skinned alive. But he agreed it was wiser to tell you the truth than to let you think I was having an affair with Jamie, which might have led to disaster. I told him you'd offered to keep an eye on things and that I was confident you had the smarts and the guts to do it."

Colby's endorsement pleased her. "What did he say?"

"He called me an idiot. Asked what I was thinking to suggest involving an amateur. I said you didn't need training to keep your eyes open. After ranting for a while, he warmed up to the idea. Truth is, we're shorthanded at the moment, and he couldn't dispute that it would be helpful to have you reporting in. They already ran that background check on you, so they know you're solid."

"So he agreed?"

"He agreed to let you help as long as you don't do *anything* we don't specifically instruct you to do. Right now, all he wants is for you to do your job like a regular employee and keep your eyes open. Agreed?"

"Yes." Elation at this provisional thumbs-up overshadowed the jitters she'd felt a moment ago. "It will be easy to take notes on customers or on things Jamie does. She *wants* me writing things down." Kate tapped the corner of her notebook sticking out of her purse.

"Yeah, that's fortunate. Did you see anything noteworthy today?"

"A strange thing happened at the end of the day, after she'd closed the store." As Colby drove through downtown, she told him about the painted doll. "I kept close watch on Jamie's face when I handed her the doll, and I could tell it startled her. She said it must be a practical joke from one of their artists and made a crack about getting revenge on them."

"Revenge?"

"Yes. She said it like a joke, but I got the vibe she didn't really think the doll was funny. She hid it in her apron pocket and quickly changed the subject."

"Huh. That's interesting."

"The doll was eerie. The clothes were normal, the apron, her hair, her features—everything was normal except the bucket of poison and the way the face was painted to make it appear she'd poisoned herself. Whoever carved and painted it is a skilled artist. It seriously looked like her."

"Can you sketch it when we get home? Just a rough sketch of what you remember?"

"I can do better than a rough sketch."

He chuckled. "True. How are you feeling after all this? Pretty crazy twist in your life."

"I'm glad I can help."

At a stoplight, he smiled at her. "You're doing great, Katie. That intel about the doll is important. We wouldn't have it without you."

The light turned green, and Colby made a hasty left turn in front of oncoming traffic. That Boston maneuver always made Kate cringe. "Can I ask if you have any idea what the doll means?"

"I can guess. My supervisor—by the way, you can call him Lorenzo. It's not his real name, but it's what I call him. He gave me permission to tell you a little more. I'm going to take a long route home, if you don't mind, to give us more time to talk. Lorenzo doesn't want us discussing things in our apartment until I scan it for bugs."

"But we already sat in the living room and discussed—"

"Yeah, he knows. Believe me, I got yelled at for it. We need to make sure the place is clean before we discuss anything else there."

"If there *are* listening devices, we need to go into hiding," Kate said grimly.

"There won't be. I'm not worried. Okay, here's what I can tell you. The group we're investigating is an antigovernment group called Eviction. They believe the national government—all parties and branches—is so corrupt that the only way to save the nation is to destroy the government entirely."

"And replace it with what?"

"Unclear. They seem to be an anarchist group more than anything. Sporadic acts of small-scope violence to rile people up. But we've received intelligence that a bigger operation is in the works, an attack involving a deadly toxin."

"A toxin?" Kate thought of the green poison staining the mouth of the Jamie doll. "So the doll . . ."

"Could be a reference to that, yeah. It could mean Jamie is in conflict with someone in the group, or more than one person, and this is a warning."

"Fall in line, or you'll be one of our victims?"

"Right."

Kate wiped her hands on her dress. The cinnamon-vanilla lotion she'd lavished on her skin from a pump in the Treasure Chest bathroom now felt slippery on her damp palms. First day at work and she'd already found evidence that Jamie *was* involved with terrorists?

Colby turned onto a street near Britteridge College. Flashing red and blue lights caught Kate's attention. Multiple police cars lined the curb. Police tape marked off a white-shingled triplex.

"That must be every patrol car in town," she said. "This looks bad."

Colby slowed the car so he could scan the triplex. "Yeah, I don't think all those cops are here busting kids for underage drinking."

"I hope it's . . . nothing to do with . . ."

Colby accelerated. "I would have heard," he said. "But check the city newsfeed. See if there's any info about what happened here."

Kate pulled out her phone and searched. "A Britteridge College student was found dead by her roommate," she reported. "No name yet, but the police say it appears to be a homicide."

Colby grunted. "What a cute little town this is."

CHAPTER 3

THE SCENTS OF SIMMERING BEEF, coconut, and ginger welcomed Jamie home. Julian experimented with different cuisines each Tuesday, and opening her front door to the aroma of whatever he'd decided to cook this week was one of Jamie's favorite things. She could use a mood boost after that freaky doll. She hung up her jacket, took the doll she'd encased in bubble wrap out of her purse, and headed into the kitchen.

"You're home early, my dearest." Julian set a stirring spoon on the spoon rest he'd made during his pottery phase. "That's a marvelous surprise."

"I was in a hurry to get out of there today," Jamie said, already feeling better. Julian's slightly old-fashioned, slightly florid speech still gave her the feeling she'd married the hero in a historical romance novel. The bow tie, now loosened, the suspenders, and the striped shirt had more of a barbershop-quartet vibe than a Mr. Darcy vibe, but he still looked glorious.

Julian came over and pressed his lips to hers. He tasted like he'd recently sampled the rich beef mixture he'd been stirring. "I don't think I've ever known you to be in a hurry to leave your lair. What happened?"

"This." Jamie unwrapped the doll. "It was in the porcelain wishing well near the book room."

Julian took it and scrutinized it, brow furrowed. "Even taking into account that some people have macabre tastes in Halloween decorations, this is unsettling."

"It's one of Niall Flanagan's personalized dolls."

"Personalized dolls?"

"He sells them himself, not through the Treasure Chest. You send him a picture of the person, and he carves and paints a wooden doll that looks like them. They're especially popular as wedding gifts—bride and groom dolls—or for anniversaries."

Julian set the figurine on the kitchen table and ran his fingers through his dark hair—a curly mass he got trimmed weekly, saying his choices were to shell out for weekly haircuts or declare his hair an independent entity and start charging it rent. "I didn't think Niall had a warped sense of humor."

"He doesn't. The original carving and painting is his work. I've seen thousands of Niall's pieces; I can identify his style. But look at this." Jamie touched the doll's face near the hairline. "The face has been repainted. White wasn't the original color."

"I'm guessing green wasn't either." Julian rubbed the top edge of the bucket in the doll's hand. "Look how the carving is uneven here, rougher than the work on the doll."

"Yes. I think Niall made the original figurine, and someone modified it. Which brings up the question of why Niall would create a doll of me in the first place. What excuse did the customer give him for wanting it?"

"I assume you've called him to ask?"

"Yes, but he didn't pick up. I left a message. If he doesn't call back, I'll talk to him tomorrow at work. He's stopping by to drop off some new owl carvings."

"Excuse me. The beef rendang is burning." Julian moved to the stove. "Do you have any idea why someone would plant a wooden image of you imbibing poison?"

"Yes. I think it's an escalation of the complaints I've gotten about changing things at the store."

"Specifically a dig at your 'hipster herbal tea' collection?"

"Yes." Jamie sat at the table. "I can't wrap my brain around how resistant some customers are to change. The way Edward Allerton and his father did things is the *only* way to do things. Since the Allertons were adamant that the Treasure Chest not sell food—not even gum or breath mints because that was one step away from making ourselves a kitschy tourist trap—my decision to add a display of handcrafted herbal tea blends and artisan chocolate bars is treason."

"It's appalling that you'd sink so low." Julian sprinkled salt into the pan. "And designating a tea or chocolate of the month is rubbing it in their faces. Soon you'll be selling hot dogs, stale donuts, and automobile parts."

"Right? I swear that's what they think."

"Buying a Niall Flanagan doll and repainting it is an expensive and elaborate way to lodge a complaint," Julian said. "Are you certain the doll doesn't mean something else?"

"I can't imagine what else it could mean. And, Julian, we're dealing with people who have sent me letters of complaint written in calligraphy on parchment to resemble historic documents and who have presented me with a handmade, two-volume scrapbook entitled *The Treasure Chest and Its Traditions: A Vital Legacy.* One volume covering Edward Allerton's years, one volume covering his father's."

"I see your point. Do you have a specific suspect in mind for the doll giver?"

Jamie didn't answer. She hated blaming someone without proof, even in conversation with Julian.

Julian set a handful of cashews on a cutting board and started chopping them. "I see. You do have a suspect but don't want to name them. I'll spare you that burden and answer my own question: Marcia Allerton-Harper."

Jamie sighed. Edward Allerton's cousin had the soft gray hair and gentle face of a cuddly grandmother and the soul of a judge at the Salem Witch Trials. With the first change Jamie had made after Allerton's retirement—offering a 15-percent-off coupon in the quarterly newsletter—Marcia had cornered Jamie in her office and lectured her for an hour on the tacky nature of coupons and how it was Jamie's responsibility to carry on Ed's legacy; he wouldn't have given the Treasure Chest to her if he hadn't thought she'd follow precisely in his footsteps. After that, Marcia had spearheaded the creation of the scrapbook and bombarded Jamie with letters, emails, and more visits each time one of Jamie's decisions had offended her. Jamie reflexively checked all possible escape routes every time Marcia entered the Treasure Chest.

"She's not the only one who's complained," Jamie said, attempting to be objective.

"She's been the most confrontational," Julian said. "She's wealthy enough that paying Niall for a hand-carved doll to use as a message wouldn't faze her. Not many people would pay for a Niall Flanagan original simply to gripe."

"I *can* see Marcia wanting to drive home the point that I'm poisoning the Treasure Chest with my tea and chocolate sales. Or rather that I'm poisoning the whole town, including myself."

"Thus the planting of the doll inside the well that symbolized your role as a source of pure water—a source you have now polluted."

"Yes, and Marcia would be likely to think of using the well to send that message. Her sister Glenda is the head of the committee that gave those wishing wells to all the major sponsors of the spring gala, and since Marcia has a finger in every town pie, I imagine she was involved with that."

"Niall will be able to tell you who ordered the doll. Even if Marcia didn't order it herself, the identity of who did will lead us to the real culprit."

"What if she ordered it anonymously? Or under a fake name?"

"My dearest, Niall would never carve a figurine of you for a random crackpot. He knows the person who requested it and why they claimed to want it, or he wouldn't have done it. This will not be a mystery for long."

"True." Jamie rose to wash her hands so she could help Julian with dinner. "Frankly, if it was Marcia, I plan to thank her for leaving the doll rather than haranguing me verbally. The doll is much easier on the ears."

Julian laughed and handed Jamie a bunch of cilantro. "Chop this, if you would. It's for the rice."

Jamie took the cilantro and selected a knife. "The good news is I think my new employee will work out fine. She was nervous today, but she worked hard and paid close attention to everything I told her."

"I'm glad to hear that."

"Tell me about tonight's dinner. It smells delicious."

"Tonight's cuisine is Indonesian. For the beef, I made a spice paste of—"

The doorbell rang. "I'll get it." Jamie wiped her hands on a paper towel.

On the porch stood a tall man in a suit and tie. Bristly dark hair, bony face—if he'd worn a stovepipe hat and a beard, he would have been a dead ringer for Abraham Lincoln. Recognition brought Jamie a spike of anxiety, and she fought an urge to shut the door with the man outside and herself peacefully inside.

"Good evening, Mrs. Stokes." Detective Aaron Powell spoke in his calm voice. "I apologize for disturbing you."

"I'd say it's good to see you again, but I'm afraid it might not be," Jamie said. "Unless you're here for a happy reason."

"I'm not, unfortunately. I need your input on a matter concerning one of your employees."

Oh no. The face of each person who worked at the Treasure Chest popped into her mind, one after the other. "Is everyone okay?"

"May I come in?"

Jamie moved so Powell could step inside.

Julian entered from the kitchen, wearing his sauce-speckled apron. "Detective Powell." He shook Powell's hand. "It's been a while. What brings you here?"

"Good evening, Dr. Stokes. I need to speak with Mrs. Stokes, but you're welcome to remain."

"Have a seat," Julian said.

Powell settled into the overstuffed chair next to Jamie's antique rocker. Jamie and Julian sat on the couch.

"I'm sorry to tell you that Valerie Mantzaris is dead," Powell said.

Jamie gasped.

"Her roommate found her dead in her apartment earlier this evening. Her death appears to have been a homicide."

Valerie had been *murdered*? Every heartbeat pumped horror and grief through Jamie. "Do you know . . . who did it?"

"The investigation is in its early stages." Powell took a notebook and pen out of his suit coat pocket. "I'm sorry. I know this is a shock, but I have some questions."

"Yes, please, ask whatever you need." Jamie scanned the room, trying to remember where her closest stash of Kleenex was located. She was going to need it.

"When did you last see Ms. Mantzaris?" Powell asked.

"Today. This afternoon." Jamie thought of college-student Valerie laughing at the abysmal puns inflicted on her by an elderly customer as she'd helped him choose a teapot for his wife's birthday. "She worked from 9:45 to 3:00."

"Did she seem upset or worried about anything?"

"No. She seemed perfectly normal."

"Was Ms. Mantzaris dating anyone?"

"Not that she told me." Tears spilled.

"Did she confide in you about her personal life?" Powell asked.

Jamie tried to contemplate that question, but the tears streaming from her eyes seemed to obscure her memory as well as her eyesight. Julian exited the room and returned with a box of Kleenex.

"Thanks." She wiped her face. Julian sat and put his arm around her.

"I'm sorry," Powell said. "I know this is painful."

"I'll get it together. Just give me a sec." Jamie drew a few deep breaths and blotted new tears from her cheeks. "Valerie was friendly with me, but it was a working relationship. I was her boss, older and married. She did talk about searching for a decent guy. If she'd started dating someone regularly, I think she would have mentioned it, but she probably wouldn't have brought up a casual date or two. She didn't seem stressed though, and nothing suspicious ever happened at work, like a guy harassing her or her getting texts or calls that visibly upset her. Or bruises she couldn't explain."

"Thank you. When Ms. Mantzaris left work today, did she say anything about her plans for the remainder of the day?"

Jamie remembered Valerie loping cheerfully toward the back door, long, crimped hair swishing. *"See you tomorrow, Jamie. Can't wait to meet the new girl."* Jamie dug her knuckles into her stomach, progressively more nauseated than hungry. "She had an evening class at seven. The history of . . . feudal

Japan, I think? She was a history major. Other than that, I have no idea. Oh, she mentioned she had a lot of homework."

"I apologize for what I'm about to ask you." Powell took a photograph from his pocket and brought it to Jamie. "Please look at this and tell me if the item is familiar."

It was a picture of a knife, the blade sullied with red. Light-headed, Jamie blinked at the picture. Valerie had been stabbed?

"Do you recognize this?" Powell asked.

"Yes." Jamie wiped her eyes and doggedly studied the image. A chef's knife, eight-inch blade, the handle carved of gray-flecked granite inlaid with tiny red, yellow, and orange stone leaves. "We sell this knife at the Treasure Chest. It's the work of a sculptor in Maine, Patricia Hendriks."

"Did Ms. Mantzaris purchase this knife at the Treasure Chest?"

Everything about Jamie was the wrong temperature: her face was freezing, her lungs were scorching, and sweat slipped down her spine in drops of ice. "I can't tell you for certain that she didn't without checking the records, but it's unlikely. These knives are expensive. Valerie was a student working her way through school. I can't imagine she would have dropped three hundred dollars on a pretty knife."

"Can you check the sales records from here, or would you need to go to the Treasure Chest to do that?"

"I can do it here. I can search for anything she purchased by using her employee login."

Julian fetched her computer. Jamie logged in and stared at the screen, straining to remember how to use the business software she could normally operate in her sleep.

Powell sat next to her. "Valerie Mantzaris," he prompted, apparently sensing she was too shaken to even remember the basics of what she was searching for.

Jamie started typing.

"She didn't buy the knife." Jamie pointed to the list of items on the screen.

"Can you tell me who did?" Powell asked.

"No. Our software doesn't track customer purchases. But I can tell you how many of that particular knife we sold and which employees handled the transactions. We haven't sold many of them." Jamie's fingers were firm now, hammering the keyboard. She'd do anything she could to help Powell nail the demon who'd killed Valerie. "Of that pattern of knife, we've sold one bread knife, a set of steak knives, and one chef's knife," Jamie reported. "The chef's knife was a cash transaction, and the . . . the employee who sold it was . . . Valerie."

Silence surged through the room. Jamie imagined Valerie swaddling the sheathed knife in bubble wrap, boxing it, and handing it to the man who . . . or it could have been a woman . . .

"I assume these knives aren't exclusive to the Treasure Chest?" Powell asked.

"They are, actually, for now." Jamie wished she had a glass of water to wet her dry mouth, but she didn't want to dispatch Julian on yet another errand. "The sculptor signed a short-term exclusive contract with us." Jamie started mentally reviewing customer faces, searching for someone who . . . who what? Looked like a murderer? Murderers looked like regular people.

Powell wrote in his notebook. "Can you tell me the time and date of the transaction, who else was working at the time, and any other information about that day?"

"It was Saturday, August 28," Jamie said. *Two weeks ago.* Two weeks ago, a murderer had walked into the Treasure Chest. "Eleven thirty in the morning. I was working, and so was Wes. Wesley Bergmann."

"May I have Mr. Bergmann's contact information, please?"

Jamie offered it. Powell jotted it down and shifted his gaze back to Jamie. His eyes were mild but so penetrating that Jamie wondered if it was necessary for her to speak or if he could read the thoughts straight out of her mind.

"Is there anything else you can tell me about the sale of the knife?" he asked.

"I . . . don't remember. I don't think . . . wait . . ." A memory snagged in her brain's filter, but she couldn't dislodge it and identify it. "There's something . . . someone mentioned . . ." Frustrated, Jamie closed her eyes. The granite-handled knives. They'd been on display for a month . . . not many sales . . .

"A new customer!" She opened her eyes. "Valerie *did* mention selling that knife. She told me she'd sold it to a new customer. She mentioned it because I'd been concerned the knives were selling so slowly, worrying I'd made a misjudgment in stocking them. Let me check . . ." Jamie typed fast and pointed to a list on the screen. "Yes, the only knife from that collection that she sold was the chef's knife. Wes sold the bread knife and the steak knives."

"Thank you. That's good information. Did Valerie say anything else about the customer? Or imply she knew him or her?"

"No, she didn't know . . . *him*. She said *he* was a first-timer at the Treasure Chest." The first thought that should have occurred to Jamie finally lit up. "Valerie carried a notebook with her. All my employees do. They jot notes about customers when they have the chance so they can provide personalized service in the future. If you check her notebook, there might be a note about the man she sold the knife to."

Powell reached into his pocket and drew out a small spiral notebook with a scene of a sunrise on the cover. Valerie's notebook. "This was at her home, in her purse. Unfortunately, there's no mention of the knife in it, but since we now know the date when she sold it—"

"Let me look."

Powell passed her the notebook. It was about half filled with Valerie's writing. Jamie flipped through it until she found August. Carefully, she scanned every entry. The notes jumped from August 25 to September 1. "Nothing for the twenty-eighth," she said grimly.

"Is it normal to skip days?"

"Oh yes. There's no mandatory framework for note taking. Some employees write a lot, others not much. If the store is busy, there's no time to take notes. Or if you're dealing with customers you already know and there isn't anything to add, you might not bother, or if you only spent a moment with most of your customers and there was no natural opening to get their names. Lots of reasons for there to be nothing on a given day." Jamie returned the notebook to Powell. "She would have invited him to sign up for our newsletter. We did that with all new customers. Of course, I doubt he would have done it if he was buying the knife to . . ." A knot in her throat squeezed the rest of her statement into silence.

"Can you give me a list of everyone who signed up that day?" Powell asked. "I'll treat the information with discretion."

The prospect of Powell approaching her customers with questions about a murder made Jamie wince, but she couldn't withhold information that might help the police catch the killer. She located the newsletter information and printed it for Powell.

"Thank you." Powell rose from the couch and accepted the list of names and addresses Julian had retrieved from the printer. "Please don't contact any of these people yourself. And please don't share the details about the knife with anyone. We prefer to keep that information confidential for now."

Jamie nodded and stood. Her legs felt as cold and heavy as the limbs of those cast-iron garden gnomes she'd sold until she couldn't endure hauling them around the store any longer. Powell set his business card on the white-oak coffee table Jamie had painted with forget-me-nots. "If you think of anything else that might be helpful, please let me know immediately."

"I will. Does Valerie's family know what happened?"

"They do," Powell said. "But they don't know any details about the murder weapon. If you call them to express your sympathy, please keep those details to yourself, as you would when speaking to anyone else."

"I will." Jamie trudged toward the door to show Powell out. It wouldn't be difficult to keep details about the weapon secret. She was in no hurry to tell Valerie's mother that Valerie had been murdered with a handcrafted knife Valerie had personally sold to her killer.

* * *

Kate switched on the Red Sox game, but she couldn't concentrate on it like she normally did. She kept brooding over the poisoned-Jamie doll and how bizarre it was that fun, vivacious Jamie Stokes might be involved with the plotting of mass murder. What about the cluster of police cars at the triplex near Britteridge College? Maybe that murder was a domestic-violence situation or drug related, but what if it had something to do with this Eviction group?

"Did I tell you Roberta at the dry cleaner's has a son-in-law who used to date my admin?" Colby asked.

"Oh, that's interesting," Kate said absently. She wasn't in the mood for a round of Six Degrees of Colby Durham. She wanted to ask him if he'd received any messages from Lorenzo about the murder, but she didn't know if he wanted to discuss it, even though the apartment was free of listening devices. He'd spent the past hour scanning it and had found nothing.

Out of the corner of her eye, she glanced at Colby next to her on the couch, now tapping on his phone. It bothered her that she'd had no clue about his work for the task force. She'd never doubted he was occupied with Durham Consulting when he traveled or worked late. Was she dumb and unobservant, or was he extremely skilled at leading a double life?

Not that skilled since you found him out. At least now she could join him in fighting terrorists. Colby and Kate Durham, secret agents. They sounded like movie characters. She ought to learn to run in high heels or buy a black leather jumpsuit.

"What's so funny?" Colby asked.

Realizing she was smirking, Kate blushed. She didn't want Colby lecturing her again about how real undercover work wasn't like the movies. "Nothing. My mind was wandering."

"Katie, you're lying."

Kate surrendered. "I was thinking I needed new crime-fighting clothes, like a black leather jumpsuit."

He laughed. "I'm totally in favor of that, babe. But that would be a big no from my boss." He reached for the remote and turned the volume of the TV up. Kate thought he was ending the conversation, but he scooted closer to her and said, "The police released the name of the Britt student who got killed. Valerie Mantzaris."

The name meant nothing to Kate. "Is she . . . involved?"

"Can't say for sure yet. But she worked part-time at the Treasure Chest."

Kate clutched Colby's arm. "That can't be coincidence."

"Yeah, I don't think it is. I don't know if she was a terrorist who ran afoul of her co-conspirators or an innocent woman who learned something dangerous, but either way, things are heating up. If they're threatening Jamie Stokes and eliminating Valerie Mantzaris, I'm betting they're planning to make their move soon. Clock's ticking."

"What can I do to help?"

"That depends. How would you feel about stepping it up a notch?"

Kate peered into his eyes. They were slightly bloodshot. He must be exhausted, handling both his business and his task-force responsibilities. "By doing what?"

"I've been going back and forth with Lorenzo." He held up his phone. "Encrypted communication channel. We can text safely. We want to search Jamie Stokes's office. We don't want to break into the Treasure Chest after it's closed. They don't have security cameras, but we think her pals are watching the place at night. During business hours is safer. Is there a time tomorrow when you and Jamie will be the only employees present?"

"Let me check the schedule." Kate picked up her phone and opened the schedule Jamie had posted. "Yes, it's only Jamie and me until four o'clock, when Wes Bergmann comes in. I'm done at five."

"Okay, great. We'll set a time to search. Obviously, we need to be sure she won't walk in on us, so that's your job—keeping her away from her office. Do you think you can do that?"

Kate focused on the TV as the pitcher walked the player at bat. A woman was dead. The terrorists' plans were accelerating. In one day, Kate's responsibilities had jumped from keeping her eyes open to actively participating in an operation.

"Sorry," he said. "If this is too much for you, I understand. Normally, we wouldn't ask you, but Valerie's murder has us scared, and we need information as soon as possible. No shame if you don't want to take this on. We'll figure out another way."

She could do this. Lives were at stake. "I don't know how I'm going to pull it off, but I'll figure out a way."

"You're the best, babe. You can handle this. Let's brainstorm tactics."

CHAPTER 4

JAMIE LEANED HER ELBOWS ON her desk in the Treasure Chest office and studied the grid on her monitor. Working out the schedule to cover Valerie's shifts was both painful and calming. It hurt to think about Valerie, but adapting the schedule was something active Jamie could do to cope with the loss of her employee. Thank goodness she'd recently hired Kate Durham. If she hadn't, they'd be in even more of a pickle now.

Today was Kate's first full shift, and Jamie hoped she'd do well handling customers on her own if Jamie was needed elsewhere. Jamie would need to hire someone to replace Valerie as soon as possible. The thought felt weirdly calloused—*Sorry you're dead. Next!*—but she couldn't leave Valerie's job unfilled while they mourned her. Lousy customer service by overextended staff wasn't the way Valerie would want to be memorialized.

She also wouldn't want to be memorialized by staff and customers gossiping about her death, but her murder would be the number-one topic in Britteridge. Inevitably, people would come to Valerie's workplace, wanting to talk about her. The best Jamie could do would be to instruct her employees not to speculate on who had killed her or why.

At least Powell hadn't publicized the fact that the murder weapon had come from the Treasure Chest. If he decided to release details about the knife, she'd have to take the remaining knives off the shelves and hope sculptor Patricia Hendriks was willing to renegotiate their contract. Continuing to offer the knives for sale in Britteridge would be out of the question.

Jamie sent the new schedule to her employees with a request for them to verify if they could cover the proposed shifts. She topped off her lukewarm cup of apple-strawberry tea with a steaming refill from the dispenser on her filing cabinet and returned to her chair.

She had forty-five minutes until the store opened. She ought to deadhead the chrysanthemums in the planter boxes near the front door or check that there were adequate hangers on the rolling rack she placed in the entryway during cold or stormy weather—rain was forecast for today. Usually, she'd be rushing around at this time of morning, doing whatever she could to make the Treasure Chest more appealing to customers. Today, a weighted exhaustion made anything that involved leaving her office sound too daunting.

She reached for her keyboard and closed the work schedule. She wanted to call Valerie's parents, but they lived in California, and it was too early to call the West Coast. Plus, they'd barely learned their daughter was dead. A call from someone as removed from them as Valerie's boss might not be welcome yet.

Had the killer chosen Valerie before he'd entered the Treasure Chest? Had he gotten a thrill out of her smiling ignorance as she'd sold him the weapon he would use against her? Or had he decided on the spot or even later that Valerie would be his victim?

The killer had left the knife at the scene. Even if the arrival of Valerie's roommate or some other interruption had scared him away, how hard would it have been to hide the knife inside his jacket as he fled? Had he deliberately left it there, a unique weapon the police would easily trace to the store where Valerie had worked? Why?

Who else had been in the store that day who might have seen the killer? She needed to dig up any fragments of information that could be useful for Powell. If she could piece together who had been in the store at what times, particularly during the morning hours and particularly in the crystal room where the knives were displayed, that might help Powell direct his investigation. Another customer might have seen the killer looking at the knives or even purchasing one.

She accessed her list of newsletter subscribers, filtered for August 28, and printed the same list she'd given Powell. Seven customers had signed up for the newsletter on that date. Next, she printed out all the transactions from the twenty-eighth and her own customer notes that she'd transferred from her notebook to her master list.

She lined up the three documents on her desk and picked up an orange highlighter. On the list of transactions, she highlighted each item that had been displayed in the crystal room. Carefully, she read through her customer notes, searching for anything that might help direct Powell to a shopper who might have seen the killer. For the first time, Jamie regretted not having a store loyalty card that allowed her to identify who had purchased what. Edward Allerton had been adamantly opposed to any type of program like that. *Personal service,*

Jamie. We don't need a computer tracking what our customers like." He would tap his forehead. *"We remember it here."*

She picked up the list of people who'd signed up for the newsletter on August 28 and read the names and addresses. She didn't recognize any of them. One of the people had a Britteridge address; three were from elsewhere on the North Shore. One was from Plymouth. Two were from out of state: Lynette Biddlestrop from Dover, Delaware, and Sanguis Etmortis from Albany, New York. Jamie pictured the Britteridge Police contacting two tourists and questioning them about anything they might have witnessed at the Treasure Chest. Instead of having pleasant memories of the delightful gift shop they'd visited in a little Massachusetts town—and sharing those memories online and with friends who might be traveling this way—the knowledge that they'd been browsing with a murderer would give them the heebie-jeebies.

Jamie spoke to the list in her hand. "Please be assured this is not typical for the Treasure Chest, Ms. Biddlestrop and Mr. . . . " She had no idea how to pronounce his name. Was it French? It was probably *San-gwee Eh-mor-tay* or something like that, but in her current state of mind, it made her think of rigor mortis.

She swapped the newsletter list for the list of merchandise she'd highlighted and studied it, trying as hard as she could not to imagine Valerie stiff and cold.

Did *Etmortis* come from the same Latin root? What an unfortunate last name. *Hello, my name is Mr. Death.*

Latin. Et. And.

Jamie slapped the merchandise list on her desk and grabbed the list of newsletter subscribers. *Sanguis*. Like *sanguine? Sanguineous, consanguinity— red, blood, related by blood*—words and definitions zipped through Jamie's mind as though she were brushing up for a vocabulary test.

Sanguis et Mortis? She pulled her keyboard forward and typed the phrase into Google translate.

Blood and death.

That wasn't a name. It was a taunt.

Jamie snatched her phone and called Detective Powell.

* * *

Kate fervently hoped the store would be so busy at the agreed-upon search time of two o'clock that an avalanche of customers would keep Jamie out of her office and Kate wouldn't have to do anything to distract her. Colby had assured her she could text him to cancel the search if absolutely necessary, but he'd also made it clear how time-sensitive this was. The task force needed immediate information on what Jamie Stokes was up to, and Kate was determined not to be the weak link, putting people at risk because she was too inept to stall Jamie for half an hour. She and Colby had worked out several possible plans for how to occupy Jamie. When the time came, Kate would choose the best one for the circumstances.

Upon Kate's arrival at work this morning, Jamie had told her about the murder of Valerie Mantzaris and instructed her not to gossip with customers—to politely thank them for words of sympathy and respond to questions with, "We don't know. The police are investigating." Kate could tell that beneath Jamie's matter-of-fact demeanor, she was under intense stress. She was friendly with customers, but whenever the store was momentarily empty, her expression tautened and darkened, and she didn't seem inclined to make small talk with Kate.

Had she been involved with Valerie's murder, or had she been frightened by it? After receiving that warning doll, was she planning to attempt reconciliation with her terrorist cronies?

Cloudy morning skies became black noontime skies, and by one o'clock, rain pounded the sidewalks. A check of her weather app told Kate the heavy rainfall would continue all afternoon. The number of customers entering the store began to ebb, and by one forty-five, Kate was alone in the main room while Jamie helped a customer upstairs in the linen room.

Kate made her final decision on which distraction to use. She hurried through the foyer and down the corridor that led to the staff-only areas and the back exit. In the kitchen that served as a break room, she opened her locker, reached into her purse, and retrieved the juice box she'd hidden inside it. She stashed the juice box in her apron pocket and went to unlock the deadbolt on the back door to make it easier for Colby's team to enter.

Grateful the front-door sensor hadn't chimed, indicating the arrival of new customers, Kate returned to the deserted main room. From upstairs came the sound of Jamie's laughter. Kate hoped Jamie's conversation with her customer would continue until Kate had fully prepped her distraction.

Praying no one would enter the Treasure Chest in the next thirty seconds, Kate rushed to the bay window that showcased a display Jamie had joked about taking hours to get perfect. If Jamie was that meticulous, she wouldn't want Katie tinkering with the display. She'd want to fix any issues herself.

Glad for the empty sidewalk outside and the partial camouflage of the rain running down the glass, Kate punched the drinking straw through the lid of the juice box and knelt on the edge of the window shelf. Listening hard for footsteps on the stairs, she crawled through the display like a rambunctious child, knocking the scarecrow off his rocking chair; scattering wooden apples, pumpkins, and sunflowers; pushing clumps of straw to the floor; and squirting grape juice as she went.

She dropped the juice box in the straw, climbed down, and brushed straw off her pant legs. Briskly, she walked into the foyer, said aloud, "Thanks for stopping in. What a storm!" and opened and closed the door so the chime would ring as though a customer had departed.

With the first part of her mission completed, she wandered mindlessly into the crystal room, hoping her galloping heartbeat would soon slow. The floorboards creaked under her feet, and blown-glass vases, crystal goblets, and hand-painted china bowls glittered around her. She loved browsing through beautiful things, and she should be paying attention and memorizing stock, but she felt preoccupied and clumsy. If she got too close to any of the breakables, she'd probably shatter them.

She checked her watch. One fifty-five. Colby must be close now, ready to slip through the back door. She wished she could feel exhilarated or patriotic right now, but she kept thinking about Valerie Mantzaris. Had Jamie caught Valerie doing something suspicious? In a news article this morning, Kate had read that Valerie's apartment had shown no evidence of forced entry.

Valerie would have opened the door to her boss.

Footsteps creaked overhead. Kate darted into the main room. She planted herself at the end of the room farthest from the trashed window display and began straightening multicolored metal chickens.

"You're welcome to linger as long as you want." Jamie's voice and multiple sets of footsteps moved down the stairs. "Unless you want to waterski home. Would Allie like to play in our playroom? We have a new wooden Noah's Ark set, which seems appropriate today."

"Thanks, but I need to pick my son up from school. We'll come back though. Allie would love that."

"I'll double-bag your tablecloth to make sure it doesn't get wet." Jamie entered the main room, followed by a woman and a preschool-aged girl. Kate smiled at them and moved to a group of pots constructed of river pebbles. She pretended to line the pots up more precisely as Jamie rang up and bagged the tablecloth.

After the woman and her daughter left, Jamie approached Kate. "How are things going?"

"Slow," Kate said. "I've only had a couple of customers since the rain got heavy. Neither of them bought anything. One had a little boy with her, and I told her about the playroom, but she said they were in a hurry."

"That Noah's Ark set is so unbelievably cute," Jamie said. "I'm determined to get *someone* to play with it today. Worst case, it'll be me."

Kate laughed, relieved that Jamie seemed more relaxed. She clearly hadn't noticed the jumbled display yet, and with no customers in the store, there was sharp danger she'd head for her office to catch up on administrative work. Kate would have to pretend to notice the display herself to draw Jamie's attention . . . No, she wouldn't. Jamie had started making a circuit of the room. Kate had seen her do this several times, taking advantage of quiet moments to check that everything was where it ought to be and to take care of anything that made the room less than pristine. Kate started industriously arranging burlap pumpkins.

"Oh my word. Oh my word, Kate, what happened here?"

Feigning alarm, Kate whirled around. "What?"

Jamie gestured to the front window. From where Kate stood, the only part of the destruction she could see was the wooden chair missing its scarecrow.

"Oh no!" Kate swooped toward the window. "I didn't notice the scarecrow had fallen—" She gaped at the sticky wreckage of the display.

Jamie rubbed her temples, her lips sealed together. A moment of panic shook Kate as she saw Jamie fighting to contain her temper. If Jamie fired her on the spot and ordered her to leave, she'd lose her ability to keep Jamie away from her office. *She won't*, Kate reassured herself. *She won't choose to fly solo right now, no matter how angry she is. She needs me to handle the sales floor so she can fix the display.*

"I'm so sorry." Kate picked up a wooden apple that had fallen to the floor. "I had no idea . . . Everything was fine . . ." Using her apron, Kate wiped a spot of juice off the apple. "I checked the whole room right before the last few customers arrived. I was with an elderly woman in the crystal room, and a mother and son were in here. I guess this explains why the mom was in a rush when they left."

"And why they weren't interested in the playroom," Jamie snapped. "Little Genghis Khan had already had plenty of playtime." She stalked toward the foyer. Kate followed her.

Jamie opened the janitorial closet under the stairs and took out a garbage sack, a roll of paper towels, and a spray bottle of all-purpose cleaner.

"I'm so sorry," Kate repeated, glad it was normal to sound shaky under the circumstances. It was past two o'clock, and the responsibility to keep Colby and his team safe was hitting hard. "The little boy was jumping up and down, but his mother was holding his hand, and I thought she had him under control. The mother said she wanted to browse and would let me know if she had questions . . . Here, let me take that." Kate claimed the trash sack from Jamie and beat her to the window ledge. She began gathering handfuls of stained straw and dropping them into the bag.

Jamie picked up a pottery pumpkin and sprayed it with cleaner. "You remember our policy is no open food or drinks, right?"

"Yes, and I did look when they came in. Neither the little boy nor the mother was carrying a juice box or other food. I . . . while I was in the crystal room, I did hear him giggling, and I heard a little thump—that must have been the apple hitting the floor. I'm sorry. I should have come to check right away, but I didn't want my customer to feel like I was abandoning her."

"Don't worry about it." Jamie drew a deep breath and smiled at Kate. "I'm sorry for barking at you. Things happen, and you can't be everywhere at once. The kid was probably restless, so his mother bribed him with a juice box, she got distracted, he bolted, and voila, Armageddon. Believe me, I've had more than my share of disasters. Like the lady who wanted to be certain the dish she chose would hold a whole recipe of her tomato soup, so she brought in a plastic pitcher filled with the soup and poured it into each serving bowl and tureen in turn, then back into her pitcher. There used to be a light gray rug on the floor in the crystal room, but it ended up in a dumpster. For the record, the *rug* could hold a whole recipe of her tomato soup."

Kate laughed, but Jamie's quick forgiveness and apology gave her the sudden feeling Colby's task force was trying to force square-peg Jamie into a round hole. Maybe they were wrong about her and she had no link to Eviction.

Don't be naive. Just because she doesn't gush hate 24/7 doesn't mean she's innocent.

"Good thing it's such a slow afternoon," Jamie said. "We'll have plenty of time to clean up before too many people see this. If customers come in, you take care of them, and I'll focus on the display, unless you need help."

"All right," Kate said. "I'm really sorry."

"No harm done, except for some juice-drenched straw, may it rest in peace." Jamie tossed a handful into the trash sack and groaned. "What's wrong with me? What a horrible time to make a death joke."

"Valerie's death must be devastating for you," Kate said. With Jamie's broaching the subject, carrying on with it would be more natural than ignoring it, and she might learn something she could report to Colby. "I wish I'd had the chance to meet her. Had she worked here long?"

"About a year and a half." Jamie set two more pottery pumpkins on the floor. "She was a history major at Britt. She loved handicrafts—had her own Etsy shop, sold sock puppets that she . . ." Jamie's voice cracked. She swallowed. "You would have enjoyed working with her. I'd better change the subject. I try not to bawl on the sales floor."

The door chimed. Kate stuffed one more handful of straw into the trash bag. "Hopefully, they'll want to look at something upstairs."

"Greet the customer, then make a quick stop in the bathroom," Jamie said. "You can't handle merchandise with Genghis Jr.'s juice all over your fingers."

Kate trotted toward the foyer. The customer was a rangy, middle-aged man with a craggy face. He folded his umbrella and tucked it into the umbrella stand. "Good afternoon." He extended his hand. "Aaron Powell."

"I'm Kate Durham. I apologize, but I'd better not shake your hand. I was cleaning up a spill, and my hands are sticky. If I can point you in the right direction, I'll run and wash my hands and be back to help. Feel free to hang up your coat."

"Thank you." Powell removed his raincoat and chose one of the wooden hangers on the rolling rack. "I'm not here to shop, so no need to hurry. Is Mrs. Stokes available? I need to speak with her."

"Yes, let me get—oh, here she is."

Jamie's expression had stiffened again, and though she smiled at the man, it was a formal smile, not a warm one. Kate guessed she was acquainted with Powell but wasn't happy to see him. *Aaron Powell.* His name sounded familiar.

"I apologize for bothering you during your workday," Powell said. "I was in the neighborhood and thought I'd come speak to you in person."

"Come into my office," Jamie said. "Kate can hold down the fort."

Kate's heart seemed to jolt out of rhythm. "Before you go, let me wash my hands. I don't want to be in the bathroom if a customer shows up."

"Yes, go ahead."

Kate shot down the hallway, stepped into the bathroom, and closed the door. It was 2:18. Twelve minutes short of the time she'd been assigned to keep Jamie away from her office. How long could she stay in the bathroom before Jamie—or Powell—got impatient and suspicious? If they caught Colby—

She turned on the tap, slipped her phone from her apron pocket, and texted, heedless of juice-sticky fingers, sending the prearranged message that would signal Colby that he was out of time: *Want to grab a burger tonight?*

CHAPTER 5

Jamie opened her office door. "Have a seat. May I offer you a cup of tea? It's an apple-strawberry blend."

"No, thank you, but feel free to help yourself," Powell said. "It's a good day for a hot cup of tea."

"Definitely."

"That's an impressive collection of mugs."

"The ones on the shelf are for guests. The ones hanging beneath the shelf are mine." She ran her finger along the seven mugs dangling from hooks, each a different color and style of pottery. "They were a gift from a potter whose work we sell. One for each day of the week." She lifted the deep-red mug on her desk and showed Powell where *Jamie's Wednesday Mug* was imprinted in the clay.

"I should commission a set," Powell said. "It would help me remember what day it is, which can be a challenge after too many hours on a case." He skimmed the office. "You've added your own touches. Very nice. When Ed Allerton retired, did he take the painting of his father?"

Jamie was impressed that Powell remembered the former décor. As far as she knew, the last time he'd been in here was over two years ago, when Jamie had been the manager, and Powell had dealt with a case involving an employee who was willing to do anything to oust her. "He did take the painting, with my enthusiastic encouragement. Since you're accustomed to shocking confessions, I'll admit I was happy to be rid of it. Old Mr. Allerton was probably the nicest man on earth, but that portrait made him look like he was ready to hang me for heresy. He wasn't good company when I was working late."

"I suspect any condemnation was in the eye of the beholder."

"Okay, I might have been a little insecure." Jamie sat in the other visitor's chair rather than behind her desk. "Did you have a chance to follow up on Sanguis Etmortis?"

"Yes." Powell took his notebook out of his pocket.

"He doesn't exist," Jamie guessed.

"That's correct."

The thought of Valerie's killer responding to her invitation to sign up for the newsletter by writing his name as *Blood and Death* kindled such rage that Jamie wanted to charge into the pouring rain and track down Mr. Death on her own. "I assume the address was fake too?"

"The address exists. We're working with the Albany police to determine why the so-called Mr. Etmortis chose it. I'm here to collect the information you told me you were gathering."

"I don't have much." She fetched the papers from her desk. "This one is a list of everyone I could identify as having been here on August 28." She handed it to Powell. "If I had contact information for a customer, I added that too. I thought that might save you time."

"Thank you."

She passed him another sheet. "This printout shows everything we sold on August 28. The items I've highlighted are located in the crystal room, which is where the knife Mr. Etmortis bought was displayed. In the margins, I've written the names of anyone I could connect to a particular purchase. If the name is in parentheses, it means I was guessing, going off my previous knowledge of a customer and their tastes or off iffy memory." She handed him the last sheet. "This one contains my customer notes from the twenty-eighth. Wes Bergmann worked that day too. I called him and left a message asking for his notes."

"Thank you. We'll follow up on that. Be aware that if none of our leads results in useful information, we'll have to publicly announce details about the knife in order to throw the net wider. I realize this will result in negative publicity for the Treasure Chest, and I apologize for that. We will, of course, leave the sculptor's name out of any press releases in hopes of minimizing repercussions to her career."

An energetic knock came at the door. "That must be Niall Flanagan," Jamie said. "He told me he'd drop off some new carvings today."

"Feel free to invite him in. I'll leave you to transact your business—unless you have anything else for me?"

"I wish I did. I'll call you immediately if I think of anything." Jamie went to open the door.

White-haired Niall Flanagan stood in the hallway, wearing a dripping raincoat and holding a rain-spattered cardboard box. The sparkle in his eyes told Jamie he hadn't heard about Valerie's death. He'd probably been holed up in his garage workshop, oblivious to anything beyond his carving tools and the piece of wood in his hands.

"It's bucketing down," he said. "I saw a fine trout swimming up the footpath—" Niall's unruly white eyebrows rose as Powell stepped up behind Jamie. "Detective Powell."

"Good afternoon, Mr. Flanagan. How are you doing?"

"Grand. Yourself?"

"I'm fine, thank you. I've finished meeting with Mrs. Stokes, so I'll excuse myself."

It was rare for Niall to stop radiating cheer, and whenever it happened, Jamie felt as though a power outage had hit the Treasure Chest. "I hope your visit doesn't mean there's trouble for Jamie or her shop," he said.

"One of my employees, Valerie Mantzaris, was found murdered in her apartment yesterday," Jamie said, wanting to get this wrenching announcement over with.

Every wrinkle in Niall's face seemed instantly deeper and droopier. "I'm sorry, love. Has the culprit been arrested?"

"Not yet," Jamie said. "But I'm sure he will be soon, with Detective Powell on the case."

"We'll do our best," Powell said. "Good afternoon." He exited the office.

Jamie beckoned Niall inside.

"I'm sorry I didn't answer your message last night." Niall set the box on her desk. "Went to bed early."

"It wasn't urgent." Niall's apology nudged Jamie with the memory of the doll. She'd been so distracted by Valerie's death that she'd forgotten about it. "Have a seat. Would you like to try my flavor-of-the-month tea? It's an apple-strawberry blend."

"I have time for a cuppa." Niall settled into a chair. "Terrible news about your girl. I met her a time or two. Lovely smile. Does the detective have any suspects?"

"Not yet." Jamie filled a mug from the dispenser. "But he has some leads."

"We know he's good," Niall said grimly.

Jamie handed him the steaming mug. "I wanted to ask you about something." She took the bubble-wrapped doll from her purse, unwrapped it, and brought it to Niall. "This was left on a table near the book room. I have no idea who put it there."

He set his mug on the desk and took the doll. For a quiet moment, he studied it from head to toe, front and back. "I carved this," he said. "But the

Jamie Stokes I carved was in fine health, not expiring from poisoning." He prodded the bucket in the figure's hand. "This was filled with daffodils, not dripping with witch's brew. Someone cut away the flowers—see the clumsiness of the cut marks. They also repainted your face."

"Why did you carve a doll of me in the first place? I assume you didn't think I'd want to sell Jamie dolls here."

Niall pursed his mouth. "Does your lad Julian have a strange sense of humor?"

"Goodness, what does Julian have to do with this?"

"He ordered the doll."

"*What?*"

"He asked me to keep it secret, but if you're bothered, I won't play his game."

"*Julian* ordered it?"

"He said he wanted it for his office, but he didn't want you to know yet because you'd press him to cancel the order."

Jamie goggled at the doll in Niall's calloused hands. Julian was quirky, but he didn't have a dark sense of humor. Even if he did, he'd have owned up the instant she'd shown him the doll.

"Ah, now, I don't want to cause strife between husband and wife," Niall said. "Sure it was a laugh, a Halloween prank."

"Did Julian order the doll in person?"

"He emailed the order."

"Did you deliver it in person?"

"I left it on your porch, following the instructions in the email, but it was a lovely work when I delivered it."

"You never spoke to him? On the phone or face-to-face?"

"I didn't. I'm sorry, love. I didn't mean to cause trouble."

"You're not the one causing trouble. Since you've already spilled the beans, may I see the email he sent you?"

Niall scraped the doll's face with his thumbnail, as though trying to remove the added-on paint. "I don't want to be in the middle, now."

"I don't think Julian ordered the doll. None of this sounds like something he'd do. The fact that he emailed rather than calling you is another wrong note. Julian actually enjoys speaking on the phone or, better yet, in person. For a request like this, he would have spoken to you directly. I think someone sent you the email, using his name. How did the buyer pay you?"

"Cash," Niall said gruffly. "Left in my post box." He took out his phone. For a few moments, he tapped the screen. "Here's the email." He passed the phone to Jamie.

Jamie didn't have to read a word of the email to confirm it was phony; the address at the top wasn't Julian's. Someone had created an email account using his name. She scrolled through the conversation between Niall and the imposter. The imposter had done a mediocre job of imitating Julian's style, but Niall had only met Julian a handful of times. He wouldn't have noticed. *Well played, Marcia.* Or *was* Marcia Allerton-Harper the culprit?

"If you'll let me, I'll take the doll back to my workshop and make it right," Niall said.

Jamie eyed the green poison staining the doll's mouth and was tempted to accept the offer. "Thanks, but I'd better leave it like this for now in case I . . . need it."

"Have you shown it to Detective Powell?"

"No, goodness, it's not a police matter. I think someone doesn't like the changes I've made here since Mr. Allerton retired, and they got creative in making their point."

"That's an expensive way to make a point. My dolls aren't a bargain, sure."

"Apparently, some peevish locals have a lot of disposable income. Or several people pooled their resources." Jamie thought of the scrapbook brigade. "I have more than one complainer."

"Jamie . . . show the detective, will you, love? That's a sick mind that'll paint you like this."

"I don't think it's meant as a threat. It's petty sulking at my selling herbal teas and artisan chocolate." She tapped the rim of her mug. "You know how the Allertons were opposed to stocking any food items? Some people have a hard time with change."

"Why should they have a say in what you do with your own shop?"

"I hope they complain so much to their friends that everyone wants to see these scandalous changes. That would be good for business." She tapped Niall's phone. "If you don't mind, I'm going to forward this email chain to myself." She did so, then returned his phone and held out her hand for the doll.

Niall scowled as he surrendered it. "I'm an old fool."

"It's not your fault." She shoved the doll into her purse. "You had no reason to doubt the order was from Julian. Don't worry about it. No harm done."

"I hope not."

Wanting to change the subject, Jamie opened the box Niall had brought. "Let's see these charming new owls."

CHAPTER 6

KATE PEELED THE LID OFF the container of hot macaroni and cheese she'd picked up on the way home. "I'm sorry I couldn't give you the full thirty minutes," she said, passing the container across the table to Colby.

He shrugged. "Things happen. We adapt. What cut the time short?"

"A man named Aaron Powell showed up. He said he wasn't a customer and wanted to speak with Jamie privately. I stalled by asking her if she could watch the sales floor long enough for me to run to the bathroom, but I couldn't take too long without making her suspicious. That's when I texted you. Did you get out in time? Were you able to put everything back?"

"Yeah, we got away clean. She won't have any reason to guess we were there."

Kate smiled in relief. "I've been getting an ulcer all afternoon, worrying. Which makes me sound like an amateur, I guess."

"You are." Colby winked. "But you're catching on fast. Pass the pepper."

Kate passed the salt and pepper shakers.

"How was Jamie today?" Colby passed the mac and cheese back to Kate. "Did she seem uptight?"

"Yes." Kate scooped pasta onto her plate. "She kept up appearances whenever customers were in the store, but when they weren't, it was obvious she was worried. And tired. She looked like she didn't sleep much last night. Have you heard of Aaron Powell? I can sketch him for you if you need me to."

"Thanks, but I know who he is. He's a cop, a Britteridge police detective."

That was why his name had rung a bell. She'd seen it in an article about Valerie's death. "So he's not involved?"

"We don't know. They might have a mole in the PD, but from everything our research turned up, Powell seems legit."

"Jamie seemed to know him."

"He questioned her about Valerie last night. He must have come back today with more questions."

Kate felt dumb for not realizing that. "Do you think he suspects her?"

"He's a smart guy, but the local police don't know about Eviction. He'll get stumped trying to figure out her motive."

They ate in silence, Kate hoping Colby would volunteer information about the search of Jamie's office without her having to ask. When the silence became more irritating than having to beg for information, she said, "Did you find anything in Jamie's office?"

He nodded.

Kate's dismay made her feel twice as amateurish. She'd hoped they wouldn't find anything, that Jamie might be innocent after all. No matter how many times she told herself Jamie was plainly guilty, she couldn't seem to give up hope that the task force might be wrong. "Can you tell me?"

He picked up his phone, worked with it, and handed it to Kate. The screen showed a picture of a sticky note with the Treasure Chest logo at the top. Written on the note in orange ink were four numbers: 5343.

Colby reclaimed his phone. "That was in her center desk drawer."

"What is it? A PIN for a bank account?"

Colby squirted Tabasco sauce on the remaining mac and cheese on his plate. "Valerie Mantzaris's apartment has a keypad door lock. 5343 is the code to her front door."

Her appetite dying, Kate drew her hand away from the spoon she'd been about to use to serve herself a second helping.

"Lorenzo got a few more details on Valerie's death. The knife the killer used was left at the scene. It has a decorative granite handle with orange, red, and yellow stone inlays in the shape of leaves. Unusual knife, made by a sculptor in Maine. The only location that sells them right now is the Treasure Chest."

Kate gulped icy water. Everything from the tip of her tongue to her stomach felt dry. She knew what type of knife Colby was talking about. She'd seen those knives displayed in the crystal room and had admired the detailed carving on the tiny, colorful leaves. "So Jamie killed her?"

"Looks like it." The amusement on Colby's face unsettled Kate. What could possibly be funny about Jamie stabbing Valerie Mantzaris?

"Maybe it wasn't her," Kate said coolly. She'd rather be amateurish than callous. "Anyone could have bought or stolen one of those knives. The Treasure Chest has lax security. Britteridge is such a low-crime place that Jamie doesn't worry much about it."

He chuckled. "Because Jamie's the one committing the serious crimes. C'mon, Katie. Who besides Jamie would choose a fancy weapon like that? Why not use whatever was already in Valerie's kitchen drawer?"

"What other evidence do you have against her?"

"What do you mean?"

"None of the evidence I've seen proves she's guilty. It could all point to someone else. Are you and Lorenzo taking into account that Jamie might not be involved?"

"Of course we are, but *you're* the one who's been handing us evidence."

"That doll could mean something else. Jamie thought it was a prank."

"Which would make it a huge coincidence. Of course she said it was a prank. What was she supposed to tell you? 'This is from my terrorist cell, threatening to murder me if I don't do what I'm told.'"

Kate shoved back from the table. "I'm going to go take a shower."

Colby grasped her hand. "Since when do you shower after dinner? Can't stand my company any longer?"

"A shower sounds refreshing." She tugged her hand away. She didn't want to admit that she felt dirty. Contaminated. Maybe it was too much thinking about the toxin. Or too much time with a woman who had blood on her hands.

"I'm sorry, babe." He kissed her knuckles. "I didn't mean to make you mad. I know it's rough learning terrible things about someone you like, and Jamie works hard to make herself likable. I'd tell you more about what led us to her, but I can't. Classified. I wish she were innocent, but at this point, the chance that she's not involved with Eviction is about one in a million."

"What now?" Kate asked, anger waning. "Do you move in on her?"

"No. We use her. We need to confirm a theory about the toxin they're using, and there's a way we can get that information from her."

"Without tipping her off?"

"Yes. Sit down, and I'll tell you about it."

Kate sat. He kissed her hand again and released it. "We suspect they're inoculating themselves against the toxin," he said.

"So it won't hurt them while they're slaughtering the rest of us?"

"These aren't suicide bombers. They don't want to die with their victims. We think we've identified the toxin, but we need to be sure. The good news is there's a way to determine if Jamie has received an antitoxin to the substance we think they're using."

"Okay. How?"

"Uh . . . well, this would boost your involvement to a level I know you didn't expect this early on. I didn't expect it either. It was actually Lorenzo who suggested it, which is pretty rash for him, but if you're willing to help, it would make this operation quick and easy."

Kate tried to mask her trepidation with humor. "I hope you're not going to tell me to spray her with the toxin and see what happens."

"Not unless you and everyone else in the Treasure Chest want to die."

"No, thank you."

He chuckled. "This won't hurt anyone except Jamie. She's overdue for some suffering anyway, right?"

Kate shrank inside. "Wait. I don't want to hurt her."

"You don't think she deserves it?"

"Yes, but . . . I mean, it's not our place . . . Let the courts take care of . . ."

"We're not asking you to torture her or assassinate her. You'll just make her sick for a few hours."

"Sick in what way?"

"Vomiting, fever, dizziness. Not even as miserable as the flu. Think of the mass murder she has planned. Think about that, Katie."

"Getting sick won't tip her off that she's busted?"

"No. She'll think she got hit with a virus, or if she does suspect poisoning, she'll blame her comrades. They're the ones who sent her the warning doll. This is important, Katie. We need to confirm the nature of the toxin. Do you understand that?"

"Yes," Kate said tersely. "What do you expect me to do?"

"I'll explain after we finish eating, but let's relax and enjoy our dinner. There's another favor I need to ask of you, but I think you'll like this one. I've decided on the painting I want for my office."

"Oh wonderful!" The reminder that Colby loved her artwork enough to want to display it in his office brightened her mood. "What would you like?"

"I'd like a series, actually, if that's the right word. A group of canvases of varying sizes, each linked to someone in my life. I haven't decided on all of them—I want your input—but I do know what I want for the first one. The idea came to me today when I was waiting at the barber's, flipping through a gardening magazine. I saw this."

On his phone, he showed her a picture of a group of white blossoms on dark-green leaves. "I've already forgotten the name of the flower, but it grew wild in the field behind my aunt's house. I remember seeing it every summer. Do you think you could start with these flowers?"

"I'd love to paint these." She hadn't thought Colby had any fond memories of being raised by his aunt and uncle. Kate flinched inside when she remembered

Colby introducing her to his aunt—a polite introduction on the doorstep, an order to remove her shoes the instant she stepped into Aunt Tanya's gorgeous entryway, and Tanya promptly dispatching her assistant to bring Kate a new pair of socks. The tiny hole in the toe of Kate's left sock was not "appropriate for luncheon"—a lunch that had included only Kate, Colby, Tanya, and her husband.

"I was thinking a small canvas for this one," Colby said. "Maybe a six-inch square?"

"Perfect."

"Do you think you . . . could start on it tonight? I want to see how it comes out to give me a feel for what would mesh well with it."

"Of course. Are you thinking oils? Acrylic?"

"You choose. Thank you, Katie. You're the best. While you paint, I'll give you the details for tomorrow's operation. Sound good?"

"I hope so. That depends on what you want me to do."

"Nothing difficult," he said. "Just have a cup of tea with Jamie."

* * *

"Bring your arm up. Don't let it droop." Julian guided Jamie across the floor of one of Britteridge College's dance rooms. "Nice, yes, beautiful."

"You'd think I'd have this down after two years," Jamie said.

"The waltz is the devil to get perfect. Whenever you want me to stop instructing, say the word. I'm capable of dancing without correcting my partner."

"No, please continue. I'm determined to knock the socks off your colleagues at the Christmas party. A dance professor should have a magnificent partner."

"You're already magnificent, my darling. Don't lean in quite so far."

Jamie curved her upper back into the proper position. Julian led her through a few more steps before saying, "I passed that phony email along to a friend in the computer science department to see what he could tell me about its source."

"I can tell you about its source. It's from a person who thinks the Treasure Chest should have stayed in the Allerton family and who relishes objecting to anything I do that alters—"

"I meant locating the computer it was sent from and so forth."

"I know." Jamie leaned in and kissed him, jarring them both out of step. "I'm joking. Is it worth pursuing that information though? It'll encourage me to have a smackdown with the culprit, and it's never good to encourage me that way."

Julian led her again into the graceful rhythm of the waltz. "I want to verify our assumptions."

"Actually, I'm not that interested in a smackdown with Marcia Allerton-Harper. What I *really* want to rage about is the fact that an evil guy walked into *my* Treasure Chest and bought my beautiful merchandise from my beautiful clerk and then used it to murder her. And look at the way he signed up for the newsletter with that horrible, taunting name, like it was all a game."

"A truly sickening touch."

"I can't express how much I want the police to catch this fiend. I wish I could be there to watch. I suppose asking Detective Powell if I could do an extended ride-along until they arrest him is out of the question."

"Dearest, even if that outlandish suggestion were a possibility, we all know you couldn't bring yourself to leave the Treasure Chest in other hands long enough for you to hover over the police."

"True. I'll settle for calling Detective Powell every ten minutes to grill him for updates."

They moved in perfect sync through a spin turn. "I can say his lines for him and save you the trouble," Julian said. "'I'm sorry, Jamie, I'm not able to share more information at this time. Rest assured that we're doing all we can to apprehend the killer.'"

Jamie admired Julian's imitation of Powell's controlled tone. "I'm behaving myself. I'm not pestering him. I only called him once today, and that was to tell him about Mr. Death's newsletter subscription. I did google that Albany address to see if I could find anything strange connected to it, but I didn't learn anything."

On top of the piano, her phone rang. She lurched away from Julian, stumbling in her dance shoes. He caught her arm.

"You'll never reach that phone if you break your ankle." He lifted her into his arms and swept her toward the piano.

"You're a show-off," Jamie said. "This isn't a cabaret competition."

"I need to stay in shape."

Jamie picked up her phone and saw Detective Powell's number on the screen. Hastily, she answered. "Hello, this is Jamie."

"Jamie, it's Aaron Powell. I wanted to let you know that in a press briefing tonight, we shared the nature of the murder weapon, the fact that it was sold at the Treasure Chest, and the date it was purchased. We also mentioned that Ms. Mantzaris worked part-time at the Treasure Chest, though I believe that had already been made public."

"Yes, I saw it in an article online this afternoon," Jamie said as Julian set her on her feet. "Thanks for the heads-up."

"I know this will be unpleasant for you, and I apologize."

"I'll deal with it. I just care about you catching Mr. Death. Do whatever you need to do."

"Thank you for your cooperation. Good night."

"Good night." Jamie wished it could be a good night and that Valerie could be at work tomorrow and that the past twenty-four hours could be a bad dream. She leaned against Julian, wanting his warmth again. "Detective Powell said—"

"I know. I eavesdropped."

"I'd better call Patricia Hendriks and warn her. It won't take long for someone to identify her as the sculptor, and I'd rather have her get the bad news from me than from a reporter."

"Let's go home, then." Julian switched off the music playing over the sound system. "You don't want to have that conversation here, where anyone could . . . ah . . . waltz in."

"If you don't mind, let's go to the Treasure Chest. I want to clear those knives off the shelf right away and fill in the gap."

While Julian drove them out of the faculty parking lot, Jamie found Patricia Hendriks's contact information and called her.

"Jamie, hello." Patricia's gravelly voice came from the car's speakers. "You beat me to the punch. I was going to call you. I'm in Boston for meetings with a new gallery, and I want to take a gander at your store while I'm in the neighborhood."

Jamie and Julian glanced at each other. "I'd love that," Jamie said. "It's about time we met in person. What's your schedule?"

"I'm here for two more days. Busy during the day, flexible in the evenings. Flexible tonight, but I assume the place is closed by now."

"We close at seven, but for you, I'll open it anytime."

"You're a sweetheart. But you called me; let's handle that first. What can I do for you?"

"I'm sorry, but I have bad news. I wanted to let you know that a chef's knife from your autumn collection was used as the weapon in a murder."

Patricia didn't speak. Jamie tried to decide whether to say something or sit in silence, picking glitter off her jacket. In the headlights from passing cars, the jacket sparkled orange and black from the Halloween wreaths she'd unpacked in the Treasure Chest's chilly basement.

"What happened?" Patricia's question was a burst of sound.

Jamie related what she knew. "I can't offer the remaining knives for sale in Britteridge right now. They're so distinctive, and in a town this size, everyone will know how Valerie died. Most people will avoid the knives, and a few oddballs might want them as creepy souvenirs. I don't want either of those things happening."

"Consider our contract canceled. We can deal with the paperwork later. I'll take the knives back."

"Thank you for your understanding."

"Her poor mother. Her poor mother. How old was this girl?"

"She was twenty."

"My knife," Patricia mumbled. "Another murder."

Startled, Jamie opened her mouth to ask for an explanation, but Patricia spoke first, her tone curt. "If you're free, I'll pick the knives up tonight. I'm in Marblehead, so I can be there soon."

"We're heading to the Treasure Chest now. When you arrive, park behind the building, and come to the back door."

"That poor girl. Her poor mother." Patricia hung up.

Jamie stared at Julian's profile. "*Another murder*? Has someone *else* been killed with her knives?"

CHAPTER 7

When the back doorbell dinged, Julian went to answer it, leaving Jamie in the office, boxing up the knives they'd removed from the shelf in the crystal room. Jamie reached for a paring knife decorated with inlays of pumpkins in the handle and absentmindedly wrapped it in bubble wrap, her attention—and apprehension—focused on Julian's voice as he invited Patricia into the Treasure Chest. Jamie needed to ask Patricia what she'd meant about "another murder." It was a dreadful thing to pry about, but she either had to pursue it herself to discover if it could be relevant to Valerie's death or relay the comment to Powell and sic him on Patricia, which sounded crueler.

Julian escorted Patricia into the office. Jamie had spoken to her on the phone many times and had seen Patricia's picture on her website, but she'd imagined Patricia as tall and athletic. Real-life Patricia was maybe five feet tall and thin in a frail-looking way, with gray-streaked red hair that reached her waist. Her face was more . . . vulnerable? . . . than Jamie had anticipated. Patricia's guttural voice had always made her sound hardened to Jamie's ears.

"It's an honor to meet you." Jamie shook Patricia's hand. Her fingers were so spidery that Jamie was impressed she had the strength to work with stone.

"Good to meet you too," Patricia said. "Great location you have here, right downtown."

"Yes, it's ideal."

Patricia held out a cardboard box. "This is for you. A little gift."

Jamie opened the box. Inside, nested in shredded paper, was a softball-sized pumpkin carved of orange stone, with a curving green stone stem. Jamie lifted the sculpture from the box. "Patricia, this is beautiful. Thank you so much."

"Soapstone," Patricia said.

Jamie rubbed the smooth stone with her thumbs. "I love it. Thank you."

"My pleasure."

Jamie set the pumpkin on her desk. "Have a seat. Would you like some apple-strawberry tea?" She gestured at the dispenser she'd switched on as soon as she and Julian had arrived.

"Thanks. I'll pass. Let me help you pack those knives."

Jamie offered the bubble wrap to Patricia. "I'm sorry our test run for marketing your knives hit a pothole."

"No worries. I'll hawk them elsewhere." Patricia swathed a steak knife in bubble wrap. "If I can stand to look at them."

"I hope they won't feel tainted to you for long. I wouldn't have told you how Valerie died, except I was sure you'd hear about it anyway, and I figured it was better to tell you myself."

"Good call." Patricia nestled the steak knife in the box. "Awful news. Heartbreaking."

Jamie waited, hoping Patricia would spontaneously explain her comment about another murder, but she said nothing.

"I'll go finish the new display," Julian said. "Excuse me, Ms. Hendriks." He left the office. Since he always bowed to Jamie's pickiness by leaving the last touches on a new display to her, she knew he was making a tactful excuse to leave, hoping his absence would make Patricia more inclined to confide in Jamie. *Thank you, sweetie.*

Jamie started disassembling the wooden rack that had held the knives. "We're replacing the knife display with your jade and jasper Christmas bowls. I usually hold off displaying Christmas merchandise until November, but I couldn't cope with the idea of my crystal room lacking a display of Patricia Hendriks's work."

"You're a doll."

Jamie reined in the urge to quip that Patricia wasn't the only one who thought she was a "doll." That wasn't a joke she wanted to explain.

Patricia picked up a carving knife and tapped her thumb against the plastic sheath protecting the blade. "Makes me sick," she said under her breath. "Using something beautiful for something evil."

Jamie figured she'd better take this opening. "When we were speaking on the phone, you mentioned another murder. I'm sorry to ask, but have your knives been used in that way before? I'm wondering if there's a pattern the police should be aware of."

Patricia kept winding bubble wrap around the knife until it was the size of a loaf of bread. Jamie wished she'd phrased the question more sensitively, but she couldn't think of a delicate way to say, *Are your knives a favorite weapon of murderers?*

"Not my knives." Patricia began unrolling the excess wrap. "You have enough pain for yourself. I shouldn't hand you mine. But I lost my stepdaughter last April. Murdered. Strangled."

"Oh my word, Patricia, I'm so sorry."

"I guess she wasn't *my* stepdaughter. She was my ex-husband's stepdaughter, from his wife's first marriage, but she was interested in sculpting, and my ex sent her to apprentice with me every summer when she was in high school. We got close. Talented young lady. Name was Annika."

"Did the police catch her killer?"

"Nope. Nothing to go on. No witnesses, no suspects. But a week earlier, she'd received a scarf in the mail." Patricia laid the knife in the box. "No return address, no card. Totally anonymous. It was an Hermés scarf."

"That's an expensive anonymous gift!"

"Yes. A beautiful scarf. She sent me a picture of it."

"She had no idea who sent it?"

"Not a clue. She assumed she had a secret admirer. A week later, she was found dead, strangled with that scarf."

"I'm so sorry. Did the police think whoever sent the scarf was the person who used it on her?"

"They couldn't trace the sender, so I don't know what they thought, but personally, I don't think the scarf was a coincidence. Some sicko thought it was funny to send her her own murder weapon."

"Valerie's murderer bought the knife from her," Jamie said. "She was the clerk who served him."

Patricia groaned. "Another sicko playing games."

"Was Annika with you in Bangor at the time she died?"

"No, she was home in New York. Albany."

"Albany?" The word released a sluice of adrenaline. *Could be coincidence . . . Albany is a big place . . .* Jamie abandoned the pieces of the display rack and opened a desk drawer to retrieve the notepad where she'd written the measly amount of information she'd gathered about Mr. Death's alleged Albany address. It was a two-story, white, Colonial-style house built in 1974. The current owners were Mason and Aria Diaz, who'd bought the house two months ago. The former owners were Kevin and Ginger Brantley; they were the original owners.

"I hadn't talked to Annika for a couple of months, and then my ex calls and tells me she's been murdered." Patricia ripped off a square of bubble wrap. "Worst day of my life."

"I'm so sorry for your loss."

Patricia stowed another knife in the box. "When we finish this, give me the tour of your store. I need something cheerful tonight."

"I'd love to. Also, I have a weird question."

"Shoot."

"Does this address sound familiar to you?" Jamie read the address off the notepad.

Patricia shook her head. "It wasn't Annika's or her family's, if that's what you want to know."

"It was an address that came up in connection with the investigation of Valerie's death. I did a little research but couldn't find anything relevant. When you said Albany, though, I wondered if there was a connection."

"Who lives there?"

Jamie handed Patricia the notepad. She read it, and her face took on the same hardness as the stone she chiseled. "Your sicko is playing games with the cops. Mason Diaz is my ex. Aria Diaz is Annika's mother."

* * *

When Jamie called Detective Powell, she expected him to summon Patricia to the police department, but within ten minutes, he was at the Treasure Chest, interviewing Patricia in Jamie's office. Jamie and Julian retreated upstairs to the book room and settled on the couch. Jamie rested her head on Julian's shoulder and wearily surveyed the nonfunctional fireplace filled with silk dahlias, daisies, and peach-colored roses in a hammered copper basket. Every time she sat here, she was tempted to make the fireplace functional again, but the cost of repairing the flue liner, combined with elevated insurance costs, didn't seem worth it.

"Poor Patricia," she murmured.

"What was her stepdaughter's name again?" Julian asked.

"Annika. I don't know her last name."

Julian lifted his arm from where he'd wrapped it around Jamie and started working with his phone. Jamie repositioned her head on his shoulder.

"This must be her," Julian said. "Annika Sandoval. Twenty-four-year-old Albany resident. Found strangled to death in her apartment last April 14."

Jamie studied the picture of a woman with short black hair, a joyful smile, and the world's cutest dimple in her cheek. "Her mother and stepfather only bought the house two months ago. That's why nothing pertinent turned up when I googled Mr. Death's address."

"Twisted creature, using that address. That sounds like a declaration that Valerie was not his first victim."

"Annika has a distant connection with Valerie. Annika apprenticed with Patricia, and Valerie sold Patricia's art. If it's the same killer, did he choose Valerie *because* of that connection? I mean, did he fly in, check out the employees at the Treasure Chest, and pick his victim?"

Julian's gaze locked with Jamie's. She knew exactly what fear her words had stirred in him: *it could have been you.*

"It's a weak connection to follow all the way from Albany to Britteridge," Jamie amended, wishing she hadn't spooked both of them with her theory.

"True," Julian said. "But it's still a connection."

For a long stretch, they sat wordlessly, Julian drumming his fingers on the arm of the couch and Jamie scanning the bookshelves.

"Maybe the killer is a student of unsolved crimes." Jamie rose and went to move a mis-shelved copy of *Gone with the Wind* from the self-help section to the classics section.

"Do you think he didn't kill Annika but tracked down her mother's address and used it for his amusement?"

"It makes more sense than a killer bopping from Albany to Britteridge. Why not pick a victim closer to home?"

"Picking victims far from home might make it harder for the police to zero in on him."

Jamie returned to the couch, where Julian was again on his phone, no doubt researching something. *Could* Valerie have fallen victim to a serial killer? Jamie had the silly thought that Britteridge wasn't big enough to harbor a serial killer, as though communities were only allowed so many serial killers per capita.

"Using something beautiful for something evil. That's what Patricia said, talking about both the knife and the scarf, I think." Jamie glanced at Julian's screen. "Why are you searching for information about Kate Durham?"

"She's new here," Julian said. "These problems are new here."

"I vetted her before hiring her, you know. Called her references and all that. Besides, it was a man who bought that knife."

"I know, darling."

Creaking footfalls from downstairs signaled that Powell and Patricia were done with their interview. Jamie and Julian stood in unison. At the base of the stairs, they met Powell.

"Ms. Hendriks said to offer her apologies, but she was tired and wanted to return to her hotel," Powell said.

"Thanks." Jamie couldn't blame Patricia for bailing out. After reliving the death of a loved one for the police, it would be hard to care about an activity as trivial as touring a gift shop.

"Thank you for immediately contacting me," Powell said. "Ms. Hendriks's information was helpful."

As Jamie debated how nosy she could be in asking for details of what Patricia had told him, Julian spoke. "Detective, Jamie received a disturbing wooden doll yesterday."

"Julian!" Heat blazed in Jamie's face. "That's not a matter the police need to worry about. Detective Powell is busy with a murder investigation."

Powell shifted his calm gaze to Jamie. "Tell me about the doll."

"It's nothing. It's a prank."

"Someone created a fake email account under my name and used that address to contact Niall Flanagan to order a wooden doll carved and painted to look like Jamie," Julian said. "The customer paid Niall with cash and left it in his mailbox. Niall left the doll on our doorstep, but the customer retrieved it before we found it and altered it so it appeared Jamie was drinking from a bucket of poison. He or she then planted the doll here at the Treasure Chest, leaving it inside a ceramic wishing well that sits on a table near the book room."

Jamie glared at Julian. "Sweetie, there's no reason Detective Powell needs to hear this. Leaving a weird doll isn't a crime."

"Why do you think someone gave you the doll?" Powell asked.

"Oh, some people in town don't like that I'm making changes here, like adding the herbal tea collection. I think that's what the poison represented. People get stuck in tradition. Do you want to see the five-page letter a ninety-year-old woman wrote to me, complete with references to the Mayflower, after I replaced the stair runner? Or the two-volume scrapbook of the Allertons' Treasure Chest traditions, compiled by concerned citizens whose stamp sets and Cricut machines are always battle-ready?"

"I'd like to see the doll. Do you have it here?"

"It's in my office, but honestly, it's nothing to worry about. Julian is being overprotective."

"May I see it, please?"

"I'll get it," Julian said.

Jamie would have pursued him but feared her interference would encourage Powell to think this was a big deal. "Sorry to waste your time," she said. "I don't expect the police to pursue the matter of who thinks I'm ruining the Allerton legacy."

"Do you know who left you the doll?"

"No."

"Do you *suspect* who left you the doll?"

Setting the police on Marcia would stir up more widespread hostility for Jamie than any change she could make. "Several people have complained, and they usually claim they have friends and family who feel the same way, so I suspect all of them, but don't worry about it. I can handle complaints. Speaking of changes, may I offer you a square of our chocolate of the month? It's from Madagascar. More acidic than last month's Venezuelan chocolate, with notes of strawberry—"

"Do you have a top suspect?"

Jamie spotted a damp leaf on the floor that she could pick up, giving her an excuse not to look Powell in the eyes. "I don't want to risk embarrassing anyone with my guesses."

"Marcia Allerton-Harper?"

Jamie squinted at the yellow leaf on her palm. "You really do read minds."

"Mrs. Allerton-Harper and I have discussed you before."

"Oh peachy. What about me?"

"About your 'stealing' of the Treasure Chest. When she couldn't talk Ed out of giving it to you, she came to me. She said you must have blackmailed him and she wanted you investigated."

"*Blackmailed* him? For what? Does she know her own cousin? That man has never even broken the speed limit."

Julian returned and handed the doll to Powell. "Niall told Jamie he painted it as a happy, healthy Jamie holding a bucket filled with daffodils. The dripping green brew and the cadaverous face were added by the customer."

"Even if it was Mrs. Allerton-Harper, I don't want anything done about it," Jamie said. "She'll calm down."

Powell examined the doll. "You found this in a table display located in the hallway upstairs, Jamie?"

"Yes."

"She didn't find it," Julian said. "Her new employee did. A woman named Katherine Durham."

Jamie gave him the stink eye. "How is that relevant?"

Julian shrugged.

"Kate is new in town," Jamie said. "She never even saw the Treasure Chest before I took over. Why would she care if I change things up?"

"Maybe the doll has a different meaning," Julian said.

"She's new to town?" Powell looked at Jamie. "How long has she been here?"

"They moved here in the summer." Jamie held out her hand to take the doll, hoping that claiming it would end this conversation.

"Where from?"

"Pennsylvania." Feeling awkward with her still-empty hand out, Jamie lowered it. "Pittsburgh area. She's only worked here for a couple days, but she's been great, learning fast, helping pick up the slack with . . .Valerie gone."

Powell placed the doll on the small table that held a bowl of Treasure Chest business cards. He took out his phone and snapped pictures of the front and back of the doll.

Jamie imagined him showing the photos to Mrs. Allerton-Harper. "I'm going to have enough bad publicity without embarrassing pillars of the community," she said desperately. "You're not going to pursue a matter this petty are you?"

"I'm not going to pursue anything petty." Powell handed the doll to Jamie. "But it's wise to document this in case your complainer escalates. Forgive your husband for sharing this with me. It was a smart thing to do. I'll leave you to your evening now."

Jamie accompanied Powell to the back door, Julian following them. When Powell had exited, Jamie whirled around and squared off with Julian. "Shouldn't you have asked me if I wanted to share that?"

"No," Julian said. "Because you would have said no, and I would have done it anyway, and I would be in twice as much trouble now."

Involuntary laughter defeated Jamie's annoyance—too much laughter for the humor in his comment, and she had trouble stopping it so she could speak. "I'm not . . . not . . . I'm not angry. I'm embarrassed. And, apparently, a little hysterical."

"You have nothing to be embarrassed about."

"I *always* have something to be embarrassed about."

"I meant specifically about the doll."

Laughter took control of Jamie a second time.

With his hand on her elbow, Julian guided her into her office and into her chair. "Powell is tactful and careful; you know that," he said. "He needs to know about the doll. Under the circumstances, I don't like there being anything strange going on here that isn't on his radar."

Anything strange here. Like a killer purchasing a pricey, decorative knife and murdering her employee. Like the sculptor who had crafted that knife standing in Jamie's office and sharing her story of losing an apprentice who was practically a daughter to murder, this crime executed via a pricey, beautiful scarf.

Jamie wiped her eyes and blinked at the doll she held. It was pricey, yes, but ghoulish, not beautiful, and it wouldn't work as a weapon—unless it was saturated in poison and every time Jamie handled it, poison seeped through her skin and did hidden damage.

Stop it. Poison is not seeping through your skin. She set the doll on the desk and fought an impulse to go wash her hands. Maybe it was a threat and the killer intended to poison her in the future. But that didn't follow the pattern of the other murders, and it was ludicrous to think two different killers were picking victims from the Treasure Chest.

Still, Julian was right. To assume the giver was a crabby traditionalist who meant no harm and to refuse to mention the doll to Powell was foolish. "I'm sorry," Jamie said. "You did the right thing. I should have told him about the doll myself."

"I understand why you were hesitant." Julian tore off a piece of bubble wrap. "I hope I haven't frightened you. I doubt the doll *is* related to the murders, but when it comes to you, I'm not taking chances."

"Thank you for watching out for me."

"Always, darling. If Detective Powell questions Kate about the doll and she gets offended and quits, I will personally find you a new employee who's even better than she."

"That's a tall order." Jamie passed him the doll. "Poor Kate. She's going to sue me for fraud after the way I presented the Treasure Chest as a fun, low-stress place to work. But it's not the doll that will drive her away. It's the fact that we sold the murder weapon. Kate liked those knives. When I showed her the crystal room, she rhapsodized about how she wished she could afford—" Jamie stopped. "Oh good grief, now it sounds like I suspect . . . I did *not* mean to imply anything."

"I know." Slowly, Julian rolled the doll in bubble wrap. He didn't usually move slowly when completing tasks. He was distracted, thinking about what she'd said regarding Kate.

"It's not suspicious to admire excellent workmanship," Jamie said.

"I admired the workmanship on those knives myself, if you recall," Julian said. "When you first put them on display."

"The killer bought the knife before Kate started working here, and I never saw her or her husband in the store before that. Plus, they're from Pittsburgh, not New York, and I really don't think they're traveling around strangling and stabbing people. I hate this conversation. Can we talk about nice things? Like sunflowers? Or apple trees or tropical fish?"

"We can discuss flora and fauna to your heart's content." Julian stowed the doll in the pocket of his jacket. "Let's lock up and get out of here."

CHAPTER 8

THE MORNING SKY WAS STEELY and the wind cold for September, but nervousness overheated Kate to the point that she removed her jacket before she reached the back entrance of the Treasure Chest. Once inside, she inhaled a few deep breaths of the cinnamon-and-old-wood air, but the scent she'd savored the first few times she'd been here now seemed to burn her throat. This assignment had felt doable last night while she'd painted and listened to Colby explain it, and the small acrylic of his aunt's flowers had pleased him so much that Kate had felt like the next Georgia O'Keefe. But afterward, she'd had trouble sleeping, and she didn't want to be here this morning. She didn't want to deal with Jamie on any level, Jamie who'd be smiling at her and faking friendliness while she conspired in a plot to poison thousands.

Help the task force stop her. If Colby had the grit to spend years putting his life on the line to pursue terrorists, she ought to be able to handle this simple operation. She'd always thought it would be a thrill to fight the bad guys, but she didn't feel anywhere close to thrilled right now. She wanted to retreat to her car and call in sick. Was she this big of a coward? Intrigued by save-the-world fantasies but lacking the ability to function once dream became reality?

She hung her jacket on one of the wall hooks near the door. Into the pocket of her apron, she tucked a small baggie of brownish powder and a pair of latex gloves, along with her peacock notebook and phone. All she needed to do was dump the powder into the hot tea dispenser in Jamie's office. It wouldn't hurt anyone who hadn't been inoculated against the toxin, but if the vaccine was present in Jamie's system, the substance would trigger a response and make her sick.

Colby's instructions replayed in her head for the hundredth time: *"Make sure you have a cup with her from the same batch and that she's the one who serves it so she knows you couldn't have tampered with her cup. When she gets sick and you don't, she'll assume the tea wasn't the culprit, and your cover will remain secure."*

Kate's throat was certainly dry enough to make apple-strawberry tea sound desirable, and it would be more than easy to have a cup with Jamie—Jamie was always offering. Kate had her plan: as soon as she greeted Jamie, she'd fake a repeated dry cough. Jamie would all but drag Kate into her office for a hot herbal remedy. This all needed to happen before the store opened. If the day was busy, they wouldn't have another chance to sit down together. Jamie would still drink the reactant at some point but not with Kate, which would leave her cover shakier.

Jamie's office door stood ajar. From the direction of the foyer came the hum of the electric broom. Perfect timing. Jamie was occupied cleaning the entryway, and Kate had an ideal opportunity to spike the tea.

Heartbeat thundering, Kate entered Jamie's office. As she'd expected, the light glowed on the hot-beverage dispenser. Jamie's Thursday mug hung on the rack; she hadn't yet had any tea. Kate drew the gloves out of her apron pocket. As she separated them, she dropped one. Quickly, she bent to retrieve it. *Hurry. Don't waste this chance.*

She pulled a glove over her left hand, but the latex stuck to her sweaty skin. Fingers only halfway into the left glove, she tried donning the right glove. It clung to her skin even worse, but at least both hands were covered. She reached for the baggie of reactant and fumbled to open it with the extra latex flapping past her fingertips.

Get your act together. She yanked and stretched the gloves, moving them into place so she could open the bag. It amazed her that Lorenzo had suggested she carry out this assignment, accepting Colby's word that she'd be capable of handling it. A few days ago, they hadn't even trusted her enough to tell her Colby was part of the antiterrorist task force, and now they were giving her vital responsibilities? Yes, they'd already done a background check on her, but shouldn't she have undergone training?

This assignment isn't complicated. It doesn't take a stint at Langley or wherever to prepare for dumping powder into a beverage dispenser.

She lifted the lid on the dispenser. Steam rose from the red-brown liquid.

She raised the bag, but her hands stalled before she tipped the reactant into the tea. Colby had sworn it wouldn't harm Jamie permanently, but the prospect of contaminating someone's drink still revolted her. Maybe she should have refused to do this, telling Colby to carry out the mission himself. He hadn't been bothered at all by the thought of Jamie suffering.

He's fighting a deadly enemy. Do you expect him to be warm and fuzzy about it?

Kate rubbed the small bag between her thumb and index finger, feeling the texture of the powder. Essentially, they were assaulting Jamie. Kate wasn't sure what the legal term was for spiking someone's drink to make them ill. She also wasn't sure what legal rights domestic terrorists had as opposed to regular criminals, but shouldn't there be due process? Innocent until proven guilty? Colby claimed to have plenty of evidence that Jamie was guilty, but he hadn't shared it with Kate. Even that keypad code to Valerie Mantzaris's door that he'd found in Jamie's desk—what if Jamie wasn't the one who'd put it there? If she had, she was sloppy about protecting her secrets.

As sloppy as Colby leaving classified information lying around in his study, then mentioning that the room needed vacuuming? He'd said he'd intended to do the cleaning himself, but he must have known Kate would beat him to it. If not for his comment, she wouldn't have bothered—the carpet had looked fine to her, and so had the baseboards, which he'd specifically mentioned as being dirty.

Colby was usually so careful. So tidy. So in control, enough so that sometimes it bothered Kate. Yet he'd flubbed something as critical as shredding a classified document? Was it truly a mistake, or had he wanted her to pull the shredder out from the wall and find that paper? Did he want an excuse to tell her about the task force?

If that's true, you ought to be flattered. He wanted to confide in you. Stop standing here steaming your pores over Jamie's tea. Dump the powder, and get out before she finishes sweeping the floor. If she's innocent, this won't make her sick. She'll only get sick if she's been inoculated, which means she's planning to murder thousands of people.

A vaccine. If the terrorists were inoculating themselves against the toxin, why would Eviction have warned Jamie about insubordination by planting a doll that illustrated her dying from poisoning? Colby had interpreted the doll as a threat to turn the toxin against her. Why would they use the toxin as a threat if she was immune? Yet Colby refused to consider that the doll might be unrelated to Eviction.

Kate shut the lid on the dispenser. She couldn't do this. She had too many questions, and the uneasy sensation in her chest kept worsening. If she was going to be involved at this level, she needed to be sure she was doing the right thing. She needed to be sure she wasn't working for people who were running a slapdash, ethically questionable operation. She needed to meet Lorenzo, for starters. She hated doubting Colby's competence, but she couldn't move forward until she had more information and clear, independent evidence.

The hum of the electric broom got louder. Jamie must be cleaning the hallway, heading toward the office. Kate resealed the baggie, peeled off her gloves, and tucked everything into her apron pocket. Rather than race out of the office in a suspicious way, she'd employ one of the excuses she'd prepared. She wiped her sweaty hands on her pants and strolled into the hallway.

Jamie smiled at her and switched off the electric broom. "Good morning, Kate."

"Good morning. You mentioned you had a needle and thread in your office that I was welcome to use. I need it now, but I can't remember where it is."

"Let me get that for you." Jamie entered her office and opened a side cabinet. She took out the kit she'd shown Kate during her orientation. The plastic tackle box contained a collection of items that might be needed during a workday, including Band-Aids, ibuprofen, safety pins, moleskin, cough drops, lip balm, and a stain-removal pen. Jamie plucked out the packet containing a sewing needle, ten different colors of thread, and foldable scissors.

"Here you go." She handed it to Kate. "I'd offer to help you sew whatever needs sewing, but I am *so* behind. I wanted to be here an hour and a half ago, but I had a flat tire."

"Oh no! What a pain. I'll fix my issue and come help you as quickly as I can. I, um, have a split in my pants. I'll go into the bathroom and stitch it up."

"This morning is a winner for both of us," Jamie said. "Good thing you discovered it now instead of at the end of the day. You don't need to hang out in the bathroom to sew. Stay in here and lock the door. When you're decent, come up to the linen room and help me arrange a batch of new tablecloths."

"Thanks," Kate said.

"Help yourself to a cup of tea and some gingersnaps." Jamie gestured to a plate of cookies on the desk. "Julian—my husband—made them last night. They're divine." Jamie took a gingersnap and exited the office, leaving Kate staring at the cookies, unable to prevent tears from welling in her eyes.

* * *

For the first couple of hours, Jamie hoped it was the gray, unseasonably cold weather keeping customers away, not the publicizing of where the killer had acquired the knife he'd used to kill Valerie. Restless and running short on stock to dust and displays to straighten, she finally left the sales floor in Kate's care and retreated to the storage room next to her office to unpack a newly delivered box of glassware.

Kate had looked flushed and edgy when Jamie had greeted her this morning, and she still didn't seem comfortable. Her smiles and perky comments had a phony vibe, and Jamie wondered if the police had questioned her about the doll. Should she be straightforward and ask Kate if Powell had contacted her? She'd like to reassure Kate that she did *not* suspect her of planting the doll, or of anything else, but the police needed to investigate all possibilities.

Jamie unwound the paper encasing a swirled-glass serving bowl and examined the piece for damage. As soon as she finished this box, she'd head back out, take a moment with Kate, and do what she could to put her at ease.

In her apron pocket, Jamie's phone buzzed. She pulled it out. Detective Powell. "Hello, this is Jamie."

"Jamie, Aaron Powell. I'll keep this short. I know you're busy."

"I wish I were busy. Business is dead at the moment—I'm sorry for that unfortunate word choice. Business is not thriving at the moment. What can I do for you?"

"I want to thank you again for connecting us with Patricia Hendriks. We're in contact with the investigators on Annika Sandoval's murder. There is a possibility that both Annika's and Valerie's murders are linked to another murder, one that happened about a year ago in Rhode Island."

Jamie closed the door of the storage room to keep the conversation private. "Linked in what way?"

"The murdered woman is Savannah Obaya, twenty-three, lived in a little town called Tiverton. Ms. Obaya's parents' house backed on the Sakonnet River. Last May, a small wooden kayak—quality thing, handmade, cedar wood—showed up in her backyard. Savannah's habit was to go out on the river every evening. When no one claimed the kayak, she took it out for a few runs. After the last trip, she was found drowned, trapped under the kayak, with injuries inconsistent with an accidental death. I'll keep the details to myself, but it was a homicide. We found out today that Savannah's family knew Annika Sandoval. The Sandoval family often vacationed in Tiverton, and they always rented a cottage next door to the Obayas."

"A distant link," Jamie said. "Like the link between Annika and Valerie, with Valerie selling the knives made by Annika's mentor and almost-stepmom."

"Yes. The choice of weapons in each case is also interesting."

"'Using something beautiful for something evil,'" Jamie quoted. "That's what Patricia said. Someone sent Annika an Hermes scarf; she was strangled with it. Someone purchased an elegant, handmade knife from Valerie and stabbed her with it. Maybe the murderer left a classy wooden kayak in Savannah's yard, knowing she'd be drawn to using it. When she did, they met her on the river. Are we talking about a serial killer?"

"Might be. We're working with the FBI, determining if any other recent murders of young women fit this pattern. You'll probably receive a visit from one of their agents today."

"Thanks for the heads-up."

"We'll be releasing information to the media about the possibility that Valerie was the victim of a serial killer, so don't feel you need to keep this secret."

"Okay, thank you for letting me know." She would never object to the necessary steps of catching a killer, but the realization that the spotlight on the Treasure Chest was about to intensify from bright to blindingly bright made her want to worm behind the boxes on the shelf and hide.

"I'll leave you to your day. Goodbye." Powell hung up.

Back in her office, Jamie took her Thursday mug from the rack, a caramel-brown piece of pottery speckled with dark brown and brick red. With the mug full of steaming tea, she sat at her desk and selected one of the gingersnaps Julian had baked last night in an effort to relax both of them.

A serial killer? If he'd killed Savannah in Rhode Island a year ago, Annika in New York last spring, and now Valerie in Massachusetts, did that mean he didn't live in the places where he committed his murders? Did he travel the East Coast, tracking down potential victims, getting a thrill out of weaving distant interpersonal connections into a web of death?

Jamie sipped tea and thought about Mr. Death slinking through the door of the Treasure Chest, seeking his next victim. How many times had he come here? He'd told Valerie he was a new customer, but that might not be true. Valerie might not have served him before, but Jamie or another employee might have, if he'd scoped the place out before settling on Valerie as his victim. Jamie needed to evaluate all her notes on male customers for the past year. That was going to take awhile. Maybe it was fortunate that business was slow this morning. She'd heard the door chime a few times, but Kate was handling customers competently on her own.

She took another swallow of tea and scowled at her mug. The apple-strawberry blend didn't taste as good as usual. She was getting tired of it. Time to start sampling new varieties for October's tea of the month.

She set her mug down. She'd check on Kate and the sales floor, then start going through her notes, preparing for a visit from the FBI.

"Oh, Jamie, good timing." Kate met Jamie as she entered the foyer. "A customer would like to speak with you. Mrs. Harper. She—"

"*Allerton*-Harper, dear." A woman with a plump face and a swirl of gray hair exited the main room and walked toward Kate and Jamie. "I'm sure Jamie has told you all about the Allerton family?"

"Good morning," Jamie said before Marcia Allerton-Harper could quiz Kate on the family tree. "What can I help you with?"

"You can help yourself, young lady, by listening to me. No, you stay here too." Marcia poked Kate's arm as Kate tried to retreat. "Everyone who works here should know so they can be on alert."

"On alert for what?" Jamie braced herself for Marcia to blame her for allowing a killer into the store. *Don't lose your temper. Smile and thank her for taking the time to come share her concerns. Don't bring up the doll.*

"I received a call from your husband," Marcia said. "He asked me about a wooden doll painted to look like a dead version of you."

On second thought, feel free to bring up the doll. Oh, Julian. "I'd be happy to talk about this, but Kate needs to get back to work."

"Psh. I'm the only customer in the store right now. Who wants to go shopping with a murderer on the loose? First of all, you ought to know better than to suspect me of giving you that doll. When I have a problem with someone, I address the person directly." Marcia took two steps closer to Jamie. Jamie didn't retreat—not that she didn't want to, but Marcia's gaze snagged her like one of the sturdy hooks Jamie used to display heavy wall décor. "I assure you, young lady, if that doll were from me, I would have signed my name."

"Thank you for letting me know," Jamie said. "I'm sure Julian made it clear I had no intention of accusing you." *A courtesy you didn't show to me when you tried to persuade Detective Powell that I blackmailed Edward Allerton.*

"Of course he did, flattering me as though gracious words would hide the insult. I told him I'd never do such a ghastly thing, and I'll tell you this, Jamie McKenzie Stokes: no one else in Britteridge who objects to the way you're treating our Treasure Chest would have left you that doll either. I was speaking to my sister—you know Glenda, of course—and we were discussing how crass people are these days when they disagree. No dignity. We know all the old guard, and not one of them would be so tasteless, or so extravagant. A Niall Flanagan carving as a message of disapproval?" Marcia shook her head. "When we see something that needs correcting, we express ourselves face to face, not by leaving an anonymous doll, and definitely not by leaving that frightful doll in the lovely ceramic wishing well Glenda's committee gave you."

Marcia had a point. She had no difficulty being forthright. "I apologize for suspecting you. You were so passionately opposed to my adding herbal teas and chocolate to our inventory that the image of me drinking poison reminded me of your objections."

"Don't be absurd. I have nothing against teas, per se, or chocolate or whatever trendy treats you're selling in hopes of appealing to college students with striped socks and beards and save-the-sea-turtles causes. I don't think food belongs on the shelves here, but that's not important at the moment. Your clerk is dead, a nice young woman, and murdered with your own knife. I heard this morning that the police think she might have been the victim of a serial killer."

Kate, who had been inching backward toward the main room, stopped and gaped at Marcia. "A serial killer?"

Marcia glanced at her. "Yes, missy, it was on the news. Some other young women have been murdered, and the police found links to Valerie Mantzaris's murder."

"Other women *here*?"

"Not here," Jamie said. "Nearby states." Kate looked so rattled that Jamie wanted to go put an arm around her. "It's awful. We'll do everything we can to help the police and the FBI—"

"Yes, we know," Marcia interrupted. "What you need to do is close the Treasure Chest and go into hiding until the police catch the murderer. You can't keep putting yourself and girls like this"—she pointed at Kate— "at risk."

Judging by the pallor on Kate's face, she was taking Marcia's warning to heart. *Thank you for scaring my staff.* "The fact that Valerie worked here doesn't mean the killer will target the rest of us. The killer's victims—"

"You're missing the point. *You've already been threatened.* If you have a brain, you'll recognize this isn't a time to take threats lightly. Your husband said you two showed the doll to Detective Powell. I'm going straight from here to the police department to inform him that none of my people planted it and he'd better find out who did, because you might be in danger. I wanted to warn you first so you can take precautions. Start by locking up the store as soon as I leave. You had the murderer in here once. He might come back."

Responses bobbled in Jamie's head, but she didn't know which one to speak. Marcia had come here because she was worried about Jamie? "It's . . . very kind of you to take the time to come warn me."

"Oh, for pity's sake. It's human decency. I'd never forgive myself if I didn't speak up and you continued risking your life because you assumed the doll was a complaint from me. Take care of yourself, child."

Speechless, Jamie watched Marcia march out the front door, flipping up the hood of her raincoat as she exited.

CHAPTER 9

"Wow." KATE GAVE A TREMULOUS giggle. "I'm glad I didn't have to handle her on my own."

"She . . . I . . . didn't expect that." How could Jamie feel so disoriented standing in the entryway of her own store? "Mrs. Allerton-Harper is always interesting to deal with, but . . . Well, it's good to know she doesn't want me to get murdered. How have things been out here?"

"Fairly quiet," Kate said.

Jamie eyed the rain spattering the glass panes on the door. "Now that the rain has started, it's going to be even quieter."

Kate toyed with the Treasure Chest business cards in their glass bowl. "You thought Mrs. Allerton-Harper was the person who gave you that strange doll?"

"She doesn't like changes I've made here and has complained many times. Sometimes in over-the-top ways."

Kate kept fiddling with the business cards, her white cheeks blushing pink. "It sounded like she thought it was this . . . serial killer . . . who might have left it."

"I'm sorry she spooked you. Come relax in the office for a few minutes. I assume there aren't any customers upstairs?"

"No." Kate followed Jamie toward the office.

"Have a seat," Jamie invited. "Tea?"

"Thank you, yes."

Jamie filled a guest mug and pushed the plate of cookies closer to Kate. Kate accepted the mug and took a cookie.

Jamie's mouth felt dry. She picked up her own mug and gulped partly cooled tea. "I'm sorry you have to deal with any of this. I promise, we usually are a quaint and adorable local gift shop." She sat on the visitor's chair next to Kate.

Kate smiled and sipped from her mug. "This blend is delicious. The tang of the strawberry comes through and the flavor of the apple, not just the sweetness of it."

Jamie took another swallow. "I was thinking it tasted off, but that's probably my stressed-out taste buds . . . or the fact that I keep thinking about poison."

Kate sipped again. "It tastes fine to me."

"So here's why I don't think the doll was from the same man who killed Valerie." Jamie started explaining about Annika's and Savannah's deaths. Her mouth kept getting drier, no matter how often she sipped between sentences. Marcia's words had apparently scared her even worse than they had Kate. *Go figure. Kate wasn't the target of the doll.*

"In all three cases, before the killer attacked, he involved the victim with the weapon on some level," Jamie continued. "Valerie sold him the knife, Annika wore the scarf, and Savannah went out on the river in the wooden kayak."

"I think I remember hearing about the kayak case," Kate said. "This is so awful."

"In every case the weapon was something beautiful. I think it's clear that a doll of me with a dead white face and green poison all over my mouth isn't intended to evoke an 'Oh how lovely.' Besides, Detective Powell didn't say anything about any of the other victims being warned beforehand. To sum up all my babble, I think Mrs. Allerton-Harper was telling the truth about not giving me the doll, but I think she's mistaken about it being the work of the killer."

Kate drank, her eyebrows furrowing. "Do you have any idea who gave you the doll, then?"

"No. Come to think of it, I should ask my brothers. I've told them about the way Marcia and her 'old guard' reacted to my selling tea and chocolate, and one of them might have thought it was funny to . . . No, never mind." Neither of her brothers would have pretended to be Julian when ordering it, and they would have sent it to her directly, making it clear it was a joke. Plus, they wouldn't have wasted that much money on a prank.

"Is your family local?" Kate asked.

"We grew up here, but we're spread out now. One brother is in Tennessee, one is in Oregon, and my sister is in Arizona. I'm the youngest. My parents retired to Florida a couple of years ago. We all keep in close touch."

"I'm jealous," Kate said. "I'm an only child. I don't remember my dad, and my mother died a few years ago."

"I'm so sorry."

"I wish my mother could have met Colby. She'd be like, 'Kate, how in the world did you manage to catch such a dreamy guy?' *Dreamy* was her favorite adjective."

"I think she'd have asked, 'Kate, how did Colby manage to catch such a dreamy girl?'"

Kate's smile was morose. "You're too nice." She picked up her half-eaten gingersnap. "What did Detective Powell say about the doll?"

"Just that Julian was wise to tell him about it in case the situation escalates." Jamie groaned. "This is insane, but I'm tempted to do what Mrs. Allerton-Harper said and lock up the store. Which is ridiculous because I just said I don't think the killer gave me the doll. It's not like he left a kayak on my lawn."

"Wait!" Kate squeaked the word. "Was the kayak murder in Rhode Island?"

"Yes, about a year ago." Jamie set her nearly empty mug aside and went to the water cooler in the corner. "In a little lakeside town."

That's why the story rang a bell. We went to Newport on our honeymoon a year ago, so we were close by when it happened. They thought at first it was an accident, but the medical examiner determined it was murder."

"So much for a peaceful and picturesque honeymoon location." Jamie filled a cup of water and drained it, but it didn't help her thirst or her escalating queasiness. Kate and her husband had been in Rhode Island a year ago when Savannah was murdered? And now, a few months after they'd come to Britteridge, Valerie was dead?

Jamie thought of Kate's husband. Sharp dresser, magnetic smile.

Of Julian mentioning to Powell that Kate was the one who'd found the doll. Of Kate admiring the granite knives.

Be reasonable. Jamie filled a second cup with water. *You know the doll doesn't fit the killer's modus operandi. And if Kate and her husband had anything to do with Savannah's death, why would Kate have told you they were near the scene of the crime?*

"This is creepy," Kate said. "Thinking the killer in Rhode Island might be the same one who struck here."

"Makes you feel like he's following you from state to state." Jamie was careful to make the words sound darkly humorous. "Annika Sandoval died in New York, in Albany. Please tell me you weren't *there* last spring."

"No, thank heavens. That really would freak me out. I've never been to Albany." Kate frowned. "Your face is very flushed. Are you okay?"

"I'm fine." Jamie gulped more water. "The last thing I need is to get sick right now. Not that you wouldn't be great running things on your own."

"I'm not ready for that. Please don't get sick."

What was wrong with her vision? Jamie squeezed her eyes shut and opened them again, but the familiar sights in her office remained smeary. "Has your husband been to Albany?"

"Who knows? He travels everywhere." Kate gave her signature nervous giggle. "I hope you're not suggesting he's the serial killer."

"Of course not. I think you'd know if your husband was a murderer." Nausea looped around Jamie's stomach. *Would* Kate know? Jamie wanted to ask if Colby had disappeared for any significant stretches of time while they were honeymooning in Rhode Island, but she couldn't push the conversation any further in that direction. She needed to call Powell and tell him to investigate Colby Durham.

Heart racing, Jamie tried to drink the rest of her cup of water but slopped it over her chin and onto her blouse. "I'm sorry, but I actually do feel lousy. I'm going to close the store and go home to sleep. You can take the rest of the day off. Go clock out. I'll lock up."

"I can help you with that," Kate said.

Jamie wanted to say she'd prefer Kate leave immediately, but a surge of dizziness and confusion wiped out the possibility of words. Wishing she had a couch in her office, she sank into a chair, but sitting down wasn't enough. She slid off the chair and stretched out on the rug between the visitors' chairs and her desk. A tickle of awareness told her this behavior would alarm Kate, but she couldn't think of a better alternative.

"Jamie?" Kate spoke softly, her voice the only sound penetrating the smothering, ruthless heat surrounding Jamie.

Jamie closed her eyes, hoping a few motionless seconds would clear her head and calm her stomach. Her pulse boomed in her ears.

"Kate," she mumbled. "Call Julian. Tell him . . ." Thirst distracted her. She pushed herself to her hands and knees and tried to crawl toward the water dispenser. Everything clouded together in blotches of color and blankness.

She needed a doctor. "Kate," she said. "Kate, I . . . need . . . Kate?" She pawed blearily in the direction of the chair where Kate had been sitting. It was empty.

Out of Jamie's scrambled thoughts, an image of Kate coalesced, Kate leaving her office this morning, claiming she'd been searching for a needle and thread. She'd given Kate the sewing kit, told her to stay in the privacy of the office to fix her torn seam. Kate had been alone in her office for a while. She could have . . .

The tea. The tea had tasted wrong.

Jamie wasn't getting sick. She'd been poisoned.

But Kate had also drunk . . .

Or pretended to drink.

The doll wasn't the beautiful weapon. Kate was.

* * *

Kate clamped her hands over her mouth as though keeping silent would make any difference. Trembling, she stood near the doorway, watching Jamie grope at the chair where Kate had been sitting. She wanted to go to Jamie's aid, to call 911, to make her comfortable while they waited for an ambulance, but Colby's voice blared in her head. *"We're not asking you to assassinate her. You'll just make her sick for few hours. Think of the mass murder she has planned. Think about that, Katie."*

Kate reached into her apron pocket and clutched the still-full plastic baggie. She hadn't given Jamie the reactant, but Jamie was sick anyway. Had Jamie's terrorist friends poisoned her? Colby must have been right about their giving her the doll as a warning.

The doll Jamie had shown to a police detective? If she knew the doll was from Eviction, why had she drawn attention to it? *Was* Powell on Eviction's payroll?

"Has your husband been to Albany?" Jamie's words clamored in Kate's memory, battering against Colby's voice. Jamie had tried to sound casual, but she'd been fishing for evidence that Colby might have killed Annika. He'd been in Britteridge when Valerie had died and in Newport when Savannah had died.

He'd looked so amused when they'd talked about Jamie stabbing Valerie. So indifferent at the thought of making Jamie suffer.

The lives of the murdered women all linked together. Interpersonal links fascinated Colby.

Get a grip, Kate. Jamie herself said you'd know if your husband was a murderer.

Kate wasn't sure she *would* know. She hadn't known he was a government agent.

How well did she know Colby?

Are you totally brainless? He couldn't have killed Savannah. That trip was your honeymoon. You were always together.

But there had been a couple of afternoons and an evening—or two evenings?—when Kate had slept heavily for long stretches, fatigued from too much vacationing, she'd assumed, or fighting off a virus . . . She usually had more stamina . . .

The chime from the front door made Kate jump. She couldn't deal with a customer now—Yes, she could. She'd rush to the customer, tell them Jamie had collapsed, and tell them to call an ambulance while Kate made Jamie comfortable. When Colby grilled her about why she hadn't contacted him instead of emergency services, she could tell him a customer had been present and she'd had no choice but to let them call an ambulance.

All the other questions in her head, she'd deal with later.

She sped toward the foyer, but her plan disintegrated at the sight of Colby stowing his umbrella in the stand near the door.

"Katie, how's your day going? Thought I'd stop by on my lunch hour." His tone was friendly, but his gaze swept deliberately in every direction, and he arched his eyebrows at Kate. The wordless questions were plain: *Where is Jamie Stokes, who else is in the store, and did you give her the reactant yet?*

Furious at her own confusion, Kate let words gush out. "I didn't give it to her."

"Be quiet," he whispered, striding toward her. "Have you lost your mind?"

"No one else is in the store, and Jamie is too sick to listen."

"She's sick? I thought you said you didn't give her—"

"I *didn't*, because this is crazy, putting me in a position like this, and I'm not doing anything else until you give me more information and training. But she got sick anyway."

"What are her symptoms?"

"She collapsed on her office floor. Her face is red, she keeps mumbling that she needs water, and she can't seem to see or move very well."

"Why didn't you call me?"

"It just happened! I didn't have time."

"Okay, babe, stay calm. First, let's make sure nobody walks into the middle of this and becomes a terrorist target." Moving rapidly, Colby twisted the bolt on the front door, flipped the Open sign to Closed, and switched off the lights in the foyer and main room.

"She needs a doctor," Kate said, the bruising pain in her head making her feel like she needed medical help along with Jamie. She wanted to trust Colby. She did trust Colby. He was her husband. "If it wasn't the reactant that did this, someone poisoned her."

"Yeah, and we know who did. If you call the EMTs, they won't know what to do for her, and neither would the hospital. The symptoms you described are symptoms of the suspected toxin. Looks like we missed the mark, thinking her pals had inoculated her."

"So she's—dying?"

"She'll die if I don't give her the antidote."

"You have an antidote?"

"As of today, yeah. Just got it. We've all been instructed to carry it. Come on." He jogged toward the office. "I don't want her dying. We need to question her. After what her friends did to her, there's a good chance she'll sell them out in exchange for a reduced sentence."

Deeply relieved, angry at herself for doubting Colby, she followed him. "I was with Jamie in her office when she started getting sick. Was I exposed—?"

"I'll dose you with the antidote too. If you're not already showing symptoms, you probably weren't exposed, but I'm not taking any chances."

"We both drank her tea. She also has a plate of cookies she said her husband made, and we both ate those."

"Okay, good to know. We'll take the tea and cookies in for analysis."

In the office, Jamie was kneeling by her desk, one hand clutching the receiver of her desktop phone, the other hand patting the keypad as though searching for the right buttons. Cookies were scattered on the carpet, and tea dribbled off the edge of the desk.

Colby ripped the receiver out of Jamie's hand and hung up the phone. Kate spotted Jamie's cell phone on the floor near the water dispenser. It must have fallen from her apron pocket. Kate picked it up. The screen showed two missed calls from Julian Stokes.

"Thanks." Colby held out a hand for the phone. "That'll have valuable information."

Kate gave it to him. Colby had removed his raincoat but not his leather gloves. "Should I be wearing gloves?"

"Yes. Where are the ones you took this morning? Your fingerprints are okay here, but if there's any residue of the toxin, I don't want you touching it."

Kate plucked the wadded latex gloves out of her pocket.

Slowly, body shaking, Jamie raised herself to her feet and made a stumbling rotation so she faced Kate. "You . . . you're . . . you're the . . ." Jamie licked her lips. "You're the weapon."

"I don't know what you're talking about."

Jamie turned her head in Colby's direction. He was closing the office door, a smile on his face that reminded Kate of the way he'd looked last night while discussing Jamie's crimes. A fresh, stinging splash of doubt hit Kate.

"The . . . he . . . involved." Jamie squinted at Colby, then at Kate. "I didn't . . . recognize it."

"What?" Not wanting to look at Colby, Kate worked at one of the gloves, trying to turn it right side out.

"The weapon," Jamie rasped. "Like the others. I brought you here, hired you . . . you . . . you planned to . . ."

"I'm not the one who poisoned you," Kate snapped. Colby might object to her being candid, but if they were planning to arrest Jamie, hiding their roles with the task force wasn't possible anymore. Kate needed the confirmation of telling Jamie to her face that she knew the truth and witnessing Jamie's guilty reaction. "Your terrorist friends are testing their toxin on you."

"What?" Jamie's dilated pupils were blank, black chalkboards, nothing written there. She took a lurching step toward Kate. "The scarf. The *knife.* You . . . Valerie. You killed . . . you and Colby . . ."

Fear stung Kate more savagely. "You can't hide it anymore. We know you're involved with Eviction."

"What? No . . . we're not . . . getting evicted. There's not even a . . . mortgage . . . I own the Treasure Chest outright."

Colby chuckled. "She's not going to confess yet, Katie. That'll come later."

Jamie wobbled, plainly about to lose her balance. Kate jumped forward to catch her, dropping the latex gloves.

Jamie's knees buckled. Kate did her best to control her fall, easing the impact as Jamie hit the floor. She would have yelled at Colby to get over here and help, but Colby was mixing powder into a small plastic water bottle, and Kate didn't want to interrupt the preparation of the antidote.

"Prop her against the desk, if you can." Colby set the doctored water bottle on the desk and unscrewed the lid on a second bottle.

Kate positioned herself behind Jamie's head. She stuck her hands under Jamie's arms, lifted, and hauled her backward until she'd pinned herself between Jamie and the desk. She wriggled out from behind Jamie, leaving Jamie braced against the solid front panel of the desk.

"Thanks, Katie." Colby shook the second bottle, mixing in the powder. "Kneel next to her and keep her hands out of my way while I get this antidote down her throat. The quicker she drinks it, the better her chances of recovering without permanent damage."

Swimming against the confusion flooding her, Kate knelt next to Jamie and grasped her wrists. Her skin was fever-hot.

"Colby has the antidote," Kate said as Colby knelt on Jamie's other side, open bottle in his hand. "You need to drink it."

Colby touched the bottle to Jamie's lips. Jamie opened her mouth, an instant, thirsty reaction. Colby tilted the bottle, pouring some of the liquid into her mouth, and Jamie turned her head sharply away, spilling the antidote down her neck.

Colby gripped Jamie's jaw and turned her head toward him. Jamie thrashed, fighting so wildly that Kate could barely hold on.

"*Jamie.*" Kate repositioned her slipping fingers before Jamie could wrench free. "We're trying to help you."

"You're . . . *disgusting* . . . evil . . . helping him kill—"

Colby sloshed more of the antidote into Jamie's mouth. She gagged and coughed, spitting so much of it onto Colby's shirt that Kate couldn't imagine she'd swallowed enough to do any good. Colby scowled at his stained shirt.

"Never mind. Let go of her," he said.

Gratefully, Kate relaxed her cramping fingers. Jamie flung herself away from Kate and Colby, crashed into the leg of a chair, and lay gasping.

"Give her a few minutes," Colby said. "When she's too weak to fight us, we'll finish up." He rose to his feet and took the other bottle off the desk. "Let's take care of you first." He offered the bottle to Kate. "Drink up."

CHAPTER 10

JAMIE TRIED TO SCREAM FOR help, but her throat emitted only a dry squawk. Water. She had to get water, clean water, untainted. She dragged herself across the floor of her office, bumping into so many things that she must have been colliding with some of them multiple times. Glinting pieces of her conversation with Kate blinked on and off in her head. Terrorists. Toxin. Weapons. Kate was the weapon. Jamie peered behind her. Shadowy figures loomed, not pursuing her but blocking the door, a barrier she could never breach. Colby and Kate Durham. Mr. and Mrs. Death.

She groped until she touched the plastic of the water cooler, then reached for the cup dispenser. She filled a cup, drained it. Filled a cup, drained it. Filled a cup, splashed it over her face.

"*Now*, Katie. What are you waiting for? We'll care for her in a minute. Drink it before you get sick too."

Drink it. Get sick. A burst of nausea made Jamie flop onto her side and draw her knees against her stomach.

"What's in it?" Kate asked.

"I don't know the chemical composition. I'm not a scientist. It'll counteract the effects of the toxin. That's all I know. Drink it, quickly."

Drink it.

Mr. Death.

"You drank tea with her. That's probably how they got her. You'll start showing symptoms any second now."

Kate's response throbbed in Jamie's skull, each word a different volume. "You said if I wasn't showing symptoms already, I probably wasn't exposed."

"I don't want to take chances with your life, all right? Drink it!"

Drink it.

Kate, the beautiful weapon.

"What's wrong with you?" Hazy strokes of motion, one figure moving away from the other, the other following. "You want to end up writhing on the floor, dying like your friend there?"

"You said you'd save her."

"I will, after you drink that."

"Kate." Jamie croaked her name. "Kate, don't."

Acrid laughter. "There's your choice, babe. Her advice or mine."

Jamie rolled onto her stomach and pushed up on her elbows. *Kate, no. He's done with you.* Her tongue shaped the words, but gasps for air eroded them. Had Kate heard her?

"I'm calling an ambulance." Kate's voice, so faint it confused Jamie. Had Kate left the room? No. Jamie dragged herself toward the murky version of Kate.

"The EMTs can't help you," Colby said. "Drink that now, or I'll force it down your throat."

"Don't . . . drink it." Jamie's lips were scraps of dried leaves. He would poison Kate, murder her along with Jamie, leave town, move on to his next victim.

"Call Lorenzo." Blurs moving apart. Together. Apart. "Call him now. Let me talk to him."

"I can't do that."

"Text him, then. Your encrypted communication channel. Let me talk to him that way."

"You don't need to talk to him."

"Yes, I do! Let me talk to him. Then I'll drink the antidote. I'll help you force Jamie to drink it. I'll do whatever you say."

Jamie fishtailed, trying to sit up. Her calf bumped something. She flung her arm to the side, and her hand smacked flat wood. Her desk. Her desk? Her sense of direction was gone. Where was Kate? That was Colby in front of her, a splotch of dark trousers, light shirt, dark hair.

"You can talk to him after we get Jamie to a secure medical facility. Drink the antidote, quickly."

"Let me talk to him *now*, or I'm calling 9—Colby!"

Jamie bent one quivering leg, drawing it up. With her foot, she searched until the sole of her shoe pressed against the leg of the desk.

Colby's voice swelled in Jamie's ears. "You're a cute little fool, Katie."

With a frantic contraction of muscles, Jamie pushed off from the leg of the desk, propelling herself toward Colby's voice. She slammed into his legs. He tumbled backward and thumped hard against something—the wall? Jamie clamped her arms around his legs and tried to tell Kate to run. She wasn't sure which words came out of her mouth, but they didn't sound like the right ones. She closed her eyes and hung on to Colby's legs, her throat and stomach on fire.

A thud vibrated through Jamie. Another thud.

Odd silence.

Long silence.

* * *

Chest heaving and tears pouring down her face, Kate picked up the phone Colby had knocked out of her hand. Colby lay slumped against the wall, eyes shut, the bridge of his nose and his forehead swelling where Kate had struck him with the stone pumpkin she'd grabbed from Jamie's desk. Jamie lay atop Colby's shins, arms encircling his legs.

Kate dialed 911 and used her foot to shove the pumpkin out of sight under the desk. She didn't want Colby wielding it. "Jamie, I'm calling the police. Let go of him. We have to get out of here." With her free hand, Kate grasped one of Jamie's arms and worked it out from under Colby.

The dispatcher spoke in her ear. "911, what's your emergency?"

Kate spoke fast, trying to enunciate clearly through tears. "My name is Kate Durham. I'm at the Treasure Chest in downtown Britteridge. I need the police and an ambulance. A woman has been poisoned, and a man has a head injury, and he's dangerous. I think he killed Valerie Mantzaris."

"Ma'am, are you in immediate danger?"

"Yes," Kate said. Colby was squirming and grunting. "He's waking up. Hurry. We're in the office at the back of the store." She pinned the phone between her cheek and her shoulder so she could use both hands to detach Jamie. Jamie mumbled something about knives and water and glitter, oblivious to Kate's efforts.

With Jamie's arms freed, Kate seized her by the ankles and dragged her toward the door. Jamie thrashed; Kate's phone slipped and fell to the floor in the middle of a question from the dispatcher about how many people were present.

Colby's eyes opened.

Kate snatched the phone, stuffed it into her pocket without hanging up, and opened the office door. She grabbed Jamie's ankles again and hauled her into the hallway. When they were a few yards from the office, Kate released her, raced to the back door, unbolted it, and yanked it open in preparation for the police.

After a frozen instant of uncertainty, she reentered the office. Colby remained flopped against the wall, groaning and feebly prodding the lump on his forehead.

If he wanted to harm Jamie further, he'd have to fight his way past Kate. She scanned the office and spotted a tall, pointed crystal award from the Chamber of Commerce. She lifted it from the bookshelf and held it by the base, ready to swing it if she had to, angry enough that she didn't doubt she could clobber Colby without hesitating.

Colby's dazed eyes gradually focused on her. "Hey . . . Katie."

"Stay where you are," Kate said. "The police are on their way."

His lips curved, shifting into a smile.

"You lied to me," Kate said. "Jamie never did anything illegal, did she? You deliberately left that paper for me to find. Do you even work for the government?"

Colby gave a wheezy laugh.

"That ID was fake. You thought it was . . . *funny* . . . to suck me into this." Kate wished she could speak the words clearly instead of forcing them out through sobs, but the triumph on his face wiped out the last of her self-control. How could everything be so clear to her now, what he was, what he'd done? "You thought it was funny to . . . to . . . trick me into playing out my silly superspy fantasy. You invented that nonsense about a domestic terrorist group to turn me against Jamie. Her life was a game to you. *My* life was a game to you."

His smile was sweet, his eyes flawless ice. "But . . . wasn't it a fun game, Katie?"

Kate stared at him—his face still gorgeous despite the swelling, his lean body graceful despite its slouching position. "You're a monster."

"Admit you enjoyed it." Swaying, he leaned away from the wall and sat unsupported. "Even more than Valerie enjoyed . . . selling me that knife."

"I don't want to hear this."

"Showing me the different inlays in the handles . . . bragging about the sharpness of the blades." Colby pressed his hands on either side of his skull. "I asked her which . . . knife was her favorite. She told me. That's the one I bought."

Kate hadn't known this level of fury was possible, rage that scorched her heart. "How many women have you killed?"

He shifted to his knees. Gripping the arm of a nearby chair, he pushed himself to his feet. "Counting you and Jamie?"

Kate hastily wiped her sweaty hands on her apron and tightened her grip on the trophy, ready to strike. "The police will be here any second. Can't you hear those sirens?"

"They're welcome." He took a teetering step toward her. "They can call the coroner."

"Get near me and I'll smash your skull in. Again."

"Oooh." He took another step. "You're a scary spy, Katie."

"Stay back!"

Their eyes met. Beneath the mockery, Kate saw darkness, frigid with hate. He would kill her if he could. His final murder.

He threw himself toward her. She leaped backward into the hallway. In her peripheral vision, she saw uniformed police officers racing up the brick walkway, but Colby consumed the center of her attention as he lost his balance and fell.

Laughing.

CHAPTER 11

THE DOORBELL RANG. JAMIE TENSED and looked at Julian, who'd immediately sprung from the couch, an alert guard-dog expression on his face.

"We should have kept our address unlisted." Jamie sank back into the comfortable recliner that had been waiting for her when she'd arrived home from the hospital—a surprise gift from Julian. He would handle the visitor, as he'd been fielding the calls and texts that had bombarded her phone over the past three days.

"I don't think an unlisted address would do much good in a town this size." Julian headed toward the door. "I'll deal with the intruder with the utmost efficiency." He checked the peephole and looked over his shoulder at Jamie.

"Kate Durham," he said quietly.

"Let her in." Jamie pushed her blanket to the floor and reached for the lever to lower the footrest.

"Stay where you are, my darling, or I'm not opening the door. You're supposed to be resting."

"I can stand up, Julian."

Julian watched her, making no move to open the door.

"*Fine.*" Jamie retrieved the blanket and draped it over her legs. The day had been warm, but at dusk, their formerly sunny living room had cooled. "The nurses were a lot less bossy than you are, you know."

"Dearest, they were equally bossy, but you were either too delirious to know it or too tired to argue with them." Julian opened the door. "Good evening, Kate. I believe we've never met in person. I'm Julian Stokes."

"It's . . . good to meet you." Kate sounded bewildered. Jamie suspected she hadn't expected Julian to answer the door in such a courteous way. "I wanted to drop this off for Jamie."

"Please come in," Julian said.

"I don't want to disturb her."

"I'd prefer you come in. If you don't, she'll attempt to chase after you, and it will be my job to stop her. Let's spare me that battle, shall we?"

Kate responded with a wispy laugh. She stepped through the doorway, carrying a tin milk can filled with sunflowers and snapdragons. Her face was haggard. Jamie figured that in a contest of who looked healthier, she and Kate would tie for last place.

"Those flowers are beautiful," Jamie said. "Thank you."

Julian took the arrangement and set it on the coffee table. "May I take your coat?"

"Thank you." Kate handed him her jacket.

He hung it in the closet. "Have a seat."

Kate sat stiffly on the couch and avoided Jamie's eyes. Jamie wondered if her own muddle of emotions showed as plainly on her face as Kate's did.

"How are you feeling?" Kate asked.

"Much, much better. Thank you. How about you?"

"I'm fine. I'm not the one who got—who nearly—" Kate's words halted.

Jamie opened her mouth to ease the painful silence, but her words stalled as well. Tears filled Kate's eyes. Jamie's sore throat contracted.

"Shall I give you ladies a moment?" Julian asked. "I have a slew of audition videos to review."

Jamie nodded, appreciating Julian's astute reading of the situation. As soon as he was out of sight, Jamie rose carefully to her feet and came to sit next to Kate.

"I'm sorry," Jamie said, inadvertently laying her words over Kate's whispered, "I'm so sorry."

"What do you have to be sorry about?" Kate wiped her eyes. "You're not the one who was dumb enough to believe she was a secret agent. Did the police tell you how I . . . what Colby told me about you . . ."

"They gave me the gist of it. Don't feel dumb. A lot of people have mistaken me for a terrorist. It's the cache of hot glue guns that always gets the NSA on my tail."

Kate tried to smile. "You and your husband shouldn't be this nice about what happened."

"Because we'd be so much happier if we were angry at you?" Jamie squeezed Kate's shoulder. "You saved my life."

"I almost poured that powder into your tea."

"But you didn't. Detective Powell told me the poison I drank was already in my Thursday mug, stuck to the interior with a sugar paste that dissolved when I filled it with tea."

"Yes, because Colby must have doubted that I'd follow through, but do you know when he probably put the poison in your mug? Remember the front window display that got trashed and I told you a little kid did it? *I* destroyed the display. Colby asked me to keep you out of your office for half an hour so he could 'search' it. That was the diversion I used."

"Oh," Jamie said. "Well . . . I'm glad to hear no customers actually violated the no-food-or-drink policy."

"Jamie! I let a murderer in and kept you occupied so he could set a trap for you."

"You had no idea he was using you as a weapon against me. You thought you were working to save lives."

"I'm so sorry. I can't believe what I did and what I *almost* did to you. I can't believe I helped Colby try to force you to drink that 'antidote.' Which would have killed you. Did Detective Powell tell you?"

Jamie's throat reverted to dry and stinging. The bottle had contained a much higher concentration of poison, enough to be lethal even without the dose Jamie had already ingested. "Yes. But you honestly thought it *was* an antidote."

"Until you started begging me not to drink it. I nearly killed you, and you were worried about me?"

"I had the sense you didn't know what was really going on."

"What gave it away? My rambling about terrorists and toxins?"

"And the fact that you didn't seem to want to hurt me."

"My ignorance almost left us both dead. Colby would have slipped away, then pretended to be devastated when he heard we'd been poisoned. I doubt the police would have found evidence against him."

"Do you happen to know if he flattened my tire that morning?"

"Your tire? Oh, the reason you were late."

"Yes. I wondered if he wanted to delay my arrival at work so I wouldn't have a chance to drink from the poisoned mug until you arrived."

"I don't know if he sabotaged your tire or not, but he probably did." Kate licked her pale lips. "He'd have wanted me there, watching you suffer, whether or not I spiked your tea."

"He got that wish, but then he got to watch you defeat him."

Kate sighed. "It rips my heart up when I think of how he used me. I don't know how many women he killed, but I'm certain there were more than Valerie and Annika and Savannah."

"Why is that?"

"Because of the way he picked his victims. Colby is obsessed with the threads that link people's lives together and always wants to trace those threads until they reach him. I'm positive that whoever he killed first was someone who had a personal connection with him, and then he followed whatever threads of her life caught his interest in order to pick his next victim, and so on. If he'd gotten away with killing us, his next victim would have had a link to you or me."

"What a devastating web."

"He's playing games with the police, giving them hints, trying to bargain. They've questioned me several times, investigating different angles. Most of the time, I don't know the answers to their questions. It's humiliating to know so little about my own husband."

Jamie couldn't think of anything to say to comfort a woman who'd learned her husband was a serial killer, so she grasped Kate's cold hand.

"Do you know what Colby wanted me to do the evening before my critical spy assignment?" Tears streamed down Kate's face. "He showed me a picture of a plant with pretty white blossoms and asked me to paint it for him. He said it grew wild in the field behind his aunt's house when he was a child, and he wanted it as part of a series of paintings representing people in his life. The painting turned out beautifully. I was proud of it."

"I'd like to see it."

"It's in police custody. The plant he asked me to paint was jimson weed."

Jamie winced. Testing had identified the poison Colby had used on her and attempted to use on Kate as jimson weed.

Kate's grip constricted, mashing Jamie's hand. "I thought maybe he wanted a memory of the field because he'd felt free there, unlike in his aunt's house. I guess that . . . wasn't the reason. He wanted to involve me with the weapon he planned to use against me, like he did with his other victims."

"The beautiful weapon," Jamie said.

"Yes."

"Kate, do you have anyone helping you out?"

"Helping *me* out? You're the one who got poisoned. I'm fine."

"I mean someone supporting you. You're not holed up in your apartment by yourself, hiding from the press, are you?"

"I'm in a hotel."

"Alone?"

"I don't have family."

"Friends?"

"I haven't been in Britteridge long enough to make a friend who'd want to deal with this garbage."

"Since the friend position is open, I volunteer," Jamie said. "The Treasure Chest will reopen next week. I'm hoping you'll be there with me."

"You can't possibly want to keep me on!"

"Of course I do. You're a fabulous employee, and I'm going to need a lot of help."

"Jamie, you're very kind, but I don't think the wife—soon to be ex-wife—of a serial killer will add to the charming ambience."

"Colby's crimes don't define you."

"In most people's minds, I'm afraid they do."

"That's their problem. People will gossip and gawk for a while, and Marcia Allerton-Harper will be in a tizzy, but we'll handle it, and everyone will move on. If you don't want to be there, I understand, and I won't pressure you, but please know it's an option. I genuinely do want you to stay."

Kate released Jamie's hand and sagged against the couch. "Thank you. I can't tell you how much I appreciate this. I was trying to figure out what to do. Colby never gave me access to his bank account, and I'm going through my savings fast. If I could keep working while I decide what to do long-term, that would help a lot."

"The job is still yours. I confess I'd rather face the gossips with you than face them alone. Strength in numbers." Jamie gestured at a plate of butterscotch-oatmeal cookies on the coffee table. "Cookie?"

"Julian's work?" Kate took one.

"No. Marcia Allerton-Harper's."

Kate eyed the cookie in her hand. "Um . . . actually, I'm not hungry."

Jamie laughed. "She visited me this morning, with her mortified sister. Remember her talking about Glenda, the sister who gave me the wishing well?"

"Yes."

"Glenda heard on the news about the doll and the suspicion that it was linked to the serial killer. She wigged out and called Marcia to admit she'd planted it. She was terrified the police would trace it to her and she'd be accused of conspiring to murder me."

"You're kidding."

"Nope. She said she'd done it to show me how I was hurting myself, along with the town."

"What an elaborate way to send that message!"

"Money's not a problem for the Allerton family. Since direct complaints hadn't convinced me to stick with tradition, Glenda thought if I saw a representation of myself drinking a bucket of poison drawn from my formerly pure well, that might wake me up to how I was contaminating the Allerton legacy."

"Good grief. She hadn't told Marcia what she'd done?"

"No. I suspect Glenda wanted to win this on her own and gloat when her quiet tactic worked after Marcia's confrontational attempts had failed. Marcia's always been so dominant. I think Glenda wanted to beat her for once. So much for Marcia's assuming her family and friends had too much dignity for the doll shenanigan."

"I can sympathize with the mistake of misjudging family. Did they tell the police?"

"Yes. Marcia marched Glenda to the police department to confess everything. Detective Powell told me they don't yet know if Colby ran with the idea of poisoning us after you told him about the doll or if poison was his choice from the beginning and the doll was convenient bling for his scheme. Either way, the Allerton sisters are profoundly remorseful and brought me fresh-baked cookies and apologies."

"Jamie." Kate pressed her thumbnail into a butterscotch chip. "I'm glad they apologized, but I hope you made them eat a few of their cookies in front of you before you tried them."

Jamie reached for a cookie. "I did," she said.

ACKNOWLEGMENTS

Many thanks to Sue McConkie and Monique Luetkemeyer for their feedback on the manuscript, to Gregg Luke for sharing his expertise, and to the members of the Storymakers Tribe for their assistance. Thank you to everyone who participated in the brainstorming threads on my author Facebook page—whether I'm on the hunt for character names, terms of endearment, or potential weapons, you're a fun and fantastic resource. As always, thank you to my editor, Samantha Millburn, and to everyone on the team at Covenant; it's an honor to work with all of you. Thank you for inviting me to be part of this compilation.

ABOUT THE AUTHOR

STEPHANIE BLACK HAS LOVED BOOKS since she was old enough to grab the pages and has enjoyed creating make-believe adventures since she and her sisters were inventing long Barbie games filled with intrigue and danger or running around pretending to be detectives. She is a four-time Whitney Award winner for Best Mystery/Suspense and a finalist for Best Speculative Fiction. Stephanie was born in Utah and has lived in various places, including Arkansas, Arizona, Massachusetts, and Limerick, Ireland. She currently lives in northern California, plays the violin in a community symphony but never practices enough, and enjoys spending time with her husband, Brian, and their family. She is a fan of homemade pizza, homemade chocolate-chip cookies, and naps. Stephanie enjoys hearing from her readers. You can contact her via email at info@covenant-lds.com or by mail, care of Covenant Communications, P.O. Box 416, American Fork, UT 84003-0416. Visit her website at www. stephanieblack.net and her author Facebook page at www.facebook.com/stephanieblackauthor.